HIGHLAND
JUSTICE

HIGHLAND JUSTICE

SONS OF SINCLAIR

HEATHER

USA TODAY BESTSELLING AUTHOR

McCOLLUM

Entangled Publishing, LLC
10940 S Parker Road
Suite 327
Parker, CO 80134
Visit our website at www.entangledpublishing.com.

Amara is an imprint of Entangled Publishing, LLC.

Edited by Alethea Spiridon
Cover design by LJ Anderson, Mayhem Cover Creations
Cover art by The Killion Group Images,
View360adv/Depositphotos, martinm303/Depositphotos
Interior design by Toni Kerr

Print ISBN 978-1-64937-076-1
ebook ISBN 978-1-64937-166-9

Manufactured in the United States of America

First Edition May 2022

AMARA

ALSO BY HEATHER McCOLLUM

SONS OF SINCLAIR SERIES

Highland Conquest
Highland Warrior
Highland Justice

THE BROTHERS OF WOLF ISLE SERIES

The Highlander's Unexpected Proposal
The Highlander's Pirate Lass

HIGHLAND ISLES SERIES

The Beast of Aros Castle
The Rogue of Islay Isle
The Wolf of Kisimul Castle
The Devil of Dunakin Castle

HIGHLAND HEARTS SERIES

Captured Heart
Tangled Hearts
Crimson Heart

To Skye – who strives for justice wherever she roams.

Skye, you will be a wonderful lawyer. I knew it since that day you stood in front of that bully at school, protecting the weaker person behind you. "Mom, if you just stare them in the eye, they usually back down." You've been staring them in the eye ever since. May they always back down, my wonderfully determined girl.

SCOTS GAELIC/FOREIGN WORDS USED IN *HIGHLAND JUSTICE*

àlainn — lovely

blaigeard — bastard

cac — shite

daingead — dammit

dòchas — hope (name of Bàs's horse)

fuil — blood (name of Joshua's horse)

magairlean — ballocks

mattucashlass — double-sided dagger

molaibh Dia — praise God

sgàil — shadow (name of Gideon's horse)

sgian dubh — black-handled dagger

siuthad — go on

tolla-thon — arsehole

BOOK OF REVELATIONS

1   *I watched as the Lamb opened the first of the seven seals. Then I heard one of the four living creatures say in a voice like thunder, "Come!"*

2   *I looked, and there before me was a white horse! Its rider held a bow, and he was given a crown, and he rode out as a conqueror bent on conquest.*

3   *When the Lamb opened the second seal, I heard the second living creature say, "Come!"*

4   *Then another horse came out, a fiery red one. Its rider was given power to take peace from the earth and to make people kill each other. To him was given a large sword.*

5   *When the Lamb opened the third seal, I heard the third living creature say, "Come!" I looked, and there before me was a black horse! Its rider was holding a pair of scales in his hand.*

6   *Then I heard what sounded like a voice among the four living creatures, saying, "Two pounds of wheat for a day's wages, and six pounds of barley for a day's wages, and do not damage the oil and the wine!"*

7   *When the Lamb opened the fourth seal, I heard the voice of the fourth living creature say, "Come!"*

8   *I looked, and there before me was a pale horse! Its rider was named Death…*

At Entangled, we want our readers to be well-informed. If you would like to know if this book contains any elements that might be of concern for you, please check the back of the book for details.

CHAPTER ONE

John Knox, Scottish theologian, 1550 AD

Christmas Day shall not be celebrated with popish joviality but be a day of godly reflection and worship.

Gideon Sinclair held up three velvet pouches. "Gifts for ye," he said, tossing one to Cain, his eldest brother and chief of the mighty Sinclair Clan of northern Scotland. Cain balanced his eight-month-old daughter, Mary, over his shoulder as he caught it.

"Your second brother is dead," Joshua Sinclair said, smiling wryly as he snatched out of the air the pouch Gideon threw at him.

"Do not believe everything chiseled on tombstones," Gideon said, referring to the false grave marker Joshua had left behind on Orkney Isle, which declared his death.

It was Christmas morning, and all four Sinclair brothers and their sister and aunt had gathered with their growing families at Girnigoe Castle, their ancestral home in the north of Scotland. Morning church services with Pastor John were finished, and they had just eaten a hearty meal to celebrate the end of the fast leading up to Christmas.

Gideon handed his youngest brother, Bàs, his

pouch. As large as the rest of them, the bag looked small in his solemn brother's calloused hand. "Open them," Gideon instructed his brothers.

"'Tis not Hogmanay yet," Ella, Cain's wife, said, referring to the last day of the year when gifts were usually exchanged. She gently pulled their daughter from Cain's shoulder. Cain met her gaze with a gentle smile on his stern face. Ella certainly had softened the mighty Horseman of Conquest.

Gideon's jaw tightened, and he rubbed at it absently. "I want my brothers to have them now," Gideon said. "To remind us of who we are." He pushed a smile onto his mouth as he turned a ring on his finger.

Cain was the first to tip the heavy ring out into his palm. It was a thick gold band. On one side was etched a bow and arrow; on the other side was the same horse head that was tattooed on each of the brothers' arms. Inside read *Eques a Conquestum*.

"'Tis Latin for Horseman of Conquest," Gideon said, even though his brothers were well versed in Latin.

He turned to Joshua, his second brother, who had brought a horde of Orkney inhabitants back to Caithness, including his wife, Kára. She sat in a chair by the hearth nursing their son. "And yours says—"

"Eques quidam de bello," Joshua pronounced perfectly. "Horseman of War." He rolled the gold ring in his fingers, holding it to the light, to see the sword on one side and the horse head on the other.

"A rich gift," Joshua said, nodding.

Gideon's smile increased. "A worthy reminder that we are God's Four Horsemen." He held up his own ring that had the scales of justice etched on one side.

"Thank ye, brother," Bàs said, his tone even. Gideon saw him slide his ring, pronouncing him the Horseman of Death, back into the velvet bag. "I must go," Bàs said. He never remained long in their presence, preferring to live alone in the forest between Girnigoe and Varrich castles.

Gideon hadn't expected his brothers to dance with joy about the rich gifts, but he hadn't expected them to study their rings with barely a smile. "Do ye not like them?" he asked.

"That depends on the meaning behind them," Joshua said, sliding the ring on the finger of his right hand. He held it up to catch the light. Hannah, their meek and mild sister, came over to study it.

Gideon pulled out another pouch. "Hannah, one for ye." He stepped forward to kiss the top of her head and laid it in her palm. The look of joy on her face made his chest tighten. She'd been ignored for so long by their father that she didn't question the insult of being forgotten.

"For me?" she asked, waiting for his nod to open it. She pulled out a thin gold ring molded with swirls along the top. The tiniest horse's head was engraved on both sides. Inside was *soror karissima*, beloved sister.

"Thank you," she whispered, sliding it onto her finger. At least *she* looked happy to receive her gift.

"Where is my rich ring?" Aunt Merida asked, inspecting Hannah's finger.

"I will have something for you on Hogmanay," Gideon said, smiling at his eccentric aunt who never failed to keep things lively in the household.

Gideon met each of his brothers' gazes in turn. "I wanted to give ye each something now to remind ye that we are the Four Horsemen of the Apocalypse that Father raised us to be: Conquest, War, Justice, and Death."

"We don't come down from the clouds, Gideon," Cain said, placing the ring on his finger. "Da thought it was the end of days when Mother died, so he raised us that way."

"My brother was insane with grief and then rage," Aunt Merida said. She passed the sign of the cross before her, something she'd done her whole life even though Scotland was now Protestant. "You were all raised engulfed in his madness."

Near the fire, Kára stood with her son, Adam, over one shoulder, patting his back. Joshua leaped up, eager to hold his bairn, something Gideon still hadn't gotten used to. The Horseman of War was a father and husband, enthralled with both son and mother. "We can be something different," Joshua said over his shoulder and then lifted the bairn high in the air.

"Not over the head," Kára said with a small laugh. "He's quite full of milk." Joshua pulled the little lad to his chest and inhaled deeply against his head as if relishing the bairn's scent.

"Again, thank ye," Bàs said, holding up the pouch. He took a step toward the door of the keep.

"I have need of my brothers' advice before ye go," Gideon said, stopping him.

Wee Adam began to fuss. Joshua dipped low and then straightened, starting a swaying type of dance while rising and falling, his knees bending and straightening. "See he likes the motion," Joshua said, glancing at his wife as he bobbed.

Ella swayed with wee Mary because she, too, began to fuss. Cain took the bairn from her. "Maybe she's fouled herself," he said, lifting the bairn to sniff her lower half.

Gideon's jaw dropped open as he watched his oldest brother sniff for possible shite. When had two of the fiercest, most brutal warriors in Scotland become nursemaids?

Gideon ran a hand down his jaw and raised his voice to be heard above the swaying, fussing, and sniffing. "The Mackays are not adjusting well to our occupation. They resist merging with Sinclairs." Gideon had been tasked to bring peace between their clan and the conquered Mackay Clan. He'd moved into Varrich Castle in the summer, trying to sort through the many layers of crime and antagonism there. Using the vast knowledge of law and guidance from philosophers, kings, and statesmen from the past, Gideon had formed his own code of ethics and laws under which the Sinclair Clan flourished. He'd researched the barbaric customs along with the compassionate rules of governing people to create the best of life for his people. Yet the Mackay Clan did not always adhere.

"Perhaps they refuse your efforts because you keep judging them so harshly," Ella said, her eyebrow rising. She patted her baby's back as Cain held Mary, beginning his own little dance opposite Joshua. Ella certainly hadn't forgotten that Gideon had judged *her* harshly when she first came to

Girnigoe. In his defense, she had lied and had been tasked to kill his brother.

"The Mackays are lawless people, used to a chief and steward with black hearts," Gideon said.

"And you judge them in public," Kára said as she hurried back from the hearth with a blanket for Adam. She tipped her head toward the flames that danced on the customary Yule log they'd lit earlier. "Do you even have greenery up or a Yule log burning to show them that you can be merry?"

"Public punishment deters other lawbreakers," Gideon said. "And there hasn't been time for frivolous decorations and old customs. Crime was rife within the Mackay Clan, and I am bringing peace."

"Perhaps ye should take the time," Cain said, changing shoulders as if one might be more comfortable for the bairn. "Merriment can lead to loyalty."

"No one comes up to the castle anyway," Gideon said. "Who would even see my holly and Yule log?"

Ella went behind Cain to smile sweetly up at her bairn over his shoulder. "Maybe," she said using the singsong voice she used only with Mary, "they don't come up to visit because you have decaying skulls flanking the gates." The bairn smiled back at her.

"Good Lord, Gideon," Hannah said, a harsh pinch of rebuke on her angelic face. "The heads are still up?"

He'd left up the severed heads of the past Mackay chief and his steward, who had abducted Hannah, Ella, and her young brother, intent on rape and murder. The grim reminder of what could befall traitors against the Sinclairs had been a warning at first. Once the heads had stopped stinking, Gideon hadn't really thought about them. But their skulls did still flank the portcullis gate.

Gideon let out a rush of an exhale that no one heard over the coos and chuckles of besotted parents. Why was he asking his brothers about integrating the two clans when they had no experience doing so? He was the one who read books that described the process. He was the one who had learned to judge right from wrong in the Sinclair clan, since his father had charged him with the duty at the age of five. In his father's opinion, it was Gideon's only purpose in life, and he'd shouldered the responsibility well.

Gideon rubbed the old scar running down his cheek then raised his hands overhead to stretch his back as if he felt the weight. He looked to Bàs. "I will exit with ye, brother. Apparently, I have a Yule log to find on my way back to Varrich."

"And holly," Kára said, smiling his way.

"Mistletoe too," Hannah added.

Joshua raised an imaginary tankard to him, since he'd left his on the table. "Let me know if ye need any help over there." He still held Adam in one arm, dipping low back and forth as his son's eyes fluttered shut.

Gideon smirked at his always teasing brother. Raised as the Horseman of War, Joshua was a trickster, even if he seemed much cheered after marrying his Orkney princess. "I don't think the Mackays have forgotten how ye set their fences and forests on fire," Gideon said.

Joshua's grin faded. "We left the cottages sound."

Bàs grabbed Gideon's arm. "Come, let us leave

them with their families."

Finding their horses in silence, the brothers rode out across Girnigoe's two drawbridges and under the impressive portcullis as snow sifted down under a heavy gray sky.

Gideon pressed his sleek black horse, Sgàil, into an easy trot through the empty streets. Most villagers would be celebrating quietly in their homes with small feasts.

The two brothers pushed into a gentle lope across the moor where Gideon and Bàs would part. Trusting Sgàil's footing, Gideon raised his gaze to the swirling sky, inhaling the fresh chill to clear his head.

"Gideon?" Bàs's deep voice drew his attention, and Gideon slowed.

"Aye?"

Bàs matched his pace, still staring straight ahead, watching the whitening landscape, his brows furrowed. "Must we be who Da said we are to be?" Bàs asked, coming to a halt. "Now that he is dead?" His pale gray horse stood as still as he sat, both serious and silent. "Cain is the leader and Horseman of Conquest, but he did not conquer the Sutherland clan. And Joshua seems much more…peace-filled now and is not always trying to start wars."

Gideon slipped the gold ring off his finger, holding it up. "Father raised us to be The Four Horsemen of the Apocalypse."

Bàs's stern face turned to him. "Only after I executed our mother with my birth."

Gideon put the ring back on his finger where it turned a bit too easily. Perhaps he should have it tightened. "We are either the mighty Sinclair horsemen or we are not. There's no partway, or we weaken. 'Twas why I gifted each of us a ring, to remind us who we are."

Melancholy mixed with the hardness in Bàs's face. He was the youngest of them all, but being the executioner for the clan had aged him. Gideon wouldn't pity him, though, for this was who Bàs was, and a man should not be pitied for fulfilling his duty.

"Who we are?" Bàs asked as if mulling over the question. "It seems who we are is not entirely made up of our actions, but also our thoughts and our hearts."

Gideon shook his head. "Our thoughts and hearts are displayed clearly in our actions if one takes the time to watch them. I was trained to watch the actions and expressions of people to administer justice for Clan Sinclair, and now for the Mackays at Varrich."

"One's heart and thoughts are reflected in one's actions?" Bàs asked.

"Aye, 'tis that simple," Gideon said. "We're taught what is right and wrong, good and evil, through the church and through our clan upbringing. Those who choose to commit crimes show their hearts to the world." Gideon started his horse walking with one hand on the reins, his other fisted on his thigh. "'Tis my duty as one of the Sinclair horsemen to judge. And we must stay the horsemen or weaken. Weakness will lead to the end of the mighty Sinclair Clan." He shook his head. "I will not let that happen." Gideon's whole life centered on making the clan stronger than any in Scotland.

"Life is simple for ye," Bàs said.

Gideon smiled, feeling how right the world was. "Aye, life is simple when ye know the rules, and I will bring that simplicity to Varrich."

Bàs nodded and turned his gaze to the forest where he would veer off toward his cabin nestled in the woods. "Happy Christmas to ye," he said. "We will meet again in a week at Hogmanay, no doubt." With a press of his heels, Bàs and his horse tore off across the snow-covered moor.

Gideon guided Sgàil west toward Varrich and entered the woods. Thick snowflakes floated down, landing in stark contrast on the horse's ebony mane and ears. All of Gideon's horses were black, since he controlled the third calvary as the third Horseman, Justice. And he worked diligently to keep Sgàil's coat glossy and sleek.

The air was frosty, and the wind ebbed and flowed in small gusts around them as Gideon let Sgàil follow the usual path between Girnigoe and Varrich castles. *Yule log. Holly.* What else was needed for Hogmanay merriment? *Mistletoe, sweets, and whisky. Bloody hell.* Making merry was costly and time-consuming.

"A Master of Revels," he murmured. He'd have to choose a jester to oversee the festivities. A Mackay lad to involve the people.

Nearly an hour later, Gideon and Sgàil broke from the forest onto the moor that stretched down to Varrich Village and the castle. Warrior's instincts made him pull Sgàil to a halt as soon as he saw movement at the far end of the clearing. A woman stood before the forest's edge, her arms open wide.

She turned slowly in a circle, her face tipped up to the sky as if she watched the snow float from the heavens.

Gideon dismounted, leaving Sgàil to wait behind. Gideon walked with deliberate smoothness, unwilling to ruin the natural peace that the falling snow created. The lass turned one way and then reversed, face still tipped to the sky. The closer he walked, the clearer he saw her. The gentle, contented smile across her face drew Gideon's full attention.

"Three… Four… Five…" She counted loudly with each turn.

Gideon stopped a few yards away. Snow dotted her free-flowing dark curls, alighting so gently that they seemed to transform into a translucent veil. The soft flakes kissed her cheeks before melting.

"Six… Seven…"

She wore a dark green costume with a short woolen jacket in blue. She paused, and he watched a snowflake land on her dark eyelashes fanned out under her closed eyes. But it was the softness of her pink lips, bent in the most contented smile, that made it difficult for Gideon to inhale. Had he ever seen such simple contentment before? He certainly hadn't experienced it.

"Eight… Ni—"

As if he'd made a sound in the unbroken silence, the woman's eyes snapped open, her gaze finding him easily, since he was the only person on the snowy landscape. She gasped and lifted two *sgian dubhs* from the pockets of her skirts, one in each hand.

...

"Halt," Cait Mackay ordered.

"I halted a full minute ago, lass," said the massive warrior who had snuck up on her. He held no weapons in his hands, but his obvious strength marked him as deadly.

Her eyes darted to the sides, but he was by himself, and the children were still hidden in the forest behind her. "Be gone with you, and leave me unmolested, else you will find yourself bloody."

He took a step closer, his palms out as if she were a fearful dog. Maybe she should growl and show her teeth. He might think her mad and leave off.

"I plan no evil toward ye. I'm but traveling to my home at Varrich and saw ye dancing in the snow."

She tracked his movements, her heart beating hard.

"Do ye need assistance?" he asked. The wind swept over the gentle hill of the moor to lift her hair. "Are ye not cold?"

Ye are nothing but a cold fish to a man. Cait pushed the plaguing words away and clasped her daggers tightly. "I have not seen you in Varrich." Handsome in face and taller and broader than most, the warrior was one she couldn't have missed. He either lied or he was a Sinclair. Both made him dangerous.

"I've not lived in Varrich Village long."

He wore the Scots plaid wrapped around narrow hips and a thin linen tunic with a short jacket. His boots laced up and had fur wrapped around them to his knees. *Lord*. He was full of muscle and wore a sword sheathed at his hip. He smiled, but he still appeared dangerous. Perhaps it was the scar down his cheek that made her think he roared a battle cry more often than he laughed. Dark hair, clipped close, and a short, well-groomed beard made him seem civilized despite how natural he stood in a warrior's stance. But she took no chances with strange men and kept her guard up.

Cait heard a limb snap in the forest behind her and talked loudly to cover it. "And I was not dancing," she said, it being the first thing to pop into her head.

"Twirling then and…counting." His eyes squinted in question.

The falling snow had been so beautiful that she'd taken a moment to herself while her children hid for their game.

The mountainous man folded his hands before him in a gesture that she supposed he used to look less threatening. As if that were possible. "I've never seen a lass older than ten twirling out in the snow."

"'Tis a way I practice my knife wielding." She held the two blades ready in her hands.

He nodded. "Ye may not want to expose your throat so much then," he said, tipping his face to the sky in imitation of her enjoyment. He sliced a finger over the masculine bump in his throat.

"I will take that into consideration. Thank you and good day." She took two steps back, listening for any sounds in the winter trees behind her where a path led to the river. The falling snow muted sounds so that she could barely hear the rush of water.

"But why were ye counting?"

Her lips opened for a long moment before she answered. "I...like to count?" Her statement came out like a question, and she tried to cover her concern with a slight smile.

A crunching sound in the woods caught her ear. "What is your name?" she asked quickly to cover it. "Perhaps I have heard of you in the village."

He kept his smile. "Ye first."

"Mistress Cait!" Libby's voice called from far away in the trees behind her. *Damn*. Cait closed her eyes for a brief second before snapping them back open. Not only had he won her name, but he now knew that there were children with her. What he didn't know was that she'd protect them with her life.

"Cait?" he said, cocking his head, his eyes merry with victory. "Cait Mackay then?"

"Come quick!" Trix screamed, tugging Cait's attention away from the warrior. The young girl ran at her from the woods. "Willa!" Tix yelled. "She's fallen in!"

CHAPTER TWO

*The Groundwork of Conny-Catching
by Thomas Harman, 1567 AD*

*A practical guide for urban dwellers to understand
the coded languages and cunning tricks of rogues
and thieves.*

Cait's heart jumped. "Willa?" she whispered, panic stealing her breath. She spun around, grabbing her skirts, and dashed into the woods.

Fallen in? Holy God!

Cait had warned them not to get too close to the river that cut through this part of Caithness. Her fifteen-year-old sister was the sensible one, and yet she'd fallen in?

Cait tore through the twiggy bramble, Trix and Libby running somewhere behind her. Heavy footfalls came up beside her as the man surged past, dodging trees to reach the river first where she could see Jack stretched out on a tree trunk bent over the rushing water.

"Jack, get back," Cait called. The only boy of her group, Jack was already taller than she, but even he couldn't reach Willa, who clung to the tree that had fallen over the raging waters.

Cait reached the edge, her gaze searching for anything to help her reach her sister. Willa dangled above broken ice over the tumbling water. Her pale face was tight, her eyes shut as she clung to the wet limb with both hands. The frigid water tugged violently at her feet and skirts. If Willa let go, her body would be swept under the thicker ice downstream, and she would drown in the frigid sweep.

No! Cait had given her life away before to save her little sister, and she would again. "Hold on, Willa," Cait yelled, as she yanked her jacket off.

"What are ye doing?" the stranger asked.

"Saving her," she yelled.

"How?"

"I…"

When she didn't give an answer, the warrior turned, dropping his belongings on the ground. "I will get her," he said above the rushing water. Trix, Jack, and Libby kept yelling encouragement to Willa to hold on. Cait's hands rose to her cheeks as she watched the stranger survey the creek below Willa. It was iced over with the water shooting down underneath. She would be sucked under for certain.

"I…I can't hold on," Willa called, terror punctuating her words. As if proving her right, her fingers slipped, and she shrieked, the water grabbing its victim.

"Willa!" Cait screamed, dashing toward her at the same time the man leaped. His bootheels, followed by at least two hundred pounds of muscle and bone, broke easily through the ice where he launched himself downstream of the branch.

Jagged ice hit him a few seconds before Willa slammed into his chest with the force of the water. His body acted like a dam, and the icy water rushed around them as he curled his powerful arms around her slender thrashing body. With slow, cautious tread he waded to the shore where Cait knelt in the muddy snow, stretching her arms out in a frantic tumbling motion to reach her sister.

"Willa, Holy God, Willa." Cait dragged her up the bank to lay against her. She was soaked and freezing, making Cait shiver, too. She yanked her cape from her shoulders and threw it around them both.

"She tripped on that root while running," Trix said, pointing along the bank. "She looked like she was flying, her arms out wide, and hit the branch that was out over the water instead of just falling in." White puffs of breath came from her mouth as she talked with wide gestures.

The man heaved himself out onto the bank and squeezed his woolen wrap, water gushing from it. "Ye need to get her dry and warm. Where can I take ye?"

Cait rose, lifting Willa against her, but the added weight of the water made her stumble. "'Tis not far. We will get her there," she said and looked to Jack. "Help me carry her."

"I have a horse," the man said. "'Twill get her home faster."

"I have found that men who help want to be repaid," she said as she struggled to hold on to Willa. "And I have nothing to pay you with."

The man frowned and lifted his hands to his mouth. Cait startled when he whistled, the single note piercing the quiet woods, but she continued to struggle to lift Willa. Jack grabbed her legs. Before they could reach the edge of the forest, thunderous hoofbeats came from the moor.

"Oh my Lord," Cait whispered, her heart pounding with effort and now fear that they would all be trampled by the huge black beast bearing down on them. But the horse slowed and stopped near the warrior. Nostrils flaring, puffs of breath billowed out as the beast surveyed them all with round, dark eyes.

In two powerful strides, the warrior was before them. He picked Willa up as if she weighed nothing. "'Tis merely a kindness. I expect no payment."

"I will see the others home," Jack said, his eyes wide as he watched the horse. None of the children had ever owned a horse, and Cait doubted Willa remembered the horse they had loved ten years ago when their parents were still alive.

"Straightaway, Jack," Cait said and traipsed right behind the man to his horse. "I will hold her," she said to him. "You're cold and wet, too."

"Climb on." He nodded to the stirrup. "The horse will remain still."

Her sweet Penny had not been nearly as large and intimidating. Cait threw her shoulders back. Yanking her skirt up high, she shoved her boot into the stirrup and lifted, swinging her leg over the massive saddle.

She held her arms out for Willa. "I'll take her." Cait embraced her limp sister before her, both wobbling in the saddle as the man mounted behind. Cait's stomach jumped when he pulled her back into the intimate space between his thighs. Before she could pull away, he threw a heavy cloak before Willa, tucking it in around all three of them. "For warmth," he murmured near Cait's ear. The brush of his breath against her skin sent an odd shiver through her. It wasn't one of revulsion or terror like the shivers that plagued her nightmares.

With a shift of his weight, the horse moved smoothly from walk to canter, and they headed across the moor. Wind and icy pecks of snow stung Cait's cheeks, and she squinted against them.

"Whose children are they?" he asked behind her as they rolled along with the horse's gait.

"Mine."

"All of them?"

"Yes. Although this clumsy one is my sister." She hugged tighter to Willa, who trembled in her arms with cold or fear or both.

Smoke danced in the breeze over the cottages in Varrich Village up ahead. "Where is your house?"

She swallowed. "Closer to the castle, at the edge of the village." She pulled an arm from the cape to point toward the right.

The horse surged forward in a thunderous run, and Cait clutched tighter to Willa under the blanket. They flew across the snow-covered ground. The warrior's arms were long enough, and Cait was pressed so close within them that he also held onto Willa.

They skirted the edge of the village and slowed upon entering to weave through the streets. Men and women, hustling along the winter road, hurried out of the way of his black charger. *Good Lord.* She and Willa would be the talk of the village after riding with a massive warrior on his pitch-black horse.

"There," Cait said, pointing toward their two-room, single-story cottage near the forest edge. Rows of stacked stone created fences behind and beside it, and a cobblestone walkway before the cottage kept the mud from creeping up to the door and dirtying Rhona's floors. There were dark spots in the thatching that looked moldy, and several areas were too thin to completely keep the elements out.

"Your husband neglects your roof," the man said and pulled his horse to a stop before the front door. Cold air hit Cait's back as he leaned away and dismounted.

She would need to climb aloft before the snow melted and dripped inside. "Yes," Cait said, meeting his gaze, "he is quite the idle bastard lying about all day in his grave."

His stern face didn't change as he pulled Willa from her arms. "I am sorry for your loss," he said, peering directly into her eyes. His were a deep gray, like summer storm clouds.

She looked away, shrugging. "He was an idle bastard before a Sinclair sword sliced through his neck." Pushing away from the horse, she jumped down. Lord, the beast was tall, just like his master.

Cait guided Willa to the door of the Orphans' Home, which flew open. "Willa! What happened?" Rhona screeched, dragging them inside. Rhona was over two score in years and helped Cait mother the four orphaned children living with them. She was strong in her convictions and full of love for any creature who needed it. Tidiness and cooking were her passions, and Cait wouldn't be able to keep the home going without her.

"She fell in the river." Cait guided Willa to a seat near the hearth fire.

Rhona fetched a privacy screen to place before

them, and Cait immediately unknotted the wet ties holding Willa's clothes, stripping her down to nothing. Rhona handed Cait a dry smock that she threw over Willa's head. Her eyes were open, but she looked pale and too weak to talk.

"And you fell in, too?" Rhona asked, her face disappearing around the edge of the screen.

"I retrieved the lass," the man said.

"God's sake," Rhona said. "Warm yourself. Take off that wet tunic else you catch your death."

Cait bundled Willa up and moved the privacy screen back so the man could reach the warmth of the fire.

Rhona was pointing at his dripping kilt. "I suppose you can't take that off."

"Not unless ye are used to naked men in your cottage," he said, making Rhona snort.

The warrior pulled his tunic over his head, revealing a perfectly honed warrior's body. His skin was golden in the firelight, a scar slashed around his side, and she saw the horse tattoo on his arm that many of the Sinclair warriors wore. There was also a tattoo at the top of his back, but he turned to face her before she could fully see it. She blinked at the chiseled muscles evident in his chest and torso that led down to his low-slung kilt. He spread the linen over a chair before the hearth and rubbed his arms before the flames.

Cait realized she was staring and yanked her focus back to his face. His gaze was on her. *Drat*. He would think she'd been staring. *I was. Bloody hell*. She was a woman, after all, and Willa's savior was every inch a man. Even though Cait was said to be cold, the obvious strength in this warrior and his golden heart in rescuing Willa stirred some warmth within her.

Rhona poured broth she had simmering into a bowl for Willa to sip. "There's another quilt in the back bedroom."

Cait hurried to the opening of the back bedroom where she paused, her hand on the doorframe. Benjamin Mackay was long gone and yet the room still haunted her. She dodged into it to fetch another quilt, shaking it before the fire to rid it of cold before settling it around Willa's shoulders.

Thump. The outer door banged the wall as the children barreled inside, huffing and sucking in air with a dramatic lifting of their shoulders. "We ran the whole way," Trix said.

"Jack made us," Libby said, bending forward to rest her hands on her knees. "How is Willa?"

"Dry and getting warm," Rhona answered.

Trix walked up to Gideon while still gulping large amounts of air. She held his satchel out to him. The unmistakable sound of coins clinking caught Cait's attention when he took it.

"Thank ye," he said, giving Trix a deep nod. She smiled back with curious eyes. Trix was the happiest of their family, always laughing and twirling about. Her name was Beatrice but, since she loved to play tricks on everyone, they had shortened it to Trix.

"Jack wouldn't let me carry the sword," Libby said with her usual pout. Slender and only eight years old, she probably wasn't strong enough to lift the man's sword, let alone carry it all that way from the river.

Libby hurried over to Willa. "She's apt to get a fever," she said.

Cait straightened. "We've handled plenty of fevers, Libby, and Rhona and I know how to fight them." She pushed several errant strands to tuck behind her ears, conscious of the warrior watching her.

Jack lifted the sword and presented it to him, his expression grim once more.

As the man took the weight, his arms bulged. Good heavens, he was built of power and strength, the thin scar on his cheek adding to his lethal look. "Thank ye, lad. Och, but what type of warrior forgets his sword in the woods?"

Libby planted her hands on her hips like she'd seen Rhona do every day. "I will never play All Hid in the forest again, even if it *is* Christmas. What a ridiculous idea, Jack."

Rhona walked closer to Cait, pretending to fetch a bowl. "There are coins in that bag of his," she whispered. "We need some for feverfew and a chicken for soup for Willa."

Cait frowned, her worry for Willa warring against the hollow feeling of guilt. She glanced his way and took a full inhale. "As you can see, we have little and nothing to pay you with except our deepest gratitude for saving our sweet Willa."

"Sweet?" Jack snorted, only to be smacked in the arm by Libby. Trix giggled.

God's teeth! The man had risked his life to save her sister, and Cait would thank him by picking coins from his pocket. She swallowed against the tightness in her throat and looked away.

She'd add it to the tally of sins she'd earned in her life and pray that God would understand she did it all to help others. Although saving her sister was also selfish, since Cait couldn't bear the thought of losing her.

"I would accept no payment," he said, showing his gallantry. "I'm just gladdened that the lass is warm and dry now and that no one else fell into the river. 'Tis a dangerous place for children to venture near in the winter. There should be a law against it." He frowned. "To protect them."

He glanced about the mid-sized thatched cottage. Did he find it lacking? They'd worked together to lay a lime ash floor in the summer, and the cottage was free of dirt and disorder, everything in its place. They had a long wooden table and a stack of sleeping pallets along one wall. The children slept with Cait in the main room and its large cooking hearth, which sat along the back wall flanked by shelves of bowls and small sacks of foodstuffs. Herbs and dried wildflowers hung from the rafters, along with woven baskets. They made the warm room smell like a summer's day. It wasn't much, but it was a happier home than it used to be when Benjamin was alive.

Drip… Drip… Drip…

The sound of the man's wet plaid dripping on the floor was loud in the sudden silence. Soaked, it tugged even lower around his taut torso, dipping to show indentations that ran below the woolen wrap to where he was no doubt just as powerful. The thought made Cait's cheeks warm. She was no virgin, but the thought of what the mighty warrior looked like completely naked made heat grow in her middle.

"I'm leaving a puddle on your floor," he said and grabbed his damp tunic from the chair. Stretching his arms to throw it over his head displayed his muscles once again.

"Holy Mary," Rhona whispered next to Cait. She couldn't agree more. Cait looked to the hearth when his dark hair pushed up through the top. She wouldn't add ogling a man, one she was planning to rob, to her long list of offenses.

"I will return to see how the lass fares," he said.

Cait's gaze snapped back to his. "No need to. Thank you," she said and walked past him to open the door. Was she being rude? Perhaps that would stop him from returning, because after pilfering a few of his shillings, any interactions between them would feel even more shameful.

He had to duck so as not to brush his head on the low lintel above the door. A mere inch separated his body from Cait's as he slid past her, and she tried to ignore the draw she felt. How long had it been since she'd stood this close to a man? One who didn't turn her stomach?

The warrior paused across from her, his hand rising to touch a dark curl laying against her cheek. The action, so gentle, tugged at her heart, and she forgot to breathe. His finger slid against her skin, capturing her breath, and she swallowed. "Ye have a speck of leaf," he said, his voice low.

She swallowed. "You won my name," she murmured. "What's yours?"

The sound of horses made her turn her face away, and the warrior stepped out the door to face the road where two horses thundered toward the cottage. No one came out this far from the village center without a reason. He drew his sword as the horses slowed to a halt before the cottage.

Cait recognized one of the men instantly. *God's teeth*. What did that crude bastard want this time? Her stomach clenched, and she drew out one of her *sgian dubhs*. If he tried to touch her again, there would be blood.

• • •

Gideon cursed under his breath. Bruce Mackay, his hired steward, pulled his horse to a stop alongside Keenan Sinclair, one of Cain's men from Girnigoe Castle.

"Children live here," Gideon said, sheathing his sword. He glanced back at Cait who stood wide-eyed. "If they'd been outside, ye could have trampled them."

Keenan nodded, his gaze going to Cait where she stood behind him. "My apologies, milady." His gaze lingered on her, making Gideon's frown deepen.

"What is it?" Gideon asked, his voice curt.

Keenan's gaze slid back to Gideon. "The chief desires ye to meet with him at Girnigoe."

Bruce's sharp eyes locked onto Cait, a hardness on his face. Was there a history between them? Years of training to read men's hearts made it possible for Gideon to pick out emotions from faces and stances. He shifted to block Bruce's line of sight. "I just departed from Girnigoe," Gideon said, watching Bruce shift his mount to the side so he could still see the lass. Why hadn't the man reported that Cait's roof needed attention?

"A letter has arrived from Edinburgh," Keenan said. His gaze lifted again to Cait. She was startlingly beautiful, even with snow-damp hair and a wet gown. But, dammit, they shouldn't be staring at her.

Gideon moved again, to stand directly in front of her. It was an obvious move to dissuade their attentions that they would be fools to ignore. "I'll return with ye at once," Gideon said, warning added to his voice. He turned to her. "Farewell."

Cait stepped back as if his serious look had surprised her, and he forced a smile. He watched her take a full breath, the gentle swell of her breasts rising against the edge of her bodice. She took a step closer, her eyes lifted to his. Did she wish to speak with him? Suddenly, her body flew forward as if she'd been pushed. He steadied her as her hands slid along his body, her feet scrambling under her to right herself.

"I'm so clumsy," she murmured, her lips mere inches from his as he steadied her.

Close up in the sun, he could see the arresting green of her eyes. The sweet scent of some flower filled his inhale. She met his gaze, her brows pinched together. "Forgive me," she whispered, a deep regret filling her voice. It was like the sound of unshed tears in the voices of people gathered at a fresh grave. There was too much heaviness in it.

He stared into her eyes. "'Twas an accident," he said and let her pull slowly away from him.

Bobbing a nod, Cait spun around, hurrying back toward the cottage. She shut the door behind her, and Gideon heard the rasp of the heavy bar slide into place on the inside.

"So ye've met the ice queen," Bruce said.

Gideon kept his scowl as he turned to his steward. "Her roof needs repair."

Bruce glanced up. "I hadn't noticed, and she didn't report it. As soon as Twelfth Night is over, I'll send some lads up there to fix it."

"I think ye should fix it today," Gideon said. "Since ye did not follow my orders to properly assess all the dwellings in the village."

"Is it not your rule that no one is to work from now until Twelfth Night?" Bruce said.

Gideon felt the tightness of his temper rising. "'Tis a guidance to be broken to fix an error." His gaze pierced Bruce's until the man looked away.

"Aye," Bruce said, his voice low.

Gideon glanced back as he gathered Sgàil's reins. "What do ye know of her?"

"Cait Mackay," Bruce said and rubbed his jaw. "From Clan Gunn in the south." His lips pursed, and he crossed his arms where he still sat on his horse. "Her parents died, and she married Benjamin Mackay when she was almost sixteen. Brought her young sister with her to live here. Benjamin died two years later in a battle with Sinclairs, and she started taking in parentless children."

"So the children aren't from her body," Gideon said.

"Nay. She has no children of her own," Bruce said. "Just the orphans. Her lady, Rhona Lindsey, was also a widow and moved in to help her about a year after Benjamin died."

"She didn't remarry?" Keenan asked. "She is

bonny enough."

Bruce snorted, a sneer on his face. "She's made it quite clear that she is not interested in the institution or any man, for that matter." Bruce fixed his hat lower on his head, covering his ears. "She's an unnaturally cold lass. No good to any man."

Nothing about Cait Mackay seemed cold to Gideon. On the other hand, Bruce's face was tight with vengeful ice.

"Then ye will hire two other lads to fix her roof today, and ye will stay well away from her," Gideon said, piercing his steward with a look that had been known to make men fall to their knees.

• • •

"They are talking about you," Rhona whispered, her ear pressed against the cold windowpane that faced the three men. The children ran over, but Cait walked to the hearth where Willa rested. Her sister's face was still pale, but she didn't feel feverish. Yet.

Cait had immediately dropped the stolen coins into her pocket on her way inside the cottage and now rubbed her palms on a small towel. Stealing from a cruel laird, who didn't care that his people were starving, was one thing. Stealing from a man who had just saved Willa's life, without asking for anything in return, was quite another.

But Rhona was right. Even with the friendships that Cait nurtured, the old apothecary would want a shilling for her cures. And if Willa became ill, Cait would do anything to save her. Years ago, Cait had sold herself in marriage to save her sister, so stealing a few shillings that would probably go unnoticed should be a trifle thing. But it still felt wrong.

"What are they saying?" Trix asked, rising onto her toes as if she were excited enough to float away like a bubble.

Rhona cursed low and scrunched her face as she met Cait's gaze. "That Bruce Mackay is saying you're cold." The simple words felt like boulders on Cait's chest, and she rubbed her fist over it as if that could lessen the tightness there. So now the warrior knew some of her shame, the one she had encouraged through the years to keep fiends like Bruce Mackay away. *I have a cold fish for me wife.* Benjamin's words still haunted her.

"And," Rhona continued, looking to the children, "that Mistress Cait is no one to meddle with."

"Good," Jack said, crossing his arms over his chest. He was truly becoming a man and had started to imitate the warriors in town, for good or for bad.

He looked over at Trix. "You should've taken a few coins out of his sack before you gave it back to him," Jack said. "Then Mistress Cait wouldn't have had to fall up against the fetid man."

"He smelled quite nice," Willa said from her spot. "Fresh air and a spice of some sort."

"Rosemary," Cait murmured and cleared her throat. "And the polish they use to keep saddles supple." She raised her gaze from the tabletop and looked at Trix. "And I do not want you stealing, even if it is for Willa."

"You do it," Jack said. "We should help you."

Cait shook her head. "I would never have that sin upon your shoulders."

"Stealing isn't a sin to save Willa," Rhona said.

That was debatable, but Cait kept silent.

"You can take a coin to Alistair Mackay to find us a chicken," Rhona said. "He is sweet on you and won't ask where it came from." She smiled broadly. "And then chicken stew tonight." The children cheered, but she shushed them, peeking out through a crack in the shudders. "They're riding away."

"How much did you get?" Libby asked. They all hurried over to the table.

Trix leaned on her stomach halfway across, propping herself on her elbows. "Perhaps he would have given us a few shillings if we'd asked nicely," she said.

Libby *tsk*ed and looked heavenward as if she were far superior even though she was barely a year older than Trix. "If he'd said no, he'd have been on guard, and then she wouldn't have been able to get anything."

"Is there enough for a chicken?" Jack asked.

Cait reached into her pocket to capture the cold metal there and pulled it out. The contents of her hand clunked on the tabletop, and the children leaned in to count.

"That isn't a shilling," Jack said.

"But the other three are," Trix said.

Cait stared down at the gold ring sitting in the middle of the table, and her breath caught in her chest.

Rhona picked it up. "Good Lord," she murmured, turning it this way and that. "'Tis…pure gold." She studied it in the light. "It has a horse's head etched on one side and…" She looked up to meet Cait's gaze, "a set of scales on the other."

Cait stood abruptly, taking the ring from her fingers. She couldn't breathe. Her lips fell open, and she stared at the cold band as if frozen with the world still moving about her.

"'Tis rich indeed," Jack said. "What's the inscription say?" He lowered his face toward it.

"She can't see with your thick head in the way," Libby said.

Cait swallowed as she studied the etched words. "*Equitis iustitiae*," Cait said, her quiet words coming out on an exhale. "'Tis Latin for...Horseman of Justice."

CHAPTER THREE

English Common Law, Warning to fellow Scotch,
12th century AD

Monday to Saturday, within the walls of the city of
York, England, 'tis legal to murder a Scotsman if he
carries a bow and arrow.

"Why the bloody hell would King James want to come here except to see if I'm actually still alive?" Joshua Sinclair said, his voice just under a roar. "If his uncle, Robert Stewart, the Earl of Orkney, sent word to him about the battle up there, and that I was the instigator, James might be coming to condemn the Sinclairs of Caithness."

Gideon held the missive up to the oil lamp that lit the table in Girnigoe's great hall. This was not how he'd planned to spend his Christmas evening. He'd rather be fixing a thatched roof over the Orphans' Home. "It says nothing about ye or the Stewart earl. Only that he wishes to inspect the Mackay holding since it was taken by us."

Cain met Gideon's gaze. "He wants to see how powerful we've grown," Cain said.

Gideon nodded. "King James may be in the middle of succession discussions with Queen Elizabeth's English counselors, but he also does not want to lose his rule over Scotland to the mightiest clan in the country."

Gideon studied Cain's narrowed eyes. His oldest brother rarely let his thoughts appear on his face, and it certainly was closed right now. "Something Da thought Sinclairs could accomplish, not in his lifetime, but in ours," Gideon said.

"Ye want us to take over all of Scotland?" Bàs asked from his position at the end of the table. Cain had called them all back to Girnigoe when the missive had arrived.

"I did not say that," Gideon said. "I merely remind ye that Da had wished for us to do so. With our four armies and Cain with his mighty bow and arrow as the Horseman of Conquest, I could win the Sutherlands, Gunns, and Campbells south of here to our side. We could take Edinburgh with twenty thousand horses. With success at the capital, we would win the support of the other clans I've been curating favor with through trade. Our joined forces would put Cain, the Horseman of Conquest, on the throne."

"Don't say *that* when James arrives," Joshua said and threw himself into a sturdy chair.

Gideon reread the brief letter that said King James would travel to survey the Sinclairs' territory sometime this winter, spring at the latest if the weather was bad. "Of course not," he murmured. "What would we do with a whole country anyway?" He looked up at Cain, shrugging in mock question, his brows rising with his shoulders. "Besides unite the people to stand strong against foreign threats and improve their daily lives with unselfish, well-planned distribution of food and care."

Joshua pointed at Gideon. "Another thing not to say."

Taught to think in terms of fairness and what was best for the Sinclair people, Gideon had helped his father and now his brother keep the peace and think ahead for the benefit of all. With Gideon's yearly goals and seasonal plans, he'd helped his clan increase yields on all crops and made certain that every Sinclair was warm, fed, and properly cared for. It all added up to creating a very strong clan to meet any challenge. He'd begun to do the same for Varrich and could do so for all of Scotland if tasked with it.

"He may want confirmation of our loyalty and to see how many troops we can contribute to the defense of Scotland when needed," Cain said. His gaze dropped to Gideon's hand. "Have ye lost your ring so soon?"

His ring? Gideon grinned when he saw that Cain was wearing his. He folded the letter, tossing it on the table. "On the way to Varrich this morn, I deviated to rescue a child from the frozen river. I didn't want to lose it to the waters." He pulled out his pouch to retrieve it, his fingers deftly slipping between the thin coins inside.

"I have mine on," Joshua said, extending his middle finger with great flourish to show where he'd decided to wear it.

"I know I dropped it in here," Gideon murmured. He lifted the bag, pouring out the coins onto the table, but there was no ring.

"Perhaps it fell through the bag," Bàs said, coming forward.

Gideon shook his head. "The bag is sound."

"Or dropped it next to the creek," Cain said.

"Stolen?" Joshua suggested, making Gideon's gaze snap to his. Could the young girl who'd retrieved the bag have taken the ring out?

Cain pushed the coins around on the surface of the table with one finger. "Are any coins missing?"

Gideon counted quickly. "Three shillings." Being raised to keep careful accounts of all that Clan Sinclair possessed, he knew exactly how many horses, beds, sacks of grain, and sheep they had. So, of course, he knew exactly how many coins were in his leather pouch, and three were missing.

Along with his golden ring.

• • •

"Can't you give it back to him?" Rhona asked as she watched Cait yank the black trews up her legs. "Tell him he dropped the ring and coins, and you found them outside."

Cait fought to control her rapid breathing as she ran through the scenario again in her mind like she'd been doing all day. Her giving it back to him. Him accusing her of stealing it, realizing that was why she'd fallen against him before he left. He was too clever not to see the truth if she brought attention to the crime.

Gideon Sinclair. *Bloody hell!* He was the brutal Horseman of Justice. Accusing and judging people as guilty was as natural to him as breathing. She'd seen his laws against stealing nailed to the chapel door along with a slew of others. She'd heard how he weighed the intentions of people in less time than they could make a plea, sentencing them to lashes or the stocks or exile or even death under the axe of his brother, the Horseman of Death. By God's holy stars, the new Sinclair leader of their clan still had rotted heads flanking the castle gates. Despite Gideon's compassion that morning, he would make an example of Cait for filching his ring.

Could she make him believe the coins fell out with the ring? If they'd been stolen, surely more would've been taken. Could she get so lucky that there was an actual hole in the bag? *Blast and dammit!* Luck was rarely with her.

No, Gideon Sinclair wouldn't believe her if she said she'd found them on the banks of the creek. Would the cruel Horseman of Justice tie her to the whipping post in town and lay the strap against her bare back? He'd ordered that punishment for Viola Finley and then exiled her because she'd been the sister of the owner of one of those rotting heads at the gate.

"You don't even need to see him," Rhona continued. "Just give the ring, and the coins if you must, to one of his guards up at the castle."

"Trust Sinclair guards? They're probably as evil as Bruce," she said. "And you know he'd pocket it all and let the blame fall on us."

Rhona looked up at the low rafters as if searching for answers. "Or say Trix took it, since she's young and easily swayed toward evil," Rhona said, making Cait stare, her mouth dropping open.

"Am I easily swayed toward evil?" Trix asked, her eyes wide.

"Yes," Libby answered.

"No," Cait said at the same time. Trix was a

trickster, but to blame the child when she hadn't even thought to do it was unthinkable. And what if the Horseman of Justice decided to take his infamous vengeance out on a wee lass?

Rhona walked over and bundled Trix up in a hug against her, a blush high in her cheeks. "Of course we cannot do that." The woman released her and pressed the heels of her palms to her forehead. "I don't know the best course of action."

"I do," Cait said, tying the black strings of her dyed tunic at her throat. "I will simply sneak into his bedchamber while he is away to Girnigoe, find the pouch, and return the ring and coins." They would have to find money for cures and a chicken elsewhere. Fiona and Evie were friends with the woman who kept a store of herbs. If anyone could talk the grumpy apothecary out of some feverfew they could. They wouldn't let Willa die.

"Jack," Cait said, looking at the boy, "reset the traps in the woods." She smiled at the others even though worry made it difficult. "A rabbit stew is as nourishing as chicken." Rhona opened her mouth to argue, but Cait continued, cutting her off. "If I return the ring and coins tonight, the Horseman may not even notice they were ever gone."

"He may have taken the pouch to Girnigoe with him," Jack said.

"Then I'll drop the coins and ring on the floor of his bedchamber where he must have changed out of his wet clothes before riding over an hour in the freezing wind. He'll think they fell out there, and even if he suspects they didn't, there's nothing to tie the mystery back to us."

Rhona grabbed her arm, her fingers digging in. "Unless he catches you."

Cait's heart hammered hard enough to make her flatten her palm against it. "He won't."

The woman's eyes were wide. "He might."

"He's gone from Varrich. Jack just confirmed it."

Jack nodded. "The guard thought the Horseman would be at Girnigoe overnight."

Rhona passed the sign of the cross before her again, her lips moving in silent prayer. "What if he comes back?" she whispered.

"Then I'll get away. I know the castle, and I have a plan for unforeseen problems." Cait nodded to her sturdy rope.

Cait pulled away to lace her boots. She was dressed in black to help her blend into the shadows. Her hair was braided and tucked into a coil at the nape of her neck. It was dark already, but her pale face stood out without her mask. She held the black wool weave across her forehead and cheeks for Rhona to tie behind her head. It left only her eyes and the lower half of her face visible.

Cait secured the strong, thin rope coil to her side, along with another she would leave outside the walls of the castle. "This will all be resolved in the next hour." She squeezed Rhona's hand. "Do not worry so."

Rhona shook her head, but her voice held surrender. "I still say 'tis too risky."

"'Tis too risky to do anything else, or nothing at all," Cait said. She had snuck into Varrich Castle before when they were desperate for food two winters ago, and the lecherous Hew Mackay hoarded riches that the common people needed. She was a thief that night, but tonight she would only be returning something. It should be easier, too, since the Horseman was away.

Gideon Sinclair. Who the bloody hell was this fabled Horseman anyway? He'd saved Willa and held them both securely as he rode them home. He hadn't even mentioned who he was when most nobles boasted of their titles and hierarchy to everyone. His actions seemed contrary to everything she'd heard about the third son of the war-loving George Sinclair.

"In and out." She patted the small coin pouch she had tied to her waist and slid her hand over the *sgian dubh* she kept in a sheath strapped to her leg. "Just keep Willa warm."

With the snow lighting the world around her, Cait did not blend into the night as easily. But luckily the moon was nearly new, allowing her to hide in the dense shadows as she moved between quiet cottages and stables in a zigzag path toward the castle near the sea. She avoided mud to hide her boot prints, but the normal traffic of the village would cover them before dawn anyway.

The conceit of the Sinclairs made them lazy about defense. Two rotted heads wouldn't deter her from sneaking over the wall facing the woods where the guards rotated only once an hour.

It also helped Cait that she'd decided at age fifteen she wouldn't be afraid of dying. Her parents had traveled beyond life, and she would meet up with them again when she followed. And with Rhona at the Orphans' Home, she knew her children and sister would continue to survive. The one thing that did scare her, though, was the possibility of one of her children being hurt. She'd continue to do anything needed to protect them from cold, famine, and now the Horseman of Justice.

She left one rope outside the wall where she could retrieve it later if necessary. Guards didn't look to the trees for people escaping. She threw the iron hook tied to the end of her longer rope upward, and it caught along the top of the stone wall. Years of climbing and swinging in the trees made the ascent easy even with the stone slick with frost. She lay on her belly along the wall's top as she unhooked her rope and lowered her legs inside the thick wall. Hanging by her fingers, she dropped, landing in a crouch.

The shadows were so thick, she could barely see her own hands as she recoiled her rope and attached it to her side. The castle was laid out in a *Z* format, three stories with walkways around the top. She kept her back to the wall of the keep as she slid along in the shadows to the rear of the castle where there had once been an herb garden. Her hands found the latch of the back door that led to a kitchen, just where it was two years ago.

Cait smiled in the darkness when it moved easily without a lock. Sinclair conceit made subterfuge simple. She paused at the deep vibration of a snore, her heart in her throat. But the man sleeping near the hearth did not stir, and she crept forward, placing one foot slowly before the next so as not to make a sound.

With the layout of the castle in mind, Cait

hurried up the winding stone stairs with light steps. She found the chief's bedchamber door on the third floor and leaned her ear against the wood. No noise issued from within. The Horseman was either gone or asleep. If the door were barred, she'd scatter the coins and ring on the stairs. *I could do that now.* But someone might steal them from the steps, and then their group would be blamed.

Cait pressed the latch and pushed gently. The door gave, and she looked inside. It was dark, too dark to properly see. She heard nothing, and she was too close to success to leave the ring outside his door.

Click. Whoosh. The sound of the walkway door opening above, letting the winter wind inside, pushed her into the room. She leaned against the closed door as she listened to footsteps, holding her breath as they marched closer, finally passing the door. *Thank the Lord.*

Her nearly blind gaze moved to the massive structure on the far wall. The heavy curtains hanging from the four posters around the bed were tied back, showing a smooth surface without the lump of a body. She took several breaths to calm her racing heart. Gideon Sinclair wasn't home.

Cait moved on silent feet, her well-worn boots soft. A table held stacks of coins balanced in both bowls of a scale, but she didn't see the leather pouch. She walked silently across to the bed and slid her hand along the thick quilt. Cait bent down to sniff it. Rosemary and something uniquely Gideon Sinclair. This was his bed, and it was massive like the man.

Her fingers curled into the warm fur draped over

the end. He had thick rugs to keep his feet warm, velvet curtains around the bed, and furs. So rich. And yet she must return the few coins with the ring. He'd hardly miss them, but she couldn't risk the consequences. She pulled out the ring and coins and dropped them on the rug by the trunk before his bed where he would likely have walked, unbuckling his belt to change into a dry plaid and tunic.

Her eyes adjusted to the near darkness of the room. The hearth was cold without embers. Two windows were large enough to allow escape if needed.

I need to go. But instead, Cait was drawn to two sets of shelves flanking the hearth, shelves that held dozens of books. Before her parents died, leaving her and her sister homeless, they'd owned books, lots of books, some in Latin, French, and English. Her father loved them, and her mother had taught Cait and Willa to read. *Information is power*, their father had said, which was why Cait's dream was to start a school in the village. The people of Varrich had lost so much confidence when the Sinclairs took over. If she could teach them to read and give them access to books, they might be able to regain some.

Her father's books would have made a school possible, even if she held it in the Orphans' Home. But when Cait's uncle arranged for her to marry Benjamin, he'd sold all the books to create a dowry for her and to pay for Willa's upkeep. Benjamin spent the dowry within the first year on whisky and the bedchamber he'd added onto the back of his cottage so he and his new bride could have privacy.

Cait's fingers moved over the leather spines.

What information lay scrolled across the pages within? Of course, Gideon Sinclair would have hundreds of books that he didn't let others read, for to read them would make them as powerful as he.

Cait stilled, her fingers resting on a thick tome, as she heard faint footsteps on the stairs. A change of guard going up to the walkway above? *Please God*.

She hurried toward the window, but her hip knocked the corner of the table. The stacked coins on the scale clanked across the wooden surface. Cait froze for a moment as her heart thumped loudly in her ears. Her fingers dropped to the table, catching two of the coins. In the darkness, she stacked them on the empty side of the scale. The coins on the other side of the scale had remained in the bowl, and she fumbled to stack them, her fingers shaking. She slid her hand across the table surface to find the others.

Plink. One fell and rolled somewhere on the floor. *Good Lord!* She stacked the third coin, but to get the scales even, she needed the fourth.

Cait's wide eyes turned to the door where the bootsteps stopped. *Go on. Keep moving.* She must still find the fourth coin. When she heard a hand press the door latch, she ran to the window, swinging it open. Working quickly, she dropped the rope down the forty-foot descent and secured the iron clamp on the stone ledge. The door swung inward, and Cait pulled herself back behind the curtain, her heart hammering painfully in her chest.

• • •

Gideon held the small dry leaf that he'd found sitting on the stone floor in the corridor. Earlier, he'd stuck it in the crack of his door when he'd closed it, his normal precaution. It'd been disturbed, meaning someone had opened the door. Perhaps one of the maids he'd asked Bruce to hire had brought in linens even though he'd ordered no one to enter his quarters. Leaving the door unlocked was a test, like leaving gold coins sitting on his desk inside. If he had a need for secrecy, he'd have locked it. He must know if there were people in his new home who broke the rules he'd firmly set.

He walked inside, holding his lantern high, his gaze taking in the simple layout easily. No one was visible, but his warrior instincts weren't fooled. Enemies often hid right before one's face. He slid the bar over the door. If someone were inside, they'd have no way out. Listening, Gideon moved casually to the hearth and bent, lighting the peat he had left stacked there.

Standing, his gaze scanned the dimness. Was the intruder still there? He walked to his desk where he'd left stacks of four coins each sitting on opposite sides of the scale his father had gifted him years ago. The scale was unbalanced, with one side higher because one gold coin was missing. He spotted it below the desk, and with ears listening to the deep silence, he crouched to retrieve it.

A whisper of fabric near one window made him pivot around to see a form in black lifting a leg over the sill. "Stad," he yelled. From the slender build, the intruder was a child or woman, both unthinkable. Who would be brazen enough to come into the bedchamber of a Sinclair Horseman?

"I order ye to halt," he said, his roar deafening in the stone room. In two strides he had the intruder. He pulled them around and stared into a masked face. What trickery was this?

Dressed all in black to blend into the shadows, it was difficult to make out the form. But the shadows couldn't hide the softness of a woman's body as he pulled her against him.

He grabbed her wrist, but with a twist and a yank, she escaped his hold and tried to turn back to the window. "We're three stories up, lass," Gideon said. "Ye will split your head on the hard ground if ye go that way."

She lunged onto the window's ledge, apparently not deterred. Was death preferable to being caught by him? He grabbed her around the waist, tugging her back inside, his face pressing against the back of her neck where a mound of dark hair was pinned. "Who are ye?" he asked.

Gideon turned the woman around to face him. Instead of rearing back, she threw herself into him, hugging around his chest with both arms as if he were a huge tree she wished to climb or uproot from the ground. He grunted, and her covered face tipped up to him. She pressed upward against his body, her arms rising as she stretched onto her toes and held his shoulders. He had no time to react as she grabbed behind his head, pulling his face down to hers to kiss him.

Bloody hell! What was she doing? Gideon certainly wouldn't let a lass dupe him like Ella had tricked his oldest brother with a kiss, to escape him when they first met.

Fingers tugging his hair, she pressed her lips hard against his. The kiss was clumsy, frantic, like a virgin caught in her first storm of passion. But when her warm palms caught his face, and she slanted across his mouth, deepening the kiss, he wondered if she possibly had some experience.

She stroked fingers through his hair, her warm lips moving over his, and her frantic desperation began to calm. As the stiffness he'd felt in her faded, so did his thoughts about Ella tricking Cain and whether this soft creature in his arms was a maiden or not. Even the questions about how she got in and her ultimate purpose washed away with the growing warmth of her response. Perhaps it was the darkness, or the mystery of who she was, or the scent that plucked at his memory, but fire ignited inside Gideon. His arms encircled her, pulling her soft body against his hard frame.

Gideon lifted her, backing her against the wall. She was all womanly curves and softness. His fingers tangled in the twist of hair at her nape. Pins fell, plinking on the stone window frame next to her, and her heavy braid slipped down over one shoulder. He pressed his face to it, inhaling along the thick length as they both pulled shallow breaths. It was silky and fragrant, tugging at that memory that wouldn't reveal itself. Who was she? Would she stay the night?

His mouth fell upon her neck, tasting the light saltiness there as he trailed kisses over her smooth skin. Her head tipped back against the wall, her breath coming in shallow rasps. He moved back to her parted lips where the kiss swept them both up again. The woman's scent, her warmth and curves, the mystery around her… It all ensnared him. Like a siren in Homer's *Odyssey*.

He held her between him and the stone wall beside the open window. Cold air had no effect on him with such fire growing inside at her response. He captured her face in his hands, feeling the mask. It was wool and tied tightly. He reached behind her head to pluck at the knot. As if the lass had been under the same spell as he, his tugging on the ties startled her into action. She gasped, turning her face away before he could free the knot. She shoved at his chest, her knee rising, but he shifted so she missed his groin.

"Hold still," he said, but her hand whipped out toward him, and Gideon felt the sting of a blade across his arm. Surprise made him release his hold for a second. Apparently, that was all the time the lass needed to hurl herself out of his window.

"Nay!" he yelled as she disappeared, leaping to her death.

CHAPTER FOUR

English codes, 16th century AD

Those who steal goods will be fined depending on the value of what has been taken. For rich items or hurt inflicted on the victim, the thief may be flogged, mutilated by cutting off one or both ears or a hand, or hanged to death.

Oh my God! Oh my blessed damning God!

Cait used the rope, winding her feet in its length to slide swiftly to the ground. There would be no retrieving it or her *sgian dubh* that she'd dropped. She didn't even dare raise her face to the window where she could hear Gideon Sinclair yelling. Would his guards hear and run around, thwarting her escape over the back wall?

Cait hit the ground and glanced up the side of the tower. The cold air lodged like wool in her throat, choking her. *Holy Lord!* The Horseman was following her down the rope.

Cait's legs acted while she coughed. Her boots churned up the logs stacked on the side of the stone stable, knocking some of them to roll so that she had to scramble with both feet and hands to the top. At the peak, she threw a leg up to catch the edge of the stable's roofline with her heel and pulled herself up to leap upon the top of the encircling wall. She took a deep breath as she dangled over it, concentrating.

"Stad!" Gideon yelled from the other side of the wall.

She grunted as she landed in a squat and took off running directly into the darkest shadows, not toward the Orphans' Home, because her footprints could be seen in the mud and snow. Arms pumping, Cait reached out to grab the rope she'd left hanging from a low branch without missing a step and raced into the woods.

The wind blew through the bare branches. *Damn.* It was easier to hide in summer when the foliage was thick. Her heart leaped as she heard a thump behind her. Gideon had jumped over the castle wall. If he caught her, would he slice right through her there in the forest for cutting his hand? *God's teeth! I bloodied one of the Sinclair Horsemen! I stole from and bloodied the Horseman of Justice. And I kissed him!*

It'd been the only thing she could think of to surprise him enough to get away. And now…*I might die for it.* She'd told herself that all would be well if she died, but in the face of it, fear tormented her. What would become of her children and Rhona? And Mistress Fiona and her sister, Evie, who barely survived on the food Cait could steal for them? And old Master Woodcroft and all the others?

Cait made for the large oak she often used to practice climbing, but it was a good five-minute sprint away. Her eyes had thoroughly adjusted to the low light, the sliver of moon giving her enough to dodge trees, but she heard footfalls crashing through the woods behind her.

"Stad!" Gideon yelled.

Like hell she'd stop. Cait searched for a place to

veer. Another tree to climb, somewhere to hide. But the winter-bare woods offered little in the way of salvation.

A large chestnut tree stood off to the right. The limbs were high, probably too high to throw her rope up to, but it was thick. A straight-out run against a Sinclair horseman would never see her as the winner. Cait reached for the tree, catching the bark with her hand to swing her around. She thumped against it, hugging her whole body in close, and willed her heart to slow. *Thin, small, silent.* She pressed her head against the wide trunk.

Blood rushed in her ears, but she could still hear Gideon running toward her. He seemed to prefer crashing straight through bramble and small trees rather than dodging them.

He will go right past. Right past. Please God, let him go right past. Returning coin was harder than stealing it.

Gideon no longer yelled for her to stop. He just ran, somehow knowing her direction. How the bloody hell could he track her at night when the moon was a sliver?

The frozen twigs snapped under his heavy boots. He could probably crush the bones in her wrist if he stepped on them. *Stop it.* If she let panic grip her, she would do something stupid like gasp or faint or die right there where she stood. Her chest hurt with her pounding heart, and she rubbed a fist against it.

Gideon ran past close enough that she could hear him take a breath while she held her own. *Past. He ran past.*

The crashing footfalls silenced, and she sucked in

a soft gasp. Gideon Sinclair had stopped. The small crunch of a footstep came from a few yards beyond her. She'd scoot around the tree to the opposite side, but she dared not move. Instead, she concentrated on becoming a part of the trunk. If only she could grow bark and moss along her back.

"I know ye are here somewhere," Gideon said. "Your footsteps pounding through the brush went silent."

Damn. In a full-out sprint, she couldn't keep quiet any more than he could. Cait looked at the limb above her. Could she reach it with her rope? Climb up there before Gideon descended upon her like a bloodthirsty wolf?

No. Perfect stillness and a miracle were the only ways to outsmart the infamous Sinclair Horseman. When stars started to spark before her eyes in the darkness, Cait parted her lips and drew in a silent stream of air and released it the same way.

She listened to his footsteps as he walked along the trail on the other side of the tree. "Your kiss was cold and hard, lass. And it didn't distract me enough for ye to escape."

You are a cold fish of a woman. Benjamin's words sneered in her memory.

"If ye come out, ye can give it another try," Gideon said, his voice just on the other side of the thick tree. When she didn't answer, not even with the crack of a twig, he went on. "What were ye doing up in my room? Did I interrupt a robbery? If you had braved my bedroom for a tryst, ye wouldn't have jumped out the window."

He walked a little farther up the trail. Could he

make out her tracks in the dim light of the moon? Damn snow made them stand out. It seemed God wasn't interested in trying to save her from this mess. It was all up to her.

Cait let her breath out slowly, listening to his footfalls crunch in the mix of snow and dead leaves. She nearly jumped when she felt a tug on the coil of rope that she held. *Damn.* The end had uncoiled several lengths on her run and lay on top of the leaves before the tree.

Cait tried to inhale, but her breath kept stuttering in her chest as Gideon slowly coiled the loose rope, which had become a trail directly to her. He rounded the side of the tree and stopped. The darkness cloaked him in shadow, making his solid form look even larger. Gideon Sinclair stared directly at her.

• • •

The woman stood so silent and still behind the tree that at first she seemed to be frozen to stone. "Checkmate," Gideon said as if this were merely a game instead of a crime.

Her mask still covered the top half of her face, leaving those lush lips bare. He'd lied about them being cold, but she hadn't fallen for that easy trick. He would've caught her eventually, leaving no tree unsearched, but her rope had given her away quite quickly. A shame. He couldn't remember being so tested in a game of chase, and he'd liked it to have gone on longer. Although not enough to let her go.

As if the rock encasing her body shattered away from her form, the woman lurched around, dashing into the darkness. The abandoned rope dangled from his hands for several seconds before he leaped after her.

The silence of the night woods broke with crashing as he dashed up the slope behind her, seeing the length of her braid. It swung like a pendulum. The woman was spry and desperate, but neither could beat his strength and stamina. He could run for hours and trained daily with steed and sword. He stayed behind her, matching her pace without exceeding it. Where would she lead him? Should he give her hope that she could get away, or was that cruel? He frowned at the thought and increased his pace, closing the distance.

Gideon reached out, his hand grazing her braid. She made a distressed sound, and her arms pumped harder, giving her a small boost. Did she see the edge of the riverbank coming up?

"Stad," he yelled, but she continued. "Stad. The river!"

With a leap, he grabbed her, pulling her into his chest as he dove and twisted in the air so that she landed sprawled across his chest. They skidded together, the snow and mud soaking immediately through his tunic, until they came to a stop just above the rushing water below. He kicked his heel into the mud, rolling her away from the bank, and pinned her. Without the layers of petticoats most lasses wore, he could feel the soft curves of her thighs and hips against him.

"In all honesty," he said, taking a deep breath to slow the beat of his heart, "ye didn't have a chance."

He reached one hand up and plucked the mask

from her face. His eyes had grown accustomed to the lack of light, and the sliver of moon shone through the thin clouds above. Her lovely face was pale, dark eyebrows arched over wide eyes. She breathed heavily, her chest rising and falling fast, and her lips were parted.

"Cait Mackay," he said. "Why would I find ye in my bedchamber?" His brow rose, and he frowned. "Were ye stealing from the Horseman of Justice?"

"No," she said, and he caught sight of the tip of her tongue as she wet her bottom lip quickly, as if her mouth had gone dry from the rapid breathing.

"No?" he repeated. "Then why would ye be in my bedchamber? Surely, it wasn't to kiss me."

The corner of her mouth hitched upward. "Maybe it was, but then your kiss was so…cold and ghastly I sought to take my life."

He smiled at her ploy. "I have had no such complaints before, so I must assume ye were there to steal my gold coins."

Her lips pulled slightly back. "I was returning your ring," she said. "And coins."

He frowned. "Which ye must have stolen earlier." Anger coiled down inside him. "When ye fell against me upon leaving your cottage."

She neither admitted her guilt nor denied it but stared straight up at him.

He dropped his gaze and gave a wry huff. "And after I saved your sister," he said and shook his head, the heaviness of immense disappointment weighing on him. "A crime against me to pay for such kindness."

She turned her face to the side. With shame?

Remorse? Or just anger for being caught in her heinous act? "I was returning them," she said.

Perhaps remorse had plagued her. "A crime to correct a crime."

Cait's head turned back, her gaze meeting his. Her large, expressive eyes glittered under the scant light. "Willa needs feverfew and a chicken. Kindness does not buy that."

"A chicken?" he asked.

"Children, especially those fighting fevers, need food, meat," she said as if explaining something to a simpleton.

Gideon had asked Bruce to distribute two chickens to each home in Varrich. One to eat and one to lay. He'd have to check his ledgers. Had the Orphans' Home already gone through their chickens?

"Stealing is never the solution," Gideon said. "'Tis a crime, which must be punished."

"Get off me," she said, and tried to shove him. "Or does the Horseman of Judgment punish through rape?"

He rolled off her. "Rape is not a punishment. 'Tis a crime," he said. "And I am the Horseman of Justice, not Judgment."

"That depends on which side of your verdict one finds oneself," she shot back and crouched. The movement surprised him enough that Gideon watched instead of grabbing her again. She leaped upward, her hands grasping a thick tree limb above his head. It was a worthy leap, but she couldn't hope to escape him. However, if she climbed the tree, then he'd be out here in the winter night for many more hours trying to get her to come down. He'd much rather question her in front of a warm hearth at the castle. And then what? Throw her in a cold dungeon? If he must.

He sighed and grabbed her leg. "Come down."

"Let go," she yelled. Raising her boots, she extended her legs with a powerful snap. She kicked him square in the chest.

Gideon felt the sodden riverbank give way under his heel, throwing his balance off even more. His arms went out as he fell backward.

"Cac!" he yelled as icy cold hit every part of him, and he was caught in the tumble of rushing, dark, frigid water. His head came up, and he took a large gulp of air. The last thing he heard before submerging under the river's icy water was his name.

"Gideon!"

• • •

The castle sat ahead, lit for the night, the portcullis down. Cait ran across the road that she'd emerged onto from the woods, her arms pumping at her sides. She hit the iron bars hard, her hands wrapping around to shake them. "Gideon's in the river! Somebody help him!"

"What say ye lass?" called down one of the guards.

Gideon had chased her. Had he not alerted the guards? "Your master, Gideon Sinclair..." She took two frantic breaths before continuing. "He's fallen into the icy river, just west of here." She threw her arm out toward the dark woods. "Come save him!"

The guard yelled down to some other men, and the portcullis began to rise as they cranked the iron chain that held it. "Hurry!" she yelled. "He was swept down the river. I don't know how far." Lord, she didn't even know if he was conscious. If he wasn't, he was already dead, drowned in the dark cold waters. *God, no.* "Save him," she whispered, but so far God hadn't paid much attention to her pleas tonight.

Cait had kicked him hard in the chest as she tried to climb away, a last effort to escape her fate. A fate that probably included public ridicule and punishment. Losing her right hand? Surely, not her head. But now, if Gideon survived, he'd accuse her of attempting to murder him.

A combination of Mackay and Sinclair warriors ran out of the bailey. Bruce Mackay stopped near her, his eyes scanning her sleek trousers and dark clothes. "What did ye do?" he asked.

Cait turned away from him and marched under the portcullis toward the doors of the castle, her boots crunching under her feet. She couldn't go home, not when she could be arrested and dragged out of her cottage, frightening the children.

She shivered with the dampness of mud and snow against her skin where it had soaked through her tunic. What would happen if Gideon died in the water? Who would rule them next? What would his brothers say? What questions would they bombard her with? *I am guilty. Guilty of so much.* She stood shivering before the wide steps leading up to the keep, unsure of what to do.

Crunch. Crunch. Crunch. Cait turned around, and

her heart leaped as she watched the forceful run of the drenched man barreling toward her. Soaked through and as mad as a poked bear. She could even hear the squish of the water in his fur-lined boots.

Gideon stopped before her, breathing hard, a mix of fury and surprise on his face. She fought the irrational urge to try to warm him.

"Ye are here," he said, his brows lowering. "Why?"

"To get help," she said. "I thought… I didn't want you to drown."

Gideon ran his hands up to his head, pushing his dripping hair back. "Every bloody time I'm around ye, I end up in the freezing river."

His voice was so surly she snapped back. "Only twice, and neither were my fault. The first was Willa's fault and the second… You shouldn't have tried to stop me from climb—"

"Ye kicked me in the bloody river!" His voice boomed, making her blink.

"Only because I needed to get away," she yelled back.

The group of men who'd run out had followed Gideon back inside the castle gates and formed a semicircle around them. Gideon glanced to the sides as if only realizing that they were not alone.

He slid out his sword, which had somehow survived the icy submersion. Cait took an involuntary step back and nearly tripped on the first rise.

"Cait Mackay," Gideon called, his voice loud enough for everyone in the bailey to hear. "Ye are under arrest for thievery and attempted murder of your chief."

CHAPTER FIVE

The Code of Hammurabi, 1750 BC

If anyone bring an accusation against a man, and the accused go to the river and leap into the river, if he sink in the river his accuser shall take possession of his house. But if the river prove that the accused is not guilty, and he escape unhurt, then he who had brought the accusation shall be put to death, while he who leaped into the river shall take possession of the house that had belonged to his accuser.

"What did she steal?" Joshua asked. "Before she threw herself out your window?"

"It seems ye found a lass who does fly," Cain said, a slight grin on his face.

Gideon ignored Cain. "My ring and three coins that were missing. She stole them before I left the Orphans' Home. Fell against me and picked my pocket."

"What was she doing in your bedroom then?" Bàs asked.

"Giving them back."

Cain lowered his bulk into one of the cushion-lined chairs by the hearth in the great hall of Varrich Castle. "She didn't take anything else?"

"Nay," Gideon said, pacing before the mantel where he'd spent most of the night. After having two of his guards escort Cait down into the dungeon with three wool blankets and a flask of weak ale, he'd changed out of his soaked clothing and spent the night in the great hall. He'd dozed on one of the guard's pallets, but for the most part he paced, trying to reason out the day's events. "Nay," he repeated. "My other stacks of coin were on my scales. Although one was on the floor"

"Ye just leave gold coins stacked about your room?" Joshua asked, throwing himself into another padded chair. "Do ye sit there at night counting them or throw them on the bed to roll around in them?"

Gideon felt his eye twitch, something that his older brother often inflicted upon him. "'Tis a test to see if anyone in my household will steal them and a reminder to them of who I am."

"Is there a reason for your people at Varrich to be stealing?" Cain asked. "They have enough food and supplies?"

"I've taken thorough accounts of the crops and animals, which were poor indeed after Hew Mackay neglected to guide his people. I gave Bruce Mackay the responsibility of distributing more chickens and grain to the villagers after ye advised I use one of their own to do so. After their gardens were burned when we attacked Varrich to save Ella, much of their food sources were destroyed."

Joshua's easy smile faded. He'd been in favor of burning the whole village to the ground then, but after returning from Orkney with his bride and her people, the Horseman of War seemed much changed. Gideon wasn't sure if he appreciated the calmer Joshua. The old one was loud and temperamental, but at least he was predictable.

"I can help ye distribute if ye don't trust your steward," Joshua said. "People who are in need must do anything they can to survive and keep their loved ones alive. Even risking their necks stealing from Sinclair warriors."

Gideon stared at the mask in his hands that one of his men had found in the woods. He held it to his nose and inhaled. *Damn.* The wool held the sweet scent that seemed to surround Cait, a mix of flowers and the herbs drying in her home.

"What are ye planning to do with her?" Cain asked, glancing down the hallway toward the door leading to the dungeon. "Ye've sent down food and drink?"

"Drink," Gideon said and stopped his pacing, also staring down the hallway. Cait hadn't said a word after he'd declared her arrest. Frown in place, she just turned and marched into the castle, waiting for someone to take her to the dungeon. "And blankets."

"Which cell is she in?" Bàs asked, also looking in that direction.

"The fresh one with solid walls, a pallet, and a privy hole in the corner," Gideon said. "So no rodents can get in and there is privacy, although there aren't any prisoners down there right now anyway."

"Will ye have Bàs cut off her head?" Joshua said, and the three of them turned frowns toward him. Joshua shrugged. "Ye make the laws, not I."

"I don't order executions for thievery," Gideon said.

"Her hand then?" Joshua said, his tone goading.

"A ring and three coins do not warrant that," Cain said, but his glance at Gideon made it obvious his brother didn't know if Gideon agreed.

"The ring was exceedingly expensive," Gideon said, his frown deepening. "Solid gold."

Silence sat between them until Gideon cleared his throat. "But she did not intend to steal the ring, only three shillings."

"So…" Joshua said, pulling the word out. "A finger then? Have Bàs chop that off with a little axe?"

"Tolla-thon," Gideon said, glaring at his grinning brother. "I'm not a tyrant."

"Perhaps we should take a poll of your people," Joshua said. "See what they think."

Gideon took three strides to reach Joshua, his hands plunking down on the two arms of the chair to lean into his brother's face. "Says the Horseman of War who wanted to burn Varrich to the ground, people and all. Just save the horses, ye said."

Joshua shoved Gideon in the chest, and he let Joshua stand up. If his older brother wanted a fight, Gideon was in the mood to accommodate him. Joshua pointed a finger at him. "I am not the real, inhumane Horseman of War, just like ye are not the Horseman of Justice sent down from a cloud by God." Joshua wiggled his fingers, and the light from the fire bounced off the ring Gideon had given him. "No matter what your trinkets proclaim."

"Father just turned over and raged at ye from the grave," Gideon said, coming nose to nose with Joshua.

"But there he will stay," Joshua said. "Because he's dead. And he was wrong. And ye might want to look at who ye really are, little brother."

Gideon, sleep deprived and coiled tight, pulled his fist back. Cain caught it, stepping before Gideon as Bàs pushed Joshua back. Gideon looked over Cain's shoulder at Joshua. "We are the Four Horsemen, the Sons of Sinclair," he said, his voice filling the great hall. "Anything less will bring doom to our clan and those who support us."

Joshua snorted and rolled his eyes. "That sounds like tyrant talk to me, that or lunacy. Either will see ye dead, something I would really rather not see." Joshua pointed at Gideon, his brows raised. "There are too many tyrants in this world. Don't add to their number."

Gideon shook off Cain's hold, keeping his gaze on Joshua. "I've no intention of doing so."

"Then be careful," Cain said, his voice low. He canted his head toward the door where a maid and Gideon's cook, Mathias, stood. "Small villages spread tales like fire through dry trees."

• • •

Cait leaned against the dungeon wall where she sat wrapped in blankets on the straw pallet. Winter sunlight lit the barred window in the upper part of the cell, and she was able to see the truth of what her senses told her last night. Gideon had a clean dungeon. It was tidier than some cottages in the village, like the one Alistair shared with his father. The dungeon floor was swept, and it even had a privy with a lid to keep the smell of sewage out.

Before she'd fallen asleep, she'd listened a long

time for the scurry of rats, but there had been none. Perhaps Gideon's fastidiousness bled over from his bedchamber to his dungeon.

She wiped her hands over her face and sighed. Rhona must be frantic. And the children. Had Gideon even let them know she was there? Had he gone to question them about her thievery? Hopefully, none of them said they were to blame because none of them were. Cait could imagine Rhona saying that she was at fault because she'd reminded Cait they needed supplies, or Jack because he hadn't caught anything in his latest trap. Or Willa for falling in the river and catching a fever.

"They could all end up in here with me," she whispered.

The scrape of the door at the top of the sloped walkway made her stiffen, and she took a fortifying breath as she rose to meet whatever appeared in the barred square in the wooden door. *Don't be Bruce.*

She let out her breath as Gideon's face stopped before the opening, his sharp gaze glancing about the cell before meeting her own. "Why do ye not have a chicken for Willa?"

Gideon apparently didn't start the day with a "Good morn." Cait crossed her arms over her chest, the blanket still wrapped around her. "The fires you set after killing Robert Mackay burned our coop and fences. What chickens survived were eaten by wolves within a week, before we could properly rebuild." It had been over a year now. "You do remember that? Setting fire to our village?" she asked, unable to keep the sarcasm from her voice.

Gideon kept his stony stare. "Ye were given two

chickens and a rooster. One hen was to be kept alive to lay eggs to eat and hatch into more chickens. Only one was to eat at the time. Did ye eat both hens and the rooster?"

"We did not receive chickens nor grain."

She watched his nostrils flare slightly as he inhaled. "I had Bruce Mackay distribute poultry to Varrich Village last summer. Two hens and a rooster per dwelling with six or more inhabitants."

Cait had seen the chickens given to some, but certainly not to anyone Bruce Mackay did not favor. Ever since she'd kicked him in the ballocks when he'd kissed her roughly behind the chapel, he did not favor her nor the orphans.

She opened her mouth to say as such, but then closed it. If history had taught her anything, it was that chiefs believed their stewards over their yeoman, especially a thief who'd kicked him in the river. And angering Bruce Mackay would just make things worse for her family. "Not all of us received them," she said, her words flat.

Cait could see only Gideon's handsomely dark face in the cutout in the door, but it hardened into something that sent a chill down Cait's spine. No wonder the villagers were terrified of the Sinclair Horsemen, especially the new chief of Varrich. Gideon didn't even need rotting heads flanking his gates to stop someone from crossing him. Yet, she'd invaded his room, and kicked him into the river. What a tangled mess.

"I'll speak with Bruce," Gideon said.

"Don't," Cait said, hurrying to the door.

"Why?"

They stared at each other through the square, her hands curled around the bars. She realized her eyes had dropped to look at his full, warm mouth, and jerked her gaze back up. "He will only say I lied."

She turned away, presenting her back. "That I'm a thief and therefore not someone to be trusted over your steward."

"Hmph," Gideon said behind her. "There seem to be quite a number of people insisting ye are trustworthy."

Cait turned, frowning. Had the children come? Rhona? "What do you mean?" But he didn't answer. He left the square in the door, making her rise on her toes to follow him with her gaze. "What people?"

The jingle of the keys was followed by his return, his dark hair looking clean and soft as he bent to shove one into her lock. "Come above." The door opened outward.

For a moment, she hesitated. Without the thick door between them, she was at the mercy of his strength. But for all the struggles last night, he hadn't hurt her, even after she'd sent him flying backward into the river.

He returned the keys to the hook on the wall and raised his arm to the side to motion for her to precede him. Shoulders back, Cait walked out of the cell, the wool blanket still wrapped around her shoulders like a cloak. Mud-stained, hair-mussed, and smelling of damp wool, Cait managed to keep her chin high and walk without hesitation up the slope, knowing that Gideon followed. She could feel him staring at her back. She stepped evenly into the great hall and stopped. It was empty and silent.

She turned to stare at him, and he pointed at the table where a cup and platter of cheese, bannocks, and cut apples sat. "Eat something," he said.

"This is a trick?" she asked, and her stomach betrayed her with a loud grumble.

He glanced heavenward. "Aye. I'm tricking ye with food and ale. My villainous desire is to see ye fed and hearty."

She walked over to the table and bit into the cheese, followed by a slice of apple. The gnawing in her stomach abated before any of it could even reach it with a swallow. She pointed the cheese she held at him. "Some tyrants do that, you know. Make their prisoners healthy before executing them."

Gideon's face hardened, his eyes narrowing. "I'm not a tyrant."

She turned back to the plate to try the bannocks. They were moist and spiced. Was this the work of Gideon's new cook? It was said the man hailed from Orkney where he'd been stationed to work for another tyrant.

"Where are these people who insist I am trustworthy?" she asked after she washed the food down with some weak ale.

"Come," he said and walked across the room, a dry set of boots strapped to his legs. He didn't turn, assuming she would follow.

The winter wind hit her in the face when Gideon opened the door, and she followed him out to stand on the top step leading into the bailey. Silence filled the space, silence and a multitude of people. Cait's breath caught on a wave of emotions. Fear for them.

Shame for herself. Gratitude for their presence. It all tangled into knots in her stomach. When she saw Gideon's brother, the Horseman of Death, standing off to the side, his skull mask in place and an ax resting against his boot, the knot slid up too high in her stomach. *Do not vomit. Breathe.*

Rhona stood near the front. "Cait," she yelled, pulling her attention. Libby and Trix were clinging to her, their eyes wide.

"Mistress Cait," Jack called next to her.

"Stay where ye are," Rhona ordered him.

Cait covered her mouth with her hand as her gaze moved over the small crowd, purposely avoiding the executioner. Alistair stood there, looking angrier than she'd ever seen him. His youthful face had solidified into the look of a warrior even if he hadn't the bulk. "Let her go," he called.

"Aye, the lass didn't steal anything," Old Master Woodcroft said from his spot on the other side. "I did." He hobbled closer on his carved support stick. "I took your ring. She was but giving it back."

So, they had all heard about her crime. Cait's cheeks heated.

"Me too," Fiona Mackay said, holding tightly to her sister's hand.

"And I," her sister, Evie, said. The two of them took a step closer. "We stole the coins. Cait was but giving them back."

Trix pulled away from Rhona. "I'm easily swayed toward evil," she called in her little voice. "I took them from your pouch."

"She did no such thing," Rhona called, pulling her back into her side, her lips moving in prayer as she lifted her eyes to the heavy clouds.

A rumble of whispers seemed to float over the crowd like a dense cloud. "I did," another called.

"Spare Cait. She's a good lass."

"I will take her place," Alistair called and strode forward, stopping in the middle of the bailey. "Let the executioner take my head instead." A gasp rose among the crowd, more of them peeking in from around the gates where grim guards stood watching.

"I'm not cutting off her head," Gideon said, his voice carrying across the gasping whispers.

"Maybe not you," Alistair said, "but him." He pointed to Bàs.

"Dear God," Cait whispered. Gideon looked at her and then back at Alistair. "Gideon," she said, "these people... Alistair—"

"I will take her place for whatever punishment you choose, Sinclair," Jack said, striding out to stand beside Alistair.

"No," Cait said.

Master Woodcroft came to stand beside Alistair, along with two hesitant men she'd helped before, men who had families who counted on them. Families not favored by Bruce for whom Cait had stolen so they did not go hungry.

"These people," Gideon said, jabbing a finger in the air at them. "They've been insisting ye are trustworthy since dawn."

He stared at her as she blinked against the emotion in her eyes. "Apparently," he said, "there are witnesses ready to swear that ye were either with them last night or that they were the ones who jumped out my window and kicked me into the river."

"They said that?" she said, her voice small.

"Not these people," he said, looking out on the waiting crowd. "These people," he said, holding up a small piece of slate with somewhat smudged names written in chalk at the bottom. "These people signed this statement of confession and are hiding from Bàs's ax and my sword."

Her lips opened and closed several times, and she shook her head. "None of—"

"Stop," he said, cutting her off. His eyes went back to the crowd who continued to yell sporadic confessions, the most repeated one being, "I'm the one who kicked a horseman into the river."

"Enough!" Gideon yelled, and a hush fell immediately under the power of that one word. It was like his sword cutting through a man.

Cait could feel the fear in the people before her, and yet they spoke up for her. She was honored and humbled and getting angrier by the second. "None of these people are guilty of any crime," she said, her words carrying across the bailey.

A round to the contrary started again.

"I said enough!" Gideon's voice thundered, punctuated by him drawing his sword. Several women screamed and Rhona grabbed Trix and Libby, dragging them to the back of the crowd.

"I'm the sole witness of these goings on," Gideon continued, his voice just slightly softer, like a rumble of thunder over the mountains instead of a death strike.

He continued, striding between Cait and the front line of people, his sword still held. It moved along his side like an extension of his arm. "I've heard enough about Cait Mackay's trustworthiness, but the fact is she still stole. I will forgive the incident with the river as the intent was not to kill, and I did not die." He looked out over the crowd as if waiting for some snide remark, but none came. "I am not a tyrant, a brute, nor a monster." He turned to look at Cait. "I've decided she will work off her punishment."

"You bastard," Alistair yelled and rushed at Gideon. Everyone gasped, including Cait.

Gideon let the rage-filled man use his own weight and momentum to fall past him with an easy dodge. Gideon's voice continued as Alistair fell on the frozen ground.

"Work as the planner of my Hogmanay festival," Gideon continued, his eyes narrowed as his gaze raked the crowd, judging them poorly for jumping to whatever dastardly conclusion to which Alistair had jumped.

He turned back to Cait and released his breath. "After careful thought, and witness of your character by these people...I am reducing your crime. Ye did not intend to steal the ring, which was worth enough to at least lose your hand."

Cait rubbed her wrist, glancing at Bàs's sword. Would she have felt the strike of such a sharp blade? She drew a slow breath, dispelling the sparks that once again popped up and moved in her periphery.

"Your crime is stealing three shillings," Gideon continued. "For that, ye have spent one night in Varrich's dungeon and will spend however many days are needed to make Varrich Castle merry for a Hogmanay Festival for the village. Ye will work with the children to put on a pageant and discuss food with my cook. Ye may return to the Orphans' Home in the evenings but must report to the castle just after dawn until the task is complete."

He looked out at the crowd. "So says the Horseman of Justice."

Cait swallowed, looking out on her friends. She was muddied and unkempt, stripped of her pride, but she stood there with her hand and her life. And anger, a growing, smoldering anger. It niggled at her stomach as she watched Gideon turn to her. Did he expect her to fall to her knees in grateful praise at his leniency?

"Before these many witnesses to your goodness in the village," he said, "do ye accept your punishment?"

Cait held her head steady, her gaze on his. "Shall I add holly crowns to the skulls at the gate?" She pointed to where the skulls of Robert Mackay and Hew Mackay sat, or rather, where they had been sitting on pikes.

Gideon followed her gaze. "As ye can see, they've been removed, but holly wreaths at the gate would be festive." He looked back at her, his piercing eyes and the white scar on his tanned cheek making her heart gallop despite her resolution to stay strong. "Do ye accept your punishment?" he asked.

"I'll need a day to gather greenery," she said.

"Of course. The rest of today and the next, but ye must arrive up at the castle the following day. Do ye accept this very fair punishment for your crimes?"

There was no other answer to give. "Yes," she said.

He nodded, his face neutral. "Go on then."

She hesitated for a mere second and then walked down the steps into the crowd, Gideon's blanket still wrapped around her. Alistair was off the ground, his cheeks stained red. Rhona, the girls, and Jack gathered around Cait as they walked out of Varrich's gates, but Cait could feel Gideon's stare on her back like a hot brand.

CHAPTER SIX

Scottish law, 1567 AD

A Scold's Bridle, a metal frame, is to be placed over a woman's head to penalize her for repeated verbal offenses and gossiping. The iron bit is to be stuck in her mouth to prevent her from talking, and she may be paraded through her town.

His father's last words to Gideon, as the warlord bled out on the battlefield, resonated within him. *Judge well without mercy. Be unbendable in your judgment. Ye know what is right from wrong.*

But did Gideon know right from wrong? He'd wanted to release Cait from his dungeon as soon as he'd put on dry clothes.

Gideon lifted his hands to rub the back of his neck but hid the telling action by scratching his head. He looked out at Bruce Mackay who stood before his desk, cap in hands.

Gideon had grown up watching the subtle signs in people to reveal what was in their minds and hearts, the truths they tried to cover up. His father would send people in to lie to him, testing Gideon to see if he could pick truth out from lies. If he was wrong, shaming and violence followed. By the time he was twenty, Gideon always deduced right. Always.

"Robbed ye?" Gideon glanced back at his

ledgers. "And ye said nothing to me?" He raised his gaze back to the man's shiny eyes.

Bruce blinked but kept a severe frown in place. "I didn't want to give ye more reason to dislike our clan. I thought ye would think I lied."

Gideon knew he lied. But a lie, with enough time in between, gave the liar time to convince himself that he had done nothing wrong. The evidence was harder to see in a person's face and stance once he'd convinced himself that he was in the right. "How many chickens were stolen last spring?"

"At least half," Bruce said. "I think it was Clan Gunn. They wore masks and looked like bandits. Stole some sacks of grain, too." Bruce rubbed his stubbled jaw. "I've been trying to help folks in the village by giving the supplies I saved to those who seemed to need them most."

Gideon stared hard for a long moment. Bruce glanced downward for a brief second before raising his eyes. Gideon turned back to his ledger, scratching the information in the appropriate blocks on his chart of food distribution. "The crop yield hasn't had time to increase. This spring, we will rotate the fields, clear a new one for planting, and burn the old barley field to cut back on the weeds that were allowed to grow freely."

"Aye, milord," Bruce said, his voice stern.

Gideon looked up. "I've sent to my brother and our allies at the Sutherland Clan for chickens to be bred. And I have lifted the old ban on villagers hunting for large animals. Any bucks brought down shall be distributed to those who did not get chickens last year. I want a list of those households." *The Orphans'*

Home had better be on it. "Is that clear?"

"Aye, milord." The man's mouth was firm, as if he fought to contain his anger. Did he resent Gideon's oversight? Apparently, Bruce Mackay needed oversight. If he lied about the Orphans' Home, that would be the final strike against him, and he would lose his position as steward and perhaps find himself in Varrich's dungeons.

"And I'll be told right away if there are any further raids, ambushes, or thieves about," Gideon said, meeting the man's hard stare with a fierce one of his own.

"Aye, milord."

Gideon leaned slightly forward over his desk to stare pointedly at the man. Why did he dislike Cait? Had she scorned his attentions? "And if I catch the meekest whisper that ye have been cheating the Sinclair Clan, I'll see ye punished without mercy."

Bruce held his stare but swallowed hard. "I'd be a fool to do anything against ye, milord, even though ye proved yesterday ye can be merciful."

Gideon paused. Was the man foolish enough to throw Gideon's compassion toward Cait in his face? "Do not prove yourself the fool, Mackay. They end up with their heads mounted at the gates."

Bruce nodded, his eyes dropping.

"Also, there will be no harassing of villagers," Gideon said. He'd grown up in the structure of the Sinclair Clan, most of which he'd established. At Girnigoe Castle and in the Sinclair village, every member respected and feared the sons of George Sinclair. Damn but he should have been watching Varrich closer.

"Of course, milord," Bruce said, lifting his gaze. He did not move until Gideon sat back in his chair. Bruce was a warrior as well as Gideon's steward, so Gideon didn't expect him to quake in his boots. A meek response would not have given Gideon any more faith in the man.

"I've given ye my trust, Mackay. Do not prove me wrong to have done so," Gideon said.

The man held his fist against his heart. Gideon looked down at the thick, bound book of accounts for the Mackay Clan. It was obvious the last chief and his malevolent steward spent no time attending to them or the health of their clan. It had taken Gideon months to sort through the numbers, and now he had to update it to show what Bruce had just admitted after his questioning. "Ye may go," Gideon said, and the man pivoted, his boots clacking on the wooden floor of the library that Gideon had set up as his office.

Gideon followed him with his gaze. The steward hesitated at the sight of Bàs standing just outside the door. Bruce continued, nodding slightly to Gideon's brother as he strode inside. "I let Cain know of your handling of Cait Mackay and the Hogmanay Festival," Bàs said. "He seemed pleased, as did Ella. She said something about sending supplies for merriment." Bàs shrugged.

Gideon grunted softly. "Proof I'm not a tyrant. Joshua's change from sinner to saint makes him judgmental."

"When ye are supposed to be the judge," Bàs said evenly.

"Aye."

"And ye judged Cait Mackay very lightly." Bàs's voice held questions to which Gideon did not have a complete set of answers. "Ye let the villagers sway ye from condemning her to physical punishment."

Gideon placed the ledger back on the shelves lining the wall behind his chair. "Cain advised that I take time to know them better. Listening to their requests is the first step. And there are precedents for doing so. Giving the populace a sense of control."

"Precedents?" Bàs asked.

Gideon turned back to him. "Aye." Bàs waited, and Gideon leaned on his desk, frowning. "Pontius Pilot, fifth governor of Judea," Gideon said.

Bàs's brow rose. "Ye use the example of Pilot releasing Barabbas because he was swayed by the crowd?"

"Aye. 'Twas a precedent in law," Gideon said, knowing it was a terrible example. He pinched his lips tighter together.

"The man who condemned Jesus Christ to crucifixion?" Bàs asked.

"I know who he is," Gideon snapped.

Rap. Rap. Mathias stood in the doorway. Mathias had been a warrior pitted against Joshua when he was on Orkney, but the man had defected and returned to mainland Scotland. Once the warrior admitted he preferred the kitchen to the battlefield, and not *just* because of bonny kitchen maids, Gideon had hired him as his cook at Varrich.

"Milord," Mathias said. "The woman ye released yesterday has arrived to…make the place merry."

Cait is here. The dark cloud that had pressed upon Gideon as he'd dealt with the ledgers and then

Bàs seemed to dissipate.

"And just so ye know," Mathias said, "she's asked me to bake a number of buns and pies to feed folks coming to practice for the pageant." His brows rose high in question.

Gideon's lips relaxed almost into a smile. Of course, she'd invite many and demand they be fed for their trouble. He nodded. "Do ye need assistance in the kitchen?"

Mathias tipped his head side to side. "Through Hogmanay. Aye. Perhaps two sets of hands."

"Can ye manage hiring some help who won't tempt ye to forget your buns?" Gideon asked, rising.

Mathias chuckled. "I'll look for the old and infirmed, preferably with warts on their noses."

Gideon and Bàs followed him out of the study but stopped. Cait stood at the top of the steps, looking about. She wore a pale blue dress that hugged her curves. Her hair was pulled back from her smooth face to tumble around her shoulders, a dark contrast to the pale wool.

"Definitely no warts on that one," Mathias said under his breath.

Gideon's brow gathered in annoyance. "And she doesn't bake, so ye will have nothing to do with Cait Mackay."

A half-smothered grin grew on Mathias's lips. It seemed Gideon was already losing his touch at frightening people.

Cait saw them and strode in their direction. "Ye can see about finding your help," Gideon said, and Mathias walked away, tipping his head to Cait as he and Bàs stepped past her. The cook half turned to check out her backside, but Bàs grabbed his shirt at the shoulder, yanking him forward.

"I have arrived as ordered," she said. "I'll need a ladder, thread, swaths of material, and hooks for hanging greenery and garland."

"Good morn to ye, too," Gideon said.

She nodded, meeting his gaze with silent fury. At what? Punishing her so lightly?

When her gaze strayed behind him, her lovely lips dropped open, her eyes widening as if she saw mountains of gold. Gideon turned to see what had captivated her.

"Books," she whispered, stepping closer. Gideon knew he should step aside, but didn't for a moment, enjoying her closeness. She looked up into his face. "How many books do you own?"

"Hundreds. Come," he said, grasping her hand.

She yanked it away and hurried forward to stand before one set of shelves, inhaling fully. "Books," she murmured.

She turned in a slow circle, taking in his desk, globe, and wall of bookshelves. He also had two small desks for scholars he wished to employ to create some translations for his collection. Cait walked along the set of books, touching their spines reverently as she bent to read them.

"Those are the classics," Gideon said. "Translations from Greek and Latin. Stories from Homer, *The Odyssey* and—"

"*The Iliad*," she said.

She knew of the classics? Perhaps she was literate. He realized that he didn't really know Cait. *She is a thief and untrustworthy*. The gruff voice of his father seemed to infiltrate his head, and he blocked it out. "Farther down are some plays that I just received from England, one by Christopher Marlowe."

Cait turned to him, her brows bent. "You like literature?"

"Aye."

"But you're a warrior."

He smiled wryly. "One occupation does not dismiss the other. Physical strength and training make one hard to kill, but knowledge is the true power. Knowledge is gained in many ways, but one is through reading everything I can obtain."

"You feel you know all about the human soul," she said, her voice hard, yet thin, as if riding her breath.

"Cait," he said, coming closer. She turned toward him, and even though her look was completely guarded, she did not step back. Cait Mackay was courageous. "About the other day..." What about the other day? He'd been very lenient, but reminding her of that did not feel wise. She waited.

"I hold no ill will toward ye," he said. "For stealing, breaking inside my room, or helping me into the river."

When he paused, she tipped her chin higher. "Is this where I am supposed to thank you?" she asked. "For humiliating me before my people? Should I kiss you for freeing me from your dungeon and not chopping off my hand?"

The mention of a kiss caught his thoughts, turning them toward the memory of the inferno that had started between them in his room. But he certainly knew better than to give her the answer that sprang to his tongue.

"Perhaps bow down and grovel, milord?" she asked.

"Cait." He let his exhale out long with her name. "Nay. That's all in the past. We move forward now."

She tipped her head. "Have you read any books on how to gain the trust of your people?"

"I'm sure I have," he said, trying not to focus on the way her curls framed her soft cheeks. "One must be predictably fair."

She seemed to ignore his statement. "For every one thing you do to frighten or intimidate people, it takes ten things that are merry, kind, and inclusive to get them to trust you again."

"Ten to one?" he said.

She nodded. "For each person. So, for your one sentencing and punishment of me before everyone yesterday, you will need to do…somewhere around three hundred acts of kindness to get your people to trust you again. Talk to you again. Show any warmth toward you."

He frowned. "Ten for each person?" She nodded. "Could I group them together like yesterday to do merry things? Would that count?"

"Perhaps," she said and turned back to the books.

"Like the Hogmanay Festival," he said.

"Mmm-hmm," she answered and continued her walk down the books. "I could also open a school here in Varrich Village," she said. "Teach the children and anyone else how to read from some of these books." Despite the brittleness of anger in her voice, he heard the undertones of deep want and passion. "Over time, they may begin to trust you again." She shrugged. "But maybe not."

Gideon tipped his head, studying her as a plan took shape. "I'd make a bargain with ye."

She snorted softly. "Not an order? Just a bargain? Perhaps you will not starve all of us in exchange for me making Varrich merry for every holiday throughout the year?"

The woman clearly did not see how lenient he had been. "Nay," he said, filtering out the irritation from his voice. "I'll let ye start a school and use this library for it if ye will help me…" He paused, unsure of what he really needed. "Help me understand the people here. I'd know them better so I can help them. If they do not tell me their roofs are poor, how will I know to have them fixed?"

Cait crossed her arms over her chest. "You want to be more accessible to your people?"

"Exactly," he said. "Accessible. That's the word."

She glanced at the books. "In exchange for giving me the funds to start a school in Varrich and access to your library?"

"Aye," he said, nodding. "Do we have a bargain?"

She looked back at him. Her frown could not hide the excitement in her eyes. "Yes."

"I would shake hands on our agreement," he said.

Cait's eyes narrowed, but she strode over to him and held out her hand. Gideon clasped it, squeezing gently. It felt small and fragile in his large paw despite her obvious strength. He felt calluses from hard work, but the back was smooth, and he rubbed his thumb across it.

"We've been twiddling our thumbs below," said a voice from the doorway. Rhona, Cait's helper at the

Orphans' Home, stared at them, her mouth remaining open and her eyes growing wide.

Cait yanked her hand away and turned to the door. "I am sorry, Rhona, but look at all of these." Cait's cheeks were pink, and her arm went out toward the books. Hope filled her eyes, allowing her entire face to open with her smile. The beauty of her happiness filled his chest as if he'd just taken a full breath of air after being underwater for far too long. She'd been beautiful in repose as she spun in the falling snow, but now…Cait Mackay was radiant.

She looked at him. "So we have a bargain?" she asked. "I can start a school?"

"Aye."

"You're a witness, Rhona. Gideon Sinclair says we can start a school and use his books."

He cleared his throat. "If ye help me become more accessible to the Mackays."

She nodded, striding away. "It will be a challenge."

"The school?" he asked as he followed them out of the room.

"No," she said, the word coming out on a huff, and she glanced back at him. "Making you into someone people want to talk to."

He smiled wryly as they walked down the spiral stairway to the great hall. Despite his power and punishment, Cait Mackay was not afraid of him. Gideon realized that he liked that.

Rhona glanced cautiously at him when they reached the bottom. The girls, Trix and Libby, were trotting around the downstairs as if they were horses. The lad, Jack, had befriended Gideon's hound and was scratching Wolf behind the ears by the hearth. His fierce dog rolled completely over to allow his stomach to be scratched, making the lad chuckle.

"Girls," Cait called. "Let us set the holly and mistletoe out along the table to see exactly how much we've gathered." Trix and Libby pulled up short when they saw Gideon. Turning, they hurried over to five large baskets of greenery, taking them to the table to dump. Their glances showed their fear.

Jack followed them but also eyed Gideon as if he might produce his sword at any moment and start slashing. "Don't drop any on the floor," Jack said to the girls. "The mistletoe is poison to dogs." He glanced back at Wolf, who stood stretching.

Wolf trotted over to Gideon, who who stroked his large head.

"He seems fond of you," Cait said as he broke away and met her at the table. "That would be one show of kindness," she whispered, indicating the children who watched.

He nodded slightly. "Wolf is a gift from my brother, Bàs."

Gideon watched Cait's nimble fingers arrange the thorny holly in rows. He would like to capture those fingers, study them. They looked delicate.

"Wolf's mother had too many pups to care for, and he was not thriving, so I nursed him along."

Cait stopped, her face tipping to the side to study him. Her gaze slid up and down his body, assessing him. "You? Nursed a pup?"

He crossed his arms, quelling the heat her perusal had shot through him. "Aye. He needed to be fed around the clock. I devised the most nutritious diet and set up times to feed him. Hannah, my sister, helped with it. Her abilities to cuddle and coo to him were better than mine, but my strategy insured that he grew strong and large." It'd been a testament to his ability to plan and use the skills he'd learned from his voracious reading. "I named him Wolf, because I knew I could grow him into a dog as large as one." He smiled at his loyal hound, who came up to his waist even on all fours. Gideon leaned down to scratch his side, hugging him around the neck before straightening to find Cait staring at him.

"A second point," she said, glancing across the table where Trix and Libby worked, but kept glancing up. Louder she said, "The children would love a dog, but we barely have enough food to feed ourselves, let alone feed one well enough to become as large as a wolf."

He frowned at her straight back. "That'll be remedied immediately," he said, making her turn back to him. He liked saying things that made her look at him. She had the most interesting eyes. They were deep green like the forest in summer, and her lashes were incredibly long. "I've sent to Girnigoe for more chickens," he said. "Ye will also have milled wheat and oats along with yeast and leavening. And some apples from the fall harvest at Girnigoe." He lowered his voice, too, bending closer to her ear. "Perhaps that'll earn me a few points for kindness."

She studied him for a long moment before going back to arranging the length of holly. "There are others in the village who need supplies."

"People who are not favored by my steward?" he asked, the roughness of his tone revealed.

She ignored his reference. "I can give you a list."

"That would be helpful." He could check Bruce's list against hers.

She stopped next to Libby, who looked at a blood spot on Trix's finger. "I have a number of villagers coming to help put on a pageant about the birth of Christ," Cait said over her shoulder and then used her apron to wipe the blood away. "Watch out for those holly pricks," Cait said to the girl and immediately looked back at Gideon. "The pageant performers will need food."

"Aye."

She turned her body toward him, leaning her backside against the table. "And when they arrive, try not to look so…brutal and warlike." She flapped her hand as if indicating his form head to toe. "You'll want to look welcoming."

"Just standing, I look brutal?" he asked, his brows pinching with his frown. "I'm not covered with blood and mud." In fact, he kept his short beard and hair trimmed and his clothes neat. Gideon liked precision and being clean. If a man looked like he rolled in mud or did not care about the appearance of himself or his belongings, it made him less powerful. Knowledge, precision, and physical strength made him arguably the mightiest of the Sinclair brothers, no matter what his father had thought.

"Especially after they watched you sentence me." She flapped a hand at him. "Fierce, frowning, like you eat kittens to break your fast in the morn."

He felt his bottom lip slide out the smallest amount in the sulk that Aunt Merida said he sometimes favored. "I look like I eat kittens?" He rubbed his jaw, his finger straying to the scar on his cheek.

One of her brows rose. "At times." She stepped closer, and Gideon remained still as she reached up to his forehead, smoothing the pinch between his brows with one extended finger. "When you frown with your whole face, Trix said she could imagine you biting off the heads of kittens."

"Or baby birds," Trix added from where she let Libby wrap her wound in a bit of cloth.

Cait lowered her finger and turned back to her task at the table while Gideon fought the urge to pull her around to him. Her fingertip had been cool and smooth, and the press on his forehead had sent a warmth through him like he'd just downed Aunt Merida's hot brew with honey. And he wanted to hear more about her ideas on how he was perceived.

Gideon cleared his throat. "I'll endeavor not to frown then." She nodded without looking at him. "And perhaps ye can tell me when I look threatening to wee animals."

Cait glanced back. "I will do so." There was a slight grin on her lips.

His breath stopped at her unguarded look. He could stare at her all day, memorizing the contours of her face. Cait Mackay, with her perfectly sloped nose, high cheekbones, and dark arched brows, was beautiful. But it was her cleverness, determination, and ability to spar verbally with him that made her unique.

Soft hearts have no business serving justice. Gideon frowned over the words surfacing in his head. They held the gruff conviction of his father.

An undertone of whispers came from the

entryway where a group of children and several mothers stood wide-eyed. "Yes, yes, come in," Cait called as if this were her castle and she wasn't, in essence, a prisoner until her sentence was served. She beckoned them as she walked over. "Thank you for coming."

These must be the children to act in the pageant, but there were only two lads.

"There will be meals and treats provided for those working through the Hogmanay festival," she said to them.

Although she spoke, they all watched Gideon as he approached, fear in the rigidness of their faces. Cait glanced at him, and her eyes opened wide in a blatant signal that he looked like he might spill kitten blood at any second.

Gideon forced the corners of his mouth to rise. Although it felt ingenuine, Cait's frown relaxed, and she turned back to her crew. "Gideon Sinclair will not harm you."

"Unless ye commit a crime," he said with a teasing note to his words.

None of the visitors smiled. In fact, their eyes opened wider, and mothers pulled their children into the folds of their skirts as if they could convey them back to the safety of their homes.

Cait glared at him. "Subtract one point," she said softly. "From each of them."

He folded his hands behind his back and looked at the group. "Mistress Cait is correct. I will not harm any of ye, and I certainly do not bite the heads off kittens or any small creatures." Cait's hand went up to her forehead as if she'd developed a headache.

Gideon forced a smile and looked back out at the cowardly villagers. "Welcome to Varrich Castle," he said. "Thank ye for helping us create a merry Hogmanay for the village." He received a few tentative nods.

One older lady in the back, whom he recognized as one who'd stood defiantly in the bailey yesterday, snorted. "I am here to make sure ye don't cut anyone's hand off, especially Cait's."

Cait's palm dropped to her cheek. "Thank you, Fiona, but Gideon keeps his promises."

"I didn't hear him promise," she said.

The gazes of the women went back and forth between him and Fiona. Gideon cleared his throat. "I promise not to harm Cait Mackay or any of ye." He kept the part about "as long as you do no wrong" inside. Cait would deduct more points if he said that.

"Come meet Wolf," Trix said from her spot behind him, and the newcomers followed her over to the fire.

Cait turned to Gideon. "Clearly you must work on your welcoming look, and you never tease about harming someone."

"'Tis good ye did not grow up in my home at Girnigoe Castle then."

She quirked one side of her mouth up. "Never."

"Cait!" The exuberant call came from the dark entryway as a few more villagers came inside. Gideon recognized Alistair, the man who'd been willing to die for Cait. Bruce had given Gideon information on the blacksmith's son. Twenty-three years old. Tall and lanky, just coming into his muscle. Mother died eight years ago. Difficult relationship with his father, Edward Mackay, who was known as a drunk. Passionate without much self-control. Alistair Mackay was someone Gideon should keep a closer eye on, especially around Cait.

She smiled at Alistair, her gaze shifting to Gideon as if checking to see if he'd drawn his sword to slaughter the young man on sight. Gideon raised his empty hands as if showing her he was unarmed.

"Good morn, Alistair. Thank you for coming to help." It was the same thing she'd said to the children, but her voice sounded different, more engaged. Gideon did not like it.

"Alistair," Gideon said, and the lad looked to him, his grin slipping into a disapproving frown.

"Sinclair," Alistair said.

"'Tis Chief Sinclair," Gideon said, keeping the steady look until Cait walked between them, her arms out. He didn't care to garner the young man's trust.

Gideon kept the lad's gaze over Cait's head. "We don't require your help."

Cait touched Gideon's arm. "I think Alistair would make a fine Master of Revels."

The touch was a mere brush, but it sparked through Gideon. He raised his gaze from her hand when she pulled it away and looked at Alistair. "The Master of Revels isn't required until Hogmanay." Although perhaps Gideon should keep his enemy close. Because Alistair Mackay was already assigned to Gideon's enemy list, even though he'd broken no law.

"I asked him to help with the children," Cait said. She stepped forward and hooked Alistair's arm with hers to lead him off toward the fire.

Gideon reached out and caught her arm. "A word," he said. "Alone."

"No," Alistair said.

Gideon looked at the obstinate man. "It was not a request. Cait is still my prisoner for her crimes." After a moment, Alistair turned and strode toward the hearth. Cait turned on her heel to glare up at Gideon in silent reproach. Which he did not deserve. He'd spoken no lies or exaggerations. She was still his prisoner.

"You'll never earn his trust looking and talking to Alistair like that," she said, her voice terse and low.

Gideon loomed slightly over Cait. "What's Alistair Mackay to ye?"

CHAPTER SEVEN

Eyre Manuscript, 1241 AD

A peasant working for a landowner must gain permission from the landowner to marry. If a peasant woman is widowed, the landowner will choose for her another husband in a timely manner. The landowner may evict a noncompliant woman from her land and home.

Cait looked up into the hard face of Gideon Sinclair. Her heart beat faster, but she wasn't frightened. It was the nearness of him that continued to shoot energy through her. It was said the Horseman of Justice could read one's thoughts just by studying the owner's face. She kept hers set in irritation.

"What is the boy to ye?" he repeated.

She looked over to where Alistair cautiously petted Wolf with the children. "He's a friend and hardly a boy. I believe he's a score and three years old, old enough to start training with your men if you ask him." She looked back to Gideon, who wore vengeance like a mask. Making Gideon Sinclair into an approachable chief was not going to be easy. But she would do just about anything to see her dream of a school come true. She poked his chest. "And you need to stop scaring him."

"He is in love with ye," Gideon said, but she already knew Alistair was sweet on her.

"He probably sees me as a replacement for his mother," she said. "She died a couple years ago, leaving him with a father who gives nothing in the way of praise or love."

"'Twas eight years ago, and he does not love ye like a mother." Gideon crossed his arms. "Has he asked ye to marry him?"

"No." Not outright, although he had hinted at it a few times before Cait could manage to escape. "He has lost his mother and has a gruff father. It makes him…sometimes rash, forgetting himself. I afford him a kindness because he's seen very little. In a way, Alistair is an orphan, too."

Gideon snorted slightly. "I lost my mother young and had a gruff father, and I don't forget myself. Ever." The man boasted too much about his perfect discipline.

"Not even when I kissed you?" she asked, because she'd felt his response when she'd kissed him in his bedchamber. Her words were out before she could swallow them, and her eyes widened. She opened her mouth to say something, anything to pull them back, but Gideon spoke first.

"I wished to see what ye were up to," he said, his voice lower. "Thievery or a night of play."

"Neither," she said. "I was returning, and I don't play that way." She tipped her chin higher.

He leaned in a bit. "Ye were married before, so I am guessing ye have…played."

Played? There was nothing playful in the rough wooing her husband, Benjamin, had forced upon her. *Ye are as cold as a dead fish. 'Tis why ye grow no bairns in your womb.*

Cait spun on her heel and traipsed across the hall toward the hearth. She plastered a smile on her face as she met the villagers there. "Let us start hanging the holly and mistletoe about. We need to string some garland also to hang on the wall surrounding the castle for the festival."

"What did he say to ye?" Alistair asked, his voice low. "Ye look upset."

She reinforced her smile. "Nothing bad," she answered. "Come, let us start working with the children."

"My father says ye can use these for the festival," Alistair said, opening a sack he'd brought with him. "Iron rings for hanging fabric and garland."

She looked upward. "We can definitely put them to use. Now we just need a ladder."

Alistair leaned closer until she could smell his stale breath. "If he's getting too close to ye, I can help ye escape this. We can go away to—"

"I'm well, Alistair," she said, placing her palm on his chest. The young man had grown during this last year. "And I could never leave my children. I'll also be starting a school here."

He glanced at Gideon with a frown. "If I was as big as he, and had his riches, I could rule this clan."

She patted his arm. "I'm sure you could."

She turned away to inspect the iron hooks. She had two similar ones that she'd bought from a traveling peddler years ago, along with the smaller hook she used on her rope, the one that Gideon must still have in his chamber.

"Pardon, ladies." Mathias, Gideon's cook, walked over to the group with some warm buns. The children squealed in delight as he set them down. Mathias was a handsome rake.

"I'm looking for two assistants in the kitchen over the festival," he said. "Some experience baking would be helpful. And"—he glanced over them, avoiding Cait— "someone matronly would be best."

"Do matrons make the best buns?" one of the lasses from the village asked. Isla was pretty and smiled sweetly at Mathias.

Mathias grinned back. "Matrons are less…distracting to my work." The ladies giggled.

Cait exhaled. "I can ask around the village."

"Thank ye," Mathias said.

"Or I can help, if need be," she added. That way none of the lasses would be in jeopardy of losing their hearts and their wits around the man who was said to *play* every night with a different lass.

"Och, but nay," he said with a chuckle, glancing at Gideon. "In fact, I might find myself bleeding just for being over here talking to ye." He was surely jesting, but Cait looked at Gideon, who watched them with a frown even though several men were bringing in another table and the ladder.

"Bleeding?" she asked.

"I have strict orders not to bother ye," Mathias said. He doffed his hat in a bow and turned on his heel to take the empty platter with him.

Three more ladies walked in and scurried around Gideon toward Cait by the fire. "Lord he is brawn," one was saying as they neared.

"Too dangerous for me," said another.

"Not for me," said Deirdre, Fiona's granddaughter. The girl was almost twenty and bonny with her blond curls. She was brave like Fiona, and could certainly attract any man, including Gideon.

"Rhona can help you get started, and we will discuss the parts for the pageant in a bit. Excuse me," Cait said, going right toward Gideon, annoyance frosting her features.

"You'll bloody Mathias if he talks to me?" she asked as she came up close to Gideon. Her heart did a ridiculous little flip as if she were foolishly baiting a wild wolf, but she didn't back down.

"Ye are asking lasses to act in the pageant?" he said in response.

"That is not an answer."

He glanced over her head toward the young girls coming inside. "Mathias is a rogue, and I have judged your heart to be vulnerable to everyone, including rogues."

Her mouth opened and closed and opened again. "You have no right to…to try to protect my heart. Maybe I want Mathias to pay attention to me."

Gideon looked back down to meet her eyes. "Lasses do not act in plays. The law states that only men and lads act on stage."

Was he *trying* to make her angry? "What law?"

"'Tis a common law. 'Tis indecent for women to act on stage. Even in London, women do not act."

"That's nonsense!"

"It might be, but 'tis a law that has always been."

God's teeth, the man just liked to argue. "I know for a fact," she said, "that Anne Boleyn acted as Perseverance in a Shrovetide pageant for King Henry of England. She was Queen Elizabeth's mother."

"And look what happened to Queen Anne," he said, his voice low as he slid a finger across his throat. The hint of a grin at the corners of his mouth made the muscles in Cait's jaw clench even tighter.

"Really!" she all but yelled, and then lowered her voice. "These girls are excited to be in the production. There's nothing crude or lewd about the roles. If you stop them now, word will circulate in the village about what you did to disappoint them."

Gideon exhaled. "Then I'll amend the law and tack it to the chapel door. Then they can act in the pageant. I'm not unreasonable, Cait. Ye but need to ask for my consideration."

Cait realized her arms were crossed over her chest, mimicking him, and she dropped them. "Do you do everything according to laws and rules?"

"Aye. Without them everything falls into chaos, crime, and destruction." He dropped his own arms. His stance reminded her of a warrior in battle except his clothes were clean and crisp. "I am the Horseman of Justice. It's always been my task to keep the laws of the land for the betterment of the people."

"Hmph. Some laws do not better people," she said, walking toward the table. "Like women not acting."

He followed her. "Then I change them. If people in Varrich Village come to me and petition for a change, I'll hear them, like the other day, and decide if the law should be amended. It keeps everything in order. If they would but come to me, they will see."

"You decide? Only *you*."

He frowned. "Aye. I've made it my life's work to

read and be knowledgeable about as much as possible, so I can decide what is safe and efficient for my people."

She stared at him over the table of greenery. "Everything is orderly in your world, isn't it?"

"It must be," he said, as she picked up a holly branch. "In order to be fair to all."

She shook her head lightly, looking down at the holly. She pushed the needle through the stem, guiding the thread through. "Judging something as fair is a personal verdict. It can't be decided by one man."

"King James would argue on my behalf," Gideon said and set another holly cluster in her upturned palm. "However…" He captured that same hand to pull her gaze. "I can be swayed by the populace, as we saw."

"So," she said, lowering her voice, "if the villagers hadn't come to…sway you about me, I would be missing a hand today?"

Gideon looked at her, and she knew he was judging. Summing her up in the little he knew about her, the evidence he'd gleaned from the scant interactions with her and any skewed information from Bruce. He was using all his book-learning skills to judge her while still knowing practically nothing about her. She was just a lass from the village who cared for children because she was a widow.

She watched his lips as they parted and tried not to remember that they'd been warm. "Likely not, but 'tis a possibility," he said. She blinked and snatched her hand away. "One who breaks laws, even for the good of others, is still a criminal."

She huffed. "Not everything in life is right or

wrong. There are areas of gray. I would think some-one of your learning would know that."

"True," he said. She kept her gaze on the holly before her. "A man who kills another who is trying to hurt his wife has still taken a life. So then I judge the life of the man killed to see if it was worthy."

She looked at him. "And how do you judge the dead man without his say? Perhaps the wife was try-ing to kill him."

"I would find that out by questioning the wit-nesses and those who know the parties involved. Then I'd decide. 'Tis simple when it is all laid out."

Gideon had an answer for everything. He al-lowed himself and everyone else only perfection. From his polished leather boots to the trimmed top of his dark hair, he was clean and cut to perfection.

"The world is not so orderly, Sinclair," she said. "People and lives are messy with emotions and rea-sons not everyone knows."

"I don't rest until I know all the details." Gideon moved his hands together, making parallel lines in the air. "Wipe off the inconsequential dust and lay out the pieces of the puzzle in precise order to de-duce the correct verdict." He dropped his hands. "'Tis what I was trained to do since I was breeched."

Cait raised her brows, letting him see her smirk. "Perhaps you need to get a little dirt on you, Gideon Sinclair."

He frowned at her wryness. "Why would I do that?"

"The best things in life are disordered and usual-ly dirty," she answered. "And you're missing out."

She almost laughed outright as he paused,

probably thinking of disorderly things that he avoided or about the virtues of cleanliness he'd read about in his hundreds of books. Cait remained silently stringing more holly onto the garland. Behind her, Alistair was moving the ladder for Trix to climb up with the first string they'd completed.

"I assume ye are speaking philosophically, because I can't think of a single best thing that is also dirty," Gideon said.

Cait chuckled softly and turned to face him. "Falling snow," she said and put her arms out to turn in a circle like he'd seen her doing on the moor. She stopped, dropping her arms. "The birth of...well, anything." She tipped her head to the side as she thought. "Babies are notoriously dirty, throwing households into disorder. Children, puppies, rolling in wildflowers, honey cakes, dancing in the rain." She reached in front of him, her arm grazing his stomach, and picked up another holly cluster. Her heart sped at the contact, but she acted as if she was not affected by his nearness. His massively strong nearness.

"Do ye dance in the rain all the time?" he asked, and she heard a slight teasing tone.

She jabbed the needle into the hard stem. "No," she said. "Not in the winter." Without lifting her head, she tipped her face to him. "Then I dance in the snow."

His mouth broadened into a smile, and a chuckle broke through. He took a big inhale and looked about the room where the children and ladies, along with Alistair and Jack, hurried about placing greenery. None of it was planned or precise or perfect.

"I argue that what a person considers the best

things in life is personal to him," he said. "Ye cannot decide for me what I feel is most excellent. That's based on how I was raised, what I've been exposed to, and something that is innate for each person born. One person can't decide overall what is best in life for everyone. Ye like dirt, and I like cleanliness and order."

She turned her whole body toward him, setting down the holly to clasp her hands. "Just like one man cannot decide for everyone what is just, fair, and good in another person." She held his stare, watching his gray eyes narrow.

"We're here, and we have poultry!"

Cait turned to see a man enter the great hall with Gideon's younger brother, Bàs. The young man who spoke was tall and lanky like Alistair and walked in with his arms bowing out to the room.

Gideon exhaled loudly behind her, which made her grin. The timing of the delivery had allowed her to win the last word in their debate.

"We're not done discussing this," Gideon said, his hand clasping her upper arm gently.

She met his frown with a smile. "Certainly. I look forward to educating you more."

"They'll need a warm place to stay until ye can distribute them," Bàs said. "We haven't enough for three per household. Only one hen until I can retrieve more from Dunrobin."

"Good morn," the lanky man said, smiling at Cait. "I am Osk Flett."

"One of the Orkney immigrants?" she asked. The whole process of settling the Orkney people had been part of what had delayed Gideon from moving into Varrich Castle, which had unfortunately left Bruce Mackay in charge.

"Yes," he said. "And Gideon's brother-in-law." He smiled broadly. "My sister is Kára Flett, married to Joshua."

She'd heard of the Orkney people coming over and the second Sinclair brother marrying their leader. Although, they'd been instructed to say Joshua had died on Orkney if ever asked. She wasn't sure who would ask, but the notice had been read before the congregation at church...several weeks in a row.

"I'm Cait Mackay."

Wolf ran directly to Bàs, skidding to a halt before him. A smile broke the seriousness of the horseman's face, and he squatted to hug the beast. He let the dog lick his cheeks, chuckling as he touched his own nose to the dog's before standing straight. He rubbed one finger against his nose where the dog had dampened it.

When the Sinclairs had taken over their clan, Gideon had Bàs publicly execute the few surviving men who had helped Robert Mackay abduct Ella Sutherland and her young brother and had tortured their Sutherland nursemaid. The one woman involved, Viola Mackay, had been spared and exiled from any clan allied with the Sinclairs.

"The barn inside the bailey is insulated with blocks of hay," Gideon said. "They'll be warm enough there."

"And make certain that anyone who receives one either butchers it soon after or, if keeping it for eggs, has a warm place to house it," Bàs said.

"Aye, brother," Gideon said. "No chicken will be tortured with freezing."

"We have bags of grain, too," Osk said, speaking more to Cait than to Gideon. "And apples from last fall's harvest."

Bàs lifted the long rolls of red and green fabric that he carried. "And these are the rolls of fabric to help ye make the place merry." He set them on a long bench at the table before heading out, Wolf following him, tail wagging.

Cait turned to Gideon. "You're truly trying to help us. With the chickens and grain, like you said you would."

The tension in his face pinched even more. "I don't say things I do not mean."

"Gideon," Osk yelled from the entryway. "Bring the older lads with you to help. There are a number of sacks."

Gideon turned on his heel, waving to Jack and Alistair to follow him out into the cold. They hesitated only a moment and then jogged across the room.

Following them, Cait stood in the doorway of the keep, watching Gideon's powerful stride. The confidence that sat in his straight back and the sure way he ordered the others to join him marked him as a leader. But the way he'd listened to her, debated with her as if she were an equal, was unexpected. And he'd followed through with his promise to help her people.

Tyrant or well-meaning chief? "Who are you, Gideon Sinclair?"

CHAPTER EIGHT

Seneca the Younger, Roman Philosopher,
1st century AD

"Some children such as those who are sick or those born defective in some way, ought to be culled from the family. Like rabid dogs or wild oxen or sickly sheep, so also we must extinguish unnatural offspring. In so acting, we thereby remove the useless from the world of the healthy and sound."

"Who is Cait Mackay?" Osk asked as they lifted sacks from the back of the second wagon that he and Bàs had driven over from Girnigoe.

Alistair frowned at him. "She's a beloved and much respected lady who runs the Orphans' Home in our village. Do not harass her."

"Cait Mackay?" Osk said, his brow lifting as he looked at Gideon. "The thief who kicked you into the river?"

Bàs nodded and Osk barked with laughter. "Really?" Osk looked toward the door where she had just turned away. "That sweet morsel kicked ye into the freezing river?"

"She's not a sweet morsel," Alistair said, his mouth hard as if he clenched it.

Gideon studied Osk. He did not look like too much of a threat, but Gideon would talk to Joshua about him anyway. "She's making Varrich festive for

Hogmanay," Gideon said.

Alistair spit on the ground. "As a cruel punishment for trying to help her people."

"Ye do not know the meaning of cruel," Gideon said, looking his way, "if ye think what she is doing right now falls under the word." He looked back to Osk. "And no one will bother her."

"What if she wants to be bothered?" Osk asked with a waggle of his brows.

Bàs looked between Gideon and Osk. "From the look on Gideon's face, I'd say that ye will be bloody if ye try to find out."

Osk glanced at him and quirked his mouth to the side before shaking his head and looking at the stacked sacks of grain. "Bloody hell. I'm not foolish enough to give one of the Sinclair brothers a reason to pummel me."

"You will bloody the boy if he tries to talk with Cait?" Alistair asked, looking at Gideon. "What does that mean?"

"I'm not a boy," Osk said, frowning at Alistair. "I might be even older than you."

Bàs hefted a one-hundred-pound bag of oats over his shoulder with little effort. "I doubt he even knows," Bàs said and walked toward the barn. "But I'd say he has already claimed her."

Gideon watched Bàs go. Had he already claimed Cait in his mind? He bloody hell didn't want anyone else claiming or doing anything to her. Not that she could be claimed without her consent. To what type of man would she consent? Probably someone who liked dirt and disorder. Someone who hadn't stood her before her village and punished her. Gideon felt an ache in the back of his neck.

"And what does that mean?" Alistair repeated, his voice insistent. "Claiming her?"

Osk dropped a heavy hand on the lad's shoulder. "That you should look elsewhere, my friend."

Alistair shrugged off the hand and went to the wagon to yank up a smaller sack.

By the time they'd unloaded the wagons and made sure the chickens were secure and comfortable, the morning had bled into afternoon. A lad ran up to Alistair with a message from his father, calling him back to the smithy to work, and Osk and Bàs followed Gideon inside the keep.

Bàs chuckled as they stepped into the decorated great hall. "Look who has traded traitors' heads at the gate for holly balls and merriment."

"'Tis what I was tasked to do," Gideon murmured as he took in the decorations. How long had they been outside anyway?

Holly was strung and hung over the mantel and along the exposed beams crossing the ceiling. Several holly balls made of evergreens and pinecones were held by bows of red ribbon. Way above the children, fabric of bright red and green was hung from the iron rings that had been attached to iron loops built into the stone ceiling. The colorful fabric ran the length of the ceiling, filling the room with waves of evergreen and cheery red. But what stopped Gideon in his stride was Cait. She stood at the top of the ladder, at the bloody top of a two-story ceiling.

Wolf leaped up to run over to greet them, his tail swatting the ladder that the children tried to hold.

Two of them jumped, giggling at the dog's antics, which bumped the ladder farther.

Gideon took off in a run before any warning could breach his lips. "Watch out!" The ladder fell over, making the children shriek and scatter. He almost plowed over a few as he ran to catch Cait, but she did not drop.

"Bloody hell," Bàs cursed under his breath as he stopped next to Gideon, both staring up at the lass. Even in her skirts, she had wrapped her legs around the length of fabric that hung down to the floor. Without floundering at all, she slid down the length until she reached the floor like a lifelong sailor lowering down a sail line.

"Huh," Bàs murmured, "and Joshua didn't believe she scaled down that wall on the rope."

Cait's cheeks were pink as she lifted her face. She wet her lips, pulling his focus.

Jack hurried over with Trix and Libby. "I should have held on to Wolf," he said.

"And those other children do not listen," Libby said, her voice scolding. Coming only to Gideon's stomach, she held her head high and stacked her wee fists on her hips like an inflamed general.

Cait wiped her hands briskly. "Let's get the last end of fabric hooked up there."

"I will hold the ladder this time," Gideon carried the ladder under the last iron loop set between the rafters and extended one arm to allow Cait access to the first rung. She hesitated but then stepped into the circle of his arms, the ladder against her front. He silently inhaled her warm scent.

Her backside grazed against him with her first

step, and he felt his jack twitch under his plaid. His grip tightened on the sides of the ladder. *Fool*. He wasn't some undisciplined rogue who pulled unsuspecting lasses to him. An educated, moral man did not trap a lass in hopes she would kiss him instead of kneeing him in the ballocks, something Keenan said she'd done to Bruce, which was why the steward disliked her and called her cold.

Cait climbed with confidence, scaling the ladder one-handed, the other firmly attached to the green fabric. Occasionally, her skirts would hitch up past her boots.

He squinted. Black stockings encased her legs. Stockings or trews, like what she'd worn in his bedchamber.

"Not a good look for ye," Bàs said behind him. "Staring up a lass's skirts."

"She wears black trews under her skirts," Gideon said, his words soft.

"Perhaps she wants to be prepared if she must jump out your window again," Bàs said, a rare grin on his face.

Cait descended. "The swaths make it quite festive in here," she said, stepping off the last rung into the circle of Gideon's arms.

He held tightly to the ladder, ignoring the whispering of children and Wolf's happy barking behind him.

"I've reached the ground safely," she said, turning to look over her shoulder at him. Up close, Cait was even more beautiful, and her cheeks were pink with exertion. The green of her eyes was arresting, and he had the urge to carry her out into the waning sun to see them more clearly. A brown freckle sat on her right cheek next to the slant of her nose.

"Ye have survived great heights once again," he said, stepping back. "Ye are like a cat who always lands on her feet."

She gave a little snort, meeting his gaze for only a second. "You've not seen me try to walk on a frozen lake." She turned and walked over to the children, who were excited by the stew that Mathias had just brought out for them all to eat before leaving.

Gideon watched the gentle sway of her hips. Cait Mackay was not an ice queen like Bruce Mackay said. Hardly. Every time he encountered her, she seemed exceptionally warm. She was a tangled knot of details that summed up into the most interesting woman he had ever met. Clever, graceful, obviously educated, sweet-smelling, hardworking, and he guessed, soft all over.

And a criminal.

• • •

Darkness was falling outside as Cait herded Jack, Trix, and Libby out of Varrich Castle. Rhona had left earlier to make certain Willa was continuing to improve. It seemed they'd not need to buy feverfew after all.

"'Tis growing dark," Gideon said, his boots crunching through the thin layer of snow in the bailey. "I'll walk ye home."

Dong…! Dong…! Dong…!

Cait jumped at the first loud bell chime from the watchtower. "God's teeth!" The children all stopped to stare up at the bell, Trix and Libby covering their ears with their child-sized, cupped palms.

"The bell about cleaved my head in two," Jack yelled over it and hurried on.

They continued after the final tone died away. "All must hear when 'tis time to get inside, bank the fires, and rest," Gideon said.

"Is that another law? Scurry inside when the bell rings?" Cait asked. "I haven't seen that one tacked to the chapel door." She picked up her stride again and waved to her elderly friend Evie. Evie frowned at Gideon and nodded to Cait, watching closely.

"That's Fiona's sister. They live together." Cait smiled brightly. "I'm well treated," she called out.

Gideon's gaze went from Cait to Evie and back to Cait. "She thinks ye are being mistreated up at the castle?" he asked.

"Probably. 'Tis why Fiona was at the castle to-day." Her gently arched brows rose. "You'd make large strides in winning the villagers over if the sisters liked you."

"Mo chreach," Gideon swore. He turned and waved at her, Evie staring back with her mouth agape. Gideon's gesture looked awkward like he hadn't ever waved before. Fiona came out to stand next to her sister, frowning.

"I treat everyone well," he called. "I mean to say, not prisoners, of course."

"Don't tease about prisoners," Cait whispered with a groan.

"Except Cait. She's a well-treated prisoner. She's not a prisoner. Any longer…because I am not… She didn't…" He stopped talking, his jaw moving as if it ached. "Cait is treated well." He turned away but then stopped, looking back. "Ye are to come to the Hogmanay Festival she is setting up at the castle," Gideon called. "Everyone must come. Let others know."

They started walking again. "Must?" Cait said. "As in, they will be judged poorly if they do not attend? Perhaps treated poorly?"

Gideon frowned. "Nay. 'Tis just…a way to say they should come."

"For a man who spouts laws and rules to his people, you need to be quite careful of the words you use."

Gideon huffed, turned on his heel, and strode back toward Fiona and Evie. Good Lord. He'd scare Evie into an early grave. Cait rushed after him.

"Excuse me, mistresses," he said. "What I meant to say is ye both should…that ye are welcome to come to my…to the Hogmanay Festival for your village, which just happens to be up at the castle. There will be food and drink and music. Everyone is welcome, not required, but welcome to participate. And if ye choose not to come, it will *not* be noted." He paused as if thinking. "Except, I would miss your kind company, gentlewomen." Gideon paused as if going over his words. "And Cait is treated well, even though she's working off her penance."

Fiona nodded. "We will come," she said, her lips pursed like they'd been most of the day as she helped Cait up at the castle.

"Very well." Gideon forced a smile. "Good evening tide." He turned, but then pivoted back in rapid succession. "And the bell is just a recommendation to close down and go inside for rest. Ye are welcome to…roam about all night if that is your wish. Let others know that, too."

Cait could barely squash her smile and met Fiona's gaze. The elderly woman had wrinkles around each eye that cut in deeper as she smiled back, shaking her head. Cait would have laughed at the ridiculous exchange, but she was still irritated. At what? That he'd caught her, put her in the dungeon with blankets and no rats? She had more privacy there to use the privy than at home. And he hadn't cut off her hand. No, but he'd shamed her before everyone. It stung, although she'd seen how those in the village cared for her.

Cait and Gideon continued walking. "You've just given them something to talk about for weeks," she said.

He met her gaze. "About how approachable and kind I am."

She couldn't contain her smile and rolled her eyes heavenward before meeting his again. "Obviously." His eyes were a light gray in daylight. She'd seen them clearly on the snowy moor. But the surrendering day made them seem darker now, almost like they could see into her. The idea made her look away.

"Ye jest?" he asked, glancing back over his shoulder. "I was quite kind and approachable. I'm certain that's what they will say. I should earn three points for that exchange."

"Words mean little. 'Tis actions that speak about the integrity of a person," Cait said. They walked in silence.

The night was crisp with winter chill and a breeze that shot through clothing like icy water, saturating her in cold. Nothing in the shadows worried Cait with Gideon by her side. Despite what had occurred, he didn't frighten her. They walked briskly, Cait not paying attention to the road. She stepped onto a frozen puddle, and her heel shot out from under her. Her arms flew out, and she gasped.

Gideon caught her arm, pulling her in to his side. "Ho now," he said. "I've got ye."

Gideon's arm was thick with muscle, as strong as the thriving limb of an oak. He held onto her even after her boots landed on dry ground. He didn't relinquish her arm, and she didn't pull it away.

"Who taught the Horseman of Judgment to be kind?" Her children had raced ahead, probably home by now, and they walked alone.

"First," Gideon said, "I am the Horseman of Justice, not judgment."

"Oh yes. I keep forgetting that." Her words were laced with the smallest hint of sarcasm. "So, who taught the Horseman of Justice to be kind? Was it your father? I know your mother died when you were young."

Gideon snorted softly. "My father was only kind to my mother, from what I have heard. After she died, his love for her turned to rage against the world. He yelled and crashed his way through his remaining years, building his army and his sons into The Four Horsemen of the Apocalypse as if it were the biblical end of days."

"Oh," she said softly. "And yet you are…controlled, disciplined."

"Aye," he said, pride in his voice. "Life at Girnigoe was loud and full of chaos. I learned early on to pick up the pieces and rebuild anything my father's rage tore apart, including relations with King James and our allies."

"He must have appreciated that."

Gideon glanced upward for a moment before helping her over another frozen puddle and around a pile of snow that someone had shoveled from before their cottage. "Cain was the oldest and was groomed by Father to be the leader. Joshua was loud and hotheaded like him. Bàs was quiet and dutiful. I, on the other hand, argued with him." Gideon chuckled. "I was *not* his favorite."

"But you kept the Sinclair Clan strong with diplomacy."

He nodded. "Oh, George Sinclair knew my value. I was also the only one who truly helped him make his plans to take the crown from King James."

She stopped, her breath, too, and glanced around to make sure no one was within hearing. The gloaming was thick with shadows, and the houses seemed closed for the night. Even so, she lowered her voice. "'Twas treason."

"Aye." He nodded. "But Father was loyal only to God, and… The Sinclairs are strong enough to take the crown if Cain wishes to put the effort into it."

"Does he wish to?" she whispered.

He looked down into her eyes. "Nay. Either way, I keep relations with James and the other clans amiable. A united Scotland is the way to keep our country strong. Civil war weakens us, opening Scotland up to foreign invaders."

They walked farther on past closed shutters as dark consumed the village. He still held her arm snug against him, as if they were lord and lady out promenading in the gardens.

"My aunt Merida and Hannah."

"Pardon?" She steadied herself on his arm, just under his short cape, feeling the thick cording of muscle there.

"Taught me to be kind," he said. "My sister, Hannah, was born kind. From what Aunt Merida says, she has our mother's temperament. And Aunt Merida, although she is not afraid to shout her mind, her heart is good, and she thinks of others before herself. For someone"—he pointed to himself—"who was urged to be cold, calculating, and judgmental, her influence prevented me from being the"—he paused to look down into her face—"tyrant that apparently Clan Mackay thinks I am."

They walked in silence several paces before Cait spoke. "You can change the way people see you. The Hogmanay Festival will invite them in to see that you want to help them. When you—" Her heel hit another icy puddle, and she tipped, but Gideon's arm held her firmly.

They stopped, mere inches apart, nose to nose. "When I...?" he murmured, and she watched his lips. There in the shadows, she wanted to kiss them again, kiss him without the panic that had gripped her in his bedchamber when she was caught. Maybe it was the darkness, or the closeness, or his clean masculine scent, or something utterly new to her. Whatever it was, circulating in the air between them, it pressed the winter chill away.

"When I what?" he murmured again.

"When you stop seeing us as the enemy, we'll stop seeing you that way," she whispered, searching his eyes in the dark. "You'll become accessible."

He leaned in, his arm sliding around her back to support her. "I do not see ye as an enemy, Cait Mackay."

She stared back. "And I'm starting to think that you might"—her words came on the faintest of breath—"not be a tyrant, Gideon Sinclair."

"Mistress Cait!"

Jack and Libby ran toward her down the dark road. "Mistress Cait. Come quick. We need you." Libby stopped before her, panting. "At the house." She tugged, and Cait hurried off with them, unsure if he would follow.

· · ·

Gideon rubbed a hand down his face. *I'm such a fool*, he thought. He'd nearly lost his mind and kissed her, there in the road. What would people think? That he'd spared her because he wanted to bed her? That she'd consider it? He glanced around but saw no one in the dark.

Gideon exhaled and started walking. He rounded the curve in the road where the stone wall began that led up to the Orphans' Home. Outside the front door stood all the inhabitants. Cait was crouched down but slowly stood, and he could see something in her arms.

Despite the crowd, no one spoke. The only sound was a soft whimper from the bundle of blankets she held against her. Cait turned her face to him. A look of worry hardened into quiet determination. "A bairn has found its way to our home."

"A bairn. On your doorstep?" Gideon looked behind him as if to find the mother.

Rhona *tsk*ed. "Abandoned here."

"That's how I came," Libby said, pulling the bundle lower so she could look into the bairn's face. "Don't worry, little one," she crooned. "We have lots of room and food for you here."

Gideon knew they did not have either, but neither Rhona nor Cait corrected the girl. Trix tried to pull the blanket away. "Are you a girl or a boy?"

"A boy, I think," Cait said, holding up a scrap of parchment. All it said was "Henry" in blocky letters.

"'Tis a crime to abandon a bairn," Gideon said. "A child is the responsibility of the parent unless they die, whether they like it or not."

Cait frowned. "You don't know the circumstances."

"The circumstances do not matter."

Her brows rose in challenge. "Yes, they do, especially when people are hungry and cold."

"I'm improving conditions." Starting tomorrow with the giving out of the food and chickens from Girnigoe.

"No one knows that yet," she said, her words snapping out. "All they know is that they are cold, harassed, and hungry. The mother might not be able to care for Henry." The bairn began to fuss in her arms, and Rhona took him. The woman smiled down into his wee face and walked inside the firelit room beyond.

"Come, children," Rhona called, and the rest followed her inside, leaving Cait still frowning at Gideon.

"Regardless," he said. "Ye have enough children to care for. Abandoning a child if the parents are living is a crime. They should ask for help first."

"Asking the enemy for help hasn't worked in the past."

"I'm not the enemy, Cait."

"Again," she said, "no one knows that." Cait turned on her heel, threw open the door, and strode inside, shutting it firmly behind her.

"Magairlean," he cursed under his breath. "I'll add a law about not abandoning children to the chapel doors," he called loudly. If she heard him through the door, she did not answer.

Blast it! The day had gone so well and the walk to her home even better until everything fell apart. Gideon ran both hands down his face and stood there in the darkness that had fully descended.

Without the firelight from inside, the shadows were thick. The moonlight, a bit more than the night before, reflected off the whiteness of the snow, and he turned around. Walking to the edge of the cobblestone footpath that stretched out from the front door, Gideon looked down at the muddied snow where they had all entered. A pair of small tracks broke off to wind away into the woods that ran behind the Orphans' Home.

He glanced back at the house. Cait was wrong. Abandonment was a sin and a crime. George Sinclair had wanted to abandon his only daughter, Hannah, after Bàs was born. She was four years old at the time and not another son. When Bàs came along and their mother died, Gideon remembered his aunt Merida defending the girl. She had pulled out book after book and used every reference she could find that spoke of the importance of having a daughter to marry into alliances. In the end, it stopped their father from turning Hannah out to be raised by one of the families in the village.

Gideon was only six years old, but he clearly remembered the power of books changing his father's mind. It was the day he started reading without being prompted by his tutor. If something was powerful enough to break through George Sinclair's madness about sending his own daughter away, then Gideon was going to embrace it.

The tracks were fresh and small, belonging to a woman. Henry's mother? They were deep, showing her stopping or walking slowly. Had she thought about returning for her bairn? He would take that into account.

Gideon's gaze slid forward along the tracks to a dark boulder up ahead. But instinct told him it wasn't a boulder. He leaped forward, charging through the snow to the body lying unconscious in the path. Wrapped in a woolen cloak, she lay on her side, collapsed. Was she dead? Was Henry truly an orphan?

"Mistress," he said. "Mistress." But she didn't move. He gently turned her onto her back, her face upward, surrounded by dark curls. The moon shone through the winter-bare trees. "Damn," he whispered, recognizing the face even in the dark.

Viola Mackay Sinclair. The woman he'd exiled a year ago.

CHAPTER NINE

Visigoth Code Book IV, Part III, 654 AD

*Persons who take an abandoned child to be
raised in their household are entitled to
the child's service as a slave.*

Europe Common Practice, 13th – 16th century AD

*Parents who do not want to raise their children may
give them to monasteries along with a small oblation
fee. Hospitals for the needy will take in abandoned
children and the care is paid by the village. Although
some institutions refuse so as not to
encourage abandonment.*

Rap. Rap.

"Cait," Gideon called through the door as he
held the unconscious woman. "'Tis Gideon." There
was a long pause, and he ground his teeth together.
"I've found Henry's mother."

The bar inside scraped across the door, and it
swung inward. Willa gasped as she stood there, apparently feeling well enough to be up. Gideon's gaze
easily found Cait where she stood holding the newborn near the hearth. "My guess is that this is she,"
he said.

Rhona flew forward. "What did you do to her?"

Do to her? People did see him as a monster.

Wasn't that what he'd wanted? For all four of the Sinclair Horsemen to be monsters, frightening people into obedience? Not if he wanted his people to trust him.

"What did I do to her?" he repeated and brushed past Willa, carrying Viola inside. "I picked her up out of the snow and carried her here."

"Is she dead?" Trix asked, both of her small hands holding her cheeks, her eyes brimming with tears.

"Nay."

Cait handed the bairn off to Libby. "Over here." She beckoned him toward a single raised bed in the corner. Gideon lowered Viola, and Cait untied the unconscious woman's cloak. She turned her face to look at Gideon. "Viola Sinclair."

He nodded, unwilling to say anything that would make him seem more of a monster. The woman had not left Sinclair territory as she'd been ordered. Had she taken on a lover or been raped? Alone and unprotected, anything could've happened to her, but exile was better than death. Wasn't it?

Cait brushed Viola's damp hair from her face. "She has a fever."

"Probably from the birth," Rhona said. "Little Henry is a fresh bairn. Still has his wee stump at his navel." She shook her head. "Did she give birth by herself in the woods?"

Cait felt the woman's pulse. "'Tis high and shallow. Willa, help me get her out of this wet cloak."

"I can help," Gideon said, moving forward to support the woman. He noticed some white spit-up on Cait's bodice. "There's puke on your shoulder."

Cait glanced there and turned back to Viola. "Remember, the good things in life are messy. That includes a bairn whose mother fed it from her weak body before she left it in someone else's care because she knew she was dying."

Bloody hell. Gideon shut his mouth, and they worked to remove Viola's wet clothes. They were filthy, as if she'd been living in squalor. Dried blood stained her smock. Rhona brought over a privacy screen, and she and Cait worked to wash the woman. Gideon felt helpless. He watched the children care for the bairn, rocking him in their arms until he fell asleep. Dammit, he was useless here, a feeling that made him itch to move.

"I'll send food up from the castle," he said. "Something warm." He pulled several coins from his purse, setting them on the table. "In case ye need some coin for the apothecary."

Cait came out from behind the screen. Her cheeks were flushed from lifting and moving the unconscious woman. She pushed a curled strand of hair from her face and grabbed a bucket. "Thank you," she said as she followed him out the door. "For bringing her here. We're her only chance."

She bent to gather snow to melt. "Allow me," he murmured and took the bucket to the side of the road where there was a pile of fresh snow.

He brought it back. "I'll send food up as soon as it is warm and some more blankets, perhaps another cauldron." Whatever he could find.

She reached for the bucket handle, but he did not let go. "Cait."

Finally, her eyes lifted to his, waiting, wordless.

Gideon inhaled, feeling unsure, which was something completely foreign to him. "I will consider your words about children and mothers."

She reached for the bucket of snow, tugging it, and he let go. "No one throws the father in the cell for leaving his child."

"And that's not right," he said. His chest felt tight, and he made himself inhale the cool air. But it did not loosen anything. "I'm sorry for angering ye. We were having…" He rubbed his chin. "Coming to an understanding."

She gave him a nod. "Thank you again for helping us. I will let you know if Viola dies." Cait turned and was through the door before his numb brain could come up with a farewell.

Gideon stared at the closed door for several long breaths. "Bloody hell," he murmured, and pivoted, striding down the path toward Varrich Castle. The paths were empty, windows and doors shut tight with the faint glow of hearth fires behind them.

Cait's whole demeanor had changed when the bairn had arrived. The only conclusion was a dark one. Cait did indeed think he was a tyrant. His hands fisted at his sides. He'd been raised to be one. Perhaps his father had succeeded.

· · ·

14 August 1589 – Trial against Viola Sutherland Mackay

Bastard-born sister to Robert Mackay, steward to Chief Hew Mackay. The woman was sent to live with the Sinclairs as a girl. Raised with the Sinclairs.

Contacted by Robert to help him take over Clan Mackay and eventually Clan Sinclair.

Viola hid a note in Ella Sutherland's bridal bouquet, telling her that her young brother, Jamie Sutherland, was in jeopardy. She tricked Ella into thinking her a friend. She delayed Cain Sinclair from chasing after Ella, thus allowing her brother to abduct Ella in crude fashion. Using tears and trickery, Viola escaped the guard set on her while the Sinclair brothers sought to figure out what happened to Ella. Viola ran directly to Varrich Castle to aid Robert Mackay in his plans, but Cain and Joshua Sinclair were already there, and Pastor John restrained her before going above with Cain and Joshua to save Ella and Jamie Sutherland.

Verdict is guilty of lying, disloyalty, and endangering an innocent woman and young man. Punishment is: two days in the stocks, one lash across the back, and exile from the Sinclair, Sutherland, and Mackay clans.

Gideon Sinclair, Horseman of Justice

Gideon sat back in his chair before his ledger. Viola Mackay had been guilty. He could have ordered her to be executed or sent to Edinburgh to prison for her heartless actions and duplicity. Exile gave her freedom to leave with her life. He tapped his fist on the table. Her only defense had been that she didn't know her brother's full plans.

It'd been three days since Gideon had found her in the snow and had sent warm chicken stew and rolls to Cait's home, along with blankets and a cauldron Mathias had found in a back room. For the last two days, he'd worked with Bàs, Bruce, and Osk to distribute chickens, indoor crates to house them through the winter, and grain to villagers after going door to door to see how they fared. Many were in desperate need, and all of them required help in some fashion.

The revenge that Clan Sinclair had inflicted, combined with Hew Mackay's mismanagement of crops and a harsh winter, had left them cold, hungry, and to-the-marrow-of-their-bones angry. Alistair had vanished when they'd stopped by the cottage behind the smithy that he shared with his father. The weathered man took the supplies with a nod and shut the door without a word.

Gideon pushed back from his desk and stood, closing the ledger. No information had come about how Viola was faring. Or her bairn. Who was the father? Why wasn't he helping care for wee Henry?

"There should be a law about that," he murmured. He glanced along the book-covered wall, sliding his gaze down the spines of the many tomes he'd basically memorized. The burden of a bairn rested on the mother, as if the fault of becoming with child out of wedlock lay entirely on her shoulders, which was a pile of horse dung. A new law was in order.

He would write it up tonight, but right now he could no longer wait to see how Cait greeted him. Cold like when she'd dismissed him the other night? Or warmer like when they had walked arm in arm over the icy road?

Gideon followed the turning steps that let out into the great hall. Mathias stood smiling at two bonny lasses. He jerked around as if found guilty when Gideon walked in.

"Gideon, Mistress Emma and Mistress Elizabeth have brought ye some tasty biscuits."

The young ladies hurried over to him. Mathias pointed at himself and then to the hall that led to the kitchen. "I have two *matronly* ladies waiting for me to bake tarts today for tomorrow's festival."

"Mathias," Gideon said, stopping him. "Alistair has resigned from his role as Master of Revels. Might you have another idea?"

Mathias thought for a second. "Osk Flett has a devilish side and will be coming with your family anyway," he said. "I can send word to him at Girnigoe."

"Aye," Gideon said, nodding. The Orkney man had even brought a smile to Bàs's dour face when they'd unloaded the chickens.

"The hall looks so bright," one of the waiting lasses said as she handed a basket over to Gideon and smiled sweetly at him. "I'm Emma." She lowered in a deep curtsy.

"And I'm Elizabeth," the other said, also curtsying. She stood, her cheeks pink, and handed him a clay jar. "'Tis jam I made last summer. Strawberry. Do you like strawberry?"

He nodded. "'Tis very kind of ye." These two apparently found him approachable.

They both smiled grandly. "'Tis to say thank you for bringing the food and blankets yesterday," Emma said. "You're the kind horseman."

"And strong," Elizabeth said and blinked several times as if trying to draw attention to her eyes.

At Girnigoe, Gideon had enjoyed the attention of several lasses in the village, their exuberance over his strength and power within the clan a natural attractant. At Varrich, most had been too frightened of his wrath to extend a smile and definitely not jam and biscuits along with whatever these two had in mind. Did they come as a pair? *Good Lord*. If Joshua weren't wed and totally smitten with his wife, Kára, Gideon would have turned the two lasses on him. Because Gideon just did not have time to deal with lasses bringing treats right now, baked or carnal. He just wanted to see about Cait.

"Thank ye again," he said, setting their offerings down. "I will return the basket and crock when empty." He would have Mathias return them. The man could charm any lass, and if they were offering more than sweets, Mathias would thank him for the chore.

They continued to stand in the hall as if waiting for something more. "I was on my way out to check on...things."

"Oh," Emma said, her arched brows rising. "We can come back this evening."

Gideon looked between them. Aye, they were offering more than jam and biscuits. He smiled. "A tempting offer, and much appreciated, but I'll be engaged elsewhere."

Elizabeth's bottom lip protruded just enough to make her look like a child who had been told that she could not have a sweet. Emma kept her smile. "We will walk with you out, then, and will definitely return for your Hogmanay Festival tomorrow evening."

They linked their arms through his as he walked
them from Varrich Castle and across the bailey
where the Sinclairs guarding the walls watched.
Would word get back to Cait that he'd had the lasses
in the castle? Did that matter? Nay. Then why did it
feel like it mattered?

A bell rang down the lane at the chapel door. It
was Sunday, and Pastor John had come to lead a
service. "I will take ye to church," he said, steering
them there. Perhaps Pastor John's words would deter
them from sneaking into his bedchamber at night. *I
need to start locking my door.* But then there'd be no
way for Cait to sneak in. *Daingead.* Perhaps he
should leave her rope dangling to the ground.

"Pastor John, this is Elizabeth and Emma, and
they will be joining ye this morn." The young pastor
nodded to them and ushered the frowning ladies inside. "A word, Pastor," Gideon called.

"Aye." They moved to the side to allow more villagers to enter. Would Cait and her troop of children
attend?

"It has come to my attention that the villagers
may not know the rules that govern the village, so
I'm planning to add more to the chapel door."

Pastor John looked at the missives nailed there
already. "More?"

"Aye," Gideon said. "Those speak of some basic
ones: no stealing, no treasonous acts against the Sinclairs…" He indicated his scrawl across the notices.
"No witchcraft or slander." He rubbed his chin. "But
there will be a new one written about fathers supporting the mothers of their children, wed or unwed.
And if a child is abandoned by living parents, both

mother and father will be held accountable." He dropped his hand. "Oh, and that females may act in plays and the nightly bell is a recommendation to settle in for the night, not a law."

Pastor John stared at him, his lips parted as he listened. He looked over his shoulder at the small chapel. "I'll have to add another door."

Gideon pointed to the wood beams flanking the entry. "I will tack them along there."

"Oh," said Pastor John.

"I'd have ye choose one missive each week to go over, for those who do not read," Gideon said. "I can't expect them to follow laws they know nothing about."

"True." Pastor John nodded to Fiona and Evie as they entered, eyeing Gideon. "Is there something ye wish me to say in particular today?" Pastor John asked.

"Aye." Gideon's gaze spotted Rhona hurrying along the road with Jack, Libby, and a skipping Trix behind her. But no Cait. "Talk about men being just as responsible as women when it comes to bringing a bairn into the world. That they must take responsibility to feed, clothe, and house the bairn and mother or they'll be held accountable for their neglect. I will post it tomorrow morn."

Pastor John followed his line of sight. "I'll work it into my message today. Will ye come to partake of God's word, too?"

"Does Cait Mackay usually come with her wards to chapel?"

"Some weeks," Pastor John said.

Gideon looked at him. "Not every week?"

Pastor John's brow rose. "It's not a law, is it?"

"In some cities, but nay, not at Varrich." But where did Cait go on Sundays when not at chapel? "She must be taking care of the new bairn who was left at the Orphans' Home."

"I will pray for the bairn," Pastor John said. "And the mother and father." He tipped his cleanly clipped head to Rhona as she and the children entered, although Rhona was staring intently at Gideon and not paying attention to the cleric.

"Good morn, Chief Gideon," Trix said, offering him a tentative smile.

"Good morn, Mistress Trix," he answered. She bobbed a curtsy and skipped inside. "How fairs wee Henry and his mother?"

"The bairn is strong," Libby said. "Viola is not, but she lives."

"Viola Mackay?" the pastor asked.

Gideon looked at the children and Rhona. "Let us keep Henry's mother out of the conversation for now."

They all mumbled their agreement, and Gideon nodded to the cleric. "Good day, Pastor," Gideon said and walked up the slope toward the Orphans' Home.

"Next week perhaps," Pastor John called after him, his voice full of hope that he might one day save Gideon's soul.

Gideon made it to Cait's door in short time, since there were no people about to whom he must greet and earn Cait's points. Being approachable took an exorbitant amount of time. Being kind was the opposite of efficiency.

Smoke curled up from the chimney on the far side of the stone cottage that now housed eight souls. Cait needed larger quarters.

Rap. Rap.

No answer. He frowned at the door.

Rap. Rap. "Good morn," he called.

The sound of a bairn came through the door. Was it left alone? Surely Cait would not leave a newborn bairn alone.

Rap. Rap.

"Mistress Cait is not in," came a young voice. It must be Willa, but where was Cait?

"'Tis Gideon Sinclair," he said. He bit back his order to open the door. Cait would surely frown over that when Willa retold the story. He cleared his throat. "I'd greatly appreciate it if ye would open the door, Willa. I'll just be a moment."

The sound of a bar sliding along the inside strengthened his patience, and he waited. He smiled at Willa, although her wide eyes made him wonder if he'd mistakenly snarled. "I would like to see the patient," he said. "And how is wee Henry?"

Her face relaxed. "He is well and eating heartily."

"Where's your sister?"

Willa's timid smile dropped away, and her eyebrows rose as if giving a casual answer. "Oh, she has gone with the others to chapel this morn. 'Tis Sunday." Even if he hadn't seen the others without Cait, he could have easily picked up on Willa's lie.

He nodded anyway, to put her at ease, and she moved aside so he could enter. The cottage was warm but not stuffy. The scent of fresh bread floated on the air. Now that they had plenty of milled flour, bread should be plentiful.

Viola lay with Henry in the same bed he'd deposited her in. Her eyes were open and filled with hatred. Of course. He was her judge and executioner before he was her savior the other night.

"I'm alive, Horseman," she said, although her voice sounded weak.

"I'm glad for it," he said, his words honest as he watched her hold her bairn gingerly over her shoulder, rubbing his back.

"You should have killed me with the rest." Her words were soft but full of venom.

Willa took up a bucket. "I must collect more snow." She nearly ran from the room.

Gideon looked back to Viola. "But then Henry wouldn't have been born." She seemed to care for her son.

"'Tis a cruel world. I would not have brought a child into it."

He picked up a chair, bringing it close. Cain's wife, Ella, had said he loomed over people, especially when he was judging them, which was all the time, in her opinion. He sat down so he'd be more on Viola's level. "The father should have helped ye. I'll ensure he does provide for the two of ye."

Viola just stared at him.

"Who is the father?"

She shook her head. "Shall I tell you so you can flog him, execute him? Nay. He showed me kindness when no one else would, fearing your wrath." Unshed tears glistened in her dark eyes. "He said he loved me."

"Then he will help with the child."

"He knows." She pulled Henry off her shoulder to hold him in her arms, his small features now relaxed in contented sleep. "But he's unable to help me further."

Unable or unwilling? "The burden should not fall solely upon ye."

Her chin tilted higher. "Why bother yourself with us? You condemned me a year ago to exile."

"But I did not condemn an innocent bairn."

Tears broke from her eyes. "Will you…will you take him from me then? Send me away?" She let the tears flow down her cheeks without acknowledging them.

Don't let a woman's tears sway ye, son. Eve wept in Eden but was still guilty.

His father's words had formed stone within Gideon as he'd grown. He thought those hard pieces of advice had made him stronger, more resistant to false sentiment. Perhaps his father's advice had made him the monster the villagers saw.

"I'm not the tyrant ye think I am, Viola. Ye have obviously suffered for your sins against my clan. Your penance is paid, and we will find a way for ye to raise your son." That was if she lived. The woman still seemed pale and weak. Were her eyes glossy with just tears, or did fever make them shine with sickness?

Her body sank back into the pillows. "Ye have much to live for," Gideon said. "See that ye follow all Cait's instructions for improving."

Her lips pinched, and she blinked back more tears, nodding as she brought Henry up to her cheek, kissing his little head.

"Is she out purchasing cures from the apothecary?" There was no business to be done on Sundays, and not between Christmas and Twelfth Night except for animal care and medical care. But it would be a likely reason she wasn't at church that morning.

"I… I do not know Cait's errands," Viola said. "I'm not someone with whom she and Rhona confide." After years of reading expressions, judging people guilty or innocent based on the dilation of their pupils, the tightness of their jaw, and their line of sight when they spoke, Gideon knew right away Viola was not telling the truth. At least not the complete truth.

He stood. "Get well, Mistress Viola. And blessings on your son."

No "thank you" passed her lips, but her face softened enough to let her appreciation shine through. Or was that just relief from escaping the executioner's block or exile without her son?

Stepping out into the chilled air, Willa grabbed up a bucket of snow, waddling under its weight to the door. "I have it," she said when he tried to take it for her. "Good day." She pushed past him into the cottage. The dismissal reminded him very much of her sister.

He looked around the empty yard. Where *was* her sister?

Gideon walked around the perimeter of the cottage. A forest sat behind it, and a set of crisp footprints led off into it. They were fresh, and he followed them between the trees.

After a quarter hour of walking, he stopped. He

was at least half a mile from her house. "Where are ye going, Cait?" he murmured. Alone in the woods? Where anything could happen to her. He gritted his teeth and continued.

Farther up, there was an outcropping of boulders that reached as high as his head. Snow covered them, and he saw what looked like a swipe around the side where the prints disappeared, the snow dislodged. It was the perfect ambush site. Instinctually, he peered around it before stepping through.

Like an owl, silently swooping down to catch its prey, Cait swung through the clear cold air. She gripped a long swath of white fabric that was anchored high into the trees. When the swinging momentum slowed, instead of sliding down, she wrapped her trouser-clad legs in the fabric, easily climbing up into the bare limbs of the tree.

Gideon stared motionless, watching her. She could climb in and out of any chamber she so desired, but the thought was fleeting as he watched her gracefully unfold before him. She wore white, slim-fitting clothing, blending in with the surrounding snow-covered trees. Reaching near the top, Gideon realized it was two pieces of fabric when Cait parted them and began wrapping one around each leg. His jaw dropped open as her legs split apart completely as she hung effortlessly in the air.

After stretching so far apart, she reached higher with her hands and brought her legs back together. Each long leg was wrapped in the fabric, and she crossed the strands behind her back. With what looked like little effort, she lifted her legs above her head until she hung upside down, her long braid hanging straight toward the frozen ground. The fabric was wrapped intricately around her in a pattern he could not fathom. She then pulled up so that her head nearly brushed the tops of the trees and paused. Gideon realized that he held his breath as she balanced there in the winter-bare canopy.

Grabbing high, Cait arched her back so that it seemed the earth was trying to pull her down. And then she let go, plunging, face first toward the ground.

CHAPTER TEN

Pope Alexander III, 12th century AD

A marriage that was brought about by an external force sufficient to elicit great fear in the woman or girl invalidates the union. Young girls shall not be forced to enter into unwanted marriages.

"Cait!" He jumped out from behind the boulders, intent on reaching her before she smacked into the frozen earth. But he was too far away, and the fall was too fast. All the muscles of his body prepared instantly for battle, but he couldn't battle the laws of nature, the very forces pulling her to her death.

The fabric caught around her as she flipped through the air, unwinding from the intricate pattern on the way down until the wrapping caught her several yards off the ground. Her gaze fell on him, and for several heartbeats they stared at each other while the momentum kept her swinging. He took a step toward her, dropping his arms that he'd held out in a foolish hope to catch her.

With a movement of limbs that was both sporadic and full of grace, she disentangled herself and climbed up the fabric into the trees faster than he'd seen any person do before. She made it look effortless even though he'd seen grown warriors unable to climb a rope despite their arm strength.

Cait reached a limb and stood upon it, looking

down, breathing hard. Her dark braid fell over one shoulder to dangle before her.

"Bloody hell... Cait? I have never... What is this?" He stared up at her with his head tilted back. Gideon had seen acrobats in Edinburgh before, ones who jumped and tumbled and even swung on a bar above the crowds, but he'd never seen anyone do what Cait had just done. Such grace and courage. "I did not know ye could fly."

"Is flying against your laws?" she asked.

"Nay."

"I'm certain you can create one that outlaws it." She was baiting him. Her surprise and wariness were turning to anger.

"Why would I do that when 'tis so beautiful?"

"Why would you punish a woman who leaves her bairn with us when she thought it would die with her?"

He exhaled. "I spoke with Viola this morn. I'm not acting against her. There were circumstances that made her act honorably. Cait, I'm not a tyrant, even if you've changed your mind."

She leaned against a branch, clutching the fabric in her hands as she watched him, judging the truth in his words. Her mouth opened, her face pinched. He waited for whatever words would come from between those lips, but then she closed them.

What had been ready to fly from those lush lips?

"Speak what sits on your tongue, Cait," he said.

She peered down at him. "Why would you afford mercy to Viola and not to others?"

His gaze dropped to the scuffed ground. "She has suffered enough for her crimes against innocents, and I will not make her innocent son suffer with the loss of his mother or clan."

"And you alone have decided that her heart has changed?" she asked.

"Aye," he said, his gaze reaching her again where she perched in the tree. "I take evidence of character and information about her circumstances and suffering and decide."

"By yourself."

'Tis your sole purpose, son, to judge and know the inner evil or good in a person. "'Tis a skill I have learned, and I do it well," Gideon said.

"Humble to your core."

"Confident in my teachings from wise books and my natural instinct for such things." He stretched his arms up to cup the back of his head as he looked at her, a snow-colored wood nymph high in the trees, the likes of which he had never seen before. "Ye do not have confidence in my judgment?"

She looked at the long swath of fabric that sat bunched around her. "I have no confidence in life and death being decided by one man. All that power in one man frightens people." She made a loop and pulled part of the fabric through, repeating the motion until the long fabric sat tied in a much shorter plait, which she secured in the tree next to a similar plait dyed dark blue, covering them both with a tarp. "If you want the villagers to speak with you, they must feel you can't just order their execution if you're having a horrid day."

Gideon moved closer to the base of the tree. He couldn't concentrate on her words as she climbed down the limbs, her small leather slippers balancing as she descended. The woman had traveled the path many times before, but even so, he held his breath until she reached the trampled snow at the bottom. It had to be at least thirty feet high.

He spotted her woolen cloak and picked it up, shaking out the folds as he walked closer to her. He held it open instead of just handing it away. "How long have ye practiced this…skill?"

Cait walked close, turning her back for him to place the cape around her shoulders. "I started climbing high when I arrived here in Varrich. No one could find me in the trees. I started swinging and trying different things because it felt like flying away."

The pain that filled her words beat at him with each heartbeat. "Ye lost your mother and father to illness back with Clan Gunn."

"And my older brother," she said, her words flat. "Willa and I were left without legal help. We had an uncle, my mother's brother, who took all our possessions, all my parents' books. He arranged a marriage for me, and Willa and I moved to Varrich with Benjamin Mackay."

"Och, but I'd have helped ye," he said. But he was a decade late. "Ye were young," he said, almost afraid to break whatever spell had loosened her tongue.

"Fifteen, the same age as Willa is now." She shook her head. "Too young to face the horrors of the wedding bed."

His hand rose to lightly touch her shoulder. "Horrors?" Had she been raped by her husband?

She looked down. "I was too young, and he was not kind."

Vengeance itched in his chest, vengeance against

her uncle and her dead husband. He guided her to turn around to face him, so she could see his face. "I'm truly sorry for what ye endured."

She swallowed, a small smile tugging at her tight mouth. "Me too, and it has made me determined never to see a child sold in marriage. I'll take them in when they have no place to go."

Cait was strong of heart. She had taken the worst situation and built conviction and good upon it. Many would have broken and grown bitter under the weight of such awfulness.

They stood close together. "I'll help ye accomplish that. I swear it," he said, realizing he hadn't known all this about her past. Pressure in his chest made him frown. Would he have changed anything in how he'd handled her punishment had he known?

Her gaze softened, and her lips relaxed into something more like a true smile. "You could do so much to help children at Varrich."

Gideon slowly inhaled the fresh scent of her hair. He'd known women who wore scents and expensive perfumes meant to attract a man. Hell, he'd given bottles of it to some. But Cait had her own natural mix of flowers and spice and musk that made him want to inhale along every inch of her skin. He'd never want to cover it.

She turned without moving out of his grasp. Could she feel this pull between them, too? He'd felt it as they'd walked in the growing shadows before Henry was found. It was a yearning as if she were a beacon of warmth in a frozen world, and he wished to be in her glow.

She walked away, prompting him to fall in step

beside her. "Ye come here to climb often," he said.

"When I can. Even if I love the children, I need to escape the pressures of life for a bit."

"Perhaps I should take up swinging from a rope."

She laughed, glancing at him. "King James may help you swing if he hears about your treasonous plans."

"He will not." Gideon raised his hand to the trees. "Your kind of swinging."

"Let us call it flying." She met his gaze.

"Aye. Flying." The words meant nothing, but something felt different. Perhaps the beginning of trust. They'd both endured trials in their youth, trials that had made them stronger.

They stepped out on the road that led back to her house. People moved along the path, since chapel had finished. "What will you do with Viola and her son?" she asked.

There were many options. He could send her to one of the cloisters that were still being run where she could be warm and raise Henry. Gideon could rescind her exile and allow her to settle in town. He could send her to live in the village of Girnigoe where she was raised from the age of ten. His word was law at Varrich, so he could make any of these scenarios come to fruition.

"I leave that up to ye and Viola to figure out," he said. "I'll support what ye think is best."

Cait stopped, looking at him. She blinked, and her lips parted in surprise. The honesty of it made him frown, but she smiled in response and nodded. "We will figure out what works best for mother and child, and I'll make certain she'll not interfere with

Mackay rule again."

Before he could reply that she could not ascertain that, she sidestepped across the road, stomping down on something, and he heard a crunch. It was too cold for beetles or bees. Barely breaking her stride, she came back to the center with him.

He glanced back but saw nothing of consequence left in the road. "What required such wrath?"

Cait chuckled, and he clung to the sound. When had making her happy become important? "'Twas just a leaf. I knew from its look it would be crunchy."

"Crunchy?"

Her smile was radiant, and he no longer cared about her answer, his curiosity swamped by the look of teasing and authentic joy in the curve of her lips. That and the fact that the anger and suspicion seemed to have faded somewhat.

She shrugged as they continued to walk. "I like to step on crunchy leaves. The smallest leaves with the biggest crunch are the best. 'Tis hard to find them in the winter when everything becomes wet. I don't let them pass when I can easily step upon them. The sound is somehow satisfying."

She laughed at his confused look and rested her hand on his arm. "You wouldn't understand. 'Tis another one of those best things in life."

"The crunch of a little leaf?"

"Everyone has their own things that make the day brighter. The crunch of a little leaf is one for me." She tipped her head. "Perhaps 'tis because something so small and without any power at all can still have a resounding voice." She shrugged again. "'Tis satisfying."

He squinted his eyes at her. "Or ye are a person who likes to make innocent little leaves scream."

She gasped, her hand to her breast. "That you would think so poorly of me!"

They arrived at her door, which flew open to reveal Willa. "You wouldn't believe—" She halted immediately when her gaze took in Gideon. "You're back. We were just about to cook two eggs that Pickle laid."

Cait looked to him. "Pickle is the hen you brought."

"Pickle? An odd name," he said.

Trix smiled behind Willa and leaped from foot to foot. "Because we're preserving her, not, you know, eating her," she ended on a whisper.

"Ohhhh," he drew out, his brows high. "I'm glad she is producing then."

Trix poked her head out to grin at him, her teeth bright. "She likes living in the house with us. Just like Boo."

"Boo?" Gideon asked.

"My bird. I named her Boo for Boudica, the Celtic warrior queen, because I hope she becomes strong again just like her." She fetched a box from the corner, bringing it close so he could see a small wren inside with an outstretched wing.

"Boo hit our door yesterday, and I'm keeping her warm until she can fly again," Trix said.

The child would probably cry when it died. "There's a law against keeping wild animals in homes," Gideon said.

Trix's easy smile dropped, and she took a step back, sheltering the little bird in her arms. "Boo will die outside," Trix said, her voice small.

"There are good reasons for laws and rules," Gideon said. "Wild animals can hurt people, and they must be fed and are dirty."

Cait moved between Gideon and Trix, flapping her hand behind her to get the girl moving away. "The bird won't hurt anyone, it eats crumbs that are too small for anyone, and the poor creature is cleaner than Jack."

"I bathed her in warm water," Trix called from the corner near the fire where she clung to her pet.

"It will probably die anyway," Gideon said, his voice lowered. "The law can be of help. She will think it flew away."

Libby stood before Trix and her bird. "We're keeping the bird inside," she said with force, as if protecting her sister and not the bird.

Cait frowned. "Your brother owns a falcon, which lives inside Girnigoe Castle. Is he breaking your law?"

"Eun is a trained warrior," Gideon said. "He flies above during battle, signaling us with colored flags that Cain gives him."

Cait stared without blinking. "Then we'll have to get some advice from your brother, since that's exactly what we're training Boo to do when she heals."

"The wren? Flying above the battlefield with flags?"

Gideon noticed all the frowns in the room. He rubbed the back of his neck. "I think I've lost more points," he said, looking at Cait.

"'Tis as easy as breathing to you, isn't it?" she said.

He exhaled, raising his voice. "I'll amend the law tonight. Wild animals being trained to aid us in battle are allowed to live indoors."

"And who can aid around the house," Libby said and lowered her hands from her small hips. "I know of a woman who had a badger who helped her around the house. She'd trained it to bring down things from up high on a shelf."

Gideon stared for a moment at the girl. Libby gave one full nod and stared back with the seriousness of a judge.

"I'll have the two of ye inspect the law before I tack it to the chapel door," he said.

Trix flew out from behind Libby. "Really? We can read it and tell you if it's a good law?"

Libby looked on expectantly, as did all of them, including Cait. "Aye," he said, earning a softening of Cait's mouth and hopefully his points back.

"I'll see ye all at the festival on the morrow?" he asked, turning to the door. He stepped out into the cold, gray day and realized that he would much rather be inside their cozy cottage.

"Oh yes," Libby cried. "We're altering some of the clothes you sent to be festive."

"I hear it will last three days," Jack said from behind.

Three days? "Aye," Gideon answered, making a note to tell Mathias if he didn't already know.

"And there will be dancing and minstrels," Rhona added.

"And sweets and presents!" Trix rushed back full of smiles.

Cait's lips pressed together as if she were trying to stop her laughter. "We will keep you no longer, Chief Sinclair, for you surely have a long list of tasks before the village shows up on your doorstep."

She slowly shut the door, meeting his eyes the whole way, even into the crack until it was completely shut, leaving him alone out in the cold. Yet her smile still brought some warmth inside his chest. Aye, he'd earned some points back.

• • •

"You're not going to wear that threadbare gown, are you?" Rhona asked as she helped Libby dry off before the fire. They'd each taken a bath and were donning their best clothes for the Hogmanay Festival at the castle.

Cait ignored the blush in her cheeks. She'd never cared about her dress and lack of possessions before, except books of course. "I haven't had time to alter the dress that was sent from the castle."

Gideon had sent warm clothing for each of them, his messenger assuring them that he was equipping all the inhabitants of Varrich with proper clothes for winter. He'd sent a green costume for Cait, but the hem was too short, making her look ridiculously tall in it. She was already tall at seven inches over five feet. The sight of her bare ankles would just enhance it.

Rhona grinned. "I know. You've spent every minute working on clothes for the children so they will look royal, but as usual you won't lift a finger to help yourself."

Cait wrinkled her nose at Rhona, who wore a new blue wool gown that accentuated her voluptuous form. "There's no help for it, because we're due there in less than an hour." She looked at Viola, who held Henry nursing on the bed. "You can come if you feel strong enough."

Viola's mouth lifted in a half smile. "Even though I'm grateful Gideon Sinclair didn't throw me back out in the snow, I have no desire to make merry with him or his brothers and Ella Sinclair, who will no doubt attend."

Everyone in town knew of Viola's sins in helping her brother try to take Cain Sinclair's bride. Until Viola forgave herself, she would not expect anyone else to do so.

Trix jumped up and down in her rose-colored dress by the door, and Libby sent her harsh looks. "Shhhh!" Willa said but smiled anyway.

"We're leaving soon enough," Cait said, pulling the long pin from her hair to let the curls down so she didn't look quite so matronly.

Jack waved Cait over to the window. "We have visitors."

Cait's stomach tightened until she saw his smile, and she strode over where he opened the shutter fully. Outside stood Fiona and Evie. When they saw her at the window, the two elderly ladies held up something green between them. A gown. "Oh my," Cait whispered, glancing at Rhona who smiled ear to ear.

"'Tis for you," Trix yelled, twirling about, her skirts going wide.

Libby opened the door. "So you can look as lovely and festive as the rest of us."

Cait stepped out into the sunny cold afternoon. "Fiona? Evie?"

The sisters smiled brightly. "'Tis one of our brother's wife's gowns that she cannot fit into anymore," Fiona said. "When Rhona said you had no time to fix a gown, we fixed this one for you. Rhona gave us your measurements."

"We added lace and the purple plaid stomacher with ties," Evie said, her rosy apple-like cheeks even rounder with her smile. "'Tis what they wear at court."

Fiona fluffed the petticoat as they held the gown between them. "Maude is rather plain, so we spruced it up."

"'Tis beautiful," Cait said, pulling the ladies inside with the gown.

Fiona and Evie paused at the sight of Viola on the bed, passing a look between them and then to Rhona. "The chief knows she's here," Rhona said.

Cait met Fiona's questioning eyes. "Gideon saved her by pulling her from the snow." The two sisters nodded to Viola, who nursed wee Henry but didn't say anything.

Rhona took the gown from them and followed Cait to the hearth. "Let us get Cait dressed. We haven't much time."

"And I will do her hair," Libby said, hands on her hips.

Cait laughed. "What's wrong with my hair?"

"You never sit still long enough for me to do a proper job," Libby said, bringing out her box of ties and pins. The girl loved to fashion hair, and Cait hoped that one day she could make a wage with her skills.

"Here now," Fiona said. "Let us get the underskirt on ye."

"I'll go on then," Jack said, looking uncomfortable. "I'll take the buns to the castle and see if Gideon needs any assistance."

Cait nodded her thanks, as the ladies laughed and talked around her. They were already unlacing her old gown as Jack shut the door behind him.

The dress was a deep green with purple plaid accents in the vee-shaped stomacher to be laced and a solid purple underskirt, which showed in the part of the green overskirt. The colors contrasted beautifully. "The material is so soft," Cait said, sliding a hand over the wool underskirt that would keep her warm, although she would probably still wear her slim-fitting trews underneath. Not only were they good for sneaking around silently and swinging through the trees, but her woven trews also kept her warm all winter. She'd gift each of the children with a pair in the morning.

"It truly is lovely," she said, smiling at Evie and Fiona.

"And our Hogmanay gift to you," Rhona said, holding out a new white smock edged in hand-knitted lace that had also been bleached pure white.

Cait stood in awe. "'Tis lovely."

"You do so much for all of us," Rhona said.

Willa hugged Cait. "And you deserve to be pretty."

Libby smiled smugly. "Jack said you'd rather have another *sgian dubh*, but he's a boy and wouldn't know about such things."

"Put it on," Trix said, still jumping around. The girl leaped as much as a hare in the spring.

Cait stepped behind a screen and slipped out of her old smock and threw on the new one, letting the thin linen float over her. "I feel like a princess," she said, stepping out. She touched the lace edging. Trix clapped her hands. Next came the underskirt that tied in the back, its fullness reaching the tops of her feet. "The perfect length."

Fiona walked around her, fluffing it. "No ankles showing."

Cait held the white stays to her, while Evie laced her in front. Next came the outer dress and long sleeves made from the same green wool. Finally, the purple plaid stomacher was added over her stays, and Rhona pinned it in place. The lacy edge of the smock peeked over the stomacher, where the swell of her breasts perched high.

"And Jack polished your leather boots," Trix said, grabbing them from where they'd been hidden in the corner.

"So that's where they were," Cait said, making a severe face that was obviously fake. She'd worn her slippers all morning, thinking one of the girls had borrowed her boots and left them outdoors. She laced up the boots that were polished with fresh beeswax and turned in a circle, making the skirts bell out.

"The bonniest lass at Varrich," Fiona said, pride in her weathered face.

Evie held her palms together as if in prayer, her smile wide. "With the bonniest heart."

"Now win the new chief, so he'll keep giving us chickens and flour," Fiona finished.

Cait snorted, shaking her head. "He is not giving

you food because of me. Gideon had been misinformed about our lack."

"'Tis that bastard, Bruce," Rhona said. "He probably sold our food for his own profit."

"That *tolla-thon*," Viola said behind her, and the two elderly sisters nodded. At least they all agreed on that.

Libby pushed on Cait's shoulder to get her to sit in the chair while she and Willa worked to pull up part of her long hair, braiding it to lie like a crown around the top.

"She needs some curls framing her face," Willa said, grabbing up a sharp *sgian dubh*. Cait caught her hand before she reached her hair. "Just a couple of strands," she said, holding out the long whisps she'd left out of the braids. "Not much and not short." Cait released her hand when she nodded.

"I'll leave them long enough to tie back in your usual braid, but today they will be curled with the poker."

"Lord help me," Cait said, but the girls were closing in as if they'd planned their assault earlier and meant to carry out their campaign.

A giddiness tickled in her stomach as she sat still, her fingers curling into the softness of her skirts. Would Gideon Sinclair think she was the bonniest lass at Varrich?

Ye are a cold fish to any man. The words swam around in her mind, quelling the giddy warmth inside Cait. Benjamin had sworn she was cold, saying that the proof was that she'd never conceived his child. And she'd believed him, because at fifteen and motherless, she had no one to teach her about such things. And he was certainly correct she'd always felt cold to the bone around him.

But Gideon Sinclair… Whenever he came close, Cait felt warm inside, either because she wanted to kick him in the shin or for a reason that made her heart beat faster. A reason that had started with that kiss in his bedchamber. Could Benjamin have been wrong, or would Gideon find out she was indeed a cold fish?

CHAPTER ELEVEN

Winter Festival, First brought to Scotland by Norsemen, 8th century AD

Hogmanay is celebrated on the last day of the year. As part of the winter celebration, giant fireballs are swung around on short and long metal poles and paraded about to signify the power of the sun. The fire purifies the world by consuming evil spirits.

"I think ye should light the second fire," Joshua said to Gideon where they stood inside Varrich's bailey.

"I will at dusk," Gideon said, scanning the villagers who were starting to breach the gates. They entered timidly, as if concerned this was an ambush instead of a festival. But the presence of Hannah, Ella, and Kára, with their bright smiles, encouraged them inside. Although most were still lacking in sustained food, everyone seemed to bring something to add to the feast. A jug of whisky or half dozen buns. One man carried a basket with two steaming fish while another brought a rabbit pie. But the one person he watched for hadn't yet appeared.

"Kára said she is cold," Joshua said. "And the bairns will need to be kept warmer."

"Kára looks comfortable out in the sun, and the bairns are with Aunt Merida inside the great hall." Gideon glanced at his brother. "I think 'tis ye who are cold."

Joshua made a face at him and marched away toward the other bonfire. Cain stood there talking with Bàs while Osk, embracing the role of Master of Revels, hopped about the bailey wearing a jester hat that Hannah had stitched for him.

The four minstrels whom Gideon had hired walked in, and he went to greet them. "Ye can set up on the platform near the stable," he said, pressing a coin into each of their hands.

"Mighty happy to bring cheer to the village," the leader of the quartet said. "'Tis time Varrich had something to celebrate." He nodded, smiling, and the four hurried over to find chairs.

Perhaps Ella had been right about having the festival. It was certainly a way to present himself as someone to whom the Mackays could come. Fear worked to deter crime, but it also stopped people from asking for help or seeking justice. Had Cait been able to ask for help when her parents died? Someone other than an uncle who sold her away in marriage at the age of fifteen?

"If *you* scowl, they'll not come through the gates no matter how much *we* smile," Ella said, walking toward him on her way to the great hall, probably to feed wee Mary. "You need to smile the whole time."

Cain's wife would always tell him and everyone what she thought, just like Aunt Merida. Come to think of it, Joshua's wife, Kára, was similar and the only one who was able to order his stubborn second brother around.

Gideon lifted the corners of his mouth, showing his teeth. Ella snorted, walking past. "And not like a wolf about to pounce."

"I'll try," he said and turned toward her as she continued. "And thank ye for coming today to help."

She paused, glancing back at him. Had she forgiven him for suggesting Cain abandon her to win the Sutherland Clan a year and a half ago? Gideon had been wrong, and he'd officially apologized to her afterward, but trust took time to rebuild. *Ten to one.* She nodded, offering him a genuine smile, and continued walking. The words seemed more to her than the gift of rich fabric that he'd given her, Kára, and Merida when they arrived. It was a start.

Bàs walked toward him from the castle. "I left your gift for Cait in your bedchamber. I hope ye don't walk in to torn bedding and pillow feathers strewn across everything." He slapped his hand down on Gideon's shoulder. Bàs smiled, something he didn't do often. Perhaps the festival was helping more than just the villagers of Varrich.

"Thank ye for that," Gideon said and watched a small group of children come in, heading toward the four horses that stood in the corner. Sgàil and his brothers' three horses represented the four Sinclair herds. "And thank ye for coloring your horse for the festival." To make Bàs's horse look pale green, he rubbed a mixture of crushed fresh leaves and grasses over his gray horse. Riding into battle with four armies, mounted on white, red, black, and pale green horses gave the enemy the impression that the true biblical Horsemen of the Apocalypse were descending straight from God.

"I found enough green leaves and grass for one horse without much trouble," Bàs said.

"Dòchas doesn't seem to mind the attention,"

Gideon said, nodding to where Bàs's horse stood still as the children came up to him, gingerly touching his coat. It'd been Hannah's suggestion for his brothers to bring their horses in for the villagers to meet so they would seem less intimidating. Their horses were so well trained that they would not move, trample, or nip, frightening the children, but just in case, one of Gideon's warriors stood with them.

Once again, Gideon was pulled between wanting to maintain the Sinclairs' fierceness and making him accessible to his people. His thumb turned the ring of the Horseman of Justice on his finger as he watched.

Joshua's bay horse, Fuil, lipped up a turnip that Joshua had cut into pieces and was now passing around to the children who stared up at him with wide eyes. Gideon's black horse, Sgàil, stood quietly waiting for his treat. He'd soon nudge Joshua if he didn't share. Cain's horse, Seraph, drew all the wee lasses, who stroked his pristine white coat. Ella had convinced Cain to let her tie colorful ribbons in Seraph's mane and tail, giving the majestic beast a magical look. It's a wonder she hadn't tied a horn to Seraph's forehead to make him into a fabled unicorn.

Several more groups of villagers walked in through the gates where Hannah and Kára greeted them. His brothers stayed back so as not to seem so intimidating, which was impossible. All four of them were over six feet tall and full of muscle from training every day. Their father had discouraged smiling and praised scowls and scars. Gideon's finger slid across the slightly puckered line along his cheek. What would George Sinclair think of this festival to win the loyalty of his people with merriment instead of fear?

A child rushed through the gates, drawing him away from such rancid thoughts. *Trix.* She skipped past the timid villagers into the bailey, followed by Libby and Willa, who walked arm in arm. They wore the festive clothes and warmer cloaks he'd sent over. Jack walked in next and headed straight for the horses. And, finally, Rhona and Cait appeared, smiles on both their faces as they stopped to talk with Hannah.

Cait's gaze followed Hannah's to land on him. She nodded, her smile deepening for a moment, enough to fill Gideon with hope. Even though he could read gestures and expressions, Cait wavered so much when she dealt with him that he couldn't be certain of anything with her. Did her smile mean that she appreciated his offerings of clothes for her children? Or did she appreciate him saving Viola and not condemning her a second time?

Gideon rubbed his jaw. *Do not let people sway ye from what ye know is right and wrong.* His father had schooled him constantly on his duty. *Damn.* Was he letting Cait sway him from justice? Was the woman a witch or had she somehow altered his perception of what was just?

Cait walked over to him, her warm cape around her. "If you frown, no one will approach you," she said, repeating Ella's prediction.

Bàs chuckled. "Happy Hogmanay," he said and walked off toward the horses, leaving them alone in the middle of the growing festive chaos.

Gideon purposely lifted the corners of his mouth, and Cait laughed. "Not so much teeth." Her comment brought on a truer smile. "Better."

She turned to inspect the bailey. "The music really adds life to the festival," she said, nodding to the minstrels, who had begun a fast tune with lute, drum, and flute.

Gideon's gaze slid across the beautiful weave of her hair, a few curls framing her face. The muted sun glinted off the dark tresses that flowed down around her shoulders over her cape. "Ye look lovely, Cait," he said.

A slight blush stained her cheeks. "Libby and Willa came at me with shears and a hot poker."

He chuckled, and her smile stretched higher. "I'm glad they left no scars behind," she said.

"Ah, but scars tell a story," he said, his smile dimming as her gaze slid to his cheek.

But then it lifted back to his eyes. "I'll let my tongue do the telling," she said and turned to survey the growing number of villagers. "Everything looks festive, and so many villagers are coming in." She spun back to him. "This is a step in bringing the clans together." She reached out and squeezed his hand. "They will begin to trust you."

"This must earn me several points," he said.

The press of her cool fingers in his palm opened his chest. "Depending on how the night goes," she said. There was something in her tone that reached inside Gideon's chest, making him want to take her into his arms. Instead, they stared at each other while the loud world floated around them. Cait had lost her smile, but some strong emotion sat in her eyes, and for once it wasn't anger.

Trix ran up to them, tugging on Cait's cape. "The white horse is named Seraph, and I think he is a unicorn! Did you see his ribbons?"

Gideon rubbed his scarred cheek. How did one have conversations with children about? Distraction was recommended in one of the books he'd perused last night in his library as he sought advice.

Gideon reached into his pocket, pulling out several bright-colored ribbons that he'd kept back from the horse. "I have these for ye, Libby, and Willa," he said, holding out three: one in blue, one in yellow, and one in light rose.

Trix squealed in delight. "Oh, thank you," she said and managed to control herself enough to wait until he placed them in her hands.

"The three of ye can decide which one for which."

"We'll all share of course," Trix said, glancing at Cait. Pinching their ends between her thumb and finger, she danced off to find the others, the ribbons trailing behind.

He looked back to Cait, but her gaze had moved on to the children, and the moment passed. He exhaled. "I have a sgian dubh for Jack and Willa, the two older ones," he said. "And will teach them how to use them. There's only one sharp side, and—"

"I know," she said but kept her smile. "I have a few."

Of course. "I know that I need to get Libby and Trix something else, too, as the daggers are much greater than the ribbons. I thought perhaps sweets?"

"Trying to balance the scales?" Her smile was teasing.

He looked out at the people filing through the gates. "I was raised to make things fair for everyone." He clasped his hands behind his back.

"Life doesn't work that way," she said. She looked outward like he did. "You can let the other children know that they will receive sgian dubhs when they reach Willa's age, if that's what you have in mind."

"Ye are wise." He nodded. "And I have another gift for them tucked away that I wanted to ask ye about first," he said.

Cait tipped her head, studying him. "Why are you giving us gifts?"

He reached out spontaneously to touch one of her curls. "Actions speak where words fail, and I have a great number of points to make up, apparently."

A slight smile turned up her lips.

"Thank you, Chief Gideon." Willa called as she hurried up wearing the blue ribbon. She curtsied.

Libby followed her, wearing the yellow-hued ribbon. "I'll teach them the proper way to weave the ribbon in their hair." She smiled brightly, and Gideon felt a tug in his chest, a bit of happiness that had nothing to do with fairness or earning imaginary points.

"Bloody hell, nay!" Joshua yelled, pulling their attention to the middle of the bailey.

"You have to," Osk said, pointing at his feet. "I'm the Master of Revels. You have to do what I say, and I say, I want those boots." Beside Joshua, Kára laughed so hard she bent forward to rest her hands on her knees. With a final curse, Joshua shed his boots. The boy traded with him, a look of satisfaction on his face.

Kára picked Osk's boots up because Joshua's feet would not fit in them. The jester danced off in Joshua's boots while his warlike brother glared in his stockinged feet. Kára patted his arm, barely able to control her laughter.

Gideon cleared his throat. "I must stop an explosion that's about to…" His words trailed off as he watched Kára pull Joshua's head down to her. She whispered something in his ear that made the fury melt away from his features, leaving only…joy? Joy in the Horseman of War? Something tightened uncomfortably in Gideon's middle. He'd felt jealousy before, when his father would honor Joshua or Cain, but never from something as simple as Joshua's happiness.

Gideon turned away from his brother and sister-in-law. "It seems Kára will keep Joshua merry."

Gideon turned back to Cait, to see her also staring in their direction. "They seem happy," she said, a subtle inflection of longing in her voice.

Hannah, one hand lifting the hem of her rich skirt, walked toward them. The wind made the curls around her face dance. "I would like to talk more with the lovely Cait Mackay who makes my very serious brother smile every time she is mentioned." She touched Gideon's arm and then turned to Cait.

Ballocks. Would Cait think he'd been talking a lot about her? It wasn't good to make a lass think he was chasing her. He'd surely read that somewhere.

"Did ye need me, sister?" he asked, his voice a warning.

She smiled even sweeter and looked to Cait. "Did ye see the gold ring Gideon had made for me for the holiday?" Cait looked closer at the band encircling Hannah's finger.

"Very pretty," Cait said.

"He commissioned rings for my brothers, too," Hannah said, grabbing Gideon's hand to show Cait, but then she stopped, dropping his hand. "Well, of course, you've seen his."

Hannah played with the thin band on her finger. "It was really sweet of Gideon to remember me with my own ring. Before, I didn't feel part of the family, since I didn't fit the legend of the Horsemen, but Gideon has included me." She turned to him and rose on the toes of her slippers to kiss his cheek. "Now," she said to him, "ye must mingle with your guests, not just stand here looking like an imposing mountain."

His meek, timid-as-a-mouse sister spoke with authority more and more with her newfound confidence. He couldn't possibly refuse her. "I will try," he said.

Hannah nodded and looked to Cait. "Despite all his diplomatic journeys to court, my brother does not mingle well."

"I'm tasked with helping him be more accessible to his people," Cait said.

Hannah's brows rose as she looked between them. "Best of luck, Mistress Cait."

"Come along, imposing mountain," Cait said. "Come meet your people." Cait tugged on his sleeve to get him walking with her. She led him from group to group around the bailey, and he learned much. Perhaps too much.

Angus had a wife named Ellen and two children, David and Paul, who wished to learn how to ride horses. Hamish had an old war injury from fighting Gideon's father but was proud that he'd outlived him. Mary had a chicken that wouldn't lay in the crate, so she had to let it wander around her cottage. Now she had eggs, but she also had shite everywhere. Gertrude had a granddaughter who was of marriageable age with wide hips for birthing sons. And Cait touched his arm nine times.

He held his breath when she slid her arm through his to lead him away from another small cluster of people who were cheerfully imbibing ale, whisky, and the many offerings the villagers had brought. He bent near her ear. "I still need to give ye your gift."

"You don't want to keep talking to everyone?" she asked.

"Of course."

She laughed at his sarcastic tone. "I believe Fiona's granddaughter, Deirdre, has some jam she'd like you to try."

"Perhaps later. I still wish to give ye your gift before it becomes late and ye suddenly disappear with the children."

Cait fingered the top clasp of her wool cape. "Rhona says I have the night to myself, so I can stay as long as I like."

"I'll be finding Rhona a rich gift," he murmured, making Cait snort softly. He grasped her hand, tugging her toward the great hall. Entering the warm room, decorated with holly and swaths of fabric, lit candles, and holly balls, the smell of cinnamon bread and apple tarts filled the air. Ella sat nursing her bairn near the hearth while Aunt Merida looked on and spoke with some of the older ladies who had come over from Orkney Isle. One of them held Joshua's son, Adam, swaying the bairn.

Cait untied the bow at her throat and pulled the cape from her shoulders. Gideon stopped. Her costume was made of green and purple wool, combed soft. It accented her lush form. The woman was made of beautiful valleys and gentle swells. Lace edged the hem and the neckline of the brilliant white smock that peeked from the top where her breasts pushed upward. She was the loveliest creature he'd ever seen.

Several dark curls slid along the soft skin of her collarbone, that he guessed would be fragrant and warm if he pressed his lips against it. His mouth went dry.

He cleared his throat. "Ye... The costume is most becoming."

She glanced down. "Fiona and her sister, Evie, altered one for me. 'Twas a surprise." She met his gaze. "I didn't have time to alter the one you sent." She studied him, frowning. "You're angered by that?"

"Nay," he said quickly. He shook his head. "There's nothing wrong, except I clearly lose my discipline around ye." He adjusted what was soon to be obvious.

She coughed softly, her hand going to her mouth. "The great Sinclair chief, undone by a mere lass."

He leaned in. "A lass with the curves and softness of a siren from the Odyssey." Had she read the book? "Do ye perchance sing?"

She dropped her hand, and in the dimness of the lamplight he thought her cheeks grew red. "I will not lead you to a watery grave or forsaken isle."

This easy banter was new between them. He'd lost track of earning points to regain her trust, and in truth, nothing about this was a game.

"Bring your friend over," Kára said as she walked past them toward the hearth to retrieve her bairn.

"Ballocks," he murmured.

"I don't think *they* are the problem," Cait whispered, nodding toward his unruly jack. "Do you need me to walk in front of you?" Laughter lurked in her voice.

He looked to where the ladies waited and called out, "I'm taking her first to ask her about the gift for the children. We will return shortly." Without waiting for her answer, he grabbed Cait's hand and led her to the stairs.

"We'll come aloft if you don't bring her back down soon," Ella said. "You have overbearing sisters now to make sure you don't disgrace the fair maidens of the village."

When they made it to the alcove at the bottom of the stairs, Cait paused. "Disgrace fair maidens?"

"She was jesting. Ella likes to make whatever trouble she can for me," he grumbled. "We had a difficult beginning."

They climbed the steps, Gideon checking to make sure she still followed as he held a lamp before them, stopping to light a few of the sconces on the way. His siblings had been assigned rooms on the floor below his bedchamber on either side of his library in case they wished to stay the entire night. His brothers would at least stay past midnight to be First Footers. 'Twas said that whoever was the first to step into your home after midnight on Hogmanay would set the luck for the coming year. Gideon surely needed luck to improve this clan. *And win another kiss from Cait.*

They stopped before his bedchamber door, and he produced a key. He glanced at Cait in the dim light. Her smile had flattened.

"Cait," he said, and she met his gaze. "I have a Hogmanay gift for ye. 'Tis not a trap to get ye in my bedchamber."

Her lush mouth relaxed into a soft grin. "Between your sisters below and my own skills with the sgian dubh, which I have hidden on me, trickery would see you bleeding. Again."

He held the back of his hand up so she could still see that he wore the scratch from a mere week ago. "'Tis healing," he said.

She glanced down at her feet. "I am glad."

The teasing mood now dampened, Gideon pushed into the room. As Bàs predicted, the wolfhound puppy had yanked one of the quilts to the floor, but there were no torn pillows. With floppy ears and large paws, the gray bundle of exuberance jumped forward to dance around them.

Cait laughed and quickly shut the door against its escape. "A pup?"

"Aye," Gideon said, lighting the lamp on a table and extinguishing the taper. He returned to her to lift the squirming dog in his arms. "She'll grow as large at Wolf, perhaps bigger. Bàs said her sire is one of the largest hounds he's seen. I will of course provide food as part of the gift, but an addition to your household, like this bundle of trouble, is something I wanted to ask ye about first before showing the children."

She walked straight over when he set the dog down, letting the beast sniff her hand. The pup immediately started licking her fingers as if she were truly as sweet as Gideon imagined. Cait laughed, the sound musical to Gideon. Lord, she *was* a siren, even if she denied it. Why else couldn't he keep her out of his daily thoughts? Her sweet smell, the softness of her hair, and the beautiful sound of her happiness. It all wrapped around him like a trap, one he wasn't sure he wanted to escape.

"I'd feel better with ye having a dog as large as a wolf protecting ye out there on the edge of the village," he said, watching her scratch through the pup's fur.

"The children will love her," Cait said, raising her eyes to his. "Thank you."

His brows rose high, and he crouched to scratch the wiggling dog. "So ye will take her?"

"How could I turn away something so adorable?" she said, laughing as the pup pawed at her dress to be picked up. Cait scooped the pup up with obvious strength. "We'll have to teach you some manners," she said, squeezing the dog and setting her back down.

Gideon fetched the meaty bone he'd hidden in the wooden chest that held his woolens. "Here, ye fluffball of mischief." The dog ran for the bone, her floppy ears bouncing. Taking the bone, she pranced over to the door to gnaw upon it.

Gideon took the basket that he'd also placed high out of the dog's reach and brought it over to Cait. "And here's the rest of your Hogmanay gift," he said. Would she like it or think he was a foolish sentimental? He'd have asked his brothers but knew they would only laugh.

"I get a ribbon, too?" she said, untying the green ribbon on top that held fabric around the basket.

"Aye, but there's more inside," he said as if she couldn't figure that out already. Gideon suddenly was at a loss as to where his hands should be as he watched her set the basket down on the table next to the lamp. He cupped the back of his head, elbows outward. Och, but he should have bought her something of value. He had the coin but had barely spent any on the gift. "And the basket is yours, too."

Gideon dropped his arms as Cait pulled out a jar of jam and a vessel that held fresh honeycomb that he'd cut from a local hive. "Sticky and sweet," he said.

"What a treat." She smiled at him. "Thank you."

"And there's something else," he said, prompting her to set her gift down.

Cait pulled out the glass jar he'd filled, holding it up to spy the little leaves inside. She glanced his way, one brow raised in question.

"They're the crunchiest, smallest leaves I could find. I picked them up and dried them before the fire. They should be quite loud when ye step on them."

Her smile melted into surprise, her lips opening as her face relaxed, her gaze returning to the jar. "You're giving me dried leaves?"

He came closer, standing before her. "'Tis a gift of the best things in life for ye. Puppies..." He tipped his head toward the wolfhound. "Sweet, sticky things." He tapped on the jar of jam and pointed to the honey. "And the crunchiest, smallest leaves I could find in Varrich Village."

"The best things in life," she murmured, staring at the jar.

Gideon crossed his arms, shoving his hands into his armpits. *Damn*. He should have given her fabric or even a new climbing rope. But, instead, he'd given her a jar of dead leaves.

"Cait—"

"I love them," she whispered, and his words stopped when she turned her gaze back to his. She blinked against the shine in her eyes, her smile soft and genuine. "I love them," she repeated. Her smile grew, and she laughed, hugging the jar to her breast. "So much potential in such little leaves that people walk past every day without giving them a thought. And yet, when given the chance to prove what they are... I bet they'll crunch so very loud."

He exhaled in relief. "Ye like it."

"Yes," she said, still clutching her jar of leaves. "All of it. And the children will be so happy."

"Which makes ye happy," he said, watching her closely. She nodded. "Well, I'd give ye your very own bairns, too, since they're also messy and therefore on your list of best things in life." He chuckled, his brows raised. "But I suppose I must get your permission for giving ye bairns," he said, teasing in his tone.

A shadow of sadness crossed over the joy in her face like a storm cloud blocking the sun. "Cait? I did not mean to imply…" He stopped when she shook her head.

"A bairn of my own…" Her words trailed off, and she met his gaze with sadness. "'Tis one best thing in life that I may never have."

CHAPTER TWELVE

*English law under England's King Henry VIII,
16th century AD*

*Acting in plays lures a woman away from her
expected roles and exposes her to sexual self-
gratification, prostitution, lasciviousness, and
indecency. Therefore, the roles of women in the
theater should be cast by young men.*

The glass jar of leaves was solid in Cait's hands. She held it against her heart as if it were a shield and turned away from Gideon's concerned face. She'd said too much. One by one, she released her fingers around the most thoughtful gift she'd ever received and set the jar back into the woven basket with her other gifts. Cait waited in the awkward silence, but Gideon didn't ask. Maybe that was why she spoke the words she never had before.

"I didn't conceive with my first husband. He said it was because I was a cold woman, like a dead fish between the sheets." She'd been so young and had taken his words as truth. Her voice had grown soft with her confession, the old memories like a lead ball on her chest. Perhaps if the words were out, they would not be such a burden.

Rap. Rap.

"Cait? Are you in there?" Rhona's voice penetrated the door. "The children are lining up for the pageant." Her voice sounded a bit frantic as if she worried that Cait was being ravished. Rhona's knocking paused when the puppy began barking. It balanced on its back legs before the door, scratching at it.

"I…am here, Rhona," Cait called and wrapped the cloth back around the basket. "I'll be right down."

"Do you have a dog in there with you?"

"Uh…yes. I'll explain when I come down."

She still hadn't looked at Gideon and turned away with her basket in her arms. "Do you have a rope for the dog?" *What have I done? Why would I say anything? Bloody hell, cold fish. He was just jesting.*

"Cait." Gideon's deep voice was like a caress over her tumbling thoughts.

"Perhaps one of the children can be responsible for watching the pup during the pageant," she said.

"Cait," he repeated, this time capturing her wrist so she couldn't scurry across the room to escape. For several heartbeats they stood there, her looking away with her arm extended out behind her, the basket caught to her chest.

She turned to face him, finally raising her eyes. She could not stand a suspicious look, but pity would be worse. Instead…Gideon's eyes were filled with a mix of many other things: anger, kindness, determination, and above all, warmth that drew her instead of making her want to run away. She held her breath.

"He was wrong," he said, his words certain.

She shook her head the smallest amount. "How

could you know that? I have no child of my own despite his...attentions." She swallowed past the dryness in her throat. "And I never felt a cinder of warmth."

Gideon released her wrist and took the basket from her, setting it down. "He was wrong, and I'll prove it to ye." He stepped closer, his finger sliding gently under her chin to tilt her face to his. "Ye are warm, every sweet inch of ye."

Cait's breath came in shallow draws, the stone in her stomach lifted by the fluttering there. Gideon lowered his face to hers, giving her time to retreat, but she did not. His warm lips settled against hers. Heart pounding, heat poured down through her, lighting the brittle kindling that caught quickly. It was like the first time, here in this same bedchamber. But without her panic, the flames of desire flared hot. The coldness of her memories turned to ash so fast she felt dizzy. But Gideon caught her to him, supporting her against his mountainous frame. It was as if the whole world could crumble, and she would still be safe in Gideon's arms. She felt herself surrender to the headiness of his support, something she had never done before.

Cait slid her fingers behind his neck to touch his cropped hair, and she heard him groan softly. The sound, the proof that he felt the same heat she did, spiraled through her, and she lifted onto her toes to mold her body against his. Their mouths slanted together, giving, taking, and tasting each other's heat. There was nothing of coldness left in her as flames danced about, bringing a breathless ache deep within her body.

Rap. Rap. Rap.

"Cait? What's going on in there?" Rhona's voice was insistent. "A dog? And the ladies below said that Gideon is in there with you. I will come in if you do not come out now."

As if waking from a dream, Cait pulled back. Gideon still held her, and the look on his face sent a shiver of need through her. Intense desire lit his eyes, and his chest rose and fell quickly, similar to her own.

His voice was like a growl. "The bastard ye were forced to wed was completely wrong." He leaned closer until she thought he might kiss her again. "Ye are fire, Cait, made of heat and passion and beauty. Never again believe the lies ye remember."

Behind her, Rhona pushed in through the door. "Unhand her," she yelled while the pup jumped around her skirts. She brandished a lit torch she'd taken from one of the sconces in the stairwell.

Apparently not seeing her as a threat, Gideon continued to gaze into Cait's eyes until she finally turned her face to Rhona. "I'm fine, Rhona." Her eyes dropped to the dog. "And look at the sweet gift Gideon is giving to us. The children will fall in love with her."

Footsteps sounded hard on the stairs behind Rhona. "Is Cait in need?" Alistair's face appeared in the doorway. "Let her go, ye bastard!"

Cait finally stepped back and picked up the basket. "I'm not in need, Alistair." Lips still damp, Cait fought to even out her breathing. Under her skirts, she rubbed her legs together to try to smother the ache that had grown.

She pushed a curl that dangled along her cheek behind her ear. "So glad you didn't abandon the pageant, Alistair. Let's organize the children below."

The man glared at Gideon, which made Cait scowl at Alistair. "Gideon has done nothing wrong. Go on now." She shooed him with a hand as if he were one of the children.

Rhona found the rope hanging from a hook near the door for the dog, the end of it chewed. "Goodness," she said but smiled anyway, tying it around the pup's neck. "We'll have to watch you in the cottage. Pickle might just peck your eyes out if you get too close." The dog tilted its head at her. "Aren't you a sweet beast," Rhona said. Luckily, the woman loved animals.

Cait's feet moved on their own as they all proceeded out the bedchamber door. *Ye are fire. Made of heat and passion and beauty.* His words were etched on her heart, making it squeeze. Somehow her feet found each step, preventing her from tumbling down the turret stairs. She felt Gideon's gaze on her back the whole way down.

"Mistress Cait," Libby called from the bottom of the stairs. "They will not listen to me!"

"That's because you aren't the one in charge," Trix said. "Mistress Cait is." She smiled up at Cait, a gap between her teeth.

"Trix?" Cait set the basket on the floor and crouched before the little girl. "You've lost a tooth."

Trix's little tongue poked through the hole in the row of bottom teeth, her eyes round. "I guess I did," she said, her words garbled around her tongue.

"It will bite you inside if you swallowed it," Jack

said, petting the puppy. "Who is this?"

"It will not," Libby said, rolling her eyes.

"The pup is a gift from Gideon for all of us." Cait knew he waited behind her. The little hairs at her nape stood up as if his gaze were a caress, making her heart tremble behind her bodice.

Trix and Libby squealed in delight, surrounding the happy dog, who leaped around on the end of its tether.

Willa rushed over. "I can't get the beard to stick to Frederick's chin."

"Look, Willa, we have a dog," Trix said, laughing as the pup licked her face.

Willa gasped and dropped before the pup. "We'll train you to protect the house."

"Her teeth are bigger than Pickle's," Trix said.

Libby patted the dog's head. "Chickens don't have teeth."

Several more children dressed in white to look like sheep ran up, and Rhona dragged the puppy away.

Gideon raised his voice above the chatter. "I'll make sure the minstrels clear the stage," he said, "and let people know the pageant will begin soon."

"Thank you," Cait said, managing to hold his gaze above the children. His handsome face held a shadow of the passion between them, but he nodded and strode across the bustling great hall. He dodged children and mothers chasing them with bits of their costumes. Even walking, Gideon's strength was obvious in the way he easily moved through the obstacles. A predator's grace. *Ye are fire*.

"Ye cannot trust him, Cait."

She jumped at Alistair's voice so close behind her and spun toward him, releasing her breath. "Truly, he was not doing anything untoward," she said. "Now help me get the children organized."

Rhona hurried back over. "I have Fiona and Evie watching our pup outdoors," she said and crouched to set a blue shawl over Trix's head.

"Do you think Mary lost teeth as a young girl?" Trix asked, her tongue sticking through the hole.

"Of course she did," Libby said, adjusting the blue shawl over Trix's head. "So did Jesus."

"Is that in the bible?" Trix asked, her eyes wide.

Cait felt Alistair grip her arm. He leaned in. "The Horseman of *Judgment* is a beast," he said, purposely renaming Gideon. "And I know about beasts and monsters. They can come across as good people, but if their hearts are ugly, cruelty comes out eventually."

Poor Alistair lived with a monster when his father drank too much whisky. "I'm sorry that you know about monsters," she said sincerely, and sighed.

He looked deeply into her eyes, making her feel uncomfortable. "Gideon Sinclair has an ugly heart."

"I've seen no evidence of it," she said, frowning, and pulled her arm away from his grasp. She rubbed at the biting ache he'd left behind.

"How can you say that?" Alistair said, his voice condemning. "After how he disgraced you before the village."

It seemed so long ago, even though it wasn't. Things were changing or she was just seeing the truth for the first time. Cait squeezed Alistair's arm.

"Gideon is trying to do right by the village. He wants people to trust him." She looked down at her feet. "I did steal from him, Alistair, and lie." She felt her cheeks warm again.

"For God's sake, Cait, he had heads rotting at his gate," Alistair said, glancing outward as if he worried Gideon was near enough to hear. "He ordered executions in the village square and exiled a woman, sending her into the wilderness with no shelter or food. It was a cruel death sentence."

"Mistress Cait," Trix called. "Did Jesus lose teeth, too?"

Cait inhaled quickly. "Alistair, I don't have time right now to debate Gideon's reasons, but I don't believe his heart is cruel."

Alistair huffed and bit down on his lower lip before speaking. "I'm thinking about leaving Varrich," he said, still trying to keep her attention by dodging into her line of sight. "Ye could come with me."

She saw Rhona bent over, talking to Trix and turned back to frown at Alistair. "I can't leave my children."

"They are not *your* children, Cait." His face was tight, and he lowered his voice. "I could give ye children, your own children."

Her mouth dropped open. Was he proposing marriage? With the chaos behind her it was hard to think beyond her surprise. Finally, she looked hard in his hopeful eyes. She had no desire to hurt him more. "I could no more leave them than I could my own children, Alistair. I thank you for thinking of me, but you must do what you need to do *on your own*," she said. "I think it is a worthy goal to leave your house and move on."

"Cait," one of the mothers called. "I think we've managed to get the costumes in place." The woman laughed, hands on her hips as she surveyed the line of angels and shepherds.

"Just think about it," Alistair said, his hands scratching through his hair as if his brain itched. He turned away, walking off, apparently not there to help with the pageant.

· **. . .**

Everyone gasped as the infant hit the stage that was set up in the bailey. Trix scooped it up. "'Tis just a poppet!" she said, fixing the blue shawl over her head. "Baby Jesus is fine."

The audience erupted in laughter around Gideon. His sisters sat on either side of him, covering their laughter politely as Trix grinned out at the villagers, a gap in her teeth. He'd never seen anything so charming before.

Cait's production of the nativity was by no means accurate with his massive dog Wolf misbehaving in his role as a donkey and the children forgetting their lines with nervousness. But the pageant filled his festival with merriment, and the people seemed full of Hogmanay spirit. So all the imperfections were perfect.

Cait looked on, her hands laid against her cheeks as she laughed at Trix's announcement with everyone else. She was such a giving, accepting mother to all children, forgiving their mistakes and protecting their vulnerable hearts with love. What would

Gideon's own childhood have looked like if Cait had been there to influence him? He crossed his arms over his chest, banishing the memory of his father's rantings before it could sour his Hogmanay.

And what did she mean that she could never have her own? Just because that old shite of a husband hadn't gotten her with child? It was likely that Benjamin was the one who was barren.

As the magi bowed before the recovered bairn, Gideon stared at Cait. Her gaze turned outward as if she felt his eyes, and she smiled at him. He nodded, smiling back until she looked away.

"She did this all on her own?" Hannah whispered, leaning in to him.

"She organized it and asked the mothers to help the children learn their lines and find costumes if they could. I provided whatever else was needed."

Hannah patted his knee. "She softens you," she whispered, making him frown. "Which is a good thing. Your edges have always been too sharp, Gideon. Cait Mackay shows great patience and mercy, qualities that can bring wisdom to justice."

Gideon watched the children as they knelt before Trix and a boy from the village who played Joseph. Trix held the poppet that was Jesus as the angel opened her wings above them. The entire bailey was quiet at the beauty the players and Cait had created under the heavy night sky. The angel, played by Libby, proclaimed the heavenly blessing on the world because of the holy birth. "Amen," she called out and people around Gideon murmured the same.

The players stood, and the audience erupted in cheers as the children bowed. Not a single person questioned the presence of lasses on the stage. When Cait started her school, she could put on performances for each holiday.

The children hurried offstage and into the keep, and the minstrels returned to begin their tunes again, having had a long break to eat.

"I'm starting the other bonfire," Joshua said as he walked by, his boots back on his feet.

"Because *I* am cold," Kára said, opening her eyes wide, a smile across her face and her arm through her husband's.

The Master of Revels was hopping around, giving out sweets to the children who had watched from the audience. Cait would probably have many more who wanted to perform after tonight's show.

Gideon paused, people moving about him, as he watched Cait accept praise for her efforts. She was probably giving all the credit to the children and helpers. She'd thrown her cape back over her gown, hiding most of her, but her hair fell about her shoulders in beautiful disarray. One of her ribbons dangled from the top braids where it had unpinned. She tucked it back up, her gaze scanning the revelers. It stopped. On him. She smiled and walked forward. Toward him. He was her first choice. The thought swelled within his chest.

Suddenly, Osk jumped before her. He gave the basket of treats that he held to a passing woman and took Cait's hands, tugging her to dance a jig with him before the minstrel stage. She went with him, laughing at his antics and dodging his pursed lips. Was the fool trying to kiss her?

"No throwing the Master of Revels into the

dungeon," Bàs said as he stopped beside him. "'Tis a law."

"I've never seen that law," Gideon murmured, striding toward the stage.

"If ye are intent on keeping the merriment going, ye best go along with him," Bàs called after him.

Several other couples had joined in the fast jig. Osk planted a kiss on Cait's turned cheek and then twirled her around, making her cape bell out. Gideon stepped close. "I think Cait is tired," he said. She did look breathless, and she'd been frantic for the last hour corralling the children.

"Pish!" Osk called. "The Master of Revels will carry her then." He stopped and picked her off the ground, his arm under her legs.

She gasped at the sudden lift, her eyes wide. She didn't laugh, her smile dropping to surprise. That was enough for Gideon, and he walked into the middle of the dancers. "Put her down," he ordered, his voice commanding. Several dancers nearby stopped to listen.

Damn. Bàs was right. Gideon needed to go along with the merriment or ruin what the night was accomplishing. "I'll take her place," he called out, trying to bend his snarl into a smile. He lifted Cait from Osk's arms. Just the feel of her there made his annoyance melt away.

She grinned up at him as he set her boots on the ground. "I think he's waiting," she said.

"Who?" Gideon asked.

"Well, I must carry someone," Osk said. "I order it as the Master of Revels." He eyed another lass on the fringe of the group that had stopped to watch.

"Someone to hold. Someone to warm. Someone to dance with me."

Cait tipped her head at Osk, who stood still, his arms out as if he still held her. "Perhaps you should truly take my place," she whispered. Her smile extended to her eyes.

Gideon chuckled. He turned, taking several broad steps to reach the Orkney man. Osk's grin turned to surprise as Gideon launched his legs up, knowing full well that Osk would not be able to hold him. Gideon landed into Osk's outstretched arms, the two of them hitting the ground, Gideon splayed out on top of a flattened Master of Revels.

The entire bailey erupted in laughter, even more so than when the wee poppet Jesus was declared sound on the stage. Osk shoved at Gideon, who remained unmoving until Cait grabbed his two hands to pull him off the poor lad.

"I think you broke my arse," Osk said and once again the audience roared. The lass Osk had been smiling at helped him stand.

"A bit of whisky and one of my tarts will help," the lass said, and suddenly Osk did not seem so impaired as he strode off on her arm, but one hand still rubbed his arse.

Cait laughed and swung his arm out between them. It was as if it were the most natural thing to do. She did not seem to care that the villagers saw her with him.

On the other side of the bailey, Joshua had lit two fireballs on chains and was twirling them around, their light making streaks in the darkness. It drew the watchers, and Gideon led Cait to where Sgàil stood with his guard. "Let's find a little quiet," he whispered.

"And where would that be?" she asked, laughing lightly.

"Just beyond the village."

"In the cold and dark?" she asked, eyeing him.

"Not for long," he said. "I'd show ye how tame Sgàil is."

She paused, glancing at the castle where Rhona had taken the children and puppy. "Just for a short time."

Anticipation swelled within Gideon, and he lifted her onto his horse's back. Climbing on behind her, he guided them carefully out of the gates where the festival had spilled. Several more bonfires had been lit with groups talking and drinking around them. Did she care that her people saw her riding into the darkness with him?

"We will return shortly," he said, leaning forward, his mouth coming close to her ear where her curls tickled against his lips.

Gideon guided them out toward the moor beyond the castle. "If it were a clear night, I would point out the constellations to ye," he said, frowning at the heavy clouds overhead in the darkness.

"My father used to show me the stars," Cait said, facing front. "It's been so long I've forgotten the patterns."

"I have a book of them in my bedchamber," he said.

The sounds of merriment began to fade, and he pulled Cait tighter in to him as they rode in silence, the wind a soft whisper over the moor, the muted moon lighting their way. "Are ye cold?" he asked and then grimaced in the darkness.

"No," she said, turning her face toward him. His gut relaxed at the soft smile he could see on her face in the darkness. Around them in the stillness, snow began to fall. She glanced up at the feathery white flakes. "Look," she whispered as if the snowfall was something holy.

Gideon secured his reins and swung his leg behind, jumping to the ground to reach up for Cait. "Are we going somewhere?" she asked as he lifted her down. She was taller than most lasses he knew, but still shorter than him by more than half a foot.

"Aye," he answered pulling her away from the horse. He took her two hands and slowly pulled her around in a circle. "I've never danced in the rain or snow, but I hear 'tis one of those best things in life. In fact, this is part of your gift."

She laughed. "You must try it." She pulled gently away and twirled, her face tipped up to the falling snow, arms wide.

Luckily, his brothers couldn't see this far from Varrich, out in the middle of a snowy night, twirling around like a wee lass. Gideon stretched his arms out, tilted back his head so the snow could land in cold pinpricks on his face, and turned. The snowfall muted the sounds from the festival even more, and the breeze stilled. Only the slight crunch of their boots could be heard as the white flakes and darkness enveloped them, tucking them away from the world.

Peace enveloped Gideon. He was doing something that had no meaning, no strategic outcome, no profit. And yet he felt richer in spirit. Gideon breathed in the chilled air. "Ye are right," he said, keeping his voice hushed. "'Tis excellent." He glanced her way and stopped because she had. She stood watching him, beautiful in the hint of moonlight filtering through the clouds.

"Keep going," she whispered and put her arms back out to resume her twirls. And he did for several more turns, inhaling and exhaling until he felt lighter and stronger somehow. He stopped to watch Cait turn, her dark hair cascading down her back. Och, but she was lovely. Would she let him kiss her again? Let him touch her?

"You're powerful enough to bring snow down for my gift," she said. "A true warrior from God."

The teasing in her tone made him smile. "Some say as much."

"And what do you say?" she asked.

What did he say? He knew he hadn't come down from a cloud on a black steed, wielding a sword and the scales of justice. Even if he *had* done everything he could to convince his father that he was worthy of being a Sinclair, one of the four brothers to make the legend true.

"I say...currently, I'm just a man staring at the loveliest lass he has ever seen."

From the distance in the dark, it was hard to see her expression in detail. Had her smile changed to dismay or the serious want that he felt within himself? Her pupils would be full circles in the darkness whether she was attracted to him or not. None of his detection methods would work out here with Cait. "What are ye thinking right now?" he asked, stepping closer.

She closed the gap between them, tipping her face up to meet his gaze. In the dim glow of the moon through the clouds, her face was pale and perfect, surrounded by the darkness of her hair that became lost in the night. "I…" She stared up at him, her teeth resting on that tantalizing bottom lip. She inhaled fully, her chest rising. She was so close that her breasts brushed his tunic that was exposed in the V of his jacket. "I have a confession," she whispered.

He watched the gentle movement of her lips over the words. "Oh?"

The wind blew around them there on the open moor, the darkness broken only by the dancing snow. She stared up into his face. "I wish to steal something more from you, Horseman of Justice. How do you judge me?"

Judge without mercy. His father's words were a mere whisper against Gideon's pounding heart.

"I'd give it to ye as a gift, so there is no need to steal."

She lifted her hand toward his face, brushing the cool pad of her thumb over his lip. "Then give me another kiss."

CHAPTER THIRTEEN

Scottish Common Law

Those believed to be guilty are considered guilty until they are proven innocent. A verdict can be rendered as 'guilty', 'not guilty', or 'not proven'. If found 'not proven' the jury believe the accused to be guilty but lack enough evidence to convict.

Gideon's warm lips came down on hers. He smelled fresh like the Highland air, wild and free, which was so unlike the disciplined, precise man. Out on the moor, alone in the darkness without people pounding on the door of a bedchamber, she lost herself in the feel of Gideon.

She relaxed into the safety of his arms and gave in to the fire of this passion erupting between them. Cait curled herself into him, melting against his muscular frame. She felt him harden against her, and it did not douse her in cold dread. Nothing about Gideon was cold, only the wind that whipped around them, covering them with the snow that now pelted down sideways.

After long minutes, he broke the kiss, his hands brushing the snow from her hair. "We'll be covered soon." His hand found hers in the darkness, and he tugged her back to his horse. Its black coat would have blended into the night except for the snowfall that was turning him into one of Cain's white horses.

Gideon lifted her easily into the saddle and climbed on behind her, pressing his beast into a loping canter across the snow-white moor. The contrast of the cold air against the heat that had spread under Gideon's kiss made chill bumps pop up over her skin. She leaned back into the safety of his chest as the world dashed by on either side, her gaze on the village with its glowing fires ahead. Lord help her. She did not want to return to it. She just wanted to stay one night wrapped up with Gideon.

Maybe he was right about her not being a cold fish after all. He had certainly set her ablaze with a kiss. All these years of thinking that Benjamin had been right, that she was at fault for abhorring his touch. Gideon was nothing at all like him. It was as if Gideon's touch could wash her clean of memories of Benjamin.

As they reached the outskirts of the village main street, he slowed, pulling his horse to a stop. She turned to look up into his ruggedly handsome face, the scar giving him the look of a seasoned warrior. "I don't want this to end," she said. "This thing between us." She swallowed against the vulnerability she was inviting.

A slight grin broke the seriousness of his face. "Then it won't."

Did she have such power over this invincible man? The thought made her giddy inside, her skin tingling. She turned back to survey the crowd up ahead. God's teeth, the whole village had attended the opening night of the Hogmanay Festival. There would be no sneaking into the castle from the front.

Gideon dismounted and reached up to help her

down. His large hands spanned her waist, the pressure adding to the thrill circulating inside her. How would it feel to have those strong hands stroke her bare skin? Cait rubbed her lips together and looked up at Gideon. "There's no easy way in?"

"Just through the bailey and the great hall filled with ladies who are no doubt finding warmth by the hearth," he said, his face growing hard with annoyance.

"Do you have my rope?" she asked.

The edge of his mouth tipped upward, giving him a roughish grin. "Aye, 'tis still in my bedchamber."

She gave him a little nod, her heart thumping wildly as she took charge of the situation. "Give me a quarter of an hour, and then throw the end down from your window." Cait walked away quickly, her eyes opening wide as her smile grew.

"'Tis a wonderous night, Sgàil," she heard him say to his horse and held her fingers to her mouth to stop a laugh that bubbled up from her happy heart.

Cait pulled to the shadows as Gideon rode past her into the bailey. She followed on foot, nodding to several ladies. She accepted gratitude from several mothers for the pageant, took a bite of a honey bun and a sip of whisky insisted upon by Osk the jester. The whisky was smooth, adding to the heat inside her. Cait quickly hugged Rhona before sliding into the shadows behind the stables. She circled the castle cautiously, but no one was about as she stole away to the space under Gideon's window.

As she stood there in the dark, her heart sped. She was no virgin, but the memories of the act were dull at best and painful at worst. *It'll be different with*

Gideon. Just the feel of his muscular chest tightened a line of want through her.

Ye are fire. She shifted, remembering his words, and pressed her fingers against the ache between her legs through the layers of her skirts and trews. She certainly had never felt that before, and if her own touch felt good, what would Gideon's touch be like? The thought and the sound of the window swinging open above made her breath stutter. Och, but she wanted Gideon Sinclair.

"Stand back," he said from above, and the rope fell like a giant snake, its end dangling just above the ground.

The cloak and skirts were cumbersome and heavy, but she couldn't leave them behind to be found. Or could she? At least some of them. She glanced around, but the only sounds came from the merriment from the front of the large stone fortification. Cait threw off the cape and the under and over skirts that were tied around her waist, unpinning the stomacher. She was left in her trews, long smock over them, and stays. Folding the layers of skirts as best she could, she ran over to the wall where several buckets hung. *Lord, please don't let Fiona and Evie ever know of this.*

Cait stuffed her clothes into two buckets, laying the stiff stomacher on top. They nestled under an overhang so the snow would not dampen them further, and she ran back to the side of the castle. Hiking up her smock, she leaped upon the familiar rope and wrapped her legs around the length. The climb was one she had done a thousand times with her lengths of fabric, and she was quickly peeking over the sill at the window casing where Gideon all but dragged her inside.

His arms pulled her cold body up against his naked chest. He'd taken his cloak and tunic off, leaving him in a low-slung kilt and boots. "I held my breath while ye climbed," he said and squeezed her tight.

She arched back, her fingers trailing over the light hair on his chest. He was magnificent. Breathing quickly from the climb, she stared up into his worried face, her brows raised high. "You've little faith in my skills for climbing? Even after seeing me practice in the trees?"

"With frozen fingers, I couldn't help but worry." He pressed her icy hands flat against his warm skin, taking the cold from them without so much as a single flinch.

Cait's gaze roamed the contours of his chiseled arms, mounds of muscle ready to move mountains. She inhaled, raising her eyes back up to his darkly handsome face. Was it the intense want in his eyes that encouraged her or the sip of whisky she'd taken? It didn't matter. She wanted Gideon Sinclair with an ache that thrummed through her with each heartbeat.

"Ah, you think I climb with my hands." Cait lifted a leg, wrapping it around one of his above the fur-lined edge of his boot. "I climb with my feet, Sinclair." She lifted her leg higher, her smock rucked up, and rested her foot on his firm arse. Her hands slid up to his shoulders, his skin hot and smooth. "And my legs."

There was no missing the invitation in her voice, but just in case, clasping his body with her powerful leg should let him know she wanted to pick right back up where they'd stopped out on the moor where only the snow had halted their natural progression.

Gideon's jaw was tight. "Are ye sure, lass?" He didn't move, as if he were a statue, a statue with a thick erection upright between the press of their bodies.

Sliding her leg down over his arse to the floor, she stood tall, meeting his gaze. "I'm no maid, and you have convinced me that perhaps I am not the cold fish I thought I was."

He touched her cheek. "There is nothing cold about ye, Cait. Just your touch sets me on fire."

Her smile grew from within. "Your words warm me like your touch," she whispered.

He searched her face. "I do not say them to sway ye."

"I know."

Still, he held himself away from her. "I want ye, Cait."

"I know." She glanced down at the hardness between them.

"But our joining is up to ye, even now in my chambers. I wouldn't—"

She rested her finger over his lips. "I want you, too." Her words were slow and succinct, whispers in the night. "Right now. Here in your chambers." She tipped up on her toes, her hands on his broad shoulders. "In every way that'll convince me I'm not cold."

Gideon's thick arms encircled her, and the giddiness within Cait plucked at the taut line of want that had been growing. She met his lips, slanting immediately to deepen the kiss. Shifting to bring her in full contact with his hard body, she heard him groan low. It was as if he'd dropped the shackles that he'd locked around himself, the ones that kept him civilized. The thought sent a pulse through her, and her arms slid up his back, holding herself there while he plundered her mouth.

Gideon was right—she trusted him. For this mighty Highlander could take anything he wanted and yet he'd asked and waited for her answer, giving her the power when his sheer strength and influence as chief could demand her complete surrender.

The muscles of Gideon's back corded as he lifted her, carrying her upright toward the four-poster bed that sat against the far wall. Fabric of crimson velvet hung from each corner, draping over the top. The fire he'd kindled crackled in the hearth, the only sound above their breath and the slide of Cait's hands over his bare skin.

Changing directions, he set her down before the hearth, and captured her face in his hands. "Ye are the most beautiful creature I've ever seen, Cait." Her heart pounded with his words. "And I am going to love every little part of ye this night." The pounding in her chest turned into a giddy flutter.

"Yes, Gideon. Absolutely yes," she breathed and began to slowly tease open the ties on her stays. He kept his eyes on her as he bent to unlace his boots, shucking them quickly before going to her own.

When he knelt to untie her boots, her breath caught. Gideon bowed before her to perform the menial task of taking off her boots. Their gazes locked, his fingers moved, and he worked one off and then the other, leaving her in stockinged feet. She watched him unfold into his full height. She was tall, but Gideon still seemed to tower above her, his muscles casually displayed under smooth, tanned skin from hours of swordplay and training. Any reluctance she might have had turned to ash and blew away with her longing.

Cait loosened her stays until they shifted downward. Her fingers pulled the string at the top of her smock, and she shrugged her shoulders. It slid lower until she felt the cool air on her bare breasts. Their fullness sat upright, the edge of her stays lifting them.

"Mo Dhia," he murmured, reverence in the deep thunder of his voice. He kissed her, his mouth leaving hers to trail along the sensitive skin of her neck as his large hands palmed first one and then the other of her breasts. When he rolled her nipple between his thumb and finger, the sensation shot down to the ache at the crux of her legs, and she moaned softly. Holding onto his mighty shoulders, she arched back, thrusting her breasts upward.

He answered her with a low groan just before his mouth came down on her nipple. Hot, wet suction plucked the cord running through her. As if he knew exactly where that line ended, his fingers moved to the crux between her legs, rubbing there over the layers of smock and trews, making her desperate for more.

"Yes, Gideon, God yes," she murmured.

With a tug on her stays, she loosened them enough to let them fall apart, landing on the floor.

He released her when she stepped back, rucking up her smock to shuck her trews underneath. She kept her smock around her, pooled under her breasts.

From the intensity of Gideon's gaze, Cait knew the light from the fire showed her form beneath the fine linen. His hand slipped under his kilt to reveal his jack, and her gaze dipped to his exposed length. Long and thick and powerful. Instead of frightening her, it seemed right. It matched the mightiness that made up the rest of Gideon Sinclair, and she took a step closer.

As if he'd been waiting to see her reaction first, Gideon pulled open the buckle of the thick belt that kept his woolen plaid in place over his hips, and it dropped with a thud to the wood floor. Gideon Sinclair stood before the fire, totally bare.

Straight and broad, the cording over his stomach showed his strength as much as the muscles in his long legs and powerful arms. Every bit of him was solid and toned. Gideon Sinclair was a warrior through and through no matter how well-groomed and refined he presented himself. The power in his form showed how deadly he could be to an enemy or how tempting he could be to a lover.

Cait's gaze moved over his body as he stood watching her, and she slowly lifted the hem of her smock. The look of building passion on his face and the clench of his fists pushed her onward. Want radiated from him, and yet he held himself back, watching her slowly expose the crux of her legs. When her fingers pressed against the ache there, Gideon slid his own hand along his jack. Just the sight made her legs weak with desire. Was the sight of her touching herself doing the same to him?

One hand at her breast, the other rubbing herself, she let the ache grow inside her. When a small moan escaped her open lips, Gideon surged forward, a beast capturing its mate. Cait gasped as he lifted her. In two strides he had her on the edge of his grand bed where he set her, letting her legs hang down toward the floor. "I'd taste your sweetness," he murmured, their gazes connected. His words, rough with want, sent prickles of sensation across her skin, making her nipples even harder. She nodded, not knowing exactly what he asked, but trusting that whatever he wanted to do to her would be full of pleasure.

Cait leaned back on her elbows, their gazes connected as he slowly rucked up her smock and spread her legs. Between them she throbbed, making her shift upon the bed. His hand came up, and her eyes closed as he touched her there. She moaned, feeling him explore her heat.

"Oh God, Gideon," she crooned and then gasped, her eyes opening when she felt the wet heat of his mouth on her. The sight of his dark head bent between her stockinged knees shot pleasure through her like lightning. She tilted, raising her heels to rest them on his massive shoulders as he loved her with his mouth and tongue. Never had she felt such pleasure.

Gideon tasted her, his mouth, and fingers in perfect rhythm, bringing her higher and higher to some peak she longed for but had never known. She pressed her hips higher against him, holding her own breasts, tugging her nipples to add to the frantic need growing in her. Faster he moved until the pleasure grew into an inferno swelling up through her abdomen. "Yes," she yelled before her breath caught, and she felt the world around her shatter. The only thing that remained was Gideon and the pulsing pleasure he gave. Wave after wave of it.

When she could catch her breath and open her eyes, Gideon stood staring down at her. There was such raw need on his face that she reached for him. "I want you now. Now Gideon," she said, her words breathless.

"Aye," he murmured in complete agreement. His strong hands lifted her, sliding her up the length of the bed, and Cait's legs opened wide across the cool coverlet as if her heat sought his hardness.

She felt him nudge against it and raised her hips to meet him. Gideon's muscular arms flanked her face as he leaned forward, his huge body over her, but she had no fear that he would crush her. She wanted him more desperately than she'd ever wanted anything. "Please," she whispered, and he thrust deep.

Her gasp turned into a breathy moan as his length filled her full. She was not a virgin, and there was no pain, only need and heat. Immediately she thrust back, pushing into the rhythm that he set. His mouth descended to hers as they strained, body against body, their muscles playing in unison to bring them together. His hands palmed her breasts, pinching lightly against her nipples, building the pleasure higher as they moved, meeting each other with powerful thrusts. What had started slow grew in pace as they strained together, racing along together.

Cait raked his shoulders and back with her nails, clinging to him. She spread her legs even wider so that he filled her, joining them together so completely that it was as if he touched her very soul. Her muscles strained, reaching with him to her peak. She felt both powerful and melting at the same time, her blood molten with desire.

"Oh yes, Gideon, yes!"

He growled low, the sound of their skin slapping together. "Ye are fire," he ground out. "My all-consuming fire."

"Fill me full, Gideon," she called out, feeling herself reach the edge of what must be the greatest pleasure.

"I wouldn't burden ye—" But she cut him off by wrapping her legs around his arse, holding him against her. He roared, pumping into her, taking her with him over the edge of reason.

• • •

"Och, but ye are exquisite, lass," Gideon said, watching Cait stand before him in the center of the bed. Not a shred of clothing hid her. Her dark hair lay across her pale skin in perfect contrast. She held her lush breasts in her hands, stroking her nipples. He groaned, his jack hard again, demanding. "If ye keep doing that, I will take ye again right now."

A grin grew across her lovely lips. "Promise?" she asked, and he saw the hunger in her eyes as she balanced on the soft mattress.

Coming forward on his knees, he held her as he kissed the gentle swell of her abdomen, marveling at the softness of her skin. Her fingers slid down to press against her sweetness, and he groaned. "Ye are a lusty wench."

"I believe I am, Gideon Sinclair," she said, and he loved the confidence in her voice. Thank God that bastard Benjamin had not broken her spirit with his lies and cruelness. If he weren't already dead, Gideon would execute him himself.

Banishing the thought of the *tolla-thon*, Gideon kissed a trail up her stomach, inhaling the combination of their scents. He loved the way his light touch brought out chill bumps along her skin. He'd be within her again and again and again if she allowed it. Her body was lush and made for a man's loving, his loving.

She turned, pulling one of the curtains hanging at the corner, coiling it around her bareness like one of her long stretches of cloth hanging from the tree. The crimson velvet against her skin somehow made her even more enticing. The rich fabric lay diagonally across her shoulder, dipping between her breasts but not covering them, to wrap around her back to her hips.

He stood, balancing on the tick under them. "Ye are wrapped like a Hogmanay gift," he said.

Her chin tilted upward slightly as she smiled. "Perhaps. I haven't given you anything yet."

He frowned. "I didn't expect a return of gifts. And especially not—"

She placed a palm on his chest. "I'm merely teasing." She pulled him closer and kissed him. "This is a gift for us both," she murmured against his lips.

Gideon grasped the end of the fabric, tugging it a

bit tighter, making her laugh. "Well then, 'tis the best gift I've ever received."

"Are you tying me up?"

His brow rose as his gaze slid down her luscious form. "So I can unwrap ye again."

She gave a little tug on the fabric. "Too bad this isn't sturdy enough to hold me."

"I'll remedy that in the morn. There are hooks in the ceiling like in the great hall." Just the thought of her tangled in the fabric, hanging in bared beauty above him, shot another arrow of tantalizing want straight through him. "Aye, first thing in the morn."

He lunged at her, and she laughed, still coiled in the velvet. His fingers found her wet and hot, and she pressed into his hand as he kissed her. She held tight to his shoulders, her fingers clutching into him as he strummed.

"Again, Gideon," she whispered, her kisses growing frantic. "I ache."

He felt the sting of her nails as she grazed his shoulders. Turning her away from him, he pulled her back against his chest and stomach, his jack sliding up between her legs. "Hold on, lass," he said. "We're going for a ride."

He felt her shudder, and she gripped the fabric up high, arching her back. Gideon thrust inside her slick, open body from behind, and his groan filled the room. He easily found her sensitive spot around the front, rubbing against it with a rapid finger as he thrust into her over and over from the back.

She clung to the fabric, raising herself higher, the two of them balanced on the bed. Even so, he lifted her with each thrust, his teeth gritted. He curved over her body, his mouth finding the nape of her neck as her hair lay to the side of her shoulder. He smashed his face into the softness there, breathing in her luscious scent.

"Oh my God, yes," she yelled.

Gideon grabbed the corner poster to give him more leverage. She moaned and arched back into him, giving him complete access to all of her.

"Oh yes," she breathed, and he rubbed faster against the hidden gem in the crux of her legs. He felt her strain, her breath stuttering as she came apart in his arms, and he pumped behind her, finding his release.

Cr…Crack!

The wooden pole gave way, breaking under the pressure. Only strength, honed balance, and warrior training prevented him from falling with Cait over the side of the bed. Gideon twisted, pulling Cait back with him, still wrapped in the length of fabric. He turned them both to the side so the pole hit him and not her. Uncaring about anything but the pleasure, they moved together as the waves of ecstasy subsided, leaving them both breathless and tangled in velvet and each other.

For several long minutes, Gideon held her, listening to her slow breathing. When she laughed, he pushed up on his elbow to look down at her. A smile lit her face. "You broke the bed," she said. "Good God."

"Me?" His brows rose in mock surprise. "I think ye had something to do with it, yanking on the curtain."

"Oh," she huffed out, her smile still broad as she

pushed up to look at the rubble. The curtain on the broken poster had yanked down the attached length of fabric halfway around the entire bed. Splintered wood sat upright, looking like jagged teeth, and the felled poster lay across the strewn blankets, the carnage reaching all the way to the pillows at the headboard.

"As if I could do all that damage." Cait turned onto her stomach and slowly crawled over his leg to slide her naked body across him like a warm, soft blanket. He wrapped his arms around her back, holding her there. Her dark hair hung down around her head like a curtain as she leaned in to give him a leisurely kiss, her pelvis pressing into him at the same time.

He growled deep in his throat and rolled her away from the broken poster to pin her once again under him. This time, their kisses were unhurried. Gideon pressed his lips gently to the sides of her face and pulled back to see her eyes open, her gaze taking him in.

Her finger touched the scar across his cheek that led down to his jawline. "Earned in battle?" she asked. "Like all the other scars I kissed earlier?" She spoke of the ones that puckered here and there along his torso and back, arms and legs.

He snorted softly before he could think to hide his shame. "Nay. 'Twas a foolish boyhood…" He swallowed, his grin wry. Only his family knew the origin of the scar on his cheek, Aunt Merida's little stitches that had sewn his face back together.

Cait's fingertip slid against it, questions in her eyes. He exhaled and squeezed her hand, bringing

her finger to his lips to kiss. "I cut myself with a mattucashlass when I was a lad."

Her brows lowered. "How?"

Gideon rolled away, and Cait threw the end of
the rumpled quilt over them. She pressed into his
side, her palm flat over his heart.

"My father didn't favor me," Gideon said. "Cain
was the eldest and the leader. Joshua had Da's temper and would drink and roar with him." He paused
and exhaled. "Once in a drunken tirade, Da mentioned I looked weak because I hadn't battle scars. I
believe I was twelve at the time." Gideon laughed,
but it sounded bitter, even to himself. "So I took my
sharpest knife and sliced my face."

Cait pushed up on her elbow to look down at
him, her face tight. "To make yourself look fiercer."
There was no pity in her tone or rebuke. It sounded
almost like…understanding.

He stared up at her. "'Twas foolish. Luckily, Aunt
Merida stopped the bleeding with stitches and kept
it from getting tainted." They stared at each other
for several breaths before she lay back into his side.

"Jack would've done the same thing," she said.
"In this society, boys have so much pressure to prove
their worth in battle. With your father being the
harbinger of war, blood, and death, it was certainly
not foolish to a twelve-year-old lad." Her hand
squeezed his, and the pressure felt like a direct link
to his heart.

Aunt Merida had ranted and shaken her head at
his foolishness. Hannah had cried with pity. Joshua
had smirked. His father had laughed. No one had
ever before made Gideon feel justified. His chest

unclenched. He brushed a dark curl from her cheek, staring into her beautiful, understanding eyes. "Cait," he whispered.

Bam! Bam! Bam!

"Gideon, are ye in there?" Cain's voice boomed through the door, and a rattle of the handle threw Cait into motion. She dove under the quilt she'd pulled over them just as Cain burst inside.

"What are ye doing?" Cain asked, his gaze taking in the destruction of Gideon's bed.

"Thinking I should have bloody locked my door." Gideon disentangled himself slowly so as not to un-cover Cait, but the angle of the quilt revealed her legs, so there was no hiding the fact that a lass was lying next to him.

Joshua appeared next to Cain. "Fok. What did ye do to your bed?"

"What do ye want?" Gideon roared. "And it bet-ter be that a horde of Englishmen is bearing down on us. Otherwise, get the hell out!"

"How about a horde of Scots?" Joshua roared back, his blasted gaze on Cait's slim, well-formed legs.

Gideon's hands fisted as he stood stark naked before them. "What Scots?"

Cain looked directly at him. "James is at your front door, brother."

Gideon's muscles clenched. "James?"

"Aye, James," Joshua said, "the bloody king of Scotland."

CHAPTER FOURTEEN

Scottish Legend of First Footer began with the arrival of the warring Norse, 8th century AD

As the year draws to an end, the first footer is the first person to cross a home's threshold after midnight on Hogmanay. They may give gifts like coin, bread, salt, coal, and whisky to represent prosperity, food, flavor, warmth and good cheer.

If the first footer is a dark-haired man, he brings good luck, whereas light-haired men, red-haired men, and women may bring ill fate, as well as physicians and clerics.

Having donned his tunic, kilt, and boots, Gideon helped Cait carefully lower out the window. *Daingead!* This wasn't how he wanted to start the new year, sending Cait away after what they'd just shared. But she was right when she insisted she needed to run home to make sure the children and Rhona were locked up tight and safe.

At the bottom of the rope, Cait waved up to him, shooing him on before turning to regain her clothes from the buckets. He wanted to walk her home, make certain she arrived unmolested by the numerous soldiers James had likely brought with him. But his brothers waited for Gideon in the library, and he must devise a strategy for dealing with James within these crucial minutes.

He pushed away from the window and surged out of his bedchamber, arriving in the library to find Cain, Joshua, Kára with their son, and Bàs standing with determination on their faces.

"What does he want?" Gideon asked, going to the window that faced the bailey. Most of the villagers had left, at least all the women and children. Mackay, Sinclair, and Orkney men stood around in small groups. James was easy to spot, standing next to a white steed decked in gold cloth. He spoke with Bruce Mackay while surrounded by soldiers from Edinburgh. Even though no weapons were drawn, they held them at their sides.

"He says he wants to be your First Footer," Cain said, setting his decorative bow and arrow, which added weight to him being the Horseman of Conquest, on the table. "He says he wants to be the first person to enter your home after midnight on Hogmanay." Cain picked up and sheathed his equally lethal sword.

"Fok," Joshua said, running a paw through his hair. "That's not a reason. He's here to see if I am truly dead."

Kára stood with him, hugging their son to her chest. "Lord Robert must've sent word about our battle at the Earl's Palace at Birsay on Orkney, and that he doesn't believe we actually died. Perhaps he dug up the graves and found only one body and a seal skeleton."

Gideon squinted, trying to see the expression on James's face from so far up. The firelight from the closest bonfire did not reveal much. "He would have gone directly to Girnigoe Castle if that were his purpose, instead of giving someone a forewarning."

"He comes to see our strength," Cain said, his hand resting on his sword.

Gideon turned back to the room and nodded. "With an overt act of friendliness."

"Friendliness?" Joshua asked. "Bringing enough troops to fill your bailey and beyond?"

"If he wished to be hostile, he'd not wait to be the First Footer," Gideon said and shook his head, his gaze going to Cain. "Aye, he's here to see if we're still loyal and to assess how powerful the Sinclairs have become. Word has reached him that we took over the Mackay Clan here at Varrich, which is why he has come here first."

He crossed his arms over his chest, the scenario revealing itself to him easily now. "He'll journey on to Girnigoe and Dunrobin Castles to make sure Sinclairs, Mackays, and Sutherlands will still stand up for him. And we'll pledge our loyalty." Gideon looked directly at Cain. "Unless ye want to be the king of Scotland."

It was a goal of their father's to see his eldest son on the throne, but Cain did not seem to covet the position despite being the Horseman of Conquest. He hardly even wore the Horseman crown that their father had made for him.

"Fok," Joshua swore again, and his son, Adam, began to cry. Kára shifted, rubbing the bairn's back and whispering motherly words of calm in his wee ear. Gideon watched her, and in his mind, Kára's pale hair turned to Cait's dark curls. How lovely Cait would look soothing his own bairn.

Gideon blinked and turned away, his thoughts scattered. He inhaled, refocusing. *James in the bailey. Cain could take the crown. We could kill the king now. Blood would mark my Hogmanay Festival.*

Joshua went to stand next to Kára and Adam. "Fok," he repeated in the waiting silence, broken only by the whimpers of his bairn.

Everything they were thinking was summed up in Joshua's curse. A civil war would weaken Scotland, giving France, England, and Spain an opening for taking control. The outcome wouldn't benefit the common people either way. The only ones who would increase their wealth and standing would be those who made it alive to the throne. And Sinclairs would be responsible for Scottish blood soaking the earth of their beloved country.

"I'll support whatever ye decide," Bàs said, his eyes on Cain. Cain was the leader, although it was the strength of all four Sinclair armies and their allies that Gideon curated that made them mighty.

"And I," Gideon said.

"Bloody fok," Joshua said, closing his eyes for a moment before looking to Cain. "And I."

Cain's face was hard with indecision. "I've never wanted the throne. James isn't a tyrant."

The tension in the room lowered, and Gideon breathed deeply. It was what he thought Cain would say. Gideon nodded slowly. "Then let us welcome him with loyalty and swear our fealty once again to strengthen his faith in us."

"Joshua and I are staying well away from him," Kára said over the head of her quieted child.

Joshua put his arm around her. "We need to get

out of the castle, but the king is standing right before the steps."

Gideon glanced at the door and then back at Joshua and his new family. "Have ye ever climbed down the side of a castle before?"

Kára's eyes opened wide. Having been raised on an isle without a single tree, she was said to be frightened of heights. Joshua grinned. "If Cait can do it, so can we."

"So can *you*," Kára said, holding Adam tighter against her breast. "I'll be walking out the front door on the arm of my lover." She stepped over to Bàs and looped one arm through his.

Their youngest brother pulled away as far as he could while still connected to Kára as if he tried not to rub against the bairn. Perhaps being the executioner for their clan made Bàs stay away from people, because he never knew who his next victim might be. Despite being uncomfortable, he would surely play along, taking Kára and Adam to safety.

"Where's Ella?" Gideon asked Cain.

"At the first sight of James, she took Mary, Hannah, and Aunt Merida back to Girnigoe. Keenan is with them. He and Ella will prepare the castle in case of siege. She's sending word to her brother and father at Dunrobin Castle."

Gideon nodded. "Let us enact our roles before James is left wondering why we haven't emerged."

Kára handed the bairn to Bàs. "Hold him for a minute," she said. Bàs's eyes opened wide, looking almost frightened of the wrapped infant. Gideon had seen Bàs filled with fury, revenge, determination, and solemn apathy, but never fear. His youngest brother held Adam at arm's length, staring at his wee face while Adam stared back, each assessing the other.

Kára strode to Joshua and kissed him soundly. With her hands fisted in his tunic she frowned up at him. "Don't you bloody fall, Highlander."

He grinned back down at her. "I'll meet ye below outside the castle wall in the shadows. Look for Fuil." He kissed her forehead. "And we will ride to the forest to climb into our home in the trees," he said, referring to the cottage Gideon had helped him build as a wedding gift for his Orkney bride.

They all filed out of the library, Joshua climbing up the tower stairs while the rest headed down. "Ye may want to give James a different bedchamber than the best in the castle," Joshua called. "He may not like a bed that couldn't hold up to your vigorous tupping."

"Vigorous tupping?" Kára asked, glancing at Gideon over her bairn's head. "Good for you, brother."

Bloody hell. It was common for a visiting monarch to take the best bedchamber in the dwelling, and at present Gideon's room had splintered wood across the bed. But there was no time to worry over details like that when the king of Scotland had still not been properly greeted. The insult was growing by the second.

The great hall was empty as the three brothers and Kára strode across. Mathias met them at the door. "I've quenched his thirst and given him and his immediate men meat, buns, and tarts. I've sent Osk to rouse my Martha and Alyce to help me start baking bannocks and more buns. His steward says they have a hundred soldiers with them."

One hundred soldiers? Aye, James was worried. Gideon patted Mathias's shoulder as he walked past. "Ye are the best of men."

Cain and Gideon walked out of the keep beside each other, Bàs and Kára behind them with her bairn. "Your majesty," Gideon said. "Welcome to Varrich Castle." He bowed deeply before the king who stood chewing a sweet bun.

James VI of Scotland was of medium height and weight. His thin legs looked even more gangly by the hose he wore under short, round trews much like English court dress. With Elizabeth I without issue, James was considered the next in line for the English throne and had already adopted their dress, down to the ruffed collar about his thin neck. His long, pointed beard accented his long, pointed nose, giving the man a triangular look. A jaunty tall hat sat on his head.

"'Tis about time the new chief of Varrich came out to greet me, his king," James said and wiped his hands together, brushing off crumbs. "I've had to amuse myself speaking with your steward after Chief Sinclair of Girnigoe left me to find you."

Bruce Mackay stood beside the king and his steward, his arms crossed. What grievances had Bruce been polluting the king's head with? If the speaker was charming in the least, James listened to him, which had already led the man down ill-conceived paths during his reign.

"Forgive me, your majesty. I was indisposed at the time of your arrival. If ye had sent word, we would've greeted ye with appropriate flourish fit for a king. I'm glad though that ye have had food and drink. More will be brought for your soldiers outside the walls."

"Good, good," James said, sounding somewhat placated. "We've ridden for several days from Edinburgh, and they'll need pallets, drink, and food."

"I'll send some provisions from Girnigoe," Cain said.

James waved his beringed hand. "Save some there. I'll be riding thence two days from now."

"Aye, of course," Cain said.

"Shall we go in where ye can warm yourself, milord?" Gideon asked, sweeping his arm wide.

"Not until we know 'tis past midnight." James smiled. "So I can bless your castle as your First Footer."

"We are honored, your majesty," Gideon said.

James watched Gideon's face closely and finally nodded before looking up at the sky. "'Tis hard to tell the time given this weather," James said, frowning at Gideon as if the snow that still swirled down was somehow his fault.

Gideon looked up, trying to judge the position of the mostly covered moon. The glow seemed appropriately overhead. "I believe we are past the hour, your majesty, and 'tis comfortably warm inside."

"Well then, let us proceed," James said with a flap of his hand.

Bàs bowed to James, and Kára curtsied before she slipped away to find Joshua and his horse in the shadows outside Varrich's wall. No doubt Joshua already watched for her.

"I'll organize the supplies for the king's men," Bàs said.

James turned his glance to Cain and Gideon and let a smile turn up his mouth. "I've a hundred men and a number of peddlers and tinkers who have followed us. They take care of themselves and bring items for purchase for your people, since there are hardly decent wares available out in this uncultured countryside." He glanced at the groups of villagers standing about. "Although your conquered people probably have little coin, if any, after you took over their lands and castle."

"The people of Varrich are being cared for," Gideon said. Could he possibly break away to make certain Cait had gotten home? There were a hundred foolish Scotsmen from Edinburgh out there in the shadows.

Cain cleared his voice when Gideon didn't continue. "We're integrating them into the Sinclair Clan."

Gideon looked to Bruce and then to several of the villagers grouped together inside the bailey, his voice growing loud. "And I'm gifting five shillings to each household to buy from the peddlers accompanying the king. 'Tis a Hogmanay gift for the families of Varrich." A murmur rose among the crowd.

Bàs moved forward as if to get to work, but Gideon delayed him with a hand. "Keep watch that Cait made it home," he whispered. Bàs nodded and strode into the crowd of Mackays. Despite his quiet ways, his height, build, and talent with a sword and executioner's ax made the men open a path for him as he walked into the night. Bàs pointed to men, choosing them to help find housing for a hundred royal soldiers. No doubt dozens would be sleeping inside the keep. Gideon kept his exasperated curse inside. If the king had mentioned the possibility of arriving this soon in his letter, Gideon would have made preparations.

Gideon and Cain walked beside James and his steward, a man named Vincent Cockburn, a watchful man of slightly larger stature than his king. Everyone stopped to let James enter the keep first, officially being the First Footer of Varrich Castle. He laughed as he entered, flourishing his arms. If the king thought he could now consider Varrich his, he would find himself quite disappointed and possibly in a civil war. As if sensing Gideon's annoyance, Cain patted his shoulder. "'Tis for only two nights," he murmured and walked forward, talking to James.

"The king and I will take your bedchamber," Vincent said.

Gideon crossed his arms over his chest. "Ye may want to see it before ye decide."

· · ·

The streets of Varrich were swollen with the king's soldiers, standing around waiting for Gideon to feed and shelter them. Some laughed. Others grumbled. Cait saw at least five pissing against cottages. All the homes were locked up tight. Fathers and husbands were probably hiding their daughters and wives and arming themselves with whatever iron poker or *sgian dubh* they could lay hands on.

The same had happened when the Sinclairs had set the village ablaze a year and a half ago, but at least the Sinclair warriors never harassed any of the women or children. Hopefully, King James had ordered his soldiers to treat the town with respect. Just in case, Cait kept to the shadows. She would've taken refuge in the trees but with her skirts she'd put back on, the climb would be hard and might draw attention, unless she withdrew to the forest. And who knew what soldiers might be hiding in there.

Cait kept her hood up over her hair and skirts close as she walked in silence, pausing every few steps to make certain no one was sneaking up on her. Bent over, she hoped she looked old and possibly hunched with a curved spine.

She exhaled in relief when she saw Bàs walking through the men on the road, talking to them in his deep, even voice. Did they know they spoke with the Horseman of Death? That he'd beheaded hundreds of people, if the rumors were true? Either way, he was related to Gideon and therefore someone who would keep order in the town. She took a step out from behind the shed where she'd stopped and gasped as a hand on her shoulder pulled her roughly back.

She twisted, her *sgian dubh* clasped in her hand, and let her exhale out in a huff. "Alistair," she said. "You startled me. What are you—?"

"Come away with me tonight, Cait," he said, pulling her farther into the shadows of the woods. "I've heard the king's men talking about raiding our houses and raping the women." He shook his head, the white of his teeth showing in stark contrast to the darkness.

"Bàs is out there," she said. "He'll not let the king's soldiers grab women. And Gideon would never allow anyone to ransack the village." She patted his arm. "Once I get home, I'll bar the door. We will be safe."

"It won't be enough." He tried to pull her into the woods, but Cait yanked her hand away from his grasp.

"Stop it, Alistair." She took a calming breath. "Why don't you help Bàs manage the king's men to help prevent such attacks if you worry over them?"

Alistair ran a hand through his hair. "I just… I want ye to be safe, Cait." He looked dejected, his gaze going to the snow at his feet.

"I'll be safe right here in Varrich, but if you worry, you can walk me home," she said, trying to build the man back up. His infatuation made him overly concerned for her, and she knew he hated being home. If Alistair held some hope she might return his affections, it made sense he'd want her to leave the town with him. She pursed her lips. How could she make sure he understood nothing would grow between them without crushing the poor man's spirit?

Alistair walked with her, leading her around the groups of men who were moving toward Bàs and his warriors to hear where they could stable their horses and bed down. She kept her hood up. Alistair might be young, but he was tall. In the dark, he probably looked formidable enough to deter anyone who might approach her.

When her boots hit the cobblestone walk before

the Orphans' Home, Cait released the breath she'd been holding. Alistair stopped with her before the door, and she knocked.

"'Tis Cait," she called. Their new dog barked, its already deep voice a deterrent to scoundrels. The bar on the other side slid away, and Viola opened the door, Rhona next to her with Jack and the children behind. Trix practically sat on their pup so she wouldn't run out. Cait smiled at Viola, who was finally strong enough to get out of the bed.

"What are ye doing here?" Alistair asked, staring at the exiled woman.

Viola's face paled. "I…gave birth to a son."

Cait turned to look at Alistair. "Gideon knows she's here and has said she may stay for the sake of the child. Don't go around telling people until Gideon has a chance to announce that she's back."

Alistair's brows bent inward as he stared at Cait, condemnation in his face. "But he judged her guilty, lashed her, and exiled her."

"She has paid the price for her wrongdoings," Rhona said, stepping before Viola, with her arms crossed.

"Do you promise not to say anything?" Cait asked him.

Alistair's gaze returned to Cait. "Bar your door." He pivoted on his heel and strode toward the village center. Cait watched him go, her face tight.

"Thank God you are well," Rhona said, pulling her in. Jack and Willa lifted the heavy bar and slid it into place. "When the soldiers marched out of the forest, my heart about stopped," Rhona said. "Jack and I rounded up the children and our new pup and brought everyone back here."

"We couldn't find you," Trix said and finally let go of the dog who ran over, prancing on her back legs to reach up Cait's skirts. She scratched the pup's head. "We looked. Where were you?"

"Why has the king come?" Viola asked. Thank God, because Cait couldn't answer Trix with "I was being thoroughly loved by Gideon until we broke his bed."

Viola walked to the cradle that had been set by the fire where Henry slept. She rocked it gently, her worried gaze going back to Cait.

"The king says he wants to be the First Footer of the new year at Varrich Castle," Cait said, peeking out the window. Blessedly, there was no one about.

"With no warning and a battalion of armed soldiers?" Jack said. He crossed his arms over his chest, looking very much like the warrior he wanted to become.

Libby's frown was heavy with fear, and Cait wrapped her in a hug. "Whatever the king wants, I'm certain Gideon Sinclair will keep us safe."

• • •

Rap. Rap.

Gideon stood outside the Orphans' Home door. It was early morning, but there were already several voices within, their pitch high and frantic. Something was wrong.

Rap. Rap. "Cait?" he called and heard the dog bark. "'Tis Gideon."

He stepped back when he heard the bar slide off

the door. It swung open, and Jack pushed past him to run outside. "I wouldn't go in there," the lad warned. He was dressed, but his hair stuck up haphazardly.

"What's wrong?" Gideon asked, glancing inside where he heard one of the girls wailing. "Is someone hurt?" He heard Cait's voice trying to calm whoever was upset.

Jack stood off to the side, his arms crossed. "'Tis the woman's curse." He shook his head. "I really need to find a place to live that's not completely made up of females." He turned to sit down heavily on an upturned log and rubbed his face as if he'd just woken.

Curse? Gideon didn't believe in witches or curses, for that matter. He stepped inside the warm room. "Cait? Is all well?" he called, but a girl's wails overrode his questions.

Trix and Libby stood near the hearth, staring at the closed door to the back bedroom. Rhona and Cait must be with Willa inside. "Does it hurt?" Trix yelled.

"Of course it hurts," Libby said. "I saw the blood, and she's crying." The girl held tightly to Trix.

Was Cait's fifteen-year-old sister in jeopardy? He remembered Cait's quest to keep her sister well, and his stomach tightened. "Shall I find the apothecary? I can send for my aunt at Girnigoe."

Viola sat in the single bed against the wall. "The girl has gotten her courses for the first time."

Gideon looked at her. "Courses?"

"Her woman's courses." Viola flipped her hand. "Her monthly bleeding."

Understanding hit Gideon. Jack had said curse, but his hasty departure made sense. "Is this…normal?" he asked, nodding toward the room where sobbing could be heard.

Viola shrugged. "I didn't wail, but some likely do. Especially when they know their sister was given away in marriage at fifteen when it was confirmed she was old enough to bear children."

"And Rhona said her insides are scraping out," Libby said, her face serious. "Which is why a lady bleeds." She held her two hands across her small abdomen. "Can you imagine?"

Gideon had seen a book of anatomy where it discussed the parts that made up a woman for her to bear children. Complicated, messy, and it did look like parts sloughed off each month to ready the womb to hold a bairn.

"The pain can be fierce for some," Viola said. "But it will not kill you. Some hardly notice, Libby."

Trix shook her head. "I never want to become a woman."

The wails had calmed enough that Gideon could hear Willa's words. "I'm not marrying anyone. I will never marry. Never."

"No one will marry you off without your consent." Cait's voice was calm, soothing.

"You could marry Jack," Trix called out, her hands cupped around her mouth. "He would never beat you, and then you'd be safe from any other man."

Libby smacked her arm. "He's like a brother to her."

"But he isn't by blood," Trix said, crossing her arms.

"But if she thinks of him as a brother, Willa won't

make bairns with him," Libby said, crossing her own arms.

"Why?" Trix asked. "How do they make bairns? Why wouldn't Willa do so with Jack?"

Libby huffed. "Well, I don't know that, but I know that brothers and sisters can't. Isn't that right?" Libby turned to Gideon, and both she and Trix waited.

"Maybe I should wait outside," Gideon said.

Viola chuckled from her position on the bed where she held her son. Her gaze moved from Gideon to the girls. "Making bairns and being a woman are complicated things to understand, girls. Mistress Cait will explain it to you when you reach Willa's age."

"I hope my courses never come," Libby said, her chin rising as if she'd just decreed her bareness. "Then I won't have to worry about bairns."

Trix shook her head. "A lady can still have courses and not have bairns, even with a husband." She smiled knowingly while Libby frowned.

"Not true," Libby said.

Trix crossed her arms. "Mistress Cait has courses but never had a bairn with her husband, so she thinks she's barren."

Gideon's gaze lifted to the door where only an occasional whimper was heard now. Cait stepped out, pulling the door firmly shut behind her. She wore a smock and stockings, her hair down and uncombed like she had just jumped out of her blankets to calm her sister. "Oh," she said, her eyes going to Gideon. "I...did not hear you come in."

"All is well?" he asked.

She nodded. "Willa is a bit upset but is not ill."

Cait grabbed a long cloak, throwing it around her shoulders to hide her smock. "Come outside," she said, walking to the cottage door.

She opened it. "You can go back in, Jack," she said, and the lad walked cautiously past them.

"If you need any help in the stables," Jack said to Gideon, "where I can also sleep, please keep me in mind." He went back inside, where Trix and Libby dashed over to him.

"Willa is a woman now," Trix said. "You could wed her. Wouldn't it be lovely if we could all stay together? You wouldn't *have* to make bairns."

Cait closed the door and leaned back against it, taking a deep breath of the morning air. "I will let Rhona handle that."

"I didn't know"—he nodded toward the door— "that it was so frightening for a lass."

"For some, yes. Rhona had never been told about it and thought she was dying until she confided in a friend."

"And Willa worries she'll be married off?"

Cait exhaled. "I've assured her she will not."

He looked at the closed door. "Trix and Libby asked how bairns are conceived."

Cait's hand went to her mouth to hide a grin. "And you sat them down and explained?"

Horror must have crossed his face because she laughed. She waved her hand. "One of their many mothers will enlighten them when they get older," she said.

He rubbed a hand along his short beard. "The girls also believe ye are barren. Do ye still worry over that?"

CHAPTER FIFTEEN

Visigothic Code Book VI, Section V, 654 AD

If a man's assertions about another should prove to be false, and it should be evident that he had made them only through hatred, and in order that he whom he attempted to accuse might suffer death, or bodily injury, or the loss of his property; he shall be delivered over into the power of him he accused, that he may he himself suffer the penalty which he endeavored to inflict upon an innocent person.

Cait glanced at the door before returning to look at him, her eyes narrowed. "How long were you inside with Trix and Libby?"

"Like I said last night, Benjamin was probably the problem," he said. "Not ye." He took a step closer and lowered his voice. "Ye saw last night how much he lied about ye being cold."

A blush infused her cheeks, and she gave a small nod. "He said it was because I was a cold woman that I did not conceive. At fifteen, with no woman to tell me otherwise, I believed him."

"And now?"

"I have had no way to find out," she said and met his gaze. "Until last night."

Gideon grasped her arms. "I will support any bairn that comes from me, Cait. I'd do anything for ye not to regret your involvement with me."

She studied his face as if memorizing what he just said. "You're an honorable man. I just don't want you to regret your involvement with *me*."

"I could never," he said. Staring into her bright green eyes, his words were an oath. No matter what came next, he would never regret one moment with Cait. He slid a finger along the soft skin at her jaw-line. An image of her holding a bairn against her filled his heart, and he suddenly hoped for things he'd never thought about before.

Behind him, a horse neighed in the distance, and the sounds of deep laughter came on the breeze from the center of the village. Cait's smile faded, and Gideon dropped his hand.

"What does the king want?" she asked, glancing past his shoulder.

He walked a few steps, looking down the empty lane. Luckily the Orphans' Home was situated on the fringe of the village. "To see our loyalties and strength," he said, "even if he admits only to be making a Hogmanay progress around his northern territory."

Her hand rested on his chest as she stared up at him. "And what will he see?" she whispered, tension clear in her features.

"That the Sinclairs are the strongest clan in the Highlands and that we're loyal to him."

She released her breath. "I worried."

He leaned in. "I discussed it at length with Cain last night, and he has no wish to weaken Scotland with a civil war when James is tolerated and fairly moderate. Even though I'm certain I could organize enough support for Cain, there'd be no victory in the bloodletting that would occur."

She placed her hands on the sides of his face. "Thank you for being so wise."

He snorted softly and slid one of her hands to his mouth, kissing the soft flesh of her palm. "'Tis the wisdom of hundreds of leaders and the follies of doomed men that give me any wisdom."

"Your books," she said.

"Aye. I've read of battles and destruction, of victories and times of peace. History is the greatest teacher if people would take their own desires out of their strategies."

"One must be taught history," she said. "We've had no access to books, and most people don't know how to read. Some rulers keep their people in ignorance so they'll believe only what they're told instead of thinking for themselves."

He frowned. "Those rulers are fearful and weak."

"Which you are not." She patted his chest in a familiar fashion, something that warmed his heart.

"Your school will help everyone at Varrich," he said. "When James leaves Caithness we can turn our efforts to planning."

Her smile broadened. "When is he leaving?"

"Two days, and then he journeys to Girnigoe." Gideon lifted his arms to cup the back of his head. "And then he'll likely go on to Dunrobin and the Sutherland Clan, since Ella was their chief before. She passed the leadership to her young brother and her father, who is acting as regent."

"Where is the king sleeping?" she asked.

"Not in my room." Gideon chuckled. "Once his steward saw the mess, he opted to house the king in the next largest room one floor down, the one Cain and Ella were going to stay in. So I have ye to thank for not being evicted from my chamber."

"Me?" She poked him in the chest, but her smile was broad.

The crunch of gravel and snow made Gideon turn, his hand going to his sheathed sword. Vincent Cockburn strode toward them from the woods. "So here you are, Sinclair."

The man stopped several feet away, his hawklike gaze directly on Cait. She wrapped her robe tighter around herself, and Gideon stepped before her. "I thought for certain you were on your way to meet with rebels, intent on murdering my king," Vincent said. He smiled, his little brown teeth looking sharp with their brokenness.

"Has the king risen?" Gideon asked, ignoring the man's casual accusation.

"Aye, and is asking to hunt with you, milord. But, first, who is this lovely creature that has drawn you away from your courtly obligations?"

Cait stepped beside Gideon and dipped briefly. "I am Cait Mackay."

The man's gaze drifted to the cottage behind her. "And you live alone here on the outskirts of the village? A private haven for your chief to visit with you?"

Gideon's hands tightened into fists. "Mistress Cait runs a home for orphans here," Gideon said, his tone harsh as he stared the grinning man down. "She's hardly alone but manages to care for four children and a bairn who have been deprived of parents."

The man's thin lips pinched. "And you were but walking all the way out here to wish her good morn?"

Gideon tipped his chin upward. "I was making certain the repairs had been finished on her roof." Which they had.

"Ah, so you were doing the duty of a chieftain checking on his populace. Forgive my misunderstanding," the man said, tipping his head to the side to study Cait. "I'm Vincent Cockburn, steward to his royal Highness, King James." He smiled broadly with no hesitation to show his neglected teeth. "And you, Mistress Cait, should bring your children with you to the feast tonight up at the castle. 'Tis to honor the king, and he would surely like to see the good that is propagated in Varrich." His arms went out to the house. "And I'd like to meet these children." His brows rose as if he questioned their true existence.

Not only did he insinuate that Cait was Gideon's lover but also a liar. Cait's cheeks pinkened with embarrassment. Before Gideon could react in a way that would make the situation more unstable, the door behind him opened.

"You can meet us now," Libby said. Rhona stepped up next to Cait, sliding her arm through hers. "I'm Rhona Mackay, Mistress Cait's helper here at the Orphans' Home. Her sister, Willa, is indisposed right now, but also lives with us."

"I am Beatrix Mackay, and Mistress Cait cares for me since my mama and papa died last year from fever," Trix said, giving a small curtsy in her hastily thrown on dress.

Libby stepped around her, hair wrapped up in a

wild bun on top of her head. "I am Libby Mackay, and she cares for me, too, although I also help with the house."

"So do I," Trix said.

"And I'm Jack Mackay," Jack said from behind, his voice sounding deeper than usual. "And we are all of this house with Mistress Cait and Mistress Rhona."

"And the bairn, Henry," Rhona said, "who is still sleeping soundly in his cradle."

Vincent's eyebrows had risen toward his receding hairline as his gaze slid across the group who had jumped to Cait's defense. "My," he said, "so many in such a small dwelling."

Cait stared indignantly at the man. "As you can see, Master Cockburn, there's no secluded haven for the chief here."

Vincent's thin lips hitched up in a wry grin. "I stand corrected in my assumption."

"Assumptions can get one skewered in the Highlands," Jack said. At his full height he was already six feet tall and had begun to fill out with muscle.

Vincent's gaze pinned the boy. "And threats to royal servants can see one hanged."

"'Twas not a threat," Gideon said, his voice still stern. "'Twas just what the lad has seen living out in this rugged land. Insinuations and veiled questions of moral character can lead to revenge. He but wishes ye safety, Master Cockburn."

Vincent Cockburn made a snorting noise and tipped his head, his gaze still locked on Jack. "In that case, I am obliged for your concern, *lad*." The last word was emphasized as if he felt that Jack was a man and not a boy anymore.

Vincent cut his eyes to Cait. "I look forward to speaking with you longer tonight when you all come up to the castle."

Cait nodded and shooed the children inside the cottage. "Thank you for the invitation." She glanced toward Gideon and then followed them inside. The bar slid across the door.

Gideon stared at the man who still wore an assessing smirk. "The Highlands are a dangerous place for men who speak before they think," Gideon said. "Tempers run hot, and blood runs easily. Ye best watch your tongue and keep your men in line as well."

The slight twitch at the corner of Vincent's eye showed his irritation with the warning. Despite his medium stature, the king's steward was obviously quite secure in his position and felt it protected him from physical harm. "Anyone who attacks me also attacks the king, and is therefore a traitor to the crown." He squinted, studying Gideon. "Are there many of those about? I hear the Highlands are rife with those wishing to gain power and topple James from his throne."

Did the king's advisor believe Gideon would throw his subjects to the wolves? Or his brothers? The calm inquisitive look tweaked a warning inside Gideon that had little to do with the actual question. It was to be expected that Vincent was tasked to ferret out traitors, but there seemed to be something more behind his words, although Gideon couldn't identify it.

"If I remember any who are dissatisfied with the way the country is being run, shall I inform ye?" Gideon asked. "And condemn them as traitors?"

Vincent's thin mouth held the hint of a smile. "Some traitors may actually be patriots looking for a stronger Scotland." He gave a small nod and walked away.

Gideon stared at his retreating swagger. Either Vincent Cockburn was trying to discover those discontented by tricking them into thinking he might sympathize or...Vincent Cockburn was a traitor himself.

• • •

"Daingead," Gideon said through clenched teeth as he stared out from the dark archway at the king laughing in his great hall. James was surrounded by several men from the village who Gideon had invited along with the minstrels who played lively tunes in the corner.

"He'll be gone soon," Cain murmured next to Gideon. His brother glanced at him. "Aren't ye used to playing the part of loyal and gracious kinsman when ye visit court in Edinburgh?"

"That's in Edinburgh, which is vastly different from northern, rural Scotland," Gideon said, watching Vincent Cockburn speaking with Bruce Mackay. The king's steward did most of the talking, even though he tried to hide it by looking out at the small groups of villagers in the room.

Gideon exhaled. "James's visit has ruined my Hogmanay Festival. It was meant to bring the village together and for the Mackays to see me as a reasonable, honorable leader of our integrated clan. But now they'll see me putting on airs like royalty." He glanced down at his finest tunic and kilt, polished boots, and gem-studded scabbard.

"There'll be more festivals and holidays where ye can sing bawdy songs and bet on piglet races with your clan," Cain said, humor in his voice. His jesting did nothing to lighten Gideon's mood. In fact, ever since Vincent's crude insinuations with Cait that morning and then his dangled treasonous comment, a foreboding had plagued Gideon.

One always felt a noose following them around when at court where the whims of a monarch, swayed by his steward and council, could see a man swiftly thrown into the dungeon or hanged. But in one's own home, where others could fall victim to royal condemnation, the feeling of being judged was prickling his instincts. Was that how the Mackays felt around him daily? Och, but that would drive him insane, even with all his diplomatic schooling. He muttered a curse beneath his breath.

"Lo now, brother," Cain said, as he dropped his hand on Gideon's shoulder. "Perhaps things are looking up." Cain nodded toward the outer doors of the great hall.

Gideon's gaze moved from the king and his beady-eyed steward to fall upon a dark-haired angel. *Cait.*

She wore the same beautiful gown she'd stripped out of last night before climbing up to his window. Somehow, it was free of wrinkles after being rolled up and stuffed into buckets. Her hair cascaded around her shoulders in dark curls, teased tighter by the damp weather. Ribbons to match her inner petticoat pulled part of her tresses up onto the top of her head. But what stole his breath was the smile that bloomed on her face when Ella and Hannah came up and started talking to her. It was genuine, free of suspicion and worry. For an instant, she looked like she had in the snow the day he'd found her twirling on the moor. What were his sisters saying to make her look so happy? He'd say it himself.

Rhona and the children followed her inside, Libby pointing to the garlands that she had helped hang. Willa even walked behind them, having recovered enough to dine with the king. Wolf ran over to greet Jack and allowed Trix to try to climb on his back for a ride until Rhona whispered in her ear. The little girl immediately righted herself, her wide-eyed gaze going to the king.

All thoughts of the children dropped away as Cait's gaze turned about the room, stopping on him. Her eyes opened a bit wider, her gaze taking in his formal dress. A teasing smile curled her lips, but it was obvious she approved.

"She'd make all the ladies at court jealous," Cain said. "And all the lads forget their heads."

Gideon watched her turn toward Alistair Mackay, who had just walked inside. Who had invited the irritating lad to dine with the king? Certainly not Gideon. "Then there'd be lads without their heads," he answered Cain.

His brother chuckled. "Violence, little brother? Over diplomacy? Father would be proud."

Cain's lighthearted words twisted in Gideon's gut.

Cain did not know the pain their father's disapproval still inflicted, like a tainted wound that never quite healed. "Excuse me," Gideon said, picking up the two wrapped gifts for the older children, and strode across the great hall toward Cait.

"Edinburgh is said to be a progressive town to live in," Alistair said and snapped around as Gideon stopped behind him. His young face pinched in annoyance.

"It is," Gideon said, his gaze meeting Cait's. "But the beauty of Scotland lies in the snow-covered moors and forests. I prefer life away from the crowds and human filth in busy towns."

"There's more opportunity for the common man there," Alistair said, his voice tight. "The common man here lives in squalor and has little ability to change his situation."

Gideon's gaze shifted abruptly to meet the young man's sharp eyes. "I've seen much squalor and crime in the large towns and cities. If ye live that way here at Varrich, ye need to petition for something better. I've made it no secret that I wish to make the lives of the people here better, be they Mackays or Sinclairs or natives of Orkney. They but need to ask."

Alistair looked away and wisely held his tongue.

"And people are starting to see that they can come speak with you," Cait said. She nodded to Gideon's sisters. "Lady Ella and Lady Hannah heard I might start a school here at Varrich. They plan to contribute books and supplies to it."

So that was what brought such light to Cait's eyes. "Aye, ye will have your school, Cait," Gideon said, "and the library here at Varrich will be open to any who wish to read or use the books there. Ye may bring a whole group if ye'd like, or they can stop in on their own."

Her mouth broadened into a wonderful smile. "Thank you," she said, her eyes tethered to his. Gideon was so taken that he nearly pushed Alistair aside to whisk Cait away to the library to see what they could explore there alone, together.

"Good Lord," Ella said, her tone half appalled and half amused.

Holy hell, was his jack tenting out his kilt? Gideon looked down. Thank the bloody lord for heavy wool. He turned toward Ella, adjusting himself covertly.

She and Hannah both held hands to their mouths, their gazes following Osk, who had just entered the great hall, dressed with even more flare than the previous night. As the Master of Revels, he seemed determined to entertain and make the place royally merry. He wore a fur-lined cape, a crown, and held a scepter with a holly ball on the top.

He made a show of holding it over various ladies and watching the closest man give the lass a kiss, usually on the cheek, but sometimes to the applause of everyone she allowed a kiss on the lips. James nodded and laughed as Osk greeted him with a bow but then came alongside him, imitating his every gesture and step.

"Give that to me then, you knave!" the king called, snatching the scepter from Osk. James began to carry it about and hold it over ladies' heads. If there wasn't a man near her, the king would deliver a kiss to her cheek or forehead. Osk ran up to him and set his own crown on King James's head to the amusement of everyone in the room, who applauded and cheered. Finally, James handed both back, and he smiled broadly at the young man from Orkney. Osk bowed deeply and dashed off to create more mayhem with a group who had just entered, James's gaze following him.

Gideon presented his arm to Cait, ignoring Alistair. "I have the gifts for Jack and Willa," he said and pulled her away from the frowning lad toward the hearth where Rhona had taken them.

"Alistair thinks you're a condemning monster," she said, her voice low.

"I care naught what he thinks, only what ye think," Gideon said, the question obvious in his tone.

Her hand squeezed his arm gently. "I think you are…nothing at all what I had imagined you to be."

"I hope then that ye imagined me to be an ugly toad with no heart or honor."

She smiled, although she looked straight ahead. "Something like that."

They stopped before the children, whom he noticed all wore the ribbons he'd gifted them the previous day. "Good eve," he said. The girls curtsied low to him, and with a nudge from Rhona, Jack bowed.

"How was that?" Trix asked, rising quickly. "Good enough for the king?"

"Aye," Gideon said. "Just like the ladies at court." Trix smiled wide, the gap where she lost her tooth making her look even younger.

Gideon turned to Willa. "I am happy to see ye

well, Mistress Willa. I have this gift for ye now that ye are older."

Her eyes grew wide as her face turned bright red. She looked mortified but took the gift. "I checked with Cait to make certain it was appropriate."

Willa's gaze snapped to Cait, whose smile had turned into a confused frown. Trix and Libby gathered closer as Willa untied the string; a silver sheath and *sgian dubh* lay in the square of fabric. "I can teach ye to wield it," Gideon said.

Trix's palms came together. "He's giving you a weapon to use against husbands and anyone who might want to give you a bairn."

Suddenly, the blush and mortification made sense. Poor Willa thought he was giving her the gift for starting her courses. "Nay," Gideon said, shaking his head. "I… I have one for Jack, too." He turned, presenting the second package to the lad.

"So he can defend himself when Willa tries to stab him for trying to give her a bairn?" Libby asked, her brows pinched.

"Nay," Gideon said, the word coming out with force.

"That would leave them both bloody and dead," Trix said, frowning at him. "How cruel."

"Nay, they're merely Hogmanay gifts, 'tis all," he said quickly. "They have nothing to do with…" Gideon ran his hand up behind his neck to rub there. When had gift-giving become so complex? First his brothers questioned the rings he got them, and now the children thought he wanted Willa to fight off swarms of men with a six-inch blade. "I'll give one to each of the lasses when they reach Willa's maturity, I mean…her age."

"I do not want to fight men off," Trix yelled out, her face aghast. Several villagers around them looked over.

Gideon lowered his voice. "They're not for that. I…" He looked at Cait, who rested a hand over her mouth. The crinkles at her eyes showed she held back laughter. "I surrender," he said, dropping his hands to his sides.

"A Sinclair never surrenders."

Gideon turned to see Cain standing behind him.

"I'll remind ye of that when your Mary grows into a woman," Gideon murmured. Cain's smile faded into a look of confusion, and Gideon thumped him on the shoulder. "Best of luck with that."

"Willa, Jack," Rhona said, "what do you say?"

"Thank you," Willa said, her voice small.

"Aye, 'tis a rich gift," Jack said. There was a bit of red in his cheeks, too.

"And if ye wish to know how to throw it or use it, I can teach ye," Gideon said. He held up a hand to Trix, who had opened her mouth. "And not to purposely bloody anyone."

"But what if—?"

He held his hand up to her again. "Unless they're being attacked. For *any* reason."

Trix shut her mouth and gave a nod as if finally consenting to the gifts.

Gideon released a breath and turned to Cait. "'Tis time to introduce ye to the king."

"Can we go, too?" Libby asked.

Cait sniffed a little laugh. "I think you should stay here with Rhona for now. A swarm of children at first might be too much for him."

Libby slapped Trix's arm. "You're too much."

Gideon pulled Cait away, and they began to walk across the room. "Ye just let me flop around like a dying fish with them."

She laughed softly. "I thought you were doing fine."

"I'd rather ride into battle outnumbered five to one."

She pressed a hand against her chest to keep her increasing laughter quiet. As they neared, she took a deep breath, and Gideon noticed that her steps slowed. "Is he kind?" she whispered, staring at the king.

Gideon leaned closer and inhaled the fresh scent of her. "He's quite fond of beautiful things, so no worries. And 'tis said he's enamored of his new wife, Queen Anne from Denmark, and is quite faithful." Otherwise, Gideon wouldn't voluntarily bring Cait anywhere near the king.

She smoothed a hand along his arm. "You're quite handsome, too, in all your crispness and shine." She glanced down at his court dress.

He grinned back at her. "'Tis not practical for anything other than standing before the king."

"I'm sure a peacock, with all its beauty strutting around, feels the same way," she bantered back.

He chuckled. "Aye, but your children have just plucked me to death."

She laughed. "You will recover, milord."

They walked together past several groups of Mackays and Sinclairs toward where the king spoke with Bàs.

Cain caught up on the other side of Cait to walk with them. He spoke quietly. "James has questions about what Joshua saw on Orkney, and I know ye have that letter he wrote."

"Aye," Gideon said. He had the missive Joshua had written earlier in the day secure in his jacket pocket.

Cain looked back out toward the king. "I think Bàs needs saving." Their youngest brother stood stiffly next to the talking monarch, looking very much like he'd cut off his sword arm if that meant he could escape.

"So Varrich's jester is one of the Orkney inhabitants then?" James was asking as they stopped before him.

Cain answered. "He's not normally a jester, and aye."

James frowned. "I'm sorry to hear about your brother being killed by my uncle over there," James said. "Lord Robert is powerful and has an army of highly trained soldiers." James probably didn't know that several of those trained soldiers had escaped his ruthless uncle with the Orkney people. One of them, Mathias, was the man who'd coordinated the royal feast they were about to enjoy.

"Even a Horseman of War wasn't strong enough to stand against a Stewart, I suppose," James continued.

Gideon watched Cain's jaw tighten, his frown more fierce than normal. Gideon cleared his throat. "I believe it was the plague that weakened our brother so that when he fought Robert's son, he wasn't at his most deadly. Although, 'tis amazing no one at the castle caught the disease."

"Aye, very fortunate," James said, frowning.

It was also fortunate Joshua wasn't anywhere nearby to hear James's comments. First off, Joshua was supposed to be dead, but secondly, Gideon couldn't see his unruly brother standing for the king or anyone to think that dandy, Robert Stewart, or his son Patrick, had truly won his life.

"Lord Robert wrote to me about the upheaval there that your brother caused," James continued.

Gideon pulled a missive from his jacket. "My brother, before he died," Cain said, "wrote this letter warning your majesty about how Robert calls himself king of Scotland over on Orkney. That he might be rallying support to overtake your throne."

Vincent Cockburn had come to stand beside the king and heard the last of what Gideon said. He reached forward to take the letter, but Gideon easily held it out of his reach. "'Tis for our king directly."

James took the letter and tucked it into his own jacket pocket. He frowned. "I'll review this. Perhaps I'll send the loyal Sinclairs to Orkney to discover the truth. There have been whisperings of my uncle's traitorous words." His eyes met Gideon's. "And I'll let nothing threaten my sovereignty."

"Of course," Gideon answered. "And the Sinclairs will journey there at your word, your majesty."

James held Gideon's gaze for a long moment, and then turned to Cait. The king's frown transformed into a pleasant smile. "And who is this lovely dove?"

Cait pulled her arm from Gideon's and sunk into a low curtsy, bowing her head so that her curls fell beautifully about her face. She rose and smiled mildly at the king. "I'm Cait Mackay, originally from the Dunn Clan closer to Edinburgh."

Vincent leaned in to the king's ear, making him study Cait with pinched eyes. "The woman recently released from Varrich's dungeon," James said.

"A misunderstanding," Gideon said. "The villagers gave witness to the wholesomeness of Mistress Cait, and she was set free in time to coordinate the festival."

"I see," James said, his smile returning. "'Tis good to have people who can come to your aid. And wholesomeness is quite desired in a marriageable woman." He tapped his chin as if thinking.

Bloody hell. Was the king going to marry Cait off? "Cait runs the Orphans' Home here in Varrich," Gideon added. "Her wards are also in attendance." He nodded toward the hearth where they had gathered, watching the room with Rhona keeping them in check. Trix waved, keeping her hand right up against her body. Jack had strayed a bit and was laughing at Osk's tumbling skills. "And she plans to start a school to teach your subjects how to read."

"Both worthy occupations," James said. "My sweet bride, Anne, loves children and hopes to have many for the good of our kingdom. She's only just turned fifteen, so she has much time to produce." He smiled. "I'll tell her of your Orphans' Home and school, Mistress Cait. She may wish to become a patroness."

Cait dipped low again, and Gideon tried to ignore the swell of her breasts so beautifully presented. "Thank you, your highness," she said.

"So, the rough Sinclair brothers are calming down now that George Sinclair has died," James said, looking away.

"Only with our families," Gideon said, knowing instantly where the king was leading. "But in battle, ye will find us just as deadly to the enemies of Scotland. One day, ye will also sit on the throne of England."

"We will see it done," Cain said, adding to his words of loyalty.

James looked between them, and then snorted softly, his gaze softening as he smiled. "If England's Elizabeth will ever die. The woman won't formally name me her heir, and she has a stubbornness that will see her ordering her counselors about until she is an ancient hag."

"When the time comes, ye can count on the support of the Sinclairs, the Sutherlands, and the Mackays," Gideon repeated. He dared not offer more, based on his covert agreements with other clans of the Highlands. For even if James didn't realize that Gideon could amass an army to take the Scottish crown right now, then his steward, Vincent, surely would. The thin, serious man stood beside them, obviously listening to every word and nuance of tone.

James nodded, his shoulders relaxing. He believed Gideon, which was all that was needed right now. Surely, before James rode away, he would ask the Sinclair brothers to take a knee and pledge their loyalty before all their people, but tonight was for celebrating the new year.

Gideon watched Rhona lead the girls, who had composed themselves, across the floor toward them. "I believe several of Mistress Cait's pupils would like to say they've met the king of Scotland." Gideon would like to see how the king of Scotland fared against an examination by Trix and Libby.

James smiled, waving them over, but the girls kept their calm pace, even though Trix walked on her toes in excitement. Had Gideon ever felt such excitement to meet the king, even when he was a lad and his father took him to Edinburgh to learn the ways of court? Nay. From the very first, his father had whispered about taking over Scotland from the weak king. That in Gideon's heart there was room for loyalty only to his brothers and the Sinclair Clan, no one else. But what about the brave woman who slid her arm back into his?

• • •

Cait hurried the children into the cottage. It was past their bedtimes, and she wanted to get back to Gideon at the castle. "Thank you, Alistair, for walking us," she said to him. He'd insisted when he saw them leaving.

"I'd not let ye walk home in the dark with those soldiers about," Alistair said. His hand caught her wrist as she was about to enter. Rhona walked around her as Alistair pulled her to the side of the doorway. "Cait," he said.

"I really must get in to help Rhona with the girls."

"Viola is still here, isn't she?"

Cait nodded.

"Then she can help Rhona," he said, his voice filled with the frown that was hard to see in the dim lighting. The air was chilled and heavy with the threat of more snow. Cait shivered even though her wool wrap was warm.

Alistair seemed taller in the darkness. "I know Gideon Sinclair worries ye, Cait. I can help."

She frowned. "He does not worry me."

"Aye, he does." He sounded so certain that she wondered what she could have said to make him think that. "And he's paying too much attention to ye even though ye have sworn not to become involved with men."

Had she told Alistair that? It was true she hadn't corrected the assumption in the village that she wasn't interested in wedding again and preferred the company of her children. But she'd never sworn anything of the kind.

"I appreciate your worry for my happiness and safety, Alistair," she said slowly and firmly, "but I don't need you to look out for me regarding Gideon Sinclair. He's an honorable man."

Alistair snorted. "He's a bloody Sinclair Horseman," he said, the words coming out with vehemence and anger.

She shook her head at a subject that had become tedious. "Has he done something to you that you dislike him so?" she asked.

"Aye," Alistair said and then paused for several moments before he spoke again. "He struck my father in a rage when Da requested payment for shoeing the Sinclair's big black steed. Said that he should shoe him for free, since he was our new chief."

Cait studied him as he shifted before her, his eyes

moving beyond her face. He looked like he was lying, but why would he? "Alistair," Cait said, laying her hand on his arm. "Do not make up stories about Gideon or anyone. It'll come back to hurt you."

Alistair yanked his arm away. "Ye call me a liar? The Sinclair is the liar here, and ye lie to yourself if ye think that dancing with him or…tupping with him will turn his black heart to truly help ye."

"I do not…" Cait hesitated, her anger making it hard for her to think straight. Heat flushed her cheeks, and her heart pounded. "I do nothing to try to turn anyone's heart, and I'd never…play with a man to gain his help." She stepped back toward the closed door. "I think 'tis time you journey home and rest. In the morning, you'll hopefully have a clearer head and I will hear your apology."

"I am not one of your children, Cait," Alistair said. "Do not rebuke me like one."

She'd never heard his voice so tight with anger before and certainly never with her. "Then act like a man, Alistair, an honorable one. Don't embellish your jealous thoughts into lies. It will lead to your ruin."

His hands went to his head, fingers spreading through his sheared hair. He turned on his heel to stride away into the darkness.

Cait almost called after him. She'd known Alistair for five years, watched him grow into a passionate young man full of ideas, but she needed to make him understand that she would only ever see him as a friend.

Cait let out a long exhale and pressed into the warm cottage, the familiar scent of baked bread and herbs calming her racing heart.

"And then he ate partridge and another bun slathered with butter," Libby said. "And then some of the boar." She nodded. "King James definitely favors wine to whisky." She frowned at Jack where he stood up near the hearth that he had just lit. "And that doesn't make him a priss."

"Maybe not, but that dandy ruff around his neck does," Jack said. He looked back at Cait where she'd gone to untie Trix's stays. "Some of the lads from Girnigoe asked if I could come back. They say there will be more of Osk's antics now that the sun has lowered."

Cait frowned. "With all James's soldiers in town, you're apt to get into trouble."

"I'm nearly a man," Jack said. The squeak that had been affecting his voice had completely vanished, making him sound older than sixteen.

Willa set water over the growing fire so they could all have a sip of something warm before bed. "I am the age of King James's queen, but you don't see me staying out late."

"'Tis different with girls," Jack said. "Ye'd be attacked by one of those soldiers if ye went out at night."

"Attacked?" Libby asked, her eyes wide.

"Aye," Jack said, "so stay inside."

"I'll learn to wield a *sgian dubh* as well as Cait," Willa said. "Then I'll be free to walk about at night and skewer any man who gets near me."

Cait inhaled through her nose, releasing Trix to twirl about in her smock, happy to be free of the tight stays. "None of us are safe walking around at night with all those soldiers in Varrich." She looked to Jack. "I need to go back to the castle to talk with Lady Ella about our school. You can escort me and then stay with the Sinclair lads." She pointed at him, her brows high. "But no trouble."

"Aye," Jack said, smiling broadly. "No trouble."

"And when I leave, you'll return home with me," she said.

His smile faltered a bit, but he nodded.

"You best be careful," Rhona said, as Cait tucked her cloak up under her chin.

"Jack or Gideon will walk me home." She lowered her voice. "And I have two sgian dubhs on me."

Rhona clasped her upper arms, a knowing smile on her lips. "Sgian dubhs won't protect your heart against the likes of Gideon Sinclair."

Rhona's warning was vastly different from Alistair's, making Cait smile softly. Rhona was part best friend and part mother, kind and clever enough to see something in the way Cait had walked with Gideon in the hall. Cait leaned in. "Maybe 'tis time I take a little risk."

Rhona smiled, her lips pursed. "I knew it," she whispered. "See, Benjamin was a dolt who knew nothing of giving a woman anything but heartache."

And a headache and bruises.

"'Tis time for you to learn from a real man," Rhona said, obviously impressed with the way Gideon comported himself. "One who is friends with the king of Scotland," she added with a nod.

Cait wasn't so sure about the friends part, but the king seemed to accept Gideon and his brothers into his circle. Even so, she would be glad when James and his soldiers left, and their simple village could return to normal. Then she could start to work on a school. And Gideon was letting them use his library. Her heart swelled.

She stepped off the cobblestone walkway with Jack, striding toward the laughter and music that floated up from the castle ahead. The breeze blew cold, and small snowflakes began to fall. "Stay warm," she said to Jack. "And act wisely. No whisky." She knew she sounded like his mother. Even though he was only nine years younger than her, she felt like she was his mother. She patted his arm. "Promise me."

"Aye," he said while staring straight ahead. "I'm to strip naked and run about yelling 'let's go for a dip in the ocean' while gulping down any spirit but whisky."

She laughed and hit his arm. "Just behave. Don't follow everything Osk does. His actions are forgivable, since he's the Yuletide jester, where yours will not be so."

"But you're friends with the chief of judgment. Surely, he will spare me for running naked."

Just as she opened her mouth to say that she would put him in the stocks herself, a hand reached out from the tree next to the road. She sucked in a breath to scream, but a large palm clamped over it as she was dragged into the dark woods.

CHAPTER SIXTEEN

Kama Sutra, Book VII by Vatsyayana,
2nd century AD

"A man should gather from the actions of the woman of what disposition she is, and in what way she likes to be enjoyed."

Bruce Mackay and Vincent Cockburn were walking toward the Orphans' Home. Gideon's grip on Cait and Jack was firm, and he pulled them back without a sound. "'Tis Gideon," he whispered, and Cait stopped struggling.

Jack, on the other hand, ripped his arm away. "Let go of us."

"Keep quiet," Gideon said, beckoning the boy to follow him deeper into the dark woods along the path. When Cait waved him to follow, the lad finally did, just as Bruce and Vincent turned the path toward them.

"I've heard nothing but that the brothers are loyal to James," Bruce said, his voice carrying easily on the breeze.

"Nothing at all?" Vincent said, his voice digging. "A comment or laughter at the king's expense?"

"The Sinclair brothers do not laugh, at least not when I'm around."

"And what of the second brother?" Vincent asked. "Is he truly dead on Orkney?"

"There's a warrior, as big as the other three, who seems to fill his place, but he calls himself Flett, not Sinclair. Rumor is that he's Joshua Sinclair."

Of course, word would get out. Gideon knew that from the start. Neighboring clans who saw Joshua would whisper about him being alive. It was only a matter of time before King James learned he lived. They'd need to turn James against his uncle before Joshua was officially confirmed alive.

Vincent walked with his hands rubbing before him as if they were cold. "The Sinclairs have thousands of horses between the clans…" His words trailed off as they moved too far to hear. Where were they headed? Toward the Orphans' Home?

"Rhona won't open the door to them, will she?" Gideon asked, his voice hushed.

"Nay," Cait answered. "She doesn't trust Bruce and doesn't know the king's steward."

"Good," Gideon said and finally released her completely. "Apologies. I saw them leave a set of stables and followed them this way. When they stopped to talk, I snuck through the woods around them to come to your cottage. When I saw ye walking and heard them continuing this way, I didn't want to interrupt whatever they were saying. The more information, the better."

"It doesn't sound like Bruce is calling you a traitor," Jack said beside him. "Even with that other dandy asking."

"But they know about Joshua," Cait said. "What will you do?"

"Joshua and Kára will stay hidden for some time. Perhaps go south," Gideon said. "But we will need to deal with Lord Robert, Earl of Orkney, rather than let it resolve on its own." He led them out through the quiet woods to the path leading back toward the castle and festival. With Jack next to them, Gideon did not try to grasp Cait's hand in case she wanted to hide their…whatever this was between them.

Gideon's hands clenched next to his sides as they walked; the crunch of their boots on the frozen ground seemed loud. He wanted to take her hand. Did she feel the same? Gideon hadn't ever felt this tension before. Wondering how a lass felt about him. Or how to keep her and those she loved safe from the king and politics. Gideon envied Joshua in that he could take his love away from all this instead of being responsible for keeping the clan together and strong.

What would happen if he took Cait and her family away from all this intrigue, giving up his responsibilities? They'd live a simple life together, away from the wars he constantly waged on the battlefield and in the halls at the royal court.

Must we always be who Da said we are to be? Now that he is dead? Bàs's question on Christmas morning roared up through Gideon's thoughts like beer shook in a vessel and then uncapped.

"Treason," Cait said beside him, making Gideon's face snap toward her. Aye. His wandering thoughts were treasonous against Clan Sinclair.

"So that's what the king's visit is all about," she said. "Looking for traitors, and as soon as he and his steward ascertain there are none in Varrich, they'll move on."

Gideon's chest held the tightness of his traitorous thoughts against Clan Sinclair. "Aye." He cleared his throat. "James will find none here because I won't allow any to be seen. We're careful to be strong but not to look stronger than the king. 'Tis a fine balance I've nurtured through the years."

Jack looked over at him through the dark. "I do not envy your job keeping the king happy when he expects treason all the time. I'd much rather be a warrior on a battlefield."

"With Cait's permission, ye can start to train with my men," he said.

"Bloody hell, aye," Jack said. Light from the first bonfire outside the walls showed his smile.

Cait didn't say anything for a long minute. "Perhaps 'tis about time, Jack."

His smile grew, and he seemed to stand taller. Cait pointed a finger at him. "As long as you listen and do not get into trouble with the other men."

"Jack!" Osk called from near the wall.

Jack leaped forward to kiss Cait's cheek, making her laugh. He ran away to join Osk and the other young men, dodging two peddler wagons set up to sell wares. She watched Jack, and Gideon watched Cait. "He's all grown up," she said softly, a touch of sadness in her voice.

Gideon squeezed her hand. "Because ye took him in and raised him to be a good man."

He drew her with him through the gathered soldiers and villagers. Once again, only men remained outside. Wives and daughters were locked up in cottages due to James's arrival.

"When is the next holiday?" he asked.

"I believe that would be Saint Valentine's Day," Cait said.

"Then we must have another festival." Gideon lowered his voice. "One without royalty and soldiers making everyone retreat home at nightfall."

They walked under the raised portcullis into the bailey. Musicians played a lively tune and the few ladies who braved the night danced around one of the fires, laughing while the men looked on. Gideon had ordered all the Mackay men and Sinclair men in attendance to keep watch over the king's soldiers. Bàs stood, his arms crossed, near his pale horse on the far side of the fire near the doors to the keep. He scanned the bailey, nodding to Gideon as they walked closer.

"Have Lady Ella and Lady Hannah already left for Girnigoe?" Cait asked. "I wished to speak with them about the school."

Bàs looked down at her. "Aye. Cain and a contingent of Sinclair soldiers escorted them out about a quarter hour ago. James accompanied them at the last minute. I doubt anyone knows he has quit Varrich."

Gideon frowned. If anything happened to James in the hands of Sinclairs, their clan would be condemned by anyone loyal to the House of Stewart. "If anyone asks, say he retired but let his steward know that he is safe at Girnigoe."

"Cockburn already knows," Bàs said and continued to stare out at the bailey.

Gideon looked to Cait. "We can still discuss the school," he said. "We can make plans in the library."

She nodded, a small smile on her lips, and he led

her into the great hall. Mathias sat at the long table with a lass on his lap, and several ladies and two Sinclair men stood near the hearth watching a chess game.

"The kitchen is closed," Mathias said, as they walked over. The poor man had been working for two days straight and even before the festival. "It will reopen at dawn."

Gideon nodded to him. "Thank ye for your efforts. There will be more coin in your pay for the unexpected royal encampment."

"We're going to look at some books in the library," Cait said. "For the school I will be starting." Her voice was a little loud so everyone in the great hall could hear her excuse for walking toward the stairs with Gideon.

Mathias smiled. "Have a lovely time *reading*."

Gideon had to quicken his step to keep up with Cait toward the archway that led above. She slowed once they reached the steps. "Would ye rather I lower a rope down outside my window?" he whispered.

She huffed. "There's no privacy at Varrich. The whole town will be abuzz that I walked up these steps with you. My only hope is that the soldiers will be up to something that will give the villagers something else to talk about."

He grinned in the darkness. "We can only hope."

She punched his arm. "You wouldn't understand. You aren't a woman with a reputation to uphold."

"The reputation of being the icy queen?" he asked softly.

"Yes," she retorted, starting to climb. "It has

taken me years to convince the men that I wish to be left alone."

"Because ye really wish to be left alone?" he asked, following her, the light from a candle he stole from a sconce lighting her way.

"Yes… No…" She stopped on the stairs, the curved walls flanking her, and turned to look into his face. At two steps above, their faces were even. "I've always wanted to be left alone, ever since I was a girl and rude men would leer at me when I walked by."

Gideon's smile faded. "No lass should be leered at."

"And then I was married off to keep Willa and myself fed and sheltered. When Benjamin was killed, I used his rantings about me being a cold fish to continue to keep people away from us. I learned to use a sgian dubh and kept myself strong, so we didn't require help from a man to survive. I lifted wood and cut peat and set traps and kept us safe. And part of my strategy was always to appear uninterested in men."

She turned back around but did not proceed. "So, if people begin to talk that I'm open to men, it will make my established way of life more difficult."

Gideon rose to the next step. "Cait," he said, softly, pulling her arm to get her to turn back to him there on the winding staircase in the tower. Candlelight flickered over her pinched features, but even so, she was beautiful. "I'll allow no lewd men to threaten your peace here in Varrich." She lifted her eyes to his, and he touched her chin. "And I don't know how anyone could ever think ye are a cold fish." He brushed his thumb against her bottom lip and watched her exhale.

"I did," she whispered. "For a very long time." She blinked as if tears pressed there, and his heart ached to take them away.

He leaned in and kissed her gently. Pulling back, he stroked his thumb over her cheek. "Sometimes," he said slowly, "we convince ourselves that we're something we're not. We bend our world around that impersonation to protect ourselves from an ugly world that requires us to be something else."

Must we always be who Da said we are to be? Gideon swallowed, the scar across his cheek feeling tight. Where his scar sat on the outside, Cait's half-healed wounds filled her inside.

"Maybe…" he started and stopped. "Ye don't need to remain alone to be safe."

She nodded the slightest amount there in the darkness, and he forced a smile. "Now let me show ye a book I have hidden away in the library."

"A book?" she asked, the sadness fading from her face. "You really want to show me a book? Alone in your library?"

He smiled. "Aye, actually."

"Well then" — she turned — "I'm curious." They continued their climb while he kept his focus on the gentle sway of her hips.

Taking her hand at the second landing, they walked down past the king's room to the library. It was cold inside, and he went directly to the hearth to start a fire with the candle he'd brought from the sconce. A bit of wool, dry peat and twigs, a flame, and a gentle stream of breath, and the fire caught and feasted, growing rapidly. He turned back to find

Cait lighting two more lamps.

She carried one with her over to the shelves and inhaled fully. "It smells like…" She turned her face to him, smiling. "Wisdom. Years of knowledge from so many brilliant minds all contained right here for anyone to acquire if they have the ability to read." The firelight glowed against her, highlighting the glossiness of the curls around her smooth face.

"Aye," he said, walking over. "I've always found such guidance in my library, whether here or at Girnigoe. I wish to bring over more books and have several translated from the ancient texts into English." He walked to the far end of the shelves and reached up to the highest level. "Like this one written in a difficult language from the far east. There are seven books in all, but one of them has… interesting drawings."

He brought it over to the table but kept his hand on the cover. "'Tis a book about…" His mouth remained open, and he frowned, closing it. "Perhaps ye would consider it lewd to show ye."

She smiled at him, her hand covering his, but he didn't budge. "I'm curious now."

"But after we just talked about men looking—"

"Are you showing these to me to make me want to do lewd things with you?" she asked.

He felt the trap easily. "Perrrrhappss," he strung the word out, and she laughed.

"After last night, I think I know what you want," she said. Her teasing smile made him relax, and he slid his hand off the volume.

"It is a text on love between a man and a woman," he said.

"Maybe I could use it to tell Willa about the act now that she is—"

"Nay," he said, his voice loud, and he lowered it. "This is only for women who have some experience."

Her brows pinched even though she held her smile. "Now I am *very* curious." She opened the book.

Gideon looked between the page and Cait's face. She stared at a graphic rendering of a man with a woman impaled on top of him. She held her bountiful breasts and he held her hips as if rocking her there. Cait blinked and turned the page to an image of the man mounting the woman from behind like they had done. "They better have a sturdy bedpost," she murmured and looked at him, laughter in the tilt of her lips.

He exhaled, relieved. "There are some wrapped-around positions." Gideon watched her turn the pages with gentle fingers, her other hand flattening against her breast. He pulled off his woolen jacket, feeling quite warm and hard beneath his kilt. "I'm looking for a translator, because the words are said to be filled with ancient wisdom on giving a lass immense pleasure."

The firelight enhanced the blush he saw rise in her cheeks, her eyes cast to the pages spread open on the table. "What would Pastor John think of this?" she asked, shaking her head. "He would probably swoon."

Gideon touched her chin, turning her lovely face toward him. "If ye are thinking about Pastor John right now, I'm definitely not presenting this book to ye the right way."

She laughed quietly, her eyes alight with mischief. "What should I be thinking about, Gideon Sinclair?"

He moved a step closer, bending his head to her ear. His lips moved slowly against the satiny skin there. He didn't touch her otherwise, letting her move away if she wished, even though he prayed to God or the devil that she wouldn't.

"Cait, lass," he whispered. "I would have ye think about your favorite picture and how delicious it will feel to have me do such things to ye." He moved back to peer into her eyes, which were dark in the shadow.

"I can choose any?"

"Or none," he said. "Or all."

Her grin broadened, and she turned back to the pages laid out before her on the table, leafing through it. She paused at a picture of a woman kneeling before a man, his erect jack buried in her mouth. Cait glanced at him. "That feels good to you?"

Bloody foking hell yes. His mouth went dry. "Aye," he said.

"Like when you…" She paused, "to me?"

"Aye." He nodded, meeting her gaze.

"Hmmm," she murmured like she was selecting fabric for a new gown and turned back to the pages, flipping slowly. Each graze of her fingertip against the pictures was like her slaking him, and he nearly groaned at the torture. When she got to the end, he held his breath as she turned to him.

Cait's teasing smile was gone. He watched her pull her bottom lip into her mouth to wet. He exhaled softly, his hand going to his hard jack. "Lord help me, lass, but just a look from ye renders me as hard as a rutting bull."

She looked down, watching him run his hand over himself through the wool of his kilt. "The lord may not help you," she said, glancing up at him with a wicked grin, "but I might." She reached for him under the woolen wrap, her cool fingers encircling him to slide up and down to the base.

"Bloody hell, Cait," he said, his eyes shutting at the pleasure of it. They snapped open when she shifted, and he saw that she'd knelt before him. He murmured a string of Gaelic about miracles granted as her mouth enveloped him, sliding along him, tasting him.

His hands tangled in her hair, as she moved against him, to and fro as if they mated. "God lass," he groaned, her tongue swirling and testing the length of him. For several feverish minutes she worked until Gideon could stand no more.

"Och, but ye will undo me, Cait," he said, his hands on her shoulders. Raising her to stand, his lips opened over hers, delving into her damp, perfect mouth. Her fingers worked the ties of his tunic, and they broke the kiss only to tug it up and over his head, leaving his chest bare for her hands to skim across. Chills of passion rippled across him, and his hands slid down to her skirts. He rucked them up, seeking her. His lips moved to her neck where her pulse raced. He reveled in her shallow breathing and stroked lower between her legs. She spread them, allowing him access to her heat, and he nearly knelt in praise at the sweet wetness that had gathered there.

Cait moaned as he rubbed against her briskly. Her legs spread even more, and when he looked up, she was unpinning the stomacher over her stays. He bent his head beneath her heavy skirts to taste her and heard her breath catch as he loved her there. Sweet. So heavenly sweet. The sounds of her pleasure and the heat of her coiled his need tighter.

She pulled at his arm, and he came out from her skirts to a sight that caught his breath. *Cait. Sweet bloody hell, Cait.* She leaned back against the table, her breasts freed from her stays to perch on top of them. She held her skirt up so that the crux of her spread legs showed, inviting him into her warm, wet body.

"Gideon," she said, her voice thick with want. "I want you in me. I don't care what way." Without so much as a glance at the book, Gideon turned her to face it on the table, his hands under her skirts on her hips. He held himself poised between her legs, bending her forward so that she braced against the heavy oak table.

He palmed her soft breasts, teasing the hard nipples until she pushed her naked arse back against him with a moan. Back arched, she beckoned him, her own fingers dipping in front to open herself even more. The sight made his crucial, all-encompassing need swell. He found her entrance and thrust into her, his hands spanning the front of her to hold her steady.

Cait's gasp turned to a moan, and she arched back into him with each thrust he sent into her, lifting her off the floor with the power. He shoved against the layers of skirts, wishing they were gone but wasting no time to strip her naked, not when they were moving in such a rhythm, building higher like a fire growing out of control. His fingers found her in the folds of petticoat, her most sensitive spot in the front as he plunged into her from the back.

"Yes, yes," she crooned as he rubbed there, his fingers moving with expert technique to wring cries of pleasure from her open lips. Her breasts hung before her, plump and pale and jiggling in a way that made him lose control.

They were beasts together. Their bodies undulating as one toward a goal of complete release. His powerful thrusts sunk in and out of her open body, her back arched, and he bent forward over her until he felt her tense around his shaft. A high-pitched moan came from her, and his own passion exploded with a deep roar that filled the room.

Holding her close against the curve of his body, they rode out the waves of pleasure together, their fast inhales and exhales slowing. He felt the slack weight of her and wanted nothing more than to pull her against him and curl up in the comfort of his bed. But they were in the library bent over a table.

He rested his lips against her nape. Hair undone, her curls hung over one shoulder, and he kissed the soft exposed skin as he withdrew, turning her in his arms. Cait's eyes were closed, a soft smile on her parted lips as she still drew in air between them. She blinked open. "We both got to choose," she said.

"Choose?" he asked, marveling in her rosy cheeks and languid happiness.

"From the book, which page to perform."

For that moment, despite the king, his treason-hunting steward, and the task of integrating the clans, despite all of that, everything was perfect in Gideon's world. "Aye," he said. He slid his fingers into her hair to cup her head. "And now I want nothing more than to carry ye above and hold ye all night."

"Just hold me?" she said, teasing in her voice.

His brows rose. "I can do a lot while holding ye."

She laughed lightly. "Perhaps you should bring along your book."

He picked up his tunic and her cape, turning to her. Breasts still out and rosy, lips damp, and hair half out of its lovely woven arrangement, Cait looked ravished. She was perfect.

Footsteps sounded loudly in the hall. *Bam! Bam!* "Gideon." Someone tried to open the library door, but he'd locked it. "Are ye in there, brother?" Bàs called from the hallway, his voice loud and full of battle. Something was wrong, very wrong to make his solemn brother race to find him.

"Aye," Gideon called back, placing the cape around Cait's shoulders before striding to unlock the door.

Bàs stood there, his face stern. It was the face of death.

CHAPTER SEVENTEEN

Visigothic Code Book III, Section I, 654 AD

If any freeman should carry off a virgin or widow by violence, and she should be rescued before she has lost her chastity, he who carried her off shall lose half of his property, which shall be given to her. But should the crime have been fully committed, he shall be surrendered, with all his possessions, to the injured party; and shall, in addition, receive two hundred lashes in public; and, after having been deprived of his liberty, he shall be delivered up to the parents of her whom he violated, or to the virgin or widow herself, to forever serve as a slave.

Visigothic Code Book III, Section VI, 654 AD

Where a Ravisher is Killed. If any ravisher should be killed, it shall not be considered criminal homicide, because the act was committed in the defense of chastity.

Cait yanked up her stays, pulling them tight. The stomacher would have to wait. She pulled her cape around her shoulders and hastily coiled her hair around her head, pins sticking in wherever she could find purchase as she flew down the winding staircase to follow Gideon and Bàs.

"His name is Eric O'Neal, a mercenary from

Ireland that James hired with his band of men to train his royal troops," Bàs said. "His brutality is known on and off the battlefield."

"Who did he harm?" Cait called.

Gideon glanced over his shoulder to see Cait catching up and waited to steady her on her flight down the stairs.

"The lass's name is Deirdre Mackay," Bàs answered.

"Holy Lord," Cait murmured. "Fiona's granddaughter." She yanked up her skirts to chase after the long strides of Gideon and Bàs as they crossed the now empty great hall. "Where is she?"

"In the bailey."

"The bailey?" Cait yelled. "What is she doing there if she's hurt?"

He didn't answer, but as they ran out the entryway, Cait stopped, eyes wide.

"She's bloody well mine," the huge man yelled from the center of the bailey. He hauled the terrified woman up against him, his paw over one of her breasts.

"Let go of her!" one of the Mackay men demanded, his sword out. Several other men stood with O'Neil, dressed in the same blue plaids with felted tams on their heads. Their swords were out, ready to defend the evil whim of their leader.

"After I'm done with her," O'Neil said, his words somewhat slurred, probably with whisky.

Deirdre's eyes were wide and wet with tears. Her dress was ripped at the shoulder, and a trickle of blood marred her lips as if the man had kissed her brutally. He now pawed her before her own people.

"Now if ye would all leave us be for a spell, the lady and I can finish what she started in private." The monster reached down and stroked himself. "Or I can fok her right here before ye all."

Gideon and Bàs drew their swords, and the Mackay men backed up, letting them through. "Unhand her," Gideon demanded, his voice like thunder. "And have a chance of winning your life against a Horseman of God."

A shiver ran through Cait as she watched the man who had lovingly pleasured her such a short time ago transform into a menacing warrior. Gideon's jaw was like granite, hard and unyielding in the firelit night. He hadn't donned his tunic, so his chest and arms were bare and mounded with thick muscle. Shoulders broad and back straight and powerful, he towered over all the men in the bailey, the tattoo on his upper back reminding them all who he was. The Horseman of Justice.

Mackay and Sinclair warriors held torches high, flooding the bailey with light as they watched the new chief of Varrich handle such wanton evil.

Bàs stood beside Gideon and said nothing. He'd grabbed an ax from somewhere. It was engraved and polished, and he swung it in an arc like he was said to do before executing the condemned. It whistled as it sliced the winter air.

The O'Neil suddenly had a *mattucashlass* in his hand, and he raised it to Deirdre's exposed neck. She gasped as he pressed it there. "Not a step closer or it slides across her lovely throat, Sinclair. Either of ye."

A line of blood sat along her neck. "Deirdre!"

Fiona's frantic voice came from the gates, and Cait ran toward her. She threw her arms around the older woman, stopping her from running headlong into the war for her granddaughter.

"Gideon will save her," Cait said as Evie ran up beside them. Together, all three hurried closer, catching Gideon's slow, unemotional words. His voice was like thunder.

"When the Lamb opened the third seal, I heard the third living creature say, 'Come!' I looked, and there before me was a black horse. Its rider was holding a pair of scales in his hand." He recited the words from Revelations. A chill that had little to do with the words and everything to do with the threat in Gideon's voice sent bumps along Cait's skin.

"Are ye going to throw a scale at me then?" O'Neil yelled, and a couple of his men laughed, although some looked serious and a bit unsure as they stared at Gideon. He didn't have the set of scales that Cait knew sat on his table in his bedchamber, but he did hold a mighty sword that seemed to thirst for blood, the firelight glinting off it as if salivating in anticipation.

Bàs began to speak, his voice just as slow and methodical. "When the Lamb opened the fourth seal, I heard the voice of the fourth living creature say, 'Come.' I looked, and there before me was a pale horse. Its rider was named Death." As he turned his ax in another arc, the other two Irishmen lost their smiles.

Gideon lowered his sword, his eyes locked on his prey. "Let her go now, unharmed, and ye may suffer only exile from Varrich. If more harm comes to her,

I'll cut your heart out, stuff it in your mouth, and mount your head on my gate." No one moved, the graphic image now in their minds. But the Irish mercenary continued to hold the frantic girl while Cait held her grandmother.

"I will kill him myself," Fiona whispered between her clenched teeth.

"I'll carve his eyes out," her usually gentle sister agreed.

Did the monster yet know his life was forfeit no matter what he did? Desperation would make him kill Deirdre.

As if realizing that, too, Gideon moved his hand to Bàs, so that his brother lowered his ax. Standing off to one side, Cait saw a dark grin cross Gideon's face. Cait couldn't see his eyes, but she guessed there was the promise of death in them. "Will ye stand before God with this innocent girl's blood on your hands, O'Neil? Ye gamble with your eternal damnation. Will God forgive ye when ye have been properly warned of His mighty wrath? Ye are not ignorant, therefore ye will be given no mercy."

"Shut your mouth," O'Neil yelled, his wicked smile gone.

"Will *your* mouth be perpetually open as ye scream in the flames of Hell?" Gideon said, his voice even, uncaring, and cold as the wind off the winter sea.

Cait felt her own throat narrow with the tension. Gideon Sinclair wielded words as lethally as he wielded his sword. He did not shift, only stared at the man as he continued his assault. "The lass is named Deirdre. She is innocent, a lamb, one of

God's sweet bairns. Not a man on the battlefield whose blood can stain your sword without God's condemnation. The lass's suffering is the key to your perpetual torture in Hell, O'Neil. Let her go, and God may still have mercy on your soul."

"'Tis not worth it, brother," the man standing next to O'Neil said. "Let her go."

"Bloody foking hell," O'Neil yelled, and shoved Deirdre away from him so hard that she fell to the ground before Gideon's feet.

Cait ran forward to grab the girl, lifting her as she sobbed. Cait glanced at Gideon's face and nearly froze. The apathy in his voice before had been a ruse. Oh, he cared, and the Irishman would die.

Pulling Deirdre away to fall into Fiona's arms, Cait turned. Her hands went to her mouth as Gideon surged forward with no warning at all, into the line of Irish mercenaries, Bàs at his side.

Without a word or a moment to consider, Gideon judged Erik O'Neil as guilty. Before the man could even lift his sword, Gideon used both hands to slice down and across, the force behind his blade strong enough to cut right through the man's neck. Gideon's roar filled the bailey as Evie screamed behind Cait. The Irishman's head hit the frozen ground and rolled, its eyes wide with surprise. God would decide the fate of his soul now.

Bàs also swung at any of the mercenaries who raised their swords, killing two immediately. Gideon skewered another one, yanking his bloodied sword from the man's chest to turn on the brother of O'Neil, the one who had encouraged him to surrender Deirdre.

Gideon's sword swung toward the brother and froze two inches from his neck. The man's eyes had closed, waiting for the strike that Gideon didn't deliver. "Ye have won your life by not lifting your sword against a Sinclair," Gideon said, his voice like God's thunder.

The remaining five mercenaries dropped their swords on the ground, not willing to risk going against the two deadly Sinclairs, who may have God's favor as His Horsemen. For a long moment, Gideon stared at them, and Cait knew he was judging them. Did they know they must win his mercy to live to see the sunrise?

"Kneel!" Gideon ordered. "Before the Sons of Sinclair."

First one and then the others began to kneel before him, last being the O'Neil brother. Gideon looked like he would lop off their heads as he lifted his sword. He raised his powerful arms, the muscles in his back and shoulders showing his massive strength. "I spare ye for following this monster against an innocent lass, but ye are to leave Varrich tonight." He turned outward toward the silent crowd of Mackays, Sinclairs, and James's men. "No one is above the law, both God's law and my law."

Several men yelled "aye." They were probably Sinclairs. The rest looked stunned and afraid of the Horseman that Gideon had become before her eyes. His only mercy given with absolute surrender.

He showed me mercy.

Gideon scanned the mass of onlookers pressing in through the gates. "Let it be known that harm and threats to innocents will not be tolerated by

the Sons of Sinclair, on any of our vast territories.
Those who viciously cause mayhem outside the
battleground or rape will find themselves presented
immediately for judgment before God by me, my
brothers, or one of our loyal warriors. If ye have an
angry and uncaring heart that yearns for such evil,
leave here now with these mercenaries while ye
still have breath and blood to do so. And may God
have mercy on your black soul."

"All hail Gideon Sinclair," Keenan Sinclair
yelled, raising his fist in the air.

"All hail Gideon Sinclair," at least half the men
in the bailey repeated, their fists in the air.

"Loyalty to the Sinclair Horsemen," Keenan
yelled.

"Loyalty to the Sinclair Horsemen," the same
men repeated, the winter wind swirling in gusts
around them. Their combined voices, hard with conviction, sent gooseflesh all over Cait's skin. Her
breath stuttered as her heart thumped hard beneath
her breast.

The king wasn't present, having gone to Girnigoe,
but his steward watched the proceedings with
shrewd eyes. What would he tell his sovereign? That
Gideon and Bàs had killed several of his mercenaries, exiled the rest, and had the bailey swearing
allegiance to the Sinclairs?

Gideon and Bàs walked over to Cait and Deirdre
where Fiona and Evie dabbed at the line of blood at
the girl's neck. Deirdre's eyes grew wide as they approached. "They're protecting us," Cait said,
stepping in front of her to stare into Gideon's stone-
cold face.

Blood had splattered across his forehead and the white scar on his lower cheek, drying there in a macabre design of power and war. He still wore nothing except his kilt and boots, the cold no discomfort to him with such rage molding him into the warrior she knew he was.

"You're frightening her," she said, putting her palm out to him.

He stopped, his gaze connecting with Cait's, and she watched him take a deep breath, his chest expanding with it. As he exhaled, the vengeance seemed to seep out of his eyes, purging the demon that had shown itself there. His face softened into one she knew. What did killing do to his soul? Even momentarily?

"Is she well?" he asked.

"She will be," Cait said.

Bàs also wore blood splatter. He nodded as if he'd waited to hear how Deirdre fared and walked back to the remaining mercenaries with Keenan and several Sinclair warriors. They'd make sure the exiled gathered their dead and departed.

Cait looked back at Gideon. "Don't put his head at the gate. You will undo all the good you've done with this festival."

He blinked, his brow furrowing. "I must calm everything back down," he said. "I do not want ye out here if there's more violence." He waved Keenan over but spoke to Cait. "Ye should go back to the Orphans' Home tonight."

A dismissal? No, it was a precaution. "Jack is here somewhere," she said, her chest hurting so that she pressed against it. People hurried about the bailey in random crisscross paths as if being set in motion again. The music was over, the mood heavy and subdued after such horror.

"I'll find him and send him home," Gideon said and turned to Keenan. "Make sure the ladies all get home without further harassment."

Keenan stopped before them. "I'm certain no one cares to cross ye further tonight by touching your woman or her ladies." *His woman?* The casual words flipped about inside Cait, adding to the mix of emotions already bubbling there. "But aye," Keenan continued, "I will make sure they are safely home."

Gideon stepped up to Cait, catching her chin gently. She looked into his eyes, trying to ignore the blood evidence of who he was. "Bar your door to all but Jack," he said. A look of pain moved across his face, and he leaned toward her ear. "I'm sorry I'm not holding ye in my bed tonight." He backed up to look deeply in her eyes. "But I must be the Horseman tonight."

"Of course," she murmured. Cait watched him walk away into the jumble of people. "Of course," she whispered again. Gideon Sinclair was the Horseman of Justice. *And I am his woman?*

. . .

"The Sinclairs are not above the king," James said as he stared at Gideon across the table in Varrich's great hall. His steward, Vincent, had no doubt told him of the events of the previous night as soon as he returned that morning from Girnigoe.

"Agreed," Gideon said, "but this is my castle and

grounds, and ye were not present. I'm certain had ye been here last night, ye would not have let Eric O'Neil rape that lass while her kinsmen watched in horror."

James rubbed his bearded chin. "Nay, I would not, but he was a damn good fighter, and you killed him and three of his men and sent the others away."

Gideon purposely lifted his cup and took a drink to give a casual impression. "Were ye planning to have a fight on your hands here, your majesty?"

"Ye think that Sinclairs could be your enemy?" Cain asked from his seat farther down the table where Mathias had provided a meal for them. Cain's severe tone was less strategic and more unveiled anger.

James chose Gideon's gaze to meet. "If I had thought that, you'd be in shackles or dead."

Years of hiding his true feelings stopped Gideon from laughing. With the network that Gideon had fostered and the territories that the Sinclairs held or had relinquished to loyal clans, Irish mercenaries or not, the Sinclairs would conquer the Stewarts. Gideon did keep a smile. "And, since I'm alive, it seems ye believe our word that we back ye and your policies as God's anointed king."

James nodded, pacified, and took up his tankard of ale. "True." He drank and set it down to point at Gideon. "But do not go around beheading any more of my men."

"Aye, your majesty, as long as they don't go around raping or murdering my people." The tone was tense, almost threatening, so Gideon smiled. "Although our Master of Revels could use some bruises, I think."

For a moment James frowned, but then he seemed to relax. He laughed. "Ho now! The handsome lad was playing his part." He pointed at Gideon. "No persecuting the crowned merrymaker at Christmastide. That is a law."

Gideon raised his cup to agree, keeping his smile. No doubt Cain was frowning down at the end, which was why he'd seated him out of the king's line of sight.

Vincent Cockburn watched the king, Gideon, and Cain closely. With as much staring the man did, Gideon was sure the king's steward, too, studied the slight changes in a person's face and stance to determine if they lied or spoke truth. Would he see that Gideon had orchestrated the king's responses?

James smiled and grabbed up a bun slathered with honey from a plate. "One more feast tonight at Varrich, and then we move on to Girnigoe and Dunrobin Castles." He'd already put the nasty business of rape and beheading behind him.

"Aye," Gideon said with a smile that he didn't even try to make genuine. Another God damn celebration when Gideon would prefer to put this whole Hogmanay behind him. The festival had started out well, but then King James's arrival had tangled everything, including whatever had started between Cait and him.

The look on her face last night in the bailey had been a mix of shock, fear, and doubt. Doubt in him? He leaned back and crossed his arms over his chest. *Daingead*. He'd allowed her and everyone in the bailey to see his deadly side. It was necessary to quell any further violence, but did Cait think he could turn that on her or any innocent?

He would talk with her about it, not let the questions stew in silence. Nothing good came from letting doubts rest. Without further information and explanation, doubts grew instead of diminishing, tainting trust that he'd nurtured with her.

"I must see to my duties this morn," Gideon said. He still needed to ferret out Jack. Cait would be frantic to find out that he hadn't found the boy. He'd sent a rider off to Girnigoe to see if he'd headed back there with Osk and the lads he'd been seen with before the incident with the mercenaries. Bàs had helped Gideon search among the soldiers last night, but none reported seeing the lad. Hopefully, he'd found a willing maid to teach him about tupping and was blissfully unaware of the worry he was causing. Gideon stood up from the table and gave a little bow to James.

Vincent Cockburn also stood. "A word, Lord Gideon."

Gideon kept his annoyance in check and walked over to where Vincent stood near Cain. "Aye."

Vincent kept his voice even so that it carried to the king. "There's a thief among your citizens."

"At Varrich?" Cain asked.

"Yes, last night," Vincent said.

"Mayhem and thievery last night," James said, shaking his head. "A sorry way to begin the new year."

Gideon frowned, waiting for the steward to continue. He looked like a cat with a bird in his mouth, pride making him stand straight, his eyes connecting with Gideon's. "During the incident with the O'Neils, someone took the opportunity to enter the king's quarters above and steal a sack of gold coins."

"Which is treason," James called, shaking his head. Although, he seemed to care more about his honey bun.

"And must be dealt with in the most severe terms," Vincent said. "In Edinburgh by a court made up of the king's counsel."

"Are ye certain it wasn't just misplaced?" Gideon asked. He wouldn't put it past the steward to take the coins himself and blame it on the populace.

"I've searched high and low in the room and the king's clothes and personal effects without discovering it," Vincent said. "Theft is the only choice left."

Gideon checked his curse, feeling the tension build again in the back of his head. "I'll make inquiries within the village. With my gift of shillings to each house, there was no immediate reason for such a crime."

Vincent's eyebrow rose. "Shillings when there's a bag of gold sitting nearby? Thirst for gold will always make men and women act unwisely."

"Finding it will be a priority," Gideon said with a brief bow and strode toward the doors. He heard Cain extricate himself as well and follow behind him. They stepped out into the early morning sun. "Damn," Gideon said as Cain stopped beside him.

Cain snorted. "Aye, bloody damn. I don't know how ye survive going to court as much as ye have. 'Tis more hellish than a bloody battle."

"By far," Gideon murmured, but his attention was caught by movement outside the gate. Bruce was striding forward with his hold on another man, nearly lifting him off the ground to keep him moving. "Jack?"

Gideon strode forward to meet them as Bruce dragged Jack inside the bailey. "Where have ye been, lad?" Gideon asked, relief at seeing the boy alive and unmaimed alleviating some of the tension of Vincent's accusations.

"I didn't do it," Jack said, his eyes wide, suddenly making him appear younger than his sixteen years.

"Do what?" Gideon asked.

Cain came beside him. "What is this about?"

Bruce threw a velvet bag on the dirt before them. "Found this on the lad. A bag of coin with the king's crest on it."

Bloody hell. The day was growing worse by the second.

CHAPTER EIGHTEEN

Magna Carta clause 39, 1217 AD

No free man shall be seized, imprisoned,
dispossessed, outlawed, exiled, or ruined in any way,
nor in any way proceeded against, except by the
lawful judgment of his peers and the law of the land.

Bam! Bam! Bam! "Cait! They have Jack!" Alistair's voice cut through the door.

Holy Lord. "Who has Jack?" Cait called as she shoved the heavy bar aside. When she'd woken to realize that he hadn't returned during the night, a sickening dread had set in right away. She'd dressed quickly, waiting for word.

Alistair stood outside, panting from his obvious haste. "The king's men, his steward. Gideon is going to have him executed."

"What? Gideon wouldn't do that." She ran inside, passing Rhona, to grab her cape, throwing it on. "What's Jack accused of?"

"Stealing from the king," Alistair said, and Rhona uttered a prayer of help behind her.

"No," Cait whispered. Had Jack taken it upon himself to take some of the king's obvious wealth to distribute to their neighbors like she had done while Hew Mackay ruled them into starvation? But things had improved since Gideon had taken over the clan. No one was starving, and Gideon had just delivered five shillings to each household to purchase supplies from the tinkers and peddler wagons.

This is my fault.

"Where is he?" she asked, following Alistair out into the frosty morning. The rare sun that shone down did nothing to thwart the chill that had settled into her bones.

"In the bailey of the castle. Bruce dragged him in, and now the king and his steward are questioning him." Alistair sneered. "And, of course, the Horseman of Justice is only too willing to pass judgment."

Gideon wasn't like that. He'd see reason. He'd have mercy if Jack were guilty. Jack was just a boy, an often-foolish boy. Cait blinked back tears as she ran next to Alistair along the road, passing neighbors and soldiers alike. Hands in tight fists, her legs hit her skirts as she hurried, ignoring the pebbles pushing through her slippers. *What have you done, Jack?* Guilt tried to trip her. What type of an example had she been to him? Had he been trying to help? Had the temptation been too great for an unthinking boy?

She and Alistair hurried into the bailey where a small crowd had gathered. "Stay back," one of the king's soldiers said, barring her way.

"He's my son," she said.

The soldier looked at her as if she were a liar since she was young.

"Cait," Gideon said, and walked toward her.

"What's going on?" she asked, staring between his face and Jack who stood with his head down, his hands tied behind his back. "You said you'd bring him home safe."

"He's judging your son," Alistair said, and she flashed her open hand at him, waving off his spiteful words.

Gideon placed strong hands over her shoulders. "Bruce found him in one of the barns this morning. There was a bag of the king's gold in his pocket."

She looked into Gideon's face. "Does he admit he stole it?" she whispered.

Gideon exhaled. "He says he didn't."

Cait closed her eyes, her head dropping in relief. "Then he didn't do it," she said, her words barely above the sound of a breath.

"But the king believes he did," Gideon continued, and her eyes snapped open.

"If he says he didn't do it, then he didn't."

Gideon's lips were tight. "I'm trying to piece this all together, but they want to take him for trial in Edinburgh."

"No!" she yelled out, causing many in the bailey to look her way. "He's just a boy." She shook her head. She threw a hand out toward Jack. "He is cold and probably hungry." She yanked off her cloak. "Put this around him."

"I'll do what I can. For now, he has to stay in Varrich's dungeon."

"The one I stayed in?" Tears filled her eyes despite the anger tightening her face.

Gideon leaned in to her ear. "Aye, and there will be food and drink and blankets."

She nodded but couldn't bring herself to utter any thanks. "Can I go to him?"

"Not now. Vincent Cockburn is still questioning him." Gideon bent to meet her eyes. "I will do

everything I can to help him, Cait. Even if that
means going with him to Edinburgh to make sure he
has a fair trial."

"And leave the comfort of your castle?" Alistair
asked and shook his head.

Gideon's concerned eyes lifted to look past Cait
toward Alistair. In a flash, the mask of anger re-
placed the softness in his features. "Ye add pain with
your bitterness. If ye do not desist, I will make sure
ye meddle no more."

"Will you kill me, too, Sinclair?"

Cait stepped between them and pushed her cape
into Gideon's hands. "Put my cape on him," she
whispered.

Gideon's face was tight with fury as he pulled his
gaze away from Alistair and strode back through the
bailey to Jack. He placed Cait's cape around Jack's
shoulders.

The boy looked up at the warmth and weight,
glancing toward her. His eyes were swollen, trails of
tears down his cheeks. It caught her breath and
twisted her heart so much, she nearly doubled over.
He gave a small shake of his head.

She sucked in a shallow breath. "He didn't do
this," she said and swallowed. She nodded, letting
him know she believed him. Because she did. He'd
never lied when confronted with his misbehavior.
"He did not."

Spinning on her heel, she pushed past Alistair.
She had plans to make, for she would do anything to
save her children, whether Gideon judged her guilty
or not.

• • •

"But you told me to get the king from his chambers," Jack said to Vincent. The boy stood before the seated king and his steward. Gideon chose to stand next to Jack so he wouldn't think he was against him. Bruce remained behind the king as if guarding him even though there were at least a half dozen royal soldiers stationed inside the keep along with Sinclairs, including Cain.

"Why would I do that when I knew our illustrious sovereign was spending the night at Girnigoe Castle?" Vincent asked, staring Jack straight in the eyes. Gideon watched every nuance and twitch of everyone involved.

"I can't answer that," Jack said.

"And how did you end up in the stable with the king's gold coins on you?" Vincent asked.

Jack raised his bound hands to the side of his head. "I... When I didn't find the king in his apartment, I went back down the hall—"

"With his bag of coins that you saw sitting on his desk," Vincent said.

"Nay," Jack said. "Something hit my head from behind. I... I don't remember anything until I woke to Bruce kicking me, and I saw I was in the stable."

Without permission that Vincent Cockburn would never give, Gideon slid his hand along the boy's head. A large bump was raised there with the crustiness of dried blood. He held some up on his finger. "The lad was hit in the head. There's proof of that."

Vincent frowned and his left eye twitched, showing that he was already bent on charging the boy guilty. This was far from a fair trial.

Bruce cleared his throat. "I...kicked him in the head to wake him this morn."

Gideon turned to him. "So, there'd be no other bruises on his body from your way of waking someone up?"

Bruce shrugged, his face drawn. "He could have other bruises. I wouldn't know. I probably kicked him elsewhere, too. I'd seen the sack of royal coins and lost my temper."

"I didn't take them," Jack said, his words like those of a child, his body curling in on itself as if he knew that no one believed him.

Gideon looked to King James directly. "I believe the lad." His voice held the strength that Jack was unable to muster. "There's no proof that he did this—"

"There's no proof that he did *not* do this," Vincent said, his voice full of condemnation. "That is the law. An accused person must prove he's not guilty to be considered so." He frowned fiercely. "As the Horseman of Justice, I was under the assumption you knew the laws of Scotland." He turned to the king. "Another reason we should bring Jack Mackay back with us to Edinburgh where he can be tried for treason."

Skewering the king's steward with his *mattucash-lass* in the middle of the great hall would not make King James trust the Sinclairs any further even if it would feel bloody good. "I know the laws, Cockburn. I've studied them since I was breeched. I've also studied the ways people proclaim without words that they're guilty with their eye twitches, higher or lower pitched inflections, dilating pupils, shifting feet and gazes. People tell the world their lies without confessing with words." He stared hard at Vincent. "And this boy is not lying. Ye, on the other hand"— he tipped his head slightly to the side as he studied Cockburn—"are."

"Nonsense!" Vincent yelled.

Gideon turned his gaze to Bruce. "And so are ye, Bruce Mackay." Not being as schooled in deception, Bruce looked down at his feet before raising his eyes to shake his head at Gideon. He just about shouted his confession. Probably without realizing it.

"Enough," James said. "I must go above to prepare for tonight's gaieties. Put the boy in the dungeons, and I'll decide what is to be done with him on the morrow."

What that meant was that James would talk with Vincent, and his bloody steward would convince James that Jack must be taken to Edinburgh for trial. And Cait would be undone with fury and grief.

What good were all his years of learning and reading if he couldn't save a simple boy from lies being said about him? Why were Vincent and Bruce so set against Jack? He was nobody of any power, and yet they had made him look like a criminal. Gideon frowned deeply, his hands fisting as he watched James's guards lead Jack back to the dungeon below that he'd occupied all day.

James walked toward the stairs, two of his soldiers with him. Vincent began to follow but stopped next to Gideon and Cain where they still stood.

"Watch yourself, Sinclair, else the king will not see your clan as loyal to the crown."

Gideon leaned toward the short man. "Watch yourself, Cockburn, else the king will see your head on the end of my pike."

Cain's solid hand fell on Gideon's shoulder. For the first time ever, it was one of his brothers restraining Gideon instead of him stopping one of them from a foolish act. His usual cool, strategic mind had burned to ash at the thought of Cait's reaction to all of this.

Vincent's eyes widened the slightest before his face pinched into a mask of indifference. "Threatening me is the same as threatening the king. Shall we add you to the dungeon with the lad?"

Cain pulled Gideon back with pressure on his shoulder. "Don't push our hospitality," Cain said, his words solemn and fierce. "Sinclairs are loyal to King James and the crown. Ye are just a soft, little man who hides behind his name."

"You dare—" Vincent began, but Cain cut him off.

"Watch yourself, Cockburn. The Highlands are a wild and dangerous place, and ye may find yourself standing before God sooner than ye think."

Without another word, Cain yanked Gideon's arm, making him follow him out of the keep, leaving the fuming steward behind. Cain dropped his hold as they emerged into the lowering sunlight, and they walked toward the stable that housed their personal horses, Gideon following as his mind churned with vengeance.

Inside, Cain huffed. "They are lying."

"He bloody foking wants to hang that boy," Gideon said, his words seething. "But I don't know why."

Cain crossed his arms to match Gideon's stance. "And ye won't until ye calm down enough to think it through."

"I have," Gideon said, running his fingers along his scalp to the back of his head that ached.

"Nay. Ye are thinking of Cait," Cain said.

When the bloody hell had his brother become so perceptive?

Gideon released a long exhale and dropped his arms. "She will be devastated if anything bad happens to Jack. He's a son to her."

"Ye need to distance your thoughts about her to help the lad."

"I know." Gideon shook his head. "I just…don't know if I can."

"Ye can, and ye will." Cain held up his hand where the ring Gideon had given him sat. "Ye are the Horseman of Justice, Gideon Sinclair, and ye will see justice done. Figure out the whys behind the deceit. Let the consequences of failure be thoughts for another day."

Gideon took a deep breath. "Aye." He must separate his feelings for Cait and what this would do to her from his objective mind. It was the only way to save the lad.

• • •

"Alistair overheard the whole discussion inside the keep today," Cait told Rhona, her voice low so that

Trix, Libby, and Willa wouldn't hear as they moved about preparing their meal. They sat with Viola on her small bed. "Alistair says Vincent Cockburn and Bruce are lying about Jack, and that the king is listening to them over Gideon."

"Bruce's soul will be damned for certain," Viola said, shaking her head. "He cares nothing for the child. There's only greed in his heart."

"If Gideon can't help Jack, I'm going to get him out of Varrich so he can run," Cait said, her throat tight. What would Gideon do if he caught her? How would she ever be able to hide her guilt from him?

Rhona murmured a prayer under her breath. "Where will Jack run?"

"I'll send him to a woman in Clan Gunn, a friend of my mother's. There he can decide which way to go. Otherwise, the king will take him to Edinburgh where the steward and Bruce's lies will see him hanged."

"Why are they doing this?" Rhona asked.

"I'm sure Bruce is getting gold for it," Viola said with a sneer. She patted wee Henry's back as she held him snuggly against her.

"But why Vincent Cockburn?" Rhona asked.

"Maybe 'tis a test to see if the Sinclairs are loyal to the crown," Cait said, her chest pinching. Had the steward seen something between her and Gideon and sought to test his loyalty? Vincent knew Jack was one of her children, and that Gideon would try to help because of their relationship, attachment, whatever this was between them. If that were the case, Cait was even more guilty in what was happening to Jack right now.

She pressed her palms together as if in prayer, touching the point to her lips. "If Gideon cannot do anything, then I will," Cait said and dropped her hands. "Tonight, before they can take Jack away."

"There will be guards," Viola said, switching her bairn to the other shoulder.

"I was in the dungeon and know where the key hangs outside the cell," Cait said.

"If they've left it there," Rhona said.

"I'll wear my thief's clothes. Maybe I can sneak past the guards."

"And maybe you'll be caught and thrown into the dungeon with Jack," Rhona said, her voice rising enough to make Willa glance over. They all looked worried, of course. A quiet tension swelled like over-risen bread dough within the cottage ever since the news of Jack's arrest.

Cait squeezed Rhona's hand. "Then you'll run this home without me, you and Viola." She glanced at the dark-haired woman. Viola nodded, a softness in her eyes. Acceptance and forgiveness of her sins may not have been something she expected.

Rhona was already shaking her head, tears in her eyes. "You could hang."

"I have to try to save him," Cait said and sniffed back her own tears. "Or I can't live with myself."

"Gideon—" Rhona started.

"Is loyal to his clan. He will not go against the crown, and even if he did, I would not have the blood of a civil war on my hands, either," Cait said. Her chest hurt. Was this what a broken heart felt like? *I cannot.* She could not let what could have been between her and Gideon weaken her resolve to save Jack.

Cait gazed between Rhona and Viola. "Pray for us tonight." They both nodded, and Cait stood. "I need to dress."

"Aye, of course," Rhona said.

Cait wore the same gown she'd been wearing, but under it was not only her slim black trews but also her black tunic. She didn't bother with stays but bound her breasts like she did when wearing her thief's clothes. If Trix and Libby wondered why Cait wanted her hair braided and wound into a tight knot instead of letting it hang free, they didn't ask.

"Be good to one another," Cait said at the door after giving them each a hug.

"You're coming back?" Willa asked, her face pinched with near panic.

"As soon as I can," Cait answered and smiled. "You, Rhona, and Viola can run the home if I'm delayed."

"And me," Trix said.

"And me," Libby said a second behind Trix.

Cait bent down, first taking Trix's hands. "You'll be the one to make everyone remember to smile and keep going with joy in their hearts." She waited for Trix's nod, even if her smile was forced.

Cait took Libby's hands. "And you will teach them all to weave hair in the prettiest way and be the voice of reason when things go astray."

Libby nodded, her face serious. "I will," she said with the gravity of an oath.

Cait stood straight, and Willa threw her arms around her. Cait wrapped her in a warm hug, kissing the top of her head. "You're a woman now, Will," she said. "You are strong, clever, and beautiful." She pulled back, looking into her sister's face. "And you never need marry if you do not wish it. I love you."

Cait looked up. "All of you." They murmured back the same, Trix wiping under her eyes. "Now go on in. I have…a royal feast to attend," she said even though they were bright enough to know that was not the agenda for the night. She turned and walked toward a lone figure who had promised to wait for her.

Alistair walked with her down the road. "You don't have to come," Cait said.

"I'll do anything to help you, Cait," Alistair said, his voice full of conviction.

"Then pray for us."

"I'd do more than that. I am not some weak woman or child. I can help you."

She placed her hand on his arm. "Thank you, but I don't want you to get pulled into this mess."

"I would lay down my life for you," he said, vehemence in his voice.

She exhaled. "Do not put more blood on my hands."

They entered the open gate with barely a nod from the guards. Most of them were James's men with a few of Gideon's stationed about, everyone watching everyone. Fiona and Evie were inside the bailey and hurried over to Cait. "What are you two doing here?" Cait asked.

"We heard about poor Jack." Fiona nudged Alistair out of the way, and the two sisters looped their arms through Cait's to escort her inside. "We're here to support ye like ye did for us when Deirdre was in harm's way."

Cait took a steadying breath. "Thank you," she whispered. "Don't make me weep now."

The sisters laughed, but it was filled with the heaviness that Cait felt. She walked inside where musicians played for the king even though their tempo lacked the gaiety of the first day of the festival. The ladies accompanied her over to the long table. On the first night of the king's visit, Cait had sat at the top of the table with Gideon. Even though she saw him standing with Cain and Bàs there, she sat with Evie and Fiona much farther down.

He'd had his back to her when she'd entered but turned as she'd walked across between the ladies. Cait's heart squeezed. He looked…magnificent. He wore his crisp white tunic with his bright plaid, the sash over his chest. The scabbard holding his sword shined at his side as if it were a part of him. Beard clipped precisely and thick hair that was given to curl, the man could attract any lass. Cait longed to walk over there.

His gaze followed her, his face hard and serious. The truth about the scar on his jaw reminded her how vulnerable he had been, but that was long ago. Gideon had a role to play that would keep the land peaceful. And for that, she must distance herself and her actions from him. *Even if you're with his child?* She banished the thought as swiftly as it came. She must focus on her eldest child right now. Jack needed her.

Before she could sit, he was behind her. "I'd have ye sit up with me," he said and then nodded to Evie and Fiona. "Good eve, ladies."

Cait turned her face to his, and her heart squeezed at the questions she saw in it. "You need to focus everything on getting Jack out of this mess. I'd not distract you."

He pulled her to the side with a gentle tug on her arm and bent his head closer. "When ye are not near me…" He rubbed his jaw. "I fear the worst and cannot concentrate, Cait."

She looked up at him. "What is the worst? That I am frightened, tortured, hanged? For that's all I can think about for Jack." She squeezed his arm, willing him to understand. "He was the first child who came to the Orphans' Home, Gideon. He was only a skinny, abandoned lad of six then, the same age as Willa. It took him a full year to trust I wouldn't withhold food from him when I was cross. Before the Orphans' Home, Jack knew only of the dark side of humanity." She shook her head. "We need to do whatever we can to win him back."

"I will," Gideon said. "With ye at my side."

She shook her head, looking down. Her plan would not work if everyone were watching her at the top of the table. "You are the Horseman of Justice," she said and met his gaze again, swallowing hard at the questions she saw there. "And you must do what you're excellent at, convincing the king of Jack's innocence."

"Gideon," Cain said several feet behind him. "James is asking for ye to start the feast. His royal gut is empty." Cain rolled his eyes heavenward.

Gideon squeezed her hand. "Trust me, Cait. I'll do everything I can for him."

"Except start a civil war," she said. "Don't bring

more bloodshed into this for me or Jack."

"Gideon," Cain said again.

"We are not done talking tonight," Gideon said, stroking her face with his thumb. He did not wait for her refusal or nod but turned away to stride purposely over toward James. Bruce sat down next to Vincent. Apparently, his new friendship had elevated him.

Cait sat between Fiona and Evie, much to Alistair's quiet annoyance. "Don't trust that monster, Cait," he said, leaning over Fiona.

Fiona shoved him back. "He saved Deirdre. He is the best of men." Evie nodded vigorously, giving Alistair a mean look.

Alistair grumbled something and grabbed a bun from the plate that had been deposited on the table. He walked off in frustration.

Cait watched as Gideon raised a toast to King James and thanked him for blessing their Hogmanay with his royal presence. James made a short speech of false platitudes and food was brought out by Mathias and the two older ladies he had hired from the village. James smiled and ate. Vincent ate and watched everyone with hard eyes. Bruce ate and drank more than any of them. Gideon spoke with Cain, his gaze taking in the occupants of the room. Once it had landed on Cait, and she held her breath. When he purposely looked away, her chest squeezed, and she could not swallow her bite for a long moment.

He is just following what I asked. Jack is the priority. But the chasm that was growing between them still hurt after she had finally let her guard down to trust. With one last drink of her wine, Cait pushed back from the table. "I think I've had enough of kingly speeches and food."

"We will go with ye," Fiona said.

"No. Stay." She leaned in to them. "Eat as much of this good food as you can. I'll take some for the children." She took two buns, sliding them in her drawstring pocket for Jack.

CHAPTER NINETEEN

*Queen Elizabeth of England, Tilbury Speech while
waiting for the Spanish Armada fleet,
9 August 1588 AD*

*"I know I have the body but of a weak and feeble
woman; but I have the heart and stomach of a king,
and of a king of England too, and think foul scorn
that Parma or Spain, or any prince of Europe,
should dare to invade the borders of my realm: to
which rather than any dishonor shall grow by me, I
myself will take up arms, I myself will be your
general, judge, and rewarder of every one of your
virtues in the field."*

"And ye, my sweet Bess, are as honeyed as your buns."

The elderly woman laughed at Mathias's words and pretended to skewer his heart with her wooden ladle as the other woman snorted.

"She's sweet for ye only, Master Mathias," the other lady said. "At home, she's quite ornery most of the time."

"That's because my sister treats me terrible," Bess said. They were Sinclairs, elderly sisters from Girnigoe who were staying at Varrich for the festival.

Cait took a full breath and stepped in the back door from the courtyard on the side, the same one she'd brooked when returning Gideon's ring that fateful night of their first kiss. *Do not think of him.*

"Good eve, Mistress," Mathias said, turning toward her with a devilish smile.

One of the sisters smacked him. "No flirting with Gideon's lass, else ye find your head at the gate."

He looked aghast. "All I said was good eve."

"'Tis the way ye said it," the second sister said, and pushed a tray of honey buns into his hands.

But Mathias still looked expectantly toward her. Cait forced a smile. "Being farther down the table, I failed to get one of your famous honey buns, and I was wondering if I could claim one to take home for the children."

"Certainly." The first sister scooped up four of them, wrapping them deftly in a square of kitchen linen for her.

"Thank you," she said.

"Ye can accompany me back out," Mathias called from the archway.

"No," Cait said. "I will… I need to stop at the privy before returning."

Mathias winked at her. "If ye need any help with your skirts—"

"Master Mathias!" the second sister yelled.

"Anne there will be happy to help ye," he finished, laughing. He turned and strode down the dark corridor toward the great hall, whistling. He would pass right by Cait's destination, the door to the dungeon. Hopefully, since the guards were changing routinely, they'd leave the top unlocked, since Jack was down at the bottom behind a locked cell door.

Trust me.

She'd trusted Gideon with her body and had started to with her heart.

He is judging your son. Alistair's warning beat at her hope. Gideon must do what was best for them all, and that meant preventing a civil war over the life of one boy. No, rescuing Jack was up to her, especially when she was the one who'd given Vincent Cockburn a reason to target him.

There were several rooms off the kitchen corridor, and Cait slipped into one that smelled of herbs and apples. A cold cellar from where she'd taken food before during Hew Mackay's rule. Her fingers shook as she untied her skirts and unpinned her stomacher that had hidden her dark tunic. Stepping lightly out of the skirts and bodice, Cait wrapped them up and set them on a barrel near the doorway. She grabbed the pocket with the honey buns from the petticoat. Fishing out her dark mask, she tied it in place and peeked out the door. The corridor was vacant and dark. Her *sgian dubh* lay sheathed along her hip where it was tied, just in case. Not that it would do her much good with a two-hundred-pound guard blocking her way.

Cait moved on the balls of her feet, keeping her boots quiet as she snuck along the corridor. *Move fast.* Mathias could come back at any moment if all the honey buns were snatched up. Fingers following the rough stone wall, she made her way to the circle of light given off by the sconce before the door that led down into the pit of Varrich Castle. And the door was cracked open.

Thank you, God.

She pushed against it, grimacing at the tiny creak

in the hinge, but no guard spoke up. Silence remained as thick as the darkness. The steps down to
the cells were uneven and completely in shadow.
Cait stuck to the left side, her fingers guiding her
against the damp wall. She shivered at the chill, remembering her night down here when she'd
remained awake as long as she could, listening for
rats.

Dim lamplight beckoned her forward, but she
took care. Falling to her death would not help Jack
in any way. Ears alert for a guard behind her, she
continued until the lamplight showed the last three
steps, and she turned the corner to hurry to the dim
cell.

"Jack," she whispered, her gaze sweeping into the
shadowed corners. "Jack, 'tis Cait." Her hand curled
around the bars of the small window at the top, and
she caught herself before she could fall back as it
swung outward. "Jack?"

The door was unlocked, and the cell was empty.
He's escaped.

Cait turned and ran, grabbing the torch from the
wall to light the steps this time. Being able to see
helped her climb quickly. Near the top, something
stuck halfway out into the path. She would have
tripped over it on the way down if she'd not stuck
close to the left side. Even so, she'd barely missed it.
Lord, she could have fallen.

As she stepped up to veer around it, Cait gasped.
It was not a spare torch or neglected weapon. No.
She held her torch higher, following the arm to
where it attached to the guard slumped against the
wall. "Oh God," she whispered. The blood that

drenched his shirtfront from the slash along his throat meant there was no reason to check for breath. The man was certainly dead, murdered for doing his duty. "Oh God, Jack."

Throwing her torch in the iron holder at the top of the stairs, Cait slipped out of the dungeon, carefully closing the door so that it looked to be locked. Was Jack still in the castle? Had he dodged out through the kitchens while she was getting undressed or before she'd even left the feast?

Down the hall, the faint sound of music told her that the meal hadn't been interrupted by anyone realizing a man had been murdered. Cait whipped around to run back where her gown was hidden and gasped as she slammed into a solid chest.

Crushing hands gripped her arms, holding her there. "What did I just catch?" Bruce Mackay asked, his breath stinking of whisky. "And what are ye wearing?"

• • •

Gideon's hand wrapped around the seat of his chair as the king droned on and on about the pleasures of Edinburgh.

"You should all come," James said. "The three remaining Horsemen, loyal to Scotland and her king." James turned to Cain. "Perhaps we can assign a fourth to act as your dead brother. It would be splendidly better to have all four Horsemen backing me."

"Perhaps I can find someone," Cain murmured, but Gideon was paying little attention.

Cait had left. She had barely stayed for the first course. Had she left because she felt guilt at eating when Jack was in the dungeon? Gideon had sent food down to the lad but hadn't mentioned it to her.

Gideon's fingers clenched the edge of the chair, partly to stop himself from rising and going after her. She wanted him to focus on clearing Jack, but her absence was more of a distraction than her presence could ever be.

Under the table, Cain's foot knocked Gideon's boot, and he looked over at King James. The man stared expectantly at him. "What say you?" James asked.

Cain spoke up. "A tapestry of the Four Horsemen would look quite rich here in Varrich." Cain turned to Gideon. "Do ye not agree, brother?"

"Aye," Gideon said, "quite rich indeed."

James looked mollified and smiled broadly. "Then as soon as I return, I'll commission one. A gift for your hospitality here at Varrich."

"Apart from beheading your best warriors," Cockburn said on the other side of the king.

"Aye," James said, his smile turning to a look of rebuke. "Apart from that."

Off to the side, where the archway led to the kitchens, a flurry of motion pulled Gideon's gaze. Bruce marched out, carrying...*Cait?* Her arms flailed about, her legs kicking as Bruce held her sideways like a slippery log.

Gideon stood, his chair toppling over behind him. Bruce held Cait dressed completely in black down to the knit mask over her face, a pocket clutched in her hand. *Bloody foking hell.* She was dressed for sneaking around. She was dressed as a thief, and he was certain he knew who she had been trying to steal away.

Gideon met Bruce halfway across the hall. "Put her down. Now."

"I caught this lass sneaking around the dark corridor," Bruce said. Unable to step around Gideon, Bruce set Cait down. "The same thief who ye caught in your bedchamber, I'd say." By now, the musicians had stopped their playing, and the whole room was hushed to hear.

Before Gideon could stop him, Bruce yanked up the mask covering Cait's face. She stood there in the center of the great hall, wearing slim black clothes, her hair tied back in a knot at her nape. Cait's cheeks were red, and she breathed heavily from her impotent exertions against Bruce's hold. Flushed and beautiful and guilty.

A murmur rose behind Gideon. He stared into her eyes. Hers were beyond worried. They were frantic. Not only had her son been seized, but now she was showing the village just how unwholesome she could be. *Damn.* She was breaking the law again, a law against the king by trying to free someone accused of treason, which was treason itself. Helping her now went against all he'd been raised to be, who he was as the Horseman of Justice. *Bloody foking hell.*

Gideon met Cait's eyes. The question lurked there. Would he let her be dragged away?

Dammit. He'd never find a credible document to justify what he was about to do. He stood tall. "Bloody hell, Bruce," Gideon called as Vincent and

James came forward. "Ye have ruined my surprise for the king."

Bruce's look of triumph dimmed. "What say ye?"

Gideon turned to James. "Cait Mackay is to provide entertainment tonight. She has an incredible talent." He gestured toward the ceiling.

James's gaze followed his hand. "What talent?"

Gideon's gaze held Cait's. "She can fly."

"Holy God," James said, taking a step back. "Is she a witch? Witches conspired to keep my young queen from me."

"Nay," Gideon said. "Cait is an acrobat." He indicated her dress and slowly uncurled her fingers to get her to drop the small sack that seemed to hold buns. "'Tis why she changed from her usual garments and wore a mask." He threw the buns at Bruce, who jumped back, dodging them. "So as not to be judged ill by her neighbors for her talent." He turned back to James. "After the last course, she was to come out and perform."

"Perform?" Cockburn said. "This sounds like a ruse. Fly?" He scoffed. "Do not lie to the king."

"We'll set up now then," Gideon said, pulling Cait's arm.

Cockburn glared at him, his neatly shaved beard unable to hide the sneer on his mouth.

"Ye will be amazed and entertained, your Highness," Gideon said.

James smiled broadly. "Good fun." He waved his fingers at Cait, and Gideon pulled her to the side.

Cain followed them. "What are ye planning?" he asked, looking between them. His brother had to know how bad this looked and that it was not planned. Cain's strategic mind would easily see that Gideon was covering up something dangerous.

Gideon met his brother's stare. It was full of questions and concern. Gideon did everything by the law. This was not in any lawbook. "There's a ladder in the bailey," Gideon said. "Get Osk and Bàs to help ye pull down one end of the two cloths tied tightly to the center iron ring."

Gideon's gaze turned to Cait. She swallowed, looking up, and pointed to the middle of the ceiling. "That iron ring holds the lengths of fabric that is tacked to the corners of the room. Drop two of them to hang straight down together."

Gideon nodded to Cain. His brother looked between them, his face a block of granite. Was he condemning Gideon? *I deserve it.* If George Sinclair was in attendance, he'd shame him, which was worse than any sword strike.

Cain turned, striding off and waved Bàs to follow him. They intercepted Osk on the way out. Bruce walked over, his arms crossed and his frown in place. Vincent followed.

"How do you come by this talent, Mistress Cait?" Vincent asked.

"'Tis…a favorite pursuit," she said. "To escape the many responsibilities of raising children at the Orphans' Home." She glanced toward Gideon, her eyes beseeching but also thankful.

"Cait," Fiona called, and she and Evie hurried over to her. "Ye did not tell us." She flapped her hand toward where the ladder was being moved.

"It was to be a surprise," Cait said weakly.

The ladder was placed, and Bàs climbed quickly

up to detach the ends of two lengths, one red and one green.

"Is that why ye wanted to leave so quickly?" Evie asked.

"Of course," Gideon said, his jaw aching. He dropped to his knee, untying Cait's boots, slipping them each off as she balanced. Cait had not sat with him because she was planning to break Jack out of the dungeon. She did not trust him to save the lad, so she had taken the task into her own hands, regardless of the risk.

A murmur rose as the two fabric lengths were dropped to pool on the floor below. Gideon grasped Cait's hand, guiding her away. He leaned in to her ear. "Just a few of your tricks should appease the king and anyone who thinks ye had other plans." They reached the fabric, and he pulled her around before him, staring her in the eyes. "For ye did have other plans," he whispered.

Cait lifted glassy eyes to his, and his anger turned to concern. She opened her lips and paused, as if unsure what to say. "Jack is innocent of all of it. *All* of it."

The musicians started up a lively tune to accompany her show, but Gideon just looked down into her pinched face. "All of it? There is more?"

She nodded. "Trust me. Please."

She turned away from him and grabbed the fabric in her two hands. The crowd gasped as she wrapped her legs easily in the length and climbed up thirty feet into the air within seconds.

Trust her? Hadn't he asked the same of her? Hadn't she decided to still take matters into her own hands? And yet she wanted him to trust her when she did not allow the same for him.

When the audience gasped, Gideon stood back, looking up. His own breath caught. Cait, legs spread in a wide *V,* was upside down. She flipped one way, her hip catching the fabric to her, keeping her aloft. She arched her back in a glorious display of flexibility and strength, and the room erupted in applause. Even the king clapped with enthusiasm.

The arch was followed by a graceful spread of her legs, splitting apart completely in the air. Her strength and grace were amazing. Everyone gasped. She brought her legs together into a narrow *V* and wrapped the lengths of fabric around each leg. Crossing the fabric in an *X* at the base of her back, she arched forward, pausing at the top. Then she fell forward, flipping down in a graceful, head-over-feet fall.

Gideon's arms went out without a thought as to how he would catch her from such height, but the cloth caught her halfway down. Everyone clapped and cheered for the executed flip. Cait climbed higher, wrapping the cloth in intricate patterns around her body. Gideon held his breath, probably with everyone else in the great hall, waiting for the drop that must be coming.

With full commitment to the fall, Cait let go, her arms out straight above her head as she unwound, falling down the length in a graceful whirl. The fabric caught her, and her legs wrapped once again, letting her straighten upright in the air. The pose brought Gideon a flash of memory, of Cait, naked and glorious with her hair draped around her shoulders, wrapped in the velvet of his bed curtain. She was utterly amazing, and brave, and strong.

By now, the people in the room were on their feet, cheering for her talent.

From the archway, one of James's soldiers hurried straight to the king. Despite Cait climbing higher, preparing for another feat, Gideon watched.

The king's smile dropped, and he looked up into the face of the soldier. Vincent, being close enough to hear, looked directly to Gideon, his eyes narrowing. Gideon stared back, not sure of what he was being accused. Vincent's gaze rose to Cait. Or of what *she* was being accused. Had she already freed Jack when Bruce found her? Had she been spotted by the posted guard?

As Cait descended to the floor, the room cheered and clapped. The smile on her face was false. Worry and desperation haunted her eyes as they fastened onto Gideon. *Trust me. Please.*

Bloody hell, Cait, what have ye done?

• • •

"His throat was slit from behind," Vincent said, his sharp eyes boring into her own. Cait sat in a chair at the table, her back straight, her eyes on her accusers.

"Are ye saying a mere lass could sneak up on one of your trained soldiers and slit his throat?" Gideon said. He stood beside her as if he were her hired councilor. Cain and Bàs stood beside him while Vincent and Bruce stood beside the king opposite her.

Vincent threw a hand out toward the fabric that

still hung in the middle of the empty great hall. "As she so displayed, Cait Mackay is no mere lass. She's unnaturally strong and able for a woman."

Gideon scoffed. "Stronger than your man twice her size?"

"Perhaps she used witchcraft to still him," Vincent yelled back.

"Nonsense," Gideon said. "Or else she'd have done the same to Bruce to escape his hold." Gideon's hands flexed by his sides as if reaching for a weapon, even though James had ordered the Sinclair brothers to surrender their swords in his presence. Gideon lowered his voice, but the seriousness in his tone still made his words demand attention. "Like I've said, and ye saw yourself...I hired Cait to entertain the king. She had nothing to do with the boy's escape or the death of your man."

Cait concentrated on keeping her breathing even. Gideon was lying for her, lying to the king to whom he'd sworn allegiance before God and his clan. He was lying to keep her from arrest and the gallows, and she wasn't helping at all.

She cleared her throat. "I left the great hall after the first course was served and walked around to the kitchen door. Mathias and his helpers can attest to my entry."

"And you didn't tell him why you were there," Vincent said.

She lifted her eyes to his. "I didn't wish for anyone to know of my talent. 'Tis not the usual comportment of a lady."

Vincent pointed at Gideon. "And yet he apparently knew to hire you."

"I saw her practicing in the forest behind the Orphans' Home," Gideon said. "I was astounded by her mastery. When the king arrived, I wished to present an entertainment he may never have seen before."

James rubbed a spot on his forehead. "'Tis true I've never seen the likes," he murmured. Vincent exhaled long.

Cait sat up straighter, looking toward the archway. "You'll find my outer clothing in one of the larders in the corridor. I donned my mask there, hoping my neighbors wouldn't know it was me performing. When I came quietly up the dark corridor, waiting for Chief Sinclair to announce me, I was grabbed and unmasked." Her eyes narrowed on Bruce, who sat casually eating yet another honey bun. "Now I may be ridiculed for wearing immodest clothing and spinning through the air."

Bruce snorted. "Ye are ridiculed already for being a thief in the village, despite Chief Gideon letting ye work off your punishment."

James stood, frowning. "Work off your punishment. What's this?"

Gideon rubbed his aching jaw. "She stayed a night in the dungeon and then worked for days to put together this Hogmanay Festival."

James stepped before Cait, his eyes squinted as if he could read guilt or innocence in her face. Didn't Gideon do the same? After a long minute, he spoke. "Mistress Cait, I see nothing but a desire to please me with a unique performance. You were ultimately in the wrong place at a time when someone else was creating mischief." His gaze slid to Bruce, who suddenly stopped chewing, his eyes growing wide.

Cait dropped her gaze to the king's pointy-toed shoes. "Thank you, your majesty." She bobbed slightly, unable to fully curtsy in trews without drawing more attention to her attire.

"I release you, Mistress Cait. Go home to your children," James said.

"All of my children except Jack," she whispered. She couldn't help it, but the frown it brought to James made the hairs on her nape rise.

"Jack Mackay is a man now," James said. "He's no longer one of your children, and he will be tried as a man, especially for his involvement in the assassination of my guard."

Before she could say anything, Gideon took her arm. "I'll see her home."

"Nay," the king said. "Send someone else. I would have you here to devise a strategy to find the culprit. I assume the entire castle has been searched."

"Aye, your majesty," Bruce said.

"Bàs," Gideon said, and his brother came forward. "See Cait home." Gideon walked with her toward the entryway of the keep, his brother following. They stopped just before the dark antechamber. Gideon's voice was low. "Did ye let Jack out?"

"No," she said. "He was already gone, and the guard was already dead." She met his gaze, his brows pinched, making his face look fierce in the torchlight. "But I would have tried to get Jack out," she whispered and shook her head, looking down. "I wouldn't have taken the guard's life, though."

"Ye do not trust me to help Jack," he said.

How could she make him understand? She took

his hand, looking at the callused palm. Just like Gideon, his hand could tease and give such pleasure, but it could also wield a sword and deliver death just as easily.

She squeezed it and met his piercing gaze. "I've been a young person at the mercy of others." She shook her head. "Jack has been set to take the blame for this, Gideon. There's more to this mess than a falsely accused theft." She pulled his hand to her chest, willing him to understand her. "Vincent Cockburn saw you with me. He thinks you're loyal to me. He could have easily set Jack up to test your loyalty."

"We've already sworn our loyalty to the king. What need would he have to test us more?" Gideon said. "And if that were the reason, why not accuse ye instead of Jack?"

She exhaled in a huff. "I don't know the workings of that man's mind, but it is not honorable." She dropped Gideon's hand. "And Jack couldn't have killed that guard while locked in a cell. Someone else helped. Who would take these risks?"

Gideon's gaze dropped to hers. "Someone who wants you indebted to them, Cait."

Her brows pinched in confusion; her lips parted but no sound came forth.

"Where did Alistair go after escorting ye inside?" Gideon asked.

"I… I do not know," Cait said. She shook her head. "He doesn't have it in him to kill someone, Gideon."

Gideon did not reply. He looked to Bàs who held back. "Take her home safely." He turned back to

Cait. "I'll have a word with Alistair and come find ye after the king releases me."

Bàs came to stand next to her as Gideon turned away, striding back without waiting for her agreement. Cait walked out into the cold night that washed through the bailey filled with royal guards waiting for orders. They spoke in clusters, their eyes ever watching. Most looked at her with either suspicion or surprise and lust in seeing her so attired. But Bàs's silent presence halted them in word and step, and the two of them walked peacefully out of the gates and up the road toward the Orphans' Home.

Cait watched the sides of the path as if she might see Jack hiding in the woods, but she saw no one. *Where is he? Is he cold and afraid? Could he be at home?* She quickened her step, and Bàs easily matched it.

He hadn't said a word the entire walk, so when he spoke, Cait startled, nearly tripping. "My brother has never bent a rule before," Bàs said, his deep voice like the low roll of distant thunder in the silent night. "His whole life has been dedicated to justice and making our clan the mightiest in Scotland. And yet he's not the Horseman of Justice with ye, Cait Mackay."

"He isn't?" she asked, glancing at him.

Bàs stared straight ahead as they walked. "Nay, or he would have punished ye in some fashion for stealing, more so than having ye decorate his great hall." He looked at her. "And he wouldn't have lied for ye tonight."

She opened her mouth to refute him but closed it. What could she say that wasn't a lie? And she would add no more to the many that she'd told that night.

They stopped at the edge of the walkway to her cottage door. "He risks the power of Clan Sinclair for ye," Bàs said, tilting his head slightly as if studying her closer.

"I…" She breathed deeply. "I am sorry for that."

Bàs's questioning expression relaxed, and a slight smile formed on his face. He shook his head the smallest amount. "Don't be." Without another word, he pivoted and walked back the way they'd come.

She watched him fade like a shadow into the night like he truly was the harbinger of death after which he'd been named.

The shutter inside the window moved, and Cait raised her hand to Viola, who peeked out. What would Cait tell them had happened? That she'd performed for the king as a lie to cover up trying to rescue Jack? That he had already disappeared, leaving blood behind? That the king would probably add murder to Jack's sentence when he was found even though he couldn't have done so from behind bars?

Cait's chest was tight, and she exhaled, dreading the questions that were soon to come. She turned slowly and gasped as a tall figure stepped out of the night. "Jack?"

CHAPTER TWENTY

Notes by Gideon Sinclair, Horseman of Justice,
5 July 1589 AD

Exile and banishment may be employed against an
offender by sending them away from their country.
This punishment is imposed by vested authority as a
punitive measure, depriving the offender of the
comfort and protection of his group. Practiced by the
Greeks chiefly in cases of homicide. Practiced in
Rome to evade execution. Before a ruling of
execution, a Roman citizen could escape by
voluntary exile.

"I need to speak with your son, Master Mackay,"
Gideon said to the blurry-eyed blacksmith. Gideon
stood at the man's cottage door behind the dark
smithy. It was late, and he may have been already in
bed.

"Alistair isn't here," the man said, looking over
his shoulder as if to ascertain that his son's bed was
empty.

When he turned back, Gideon's torchlight lit his
face where a large bruise covered one of his eyes.
The older man's lip was also split and swollen.

Gideon held his torch out to him. "I'd inspect for
myself."

As most people do, the man took the torch that
was thrust at him, and Gideon was able to see that

the knuckles of his dominant hand were not bruised or cut. So, he hadn't been brawling. Someone had hit him without him fighting back.

Gideon's gut tightened. He walked past the old man into the scantly furnished home and turned to take back the torch, casting its glow over the room to beat back the shadows. Two beds, both rumpled, sat on opposite sides of the one room that had a table with some dirty dishes on it. A miniature portrait of a woman sat on a small table by the hearth where the man sat back in a chair. Shoulders bent, Alistair's father looked broken.

"I haven't seen Alistair since before dinner," the blacksmith said. "But that's not unusual. He's a man and often stays out all night."

"Ye don't question him about where he goes?" Gideon asked, watching closely as the man set his gaze on the portrait of the woman.

"He doesn't like to be questioned."

"It is said he wishes to leave Varrich," Gideon said.

Edward Mackay snorted softly. "That would be a blessing." He looked to Gideon. "My boy has an unsettled heart. It makes him...angry."

"Did he do that to your face?" Gideon asked, his words even and without pity or accusation.

Edward returned his gaze to the coals of his peat fire. "I'll let him know ye stopped by when he returns."

A proud man, Edward Mackay wasn't going to say that his son mistreated him. "Thank ye," Gideon said.

The man grunted in reply but did not look away

from the miniature of the woman.

Damn. Alistair Mackay was more dangerous than Cait knew. Gideon stepped out into the night. "Where are ye?" he murmured, his gaze sliding from shadow to shadow along the winding path through Varrich. And even more important, did he have Jack?

Gideon strode toward the Orphans' Home. It had been over an hour since Bàs returned from walking Cait home. It had taken most of that hour to convince James that Gideon wasn't going out to organize his troops to attack more of James's men. Cockburn whispered words of unease into the king's ear. Had the steward been the reason for James's sudden appearance at Varrich when his original missive didn't announce a Hogmanay visit?

The windows were lit from within Cait's cottage, and voices talked on top of one another. They were too soft to hear, and he knocked on the door. "'Tis Gideon."

Footsteps sounded, and the shutters opened. Viola and Willa pressed close to the windowpanes to look out at him.

"I would see Cait," he said.

The bar slid off the door, thumping to the ground. Rhona opened the door. "We heard from Fiona and Evie that Jack is missing, taken from the dungeon, and a guard is dead."

"Aye," Gideon said.

Her eyes met his. "Is Cait with you?" she asked.

Gideon's muscles tightened as if anticipating a blow. "She's not here?" His hands fisted. Rhona shook her head, her eyes wide. "But Bàs brought her here."

Viola came up behind Rhona, and they looked at each other. "She… She did not come to the door."

Trix whimpered behind her.

Viola met Gideon's gaze. "I heard voices. When I looked out, I thought I saw Cait." Her eyes were wide with guilt. "I… I went to see why Henry was fussing, expecting that she would knock." She looked at Rhona. "When I said I thought Cait was here, and we opened the door—"

"No one was outside," Rhona cut in. "We looked all around the cottage, but Cait wasn't there." She dabbed at her eyes. "We thought maybe she ran back to the castle."

"We were going to get you," Trix said.

"Gideon," Viola said, looking past him into the night. Her gaze slid to his. "Do you think Alistair Mackay might have anything to do with her being missing?"

Gideon grabbed her shoulders. "What do ye know about Alistair?"

She shook off his hands and pointed. "My hut is in a dense grove about half a mile that way. There is a large boulder that stands as tall as you and then behind it there are two dead birch trees toppled against each other." She swallowed, her small fist curling to lie against her breastbone. "If Alistair has anything to do with all this… Well, he might be there. Jack and Cait, too."

. . .

"Jack is out here?" Cait asked.

"Aye," Alistair said, lifting his glass-enclosed

lamp to shine light on the felled limbs before her. "I saw him in the village and brought him here to hide."

"How did you even know this place was back here?" Cait asked as she maneuvered through the bramble toward a shelter made of logs, branches, and thatching.

"I built it," Alistair said, pride obvious in his voice. "'Tis watertight and hidden away. I'm very capable, Cait. I can build us a shelter out of anything when we leave Varrich."

She sighed softly. "Alistair, I am n—"

"Mistress Cait?" Jack's voice cut through her words.

"Jack?" She ran forward, her trews making it possible to dodge the reaching limbs that surrounded the hut like a fence. "Oh Jack." She threw her arms around the lanky boy standing in the open doorway. He trembled, holding her tightly.

He wore her cape that Gideon had laid about his shoulders in the bailey. "Are you hurt?" she asked.

"No," he answered, although there was pain in his voice, and fear. The same had lurked in her own voice years ago when Benjamin had carried her to Varrich. How could she wipe it away?

She held his face in her palms. Grime and sweat covered his skin. "How did you get out? I went down to see if I could free you, but you were already gone."

His gaze lifted over her head. "Alistair unlocked the door."

A chill started at Cait's nape and trailed down her spine. "Alistair," she murmured. He'd said he'd found

Jack in the village.

"I freed him," Alistair said behind her, "for you, Cait."

Cait turned away from Jack, keeping him at her back. The stark light from the lamp cut across Alistair's face, giving the young man a sinister look. "Did you slice that guard's throat, Alistair?" she whispered.

"What?" Jack said. "You said you'd just knocked him unconscious."

Alistair kept his gaze on Cait. "You need to know, Cait, that I can take care of us once we are together. I can protect you and build you a home. We will have our own children, and we will be happy."

She swallowed hard and shook her head. "I don't feel the same for you. I never will, Alistair. We are… friends, nothing more." And after he'd just killed an innocent man, she could not fathom being friends with him.

Alistair took the few steps between them with rapid strides, his legs tearing through the bramble without care. He grabbed Cait by the arms, squeezing them until she grimaced. "We will be together, Cait," he said through clenched teeth, a crazed look tightening his face, half cast in shadow. "I killed for you. I'll do anything for you." He shook her, his strength evident.

"Let her go!" Jack yelled.

Cait's teeth hit together, and she grabbed for Alistair's forearms. He stopped, and she tried to calm her rapid breathing. *Holy God.* She swallowed, still holding onto his arms, and met his sharp gaze. "I… I see that now," she said, her words breathless with tension.

"Finally," Alistair said, a large smile blooming on his boyish face. He released her, and she nearly fell backward. Jack steadied her.

She needed a plan, but she didn't even know the goal now. Get Jack back home only to be arrested again? Retrieve supplies for Jack and somehow elude Alistair? Could the two of them even get past Alistair without a weapon? Her *sgian dubh* had been confiscated by Bruce and not returned. "Perhaps," she said, "you should give me a dagger, so I can protect myself and whatever children we have."

"Foolish Cait," Alistair said. "*I* will protect you." She took his answer as a no.

"What are your plans?" she asked Alistair. "The king's soldiers are looking for Jack and whoever killed their friend."

Alistair raised two fingers. "I have two horses waiting." He bent them and stroked the back of his knuckles along her cheek. Rough scabs on them scratched against her skin.

"You stole two horses?" she asked.

He shrugged. "They're Sinclair horses," he said as if that made them acceptable to steal.

Behind her, Jack took a small step back, pulling Cait with him. Alistair frowned, his gaze rising to Jack's, and he drew a *mattucashlass*. Cait gasped softly at the sight of blood on the blade.

Cait stood before Jack. "Why don't you retrieve the horses then?" she said. "And supplies for our trip away?"

Alistair's gaze dropped to her, and he smiled but didn't lower the knife. "Aye. I'll get the horses and the food I've packed. Jack can escape on one horse with his pack, and you and I will go on our own."

"I'd stay with Mistress Cait," Jack said. The feel of his support behind her was both reassuring and frightening.

"Nay," Alistair said, his voice snapping.

Cait nodded. "We'll figure that out when you return with our supplies."

After a long pause, Alistair stepped forward and grabbed Cait's wrist, yanking her away from Jack. "I'd speak to you before I go," he said, pulling her into the hut.

"Cait," Jack said.

"'Tis fine," she said, not wanting to push Alistair further.

The glow of Alistair's lamp pressed back the shadows. There was a crudely made table along one side and a central fire pit with an open hole in the thatching over it. There were charred logs in it. The floor was dirt, and a pallet lay on the ground with rumpled bedclothes. Cait inhaled swiftly as she saw the dark stains of blood all throughout the bed and twisted sheets. A small nest made of blankets sat next to the bed as if it once held a bairn.

"Is this Viola's hut?" Cait asked and turned to Alistair. "Did you build this hut for her?"

He seemed to consider the question. "Aye, to both. She was exiled by that devil. Gideon Sinclair is evil, Cait." He leaned forward. "You need to know that." A hardness came over Alistair's face as if some demon had surfaced, brought forth by Gideon's name on his tongue.

Cait's chest squeezed tight. What had Alistair

asked Viola for in payment? "Are you Henry's father?"

"Henry?" Alistair asked.

"Viola's infant son."

Alistair stuck a fingernail between his teeth as if to pick a seed out. "I didn't know she named him that." He dropped his hand. "Aye, I fathered the bastard." He smiled at Cait. "Proof I can give you children." His smile faded. "Unlike that crusty old beggar Benjamin. I hate the thought of him rutting between your legs, Cait, his cock half dead. He said you were a cold fish in bed, but I know you have a fire in you." Alistair rubbed a hand down his front to his obvious erection. "And I'll get you with child without delay," he said proudly.

The thought poured like icy water through Cait's veins. "I don't want to have your children, Alistair. I don't think of you that way."

His face hardened, the stark lamplight making him look even more like the monster he was. "You see me as a boy." With a flip of his hand, he raised his plaid to expose himself, his hand fisting around his length. "I am no boy, Cait. You will see that soon enough." He stroked himself several times, making her back up until the wall of the hut stopped her.

Alistair cursed, but a smile came back to his mouth. "Och, but you make me ache, woman. We must get our mounts before we are discovered." He dropped the front of his woolen wrap. "There will be time to love each other later."

Lunging forward, he grabbed her wrist with the same dirty hand.

"Let go," she said, but he wouldn't be deterred as

he dragged her toward the doorway.

Alistair yanked her up to him, his face looming over hers. "Come now, Cait, don't be a child. You want to save Jack, don't you? Let us get the horses, and I will give him one to escape the hangman's noose. Otherwise, they'll catch him, and I will swear I saw him leave the dungeon with a bloody knife."

"Mistress Cait?" Jack asked from the doorway, having heard her call out.

"Is perfectly well," Alistair said, still looking in her face. "Tell him how well you are."

"I… I am well, Jack," she said. She needed time to think of a way out that would save Jack while also saving herself. She couldn't let Alistair spread lies about Jack, and she needed to give Jack a chance to flee.

"Stay here, lad," Alistair said. "We'll be back quickly with supplies."

"You can move faster if you leave her here," Jack said. "She's a slow walker."

Alistair gave him a wry grin. "Cait is tender and easily hurt. I don't feel she is safe out of my sight." He pulled her close against him. "Let's go quietly, sweet Cait. We wouldn't want to alert anyone to where Jack is hiding."

She stopped herself from struggling and looked back at Jack, standing there, his hands fisted at his sides. "If you think we've been found out, run. Run south toward Clan Dunn." He didn't nod, just stared after her walking away tethered to a madman.

The forest was damp, the snow crunching underfoot as it refroze with the nighttime temperature drop. Behind her, she heard a snap and crunch, and

she spoke to cover it. "Where are the horses?"
Please run the other way, Jack.

"In Fiona and Evie's garden. In case the horses
were discovered missing after I shoed them, there
would be nothing tying me to their disappearance."
He smiled at her and tapped the side of his head
with one finger. "I'm clever, too."

Clever in a self-serving, chilling, monstrous sort
of way. Cait continued to scan the woods as they
walked, their footfalls loud no matter how slow
Alistair led them. *I will scream when I see anyone.*
But then Alistair would say he'd found Jack and that
Jack had killed the guard.

I will say Alistair is lying. Would Vincent
Cockburn believe her? Surely Gideon would.
Wouldn't he?

The worry kept her mouth shut as they emerged
from the woods below the Orphans' Home. *Gideon!*
He ran out of the cottage, and she opened her
mouth to scream.

Alistair covered her mouth with his hand, practically twisting her head to breaking as he yanked her
back into the woods. Cait bit down on Alistair's dirty
palm and twisted in his grasp.

"Be still," he said, spittle hitting her ear. "Or I'll
punish you, Cait."

Crack. Alistair's body jerked, and he groaned.
His hand dropped away from her face as he fell.
Behind him Jack held a large rock, his chest rising
and falling with fright or exhilaration. He shook his
head. "He was not going to help us."

"Gideon," she yelled.

"There!" Bruce yelled from farther down the

path, waving his arm. Several guards were with him.

Jack dropped the rock. It rolled next to the unconscious Alistair, who lay slumped in a heap.

Cait threw her arms wide, blocking Jack as the guards ran toward them. "Alistair killed the guard," she yelled. "He let Jack out after slitting the guard's throat."

Gideon reached her first. "Cait?" His gaze dropped to Alistair and rose to her. Dread mixed with fury on his face. "Are ye well?"

She nodded, wanting only to run into Gideon's arms. Opposite of Alistair in every way, she longed to wash away his touch with Gideon's warmth, but she held back, keeping Jack behind her as Bruce and the guards stopped before them, short swords drawn. "Jack saved me. Alistair had some insane plan to prove himself worthy and take me away. He stole two horses that are in Fiona and Evie's garden."

"Take him and the lad," Bruce said, but Cait held her arms out to block them.

Cait looked between Gideon and Bruce. "Jack did nothing wrong."

"That has yet to be proven," Bruce said. The guards walked behind them, and she could not keep her body between them and Jack.

Two strong arms pulled her forward. She fought against them even though she knew she would not be hurt. Gideon hugged her to his chest. After a moment, she stopped struggling, her body going limp except for slight tremors running through her. His warmth and scent warred against her need to pull away and blame him for letting Bruce and the soldiers take Jack again.

Gideon said nothing, just held her to him. The guards were quiet as they led Jack away and hefted Alistair. "Don't lock them away together," she murmured against Gideon's chest.

"I'll see Alistair in the dungeon and will lock Jack in a room above. He will have a bed and blanket and food. I swear it." The deep rumble of Gideon's words brought a calm to her frantically beating heart.

"Thank you," she whispered, her words small and numb.

He relaxed his hold on her, and she looked up into his face. It was hard to read his expression in the dark now that the torches were gone, marching with Jack back toward the castle. "Jack did not steal those coins," she said. "And he didn't ask Alistair to kill anyone to get him out. Jack just saved me by following me back to town and hitting Alistair when he could have stayed hidden and ran. He sacrificed his freedom for me. You must help him."

"I will," Gideon said. "But I have to do it through negotiation and cleverness. I'll follow him to Edinburgh after the king tours Girnigoe on the morrow. Ye must stay out of this mess, Cait."

"I want to help," she said.

"Ye cannot."

"Why?" She pushed at his chest until he released her.

"Because they may try to seize ye, too," he said and leaned forward, holding gently to her upper arm. "And I'll not let that happen."

"But you will let them take an innocent boy whom I love and have raised?"

"Ye must trust me to handle this without starting a civil war, Cait."

He had asked her to trust him before, and she'd snuck inside to free Jack instead. She had asked him to trust her about not killing the guard, and he had. She pressed her hands to her head. "I'll try."

She heard him exhale, and some of the tension drained out of his frame. He raised his palm to her cheek, holding it gently. She wanted to turn in to it, to push into his embrace, but she held her place.

"Come up to the castle," he said, his voice as alluring as the heat of a flame. "Stay with me tonight."

She closed her eyes for a moment as her traitorous body came to life in anticipation of a night with Gideon. Pleasure, giving and taking, would make the world and all its horrors and anguish fade away. Like strong whisky.

She rubbed a hand across her chest that clenched with worry and despair. *Trust me.* She had told him she would try to stay out of this mess with Jack. Cait looked into his face. "I will likely try to release Jack again if I get too close, and I've just promised to try to trust you to save him legally." She shook her head. "I must go home tonight." With every ounce of mental strength left, Cait turned away from the man who had become her mountain of strength.

I can manage on my own. She had, all her life, before meeting Gideon Sinclair, and she would again. Tears ran down her cheeks as she walked away into the darkness.

CHAPTER TWENTY-ONE

Eyre Roll, Scottish, 1241 AD

A person finding a dead body is named the first finder. If the body was killed in suspicious ways, the first finder shall attend court as witness of the finding. If the first finder does not attend, the entire village where the body was found will be fined.

"No," James said, staring directly at Gideon. "You'll accompany me with your other two brothers to Girnigoe and Dunrobin."

"I promised his mother I'd accompany Jack to Edinburgh," Gideon said, feeling the thump in his chest as his teeth clenched.

"You can catch up to the man after he is held there," James said. "My steward and my small band of faithful soldiers will escort him and Alistair Mackay while we journey on," James said, waving his hand, indicating that his word was final.

Gideon sucked air in through his nose so strongly that James glanced at him, pausing, no doubt, at the look of mutiny on Gideon's unguarded face.

James narrowed his eyes. "Any deviation from my direct order is treason, Sinclair, and I order you to accompany me with the other Horsemen while I am on Sinclair territory. The prisoners leave in a quarter hour, and we set forth to Girnigoe directly afterward."

Gideon stared back, but all he could see was the crushing worry in Cait's face. Without changing his features, Gideon said, "I'll secure my room."

James smiled, although it didn't reach his eyes. "Perhaps someone can fix your bed while you are gone." He turned away to stride with purpose out of the keep.

Vincent Cockburn, a smug grin on his thin lips, nodded to Gideon. "The boy and his mother or the king." He tipped his head and squinted his eyes as if peering into Gideon's mind. "Love and treason or loyalty and loneliness." He shrugged. "I thought you'd choose the woman." He turned around and strode after James. "The lad will be fine as long as he keeps his head." He laughed.

Rage roared up through Gideon, rage so thick he almost drew his sword right there. It must have registered on his face because Cain placed his arm on his shoulder. "He's not worth your neck."

Gideon turned away from Cain's grasp and strode out of the hall, taking the stairs with a vengeance. It was all he could do to keep the beast eating away at his composure inside until he threw open the door to his bedroom. The force sent the door crashing into the wall. He stopped before the still broken bed.

Cait. All he could see was Cait. Cait wrapped in the curtain. Cait smiling or panting with pleasure. Cait holding wee Henry, comforting Willa, and defending Jack. "Oh God, Cait."

He'd lose her if he let Jack go with Vincent. Gideon felt it in his gut. Even if he could somehow follow after the delay and save the boy, she would know he chose to go with James.

Justice is your purpose, lad. Laws, not emotions, make us strong. Decide what is right for the clan and do not waver from it for anyone, especially a woman. They are fragile creatures and make men weak.

His father's words had been heartfelt, one of the few times he'd spoken to Gideon without seeming to wish he were Cain or Joshua. The woman he spoke of was their mother. George Sinclair loved her, and when she died it nearly killed him. He felt weak and despised it, so he became the monster they remembered.

Had Cait made him weak? "Nay!" he yelled to the room.

Ye are my weakest son.

"Nay!" Anger welled up inside, leaking out of his cold bones, infiltrating his muscle and sinew. Fists clenched and teeth bared, Gideon strode over to the polished set of scales sitting on his desk, two stacks of coins balanced on either side. A gift from his father.

Your only purpose is to strengthen the Sinclair Clan. You are the Horseman of Justice.

"Nay!" Gideon swept his arm out, catching the delicate golden instrument. It flew across the room, the coins scattering like rapid bullets.

Crash! The scale hit the stone wall, exploding into pieces, falling to the floor with the coins.

"'Tis not my only purpose!" he screamed, turning around to see Cain standing in the doorway, watching. "I'm a man, not the foking Horseman of Justice!" Gideon sucked in large gusts of air to feed his pounding heart, as if he readied to charge into battle.

Cain kept his stoic features in place and inhaled slowly. He gave one slow nod but didn't say anything.

Gideon's fists, still clenched, rose to press against his forehead, sliding up to the top as his eyes squeezed shut. "Dammit! I'm a man." He opened his eyes to stare at his brother and dropped his hands. "I'm saving that boy for Cait."

Cain nodded, even though he held his grim frown. "I support ye, brother. I will try to appease James even without your skill."

"He will call me traitor, especially if I must steal the boy away."

Cain's brow rose. "'Tis good ye have curated our allies over the years, then." He nodded. "We are prepared for war."

"Cait doesn't want war," Gideon said, doubt and indecision pressing in on him. Everything had been so easy to see before, good and bad, the right action and the wrong action. But now right and wrong were twisted.

"We'll endeavor to avoid it," Cain said. "But ye do what ye must, not because Da told ye how to be, but how your soul tells ye how to be a man of honor."

Gideon took a deep breath. He walked up to Cain, sliding his gold ring from his finger. "Then let it begin," he said, pressing the ring against Cain's chest where it fell, clanging on the floor. He walked out of the room, Cain behind him.

Outside, in the bailey, James walked about, head high, cloak billowing royally in the wind. "Let us off to Girnigoe," he said, smiling as if the whole world and everyone in it were aligned to his purpose.

"Aye," Cain said and went with him toward their readied horses. "The weather will be good for the ride."

James breathed deeply of the chilled air. "I must get to the country more. The air does me good." He looked down at Gideon from where he sat on his mount. "I see why ye are drawn back here away from Edinburgh."

Gideon nodded and took Sgàil's reins from the lad holding them. He mounted.

James looked about. "Where is your brother named for death?"

"Bàs has scouted ahead and will meet us," Cain said.

"Good," James said. "I'll have all three remaining Horsemen by my side as we ride across Girnigoe's two drawbridges." He frowned. "We should choose a fourth horseman, say he's an illegitimate brother, perhaps."

Cain led their procession out of the gates, talking to James, easily distracting him from the fact that Gideon was not beside them. As soon as they turned to ride along the wall, Gideon turned Sgàil in the opposite direction, the direction Cockburn had ridden out ten minutes prior with his band of twelve soldiers and two prisoners.

Gideon pressed in on Sgàil's sides, and his black steed surged forward as if feeling Gideon's need to go to war.

No more blood on my hands. Cait's words helped him to breathe and not just draw his sword and start slashing. He'd use his discipline, learning, and cleverness to prevent war if he could.

Sgàil galloped through the streets of Varrich, making people press back against their cottages to stay out of the way. Gideon focused over his horse's flared ears toward the moor beyond the village. The group under Cockburn's direction had stopped in the middle, and another horse approached.

Gideon slowed his horse and squinted, making out Bruce riding out to join Cockburn. "Damn," he murmured, and leaned forward, pushing Sgàil to catch them. He tore out of the woods, riding directly toward them. Cockburn saw him and directed the soldiers to form a line between Gideon and him with the prisoners who sat with two of the guards.

Out of the corner of his eye, Gideon saw another rider flying along with him, a rider on a pale green horse. Bàs wore his skull mask and black cloak that flapped in the wind. Tilting his head to glance at Gideon, Bàs gave him a nod. As they neared the group, Gideon slowed, and he and Bàs trotted together toward the group.

"Ye are to ride with the king," Gideon said.

"And so are ye," Bàs answered. "Fourteen against one, even one Horseman, isn't fair odds. Cain agrees."

Gideon breathed deeply. Aye, his brothers would go to war for him. He was both angry and thankful at the same time. He nodded. "Two Horseman, back-to-back, though, could win against a hundred."

With the lower half of his face exposed, Gideon saw Bàs smile at the boast. "Easily," he said.

Sgàil walked to meet the group on the moor, his gait slow and restless. He had ridden into battle with Gideon so many times that he could feel the readiness in his rider's seat.

Cockburn held up a hand for them to stop. "Ye two are to go to Girnigoe, Sinclair," he yelled.

"My brother is with the king. God told me to follow ye," Gideon said.

"And God told me to follow my brother," Bàs said, his deep voice and skull mask as intimidating as ever.

Sgàil snorted, his nostrils flaring, and shook his black head. He knew the press of Gideon's heels in the stirrups meant they were about to charge. The display had the desired effect on several of the guards, fear tightening their faces. One glanced upward as if to see an angel watching.

Cockburn brought his horse around, his eyes narrowed in judgment. "You're not needed for the trial."

Bruce pulled his mount up next to Cockburn. "I'm the First Finder. I found the soldier with the slit throat, so I must come to court to present what I saw."

"And I watched Jack hit Alistair with the rock," Gideon said. "So let us head south to Edinburgh."

Cockburn looked at Gideon for a long moment. "We're not going to Edinburgh."

The implications made Gideon's hand itch for his sword. "Ye do not follow the orders of your sovereign, either?"

"I've a different mission, Sinclair," Cockburn said. "One James knows nothing about, although he will soon enough." He lifted his chin as if he could look down on Gideon. "You can join us, or you can die out here right now." The guards pulled their swords. "James already thinks you are a traitor."

"It seems there are a number in his midst," Gideon said casually.

Cockburn smiled a vicious little grin. "I've been whispering about your traitorous leanings into James's ear for months and told him last night that if you didn't ride with him to Girnigoe as he ordered, you were a traitor." His gaze shifted to Bàs. "You and all your clan."

Bàs shifted his battle-ax to his other shoulder. "That was an unwise thing to do," he said.

Gideon studied Cockburn, his eyes narrowing. "Unless getting James to declare war against the Sinclairs is your aim. So we can unseat him."

The wind blew the thick clouds overhead. Horses shifted, their tack rubbing. Tension lay thick around them, like fog blanketing a battlefield at dawn. Finally, Cockburn began to talk, his voice firm.

"There are many Scots who tire of James and his Protestant ways on the throne. He's untried and has been ruled by his regents for so long he doesn't act on his own. He has turned his back on Catholicism, the religion of his mother, the true religion. And he's led by anyone he fancies."

"Does he not fancy ye. then?" Gideon asked, using the steward's word.

Cockburn's smile slipped. "Not as much as others."

Gideon crossed his arms over his chest. "What's your plan?"

"You'd join us?" Cockburn asked. A slow glance at the soldiers and Bruce showed that they were all part of this mission, whatever it was.

"With the Sinclair armies backing ye, ye can't help but be successful," Gideon said.

Cockburn smiled. "It has been said that the Sinclairs desire more glory than James has given you."

"And the boy goes free," Gideon said.

Cockburn looked between Alistair and Jack. "'Tis good to keep another player to take the blame in case the first is a coward."

Take the blame? The details fell into place. Cockburn needed a scapegoat, a sacrifice who could be blamed and executed for treason if things went wrong. Cockburn's mission was to assassinate the king, and he'd chosen Jack to be the one to do it.

• • •

Cait held one arm around the trunk of the oak as she watched the group on the moor. Praise God, Bàs had joined Gideon, although the odds were still against them.

Fiona had run directly to Cait with news that the king had ordered Gideon to ride with him. Yet, here he was, keeping his promise to follow Jack. Cait's heart squeezed. Gideon was doing something that went against everything he believed in, everything he'd been raised to do—that rules and laws were to be upheld unless they could better the Sinclair Clan. Saving Jack and risking King James's anger didn't better the Sinclair Clan. No, Gideon was doing this for her.

She blinked against the tears, and one spilled out to slide hotly down her cheek.

The group remained in conversation on the moor, and then Gideon and Bàs rode up front with Vincent. Cait watched them as they turned toward the northeast. She frowned. Edinburgh was south. Why would they travel north? Only moors, forests, and eventually the sea lay that way. And Girnigoe Castle.

Her breath caught. Gideon's brother, Cain, was leading James through the woods along the creek where Willa had fallen in. Cait looked in the direction where Girnigoe lay. The majority of the king's soldiers were there already, setting up a perimeter of protection for the king under the guidance of the Sinclairs. Vincent Cockburn's group was supposed to be going to Edinburgh, but it looked like they were circling around to head toward Girnigoe, too. Had Gideon convinced the king's steward that Jack was innocent?

"No," she whispered, her lip brushing the bark on the tree. Cockburn would have just released Jack, and Gideon had already tried to convince the steward without success.

The group began to ride across the moor toward Girnigoe. "What are you doing?" Whatever it was involved Jack and Gideon. It was a change in a plan that had been set in stone. A brief conversation would not change it. "Unless it was the plan all along," she whispered, her mind running ahead to scenarios that would make Vincent Cockburn decide to ride toward the king. He could cut off James's party before he reached Girnigoe. *Treason?*

A thought-out plan by James's steward? A deadly deed done on Sinclair soil? She gasped, her hand going to her heart that beat hard like a falcon taking flight. "With Jack." Set up to look guilty by Cockburn. Now the steward had two scapegoats, Jack and Alistair. If something deadly happened to the king, one or both would take the blame.

Cait pushed away from the trunk, climbing down the limbs to land on the ground. She sprinted toward the Orphans' Home. *I need a horse.* Could she convince a guard at the castle of her suspicions so she could borrow a horse and ride to Girnigoe to warn Cain? "Bloody hell," she cursed, her legs pumping, snapping her skirts until she raised them up to her knees. She barreled into the Orphans' Home door, pushing it open. "I need a horse," she called out.

Rhona and Viola stood with Willa, eyes wide. "Trix and Libby went to get one of the two you said Alistair had hidden in Fiona and Evie's garden," Rhona said, wringing her hands.

Yes! She could take one of the stolen Sinclair horses. Hopefully, it was docile. "How long ago?"

"Too long," Viola said and grabbed Cait's trews and tunic. She nearly threw them into Cait's hands and started unlacing her dress. "They overheard Bruce talking with that traitor Cockburn after you left to see Jack ride away. Cait." Her fingers paused as she looked in her eyes. "I think Cockburn and Bruce are planning to kill the king and take the throne of Scotland."

Cait swallowed. "I saw Bruce join the group taking Jack and Alistair to Edinburgh. But they turned northeast instead of south. If they kill the king…" Cait slammed first one leg into her trews and then the other. "They are going to blame Jack."

Rhona gasped, her hand going to her mouth. "He'll be gutted alive and beheaded in Edinburgh."

"Gutted alive?" Willa squealed and grabbed her stomach as if feeling the blade.

"Gideon is with Jack now, and Bàs Sinclair. They won't let Jack be blamed," Cait said. But at what cost? Civil war? The Sinclairs being labeled traitor along with Jack?

Willa shook Cait's arm. "And Trix and Libby haven't returned with the horse. Cait, what if they decided to ride to Girnigoe on their own?"

The young girls always wanted to help, wanted to prove their worth despite all the times Cait told them they were needed, special, and loved. The two of them together, building each other up, could've easily convinced each other to ride on themselves to warn the king.

Cait met Willa's panicked gaze. "Then I hope they left one horse for me."

• • •

Gideon held Sgàil back to match the slow gallop of the traitorous soldiers led by Cockburn. A quick glance at Bàs showed he did the same. They hadn't needed to confer before Gideon had accepted Cockburn's foolish scheme to assassinate the king. Bàs would go along with Gideon's course.

With James dead, it would require an all-out war to evict the likes of Cockburn from taking over Scotland, something Gideon would never allow. The man represented the selfishness and perfidy in James's advisors. A nest of serpents bent on taking the king down without him being aware of the danger around him.

If Jack hadn't been set up to take the blame for the assassination, Gideon would already be with the king, although unaware of the treachery riding toward him. Traveling at this speed, Gideon calculated they would intercept James and Cain, with their six soldiers, before they reached Girnigoe. Were the soldiers riding with the king also traitors? Could they have already attacked? More likely, Cockburn had ordered the king to remain alive until they reached him with their scapegoat, Jack or Alistair.

Cockburn raised his arm, and the group slowed. Gideon rode next to him with Bruce on Cockburn's other side. "They may reach Girnigoe before us," Gideon said.

"Two of the soldiers know we're coming and will slow them down," Cockburn said.

Only two? A good thing to know.

"They'll delay at the edge of the forest just west of the moor leading to Girnigoe," Bruce said. He sat his horse as if proud to know the plans before Gideon. How easy it must've been for Cockburn to convince Bruce to assist, his oath to the Sinclairs and therefore to James meaningless.

They rode on for nearly an hour before Bruce halted them just inside the forest's edge that lay to the south of the moor. "There they are," he said, pointing for Cockburn to follow. Cain sat his white steed as they walked along the edge of the forest on the far side. He spoke to some of James's men in the tree line, but he kept looking around as if his warrior instincts picked up on the treachery nearby.

"Why attack here?" Gideon asked. "Girnigoe is below with hundreds of Sinclair and the king's warriors who can jump in to save the king."

"Why do you think I let you and your brother live when joining us?" Cockburn asked.

Because you didn't want to die on my sword. "Why?" Gideon said instead.

"I want the Sinclairs to see you and your brothers siding against the king." He smiled as if he relished his own cleverness. "They'll support our mission then."

Cockburn motioned to the soldier holding the boy on his horse to come near. "Jack, I have a job for you, young man."

Jack breathed quickly, his chest rising and falling fast with panic.

Cockburn nodded, and the guard cut the rope around Jack's wrists. The boy rubbed at them and flexed his fingers as if they'd fallen asleep. "You'll be remembered today as the hero who saved Scotland."

All the muscles in Gideon tensed. Cockburn wanted Jack to be the one to kill the king.

Jack shook his head, obviously having come to the same conclusion. Cockburn frowned. "If you don't do exactly as I say, I'll tell all of Edinburgh how you killed the king today."

"You'll tell them that either way?" Jack said.

"Yes," Cockburn said. "But if you're brave enough to follow through, you'll be free to go wherever you wish today. I will even give you a horse and provisions. If not…" Cockburn gave him a pitiful look. "Your head, detached from your body, will make it to Edinburgh to take the blame."

The boy's eyes widened even more, his nostrils flaring like a colt catching the scent of a pack of wolves. Gideon pulled his sword, the sound stark and chilling in the quiet.

"Put it back," Bruce said, and Gideon saw that he held a nocked arrow pointed straight at Jack. It would pierce the boy before Gideon could reach either of them.

"I'll kill the king," Alistair said. "I'd be happy to if you give me a horse and provisions." He smiled.

Cockburn looked between them, his mouth pinched. He apparently didn't like to change plans once they were set. Alistair had fallen into their hands, making Jack unneeded.

"Aye," Gideon said. "Let the madman act. Jack is just a boy who has no lust for blood yet."

Cockburn looked out onto the field, and Gideon could see he was anxious to begin so as not to lose the opportunity. "Very well, cut his rope and give him a dagger. Malcolm will ride you close to the king's party and dismount. You'll ride right up to James and stab him." He looked back at Gideon. "I will leave it up to you and your brother to stop Cain Sinclair however you wish. But make sure that James is unprotected."

Cockburn held Gideon's gaze. "If the Sinclairs help rid Scotland of Stewart rule, Sinclairs can help me set up a stronger rule to keep our country safe from foreign influence. You'll be the mightiest clan in all of Scotland."

"We already are," Gideon said.

Bruce snorted, but Cockburn just smiled. "I believe you are, and your strength will benefit

Scotland, or I would've ordered you and your brother dead already."

Bàs snorted but didn't say anything. Gideon knew his brother was close to losing his stoic calm and slaughtering them all. But if he and Gideon did that, James would see them as murderers of his men.

Cockburn turned to Alistair. "Once you kill the king, keep the horse and ride back to Varrich for provisions."

Alistair glanced toward Gideon. "How do I know he won't try to kill me?"

Cockburn shrugged. "You might want to flee quickly before this mess here is untangled enough that he can find you."

Gideon's jaw ached, and he stared hard at Alistair. "Don't go anywhere near Cait when ye go back there or I'll hunt ye down and rip your heart from your screaming throat."

Alistair tried to smile, but it wavered, and Gideon watched him swallow before he gave a nod. But Gideon didn't believe him. He'd make certain Alistair didn't make it to Varrich.

Gideon looked to Cockburn. "Leave the useless boy here."

"No," Cockburn said. "He'll ride with us." He looked to the guard holding Jack. "If Gideon or Bàs Sinclair act against us, cut the boy's throat."

The soldier drew his dagger, holding it in front of Jack. The lad looked too frightened to act against the soldier, who probably weighed a hundred pounds more than him.

Cockburn turned his mount to the field before them and pulled his sword. "To arms, men, and may we be victorious in ridding our country of this misfit king and bringing the true religion back to Scotland." He held his sword up, a glaze of blood lust tightening his face into zealous determination. "Ride!"

Sgàil lunged forward with the shift of Gideon in the saddle. But Gideon and Bàs did not raise their swords.

The familiar pounding of hooves against dirt shot through Gideon as they raced onto the field. He watched the far end, knowing that Cain would quickly deduce what was happening. Without Bàs's and his swords raised, Cain would know they did not join the battle with Cockburn. Would the two traitorous soldiers react against the others, killing their own men to distract them from the oncoming dozen?

Suddenly another horse broke from the forest from the direction of the stream that led to Varrich. It was a bay horse, unsaddled and flying in a mad gallop, barely controlled. On its back clung two lasses, two little lasses. His heart pumped with a deep thud. Trix and Libby were riding into the middle of a battle to assassinate the king.

CHAPTER TWENTY-TWO

Treason Act, England, 1351 AD

Those convicted of treason shall be hanged but not until they are dead. Still alive, they shall be cut from chest to lower abdomen, their entrails removed. Then they will be beheaded and their body cut into four quarters to be separated across the kingdom.

The remaining horse behind Fiona and Evie's cottage was older and stubborn. The mare didn't want to move faster than a slow run. "Come on, girl," Cait urged as they loped across the frozen ground toward another stretch of trees. On any other occasion, Cait would've thanked God for a slow, steady mare who seemed incredibly gentle. But racing after Trix and Libby to warn Cain and save Jack, Gideon, and King James, she cursed her luck.

"Faster!" she yelled, but patted the mare's neck sweetly. "You can do it."

The horse seemed to pick up speed, its front legs pulling hard as Cait clung to her, lying down low over her neck. If she fell from here, she'd surely die. *God protect my girls*. Trix and Libby had only ever ridden gently plodding horses at fairs. Cait's heart felt like it would fly away with the speed of its beating. In one day she could lose Jack, Trix, and Libby. *And Gideon*.

Cait slowed as she entered another swath of

forest. Following the creek, she should come out above Girnigoe Castle. She and the horse moved swiftly between winter-bare trees, Cait squinting to see, her ears straining to pick up any sign of the girls or the king's group.

"An attack!" she heard a man yell up ahead.

"No!" Where were Trix and Libby? Her heels kicked against the horse, Cait's desperation spurring her forward to break through the trees onto the frozen moor. She pulled back on the reins, circling the horse. Trix and Libby clung to a large bay horse standing beside King James. "No. No. No. No. No," she whispered in rapid succession, her mind taking the scene in through wide eyes.

Cain and the small group of Sinclair and king's soldiers encircled them, facing the oncoming horses. Gideon rode with the traitors, and Jack sat before a large royal soldier as if trapped there. Alistair rode alone on another horse.

Cait must put herself between the oncoming blades and her children. She surged toward Trix and Libby, coming in from along the tree line. Before she could reach the girls, Gideon's horse leaped forward, galloping from the moor, faster than the rest. Powerful chest barreling closer, Gideon's horse seemed to barely touch the ground as hundreds of pounds of force flew straight toward the girls.

"Save them!" Cait screamed. Gideon's face pinched with gritty determination. Teeth clenched, he rode like a warrior angel straight from God, his black horse flying in contrast against the field of white snow.

Libby and Trix hugged tightly to each other on

their horse. Even together, they looked small seated bareback, surrounded by huge men, in a place where no little girl should ever be caught. Cait watched in horror as Gideon barreled toward them. He held no sword, only the reins of his warhorse.

Bàs flew with him, also without his usual sword or ax, but all the men behind them held their weapons ready to strike. Gideon threw his arm across as he neared, signaling Cain. Cain moved away from the girls seconds before Gideon turned at the last moment so as not to crash into them. Snow shot up from the horse's hooves as he came to a halt, blocking Trix, Libby, and the king with the large bulk of his horse and himself. The girls screamed.

"Blast it, Sinclair!" the king yelled.

Cait rode toward them, not sure what to do. She had only one dagger, but she pulled it from its sheath lying against her hip. One of the king's men raised his sword behind the girls, his gaze on the king. "Traitor!" Cait yelled. She leaned low over her horse's neck as the brave mare rode directly toward the soldier. James turned to see the mortal blow coming.

Before Cait reached them, Gideon stood in his stirrups, twisting in time to see the blow coming. The girls screamed again as Gideon's blade cut through the air over their heads, hitting the man's shoulder with enough force to throw him off his horse. "Your steward is a traitor," he yelled to the king. "Stay behind us," Gideon said.

Yanking back around, in that instant as Cait reached them, their gazes connected. She saw so much in the space of heartbeats: complete commitment to saving her girls, strength, honor, and yes, love. He'd do anything to save her children, throwing down his life to do so. His strength and conviction filled her with strength.

"Cockburn!" yelled James over Gideon's shoulder. "You will hang for this!"

Cait pulled her mare to a stop on the other side of the girls, blocking them between her and Gideon. Gideon turned back outward toward the battle that had begun.

"I knew you lied!" Vincent Cockburn yelled at Gideon. His head swiveled around toward the man who stayed back, holding Jack. "Kill the boy."

"No!" Cait yelled.

Gideon's horse leaped forward, leaving the king, rushing through the fray within seconds.

"The king!" Libby yelled and banged her heels into her horse to get it to move before him as if to replace Gideon.

Gideon's black horse dodged swords and horses on its one-way course directly toward Jack and the traitor lifting a blade to his neck.

"No, Jack!" Cait called.

Trix opened her mouth wide and screamed, a high-pitched cry that caught everyone's attention for a split second.

Jack threw his body forward along the horse's neck.

"Take thee to Hell!" Gideon's roar reached Cait over the guttural yells of the fighting men. Jack, arms wrapped around the horse's neck, fell to the side, swinging under the horse's neck as Gideon rose again in his saddle, his bloody sword flying in an arch that intersected the soldier's neck. In one hit, the man's head toppled from his shoulders.

"Take the horse," Gideon yelled at Jack. "Go!"

Cait would take the girls away, too, but the fighting was all around them as the traitorous steward and his men tried to cut a path to the king.

Bàs took on two at once, as did Cain. "I'll not hide behind children," James said, finding his courage. He was the target, and his death would cause many more deaths with civil war. But he drew his sword.

"Help me protect the girls," Cait called. "Please, your majesty."

"Use the horses to keep them blocked," James ordered, pointing to the ground. "I'll guard their backs."

Cait dismounted, helping Libby and Trix down. They clung to her on the ground, protected by the bulk of the two horses. It was harder to see, but the screams and groans and banging of steel against steel would remain in their nightmares.

"Make way!" Alistair yelled, and his horse barreled toward them.

"Enemy to Sinclairs! Enemy to James!" Gideon yelled, signaling his horse to jump forward to meet the threat.

Alistair's eyes were wide and wild. As Gideon struck his sword, Alistair slid to the ground, landing in a crouch. He ran straight toward the king, a short sword clutched in his hand. As he reached them, he grabbed the king's leg alongside his horse, yanking hard.

James yelled as he lost his balance, sliding over

the horse's back to the ground, his sword jarred from his grasp. James stared up at Alistair, a look of disbelief on his face that this country boy, just turned man, was going to kill him. Alistair raised the sword in two hands. "See, Cait," he yelled, "I will be king."

Crack!

Alistair's face pinched in pain, and he dropped to the ground, falling upon James, who shoved him away. Jack stood behind him, holding a large rock.

Jack stared wide-eyed at Cait. "He never looks behind him."

The king pushed himself back up, grabbing his sword. He turned toward the continuing battle as Jack ran to Cait and the girls. Horses stood behind them, and Cait stared up at Gideon upon his black horse stationed before them. Gideon remained there, glancing behind them and then forward again, guarding them. He held his sword but didn't move away to finish the battle with his brothers and the soldiers loyal to James.

The strength in Gideon was without doubt as he remained. He'd dropped his cape, and the muscles of his back and arms stretched against his tunic as he held himself ready, calling to Cain and Bàs when needed.

"James!" Gideon yelled but didn't move.

The king ran to the side where Vincent had dismounted in an attempt to sneak up on him. Their swords clanged as they hit together, full force. "Traitor!" James yelled.

"Sinner!" Vincent yelled back, spit flying from his face. "I will kill you as you have killed the true religion in Scotland."

Jack tried to pull away from their huddle in the middle, but Cait kept her hold on him.

James battled back at Vincent, moving him farther away from them with blow after blow against his sword. The zealous look of confidence turned to hatred in Vincent's pinched features. Behind him, Cain ran up, grabbing Vincent's arms while knocking his sword from his hand.

James pointed his sword tip into Vincent's exposed throat. Breathing hard, the king stood there, ready to pass his judgment. He glanced at Gideon, who still blocked them even though the sounds of battle had silenced. "What say you, Horseman of Justice?"

Bàs stepped up with the ax that had been held in a special harness tied to his horse. With his skull mask, grim frown, and blood across his tunic, he was everything the Horseman of Death ought to be. Cait pressed the girls' faces into her middle, not wanting them to witness the execution.

Gideon looked behind him, his gaze on Cait, dropping to the girls. He turned to the king. "Before these many witnesses, and by his own words, Vincent Cockburn is guilty of treason against James, King of Scotland." The low thunder in his voice sent a shiver up Cait's spine. Gideon bowed his head to the king. "The punishment is at the discretion of his majesty."

James rubbed an arm across his sweaty brow, the tip of his sword bobbing as if he found it heavy. He let it drop, since Cain had ahold of his steward. "How many who came with me to Varrich are against me? How many walk my halls back at Edinburgh?"

Vincent's face tightened in a dark grimace full of loathing that bordered on madness. "More than you know. Your mother followed the true religion, and so do we."

Cait held tightly to the girls as the man spoke of Mary Stewart, Queen of Scots and Catholicism and how easily Scotland could slip back into civil war.

James stared Vincent in the face as if he wished to cleave his skull and pull out the names of the traitors around him. "I'd slay you here," he said, "but you don't deserve to die as a warrior. You will give me names and then reap the consequences of being a traitor before the people of Edinburgh to send a message to those plotting against me and the peace of Scotland."

Cain yanked Vincent around, marching him out toward the field where bodies lay, and other soldiers and the few Sinclair warriors stood. Breathing heavily, most still sat their horses, blood splatter across them and their steeds. Two had dismounted to stand over Alistair where he began to rouse, groaning as he turned over to look up at their grim expressions.

A group of soldiers rode toward them from Girnigoe. "They are loyal to the king," Bàs called out as the royal soldiers raised their swords, bravely waiting to meet a possible enemy they had no hope of surviving. "But some of the king's men may not be."

Gideon dismounted, moving behind his black horse to Cait. Jack pulled the girls aside as Gideon walked up to her. He searched her face, evidence of violence and worry on his hard features. "Ye are well and whole?"

She nodded quickly as anxious energy still shot through her. He shut his eyes for a second, almost as in prayer, and then opened them to search her face, his hands coming up to reach for her. He hesitated, and she could feel the question in it.

Cait ran to him, throwing her arms around his middle as she hugged him tight. Surrendering her worry and constant vigilance for the moment, tears coursed from her eyes. He wrapped her up against him. "My foolishly brave, determined lass," Gideon said.

She looked up. "I couldn't leave them in jeopardy."

He nodded once slowly, his gaze never leaving hers. "As it should be for a mother."

His words burrowed into her, making her heart swell. He understood. These were her children as much as if they were born from her own body. He'd ignored the king's order for him to accompany him to Girnigoe. He'd acted the traitor to stay with Jack. He'd stood before her and her children, protecting them while others fought for the king.

Cait's mouth relaxed into a smile. "You broke the rules for me."

He stared into her eyes. "Aye."

Cait's hands reached up, her palms lying over his cheeks. "I love you, too, Gideon Sinclair," she whispered and pulled his face down for a kiss.

• • •

"To Jack Mackay, I present this sword," King James called out in the bailey at Varrich Castle where they had returned. "For saving his sisters and coming to the aid of his king." He held out the richly decorated sword. It had been raised against James but was now washed clean from the battle. Jack walked forward, standing taller than Gideon had ever seen him. "It hopefully works better than a rock," James said.

Jack smiled and bowed low, receiving the sword with such pride before the entire clan. Cait clasped her hands before her mouth as she stood behind them, her face lit with happiness. Rhona openly cried, her smile in contrast to the tears.

James turned and beckoned forward Trix and Libby. Wearing their festival best with the ribbons tied in their woven hair, the girls came up together, joined by their hands. They curtsied deeply in unison as they'd been practicing since they'd been asked to attend the king's ceremony the morning after the battle.

"For the two maidens of tender age and great bravery, Beatrix and Libby Mackay, I present these daggers." He turned, retrieving a pair of short daggers, their blades polished and their handles each with tiny gems in them. His new steward brought forth the scabbards for each, which were just as beautifully wrought.

Trix gasped, and Libby held her hand flat against her mouth as if stopping herself from doing the same. They each took the blade and sheath, sliding them in place, and curtsied low again as they murmured their thanks.

"To Cait Gunn Mackay," James called out, prompting Cait to walk forward. "For acts of bravery for riding to my aid…" He narrowed his eyes at her, reminding her that he knew she'd really ridden to come to her children's aid. "I pledge to send ink, quills, parchment, and books for your school. My bride and queen will surely become your patron, as she loves children and learning."

Cait's smile grew genuine at the rich gifts. "Thank you, your highness." She lowered into her own curtsy.

James turned to Gideon where he stood in his crisp, clean tunic and woolen plaid, polished sword at his side. Cain and Bàs stood on either side of him in the order of their births. "And to the Sinclair Horsemen…" He met each of their gazes directly. "I give you my trust. In a world where disloyalty is often cloaked in lies of support, I've seen firsthand how you back me, the true leader of Scotland."

"Our strength and swords are yours, your majesty," Cain said as the chief of the Sinclair Clan. He bowed, his fist going to his chest. Gideon and Bàs repeated the oath, bowing also. James's serious look lightened at the display.

Gideon raised his sword in the air. "Loyalty to King James! Strength to Scotland!" he called out. All the warriors in Varrich's bailey and spilling out of the gates and around the walls, lifted their swords. "Loyalty to King James! Strength to Scotland!" they yelled, their words in unison.

The sound vibrated along Cait's spine enough to raise chill bumps on her skin. Even Jack raised his sword. Trix and Libby raised their daggers, their faces serious enough to make Cait think they would follow James into another battle if given the option.

The gathered people erupted into cheers, and the

king smiled broadly. As the fervor receded, Gideon moved toward Cait. The girls had run over to Rhona and Viola to show them their daggers, and Jack strode toward Osk and several Girnigoe boys, his sword at his side.

Gideon stopped before her, and she smiled up at him. His stony expression softened.

Before either of them could say a word, James walked up beside them. "You will certainly follow me to Edinburgh," he said, his gaze on Gideon. The words, said so casually, had an undertone of an order, and Cait's stomach tightened.

Gideon's gaze remained on her. "Certainly, your majesty," he said, "after I fully integrate the Mackay and Sinclair clans." He finally turned toward the king.

James frowned. "When will that be?"

"It takes some time, but to make your Scotland strong against her enemies, I will do my duty to bring us together and train us to protect your realm." The way Gideon spun his refusal would make it hard for any loyal Scotsman to refuse his plan.

"I could order you to come with me now," James said, his eyes narrowing.

Gideon met his gaze with unblinking calm. "Aye, ye could, but I know ye are a man of keen intelligence who sees the value in my work in uniting the clans of your northern territory."

James snorted, his gaze resting on Cait. "Mistress Cait could come with you."

She bowed her head. "I'd like to bring my children to court to meet your queen, your majesty, but

I will need time to prepare them."

He exhaled and looked back at Gideon. "I always thought you to be a rigid man of law, and yet you break rules." He held his hand up as if expecting Gideon to argue. "I expect you to uphold my laws when you come to court, eventually." James didn't wait for a reply. He turned and walked away.

Gideon's face relaxed into a smile as he stepped closer to Cait. Around them, men and women talked and laughed. Horses were readied for the king's army to depart. Vincent, Bruce, and the remaining traitors had been ridden out earlier, surrounded by James's loyal men and a group of Sinclairs who would ride with them to the edge of their territory.

Everywhere noise and jostling pervaded, yet Cait stood still before Gideon. Complex, intelligent, incredibly brave and giving, Gideon Sinclair was a man worthy of her love. She'd told him as much, but they'd had no time to talk since the scene on the moor. She raised her palm to his cheek, her thumb gliding along the scar that he'd given himself as a child, desperate to prove himself.

Gideon leaned down, his lips finding hers. His kiss was warm and strong, just like the man. Around them, a cheer rose, but Cait cared only for the strength and warmth with which Gideon surrounded her. The future was still undecided with questions and hard decisions, but right then with his arms around her, hope swelled inside Cait. And the feeling melted every bit of ice within her.

• • •

"Have ye told her?" Cain asked.

"About the school?" Gideon asked as he and Cain walked out to the center of the bailey where Alistair stood with his hands tied behind his back.

"Nay," Cain said, his rare grin stopping Gideon. "About being in love with her."

"Actions mean more than words," Gideon said, his gaze searching for Cait in the gathered crowd that included Edward Mackay, Alistair's father.

Cain dropped a heavy hand on his shoulder. "Cait wants the words, brother." Cain's brows rose high. "All women want to know what's in their man's heart. At least that's what Ella says."

"Do ye profess your love to her all the time then?" Gideon teased, though his stomach remained tight. Would Cait come to see the proceedings over her one-time friend?

Cain grinned. "Aye, every chance I get, especially when she grants me a view of her lush curves." His brother was still completely enamored of his wife. How would life be with Cait at Gideon's side? He had thought of little else since he'd kissed her in the bailey yesterday to the cheers of Sinclairs and Mackays alike. Even though he was supposed to be deciding the grim fate of Alistair Mackay.

They stepped up to the platform that had been built that morning. Alistair stood at the center, his eyes trained on his father. Gideon studied the young man. Remorse weighed on his face, but he held a strange smile, as if he already knew he would stand in judgment before God today.

Beyond him, Cait and Rhona pushed through the crowd toward the front. Would Cait agree with his plan after all the man had done to her and those she loved? He forced his gaze to Alistair as Bàs walked over, dressed in his executioner's black, the skull mask in place, his ax over one shoulder.

Without a word, Bàs stood, his booted feet braced apart, ax-head down, waiting for the proceedings to begin. Gideon hadn't told any of them his plan. He'd wrestled with it all night, thinking about Cait's words but pulling the decision out of them, making it truly his own.

Rhona came over, leaving Cait. Gideon looked down at the woman. "He is the father of wee Henry," she said. "He told Viola he loved her and would marry her, all the while he was trying to court Cait." She shook her head. "I don't know if you knew that. He abandoned her once she told him she was with child. The poor lass endured the whole confinement alone in that shack in the woods. Shameful," she said and looked to Bàs. "You should use a dull blade against his neck," she said, obviously wanting Alistair to suffer before he died.

Bàs stood with his arms crossed over his chest, completely taking on the persona of death. He slowly shook his head, his gaze dropping to the woman. "My blade always strikes death with a single blow. 'Tis the same for all, no matter the crime."

Rhona swallowed hard, her eyes wide. She bobbed her head and looked back at Gideon. "I thought you should know the extent of his crimes before you pass judgment."

"Thank ye," Gideon said, and Rhona hurried back through the crowd, stopping with Fiona and Evie. Cait stood with Jack and Viola, but the other children were not present.

Gideon stepped up onto the platform, and the bailey hushed. Gideon's gaze moved over the crowd of mostly Mackays and some Sinclairs. Alistair was clearly guilty of many acts that warranted his immediate death. Swift justice had always been Gideon's duty, in which he prided himself. It had proved his worth to his father.

Must we always be who Da said we are to be? Now that he is dead? Bàs's question on the moor beyond Girnigoe as the snow fell, the day he first saw Cait twirling in icy glory... His question had set the spike in Gideon's resolute ideas about his duty. And Cait's ideas had been the hammer to split his convictions into shattered pieces. Now he must build something new with them.

"Alistair Mackay," Gideon said, his voice like thunder in the waiting bailey. "Ye are charged with treason against King James, killing a solider of the king, abuse of Mackay citizens, and abandoning your own child without support." A murmur rose within the crowd at his offenses. "Do ye have anything ye would like to say?"

Alistair stared straight out at Cait. "I did it all for love," he said. "To prove I could provide for the only woman I care about, Cait Mackay."

Gideon watched as Viola took Cait's hand, the two of them holding tightly as another murmur rose in the crowd. Gideon raised his arms, lowering them slowly to get the crowd to quiet. "I am Gideon Sinclair, Horseman of Justice." His voice rang out across the heads of the people, his people. "And..." He paused for several heartbeats. "And I'm inadequate to decide this man's fate."

Stunned silence sat among the people as if they had all gasped in unison, sucking in every drop of noise in the air.

"I am one man," Gideon continued, and his gaze searched for and found Cait's. "I have my own history that sways me to see those being judged in a certain light, making me merciful or cruel in my judgment of guilt. But I do not speak for God." He looked out at the crowd. "Alistair Mackay's sins are many, and his people, those he lives with, shall choose his fate."

"Hang him!" one man yelled toward the back.

"Cut his head from his shoulders," Fiona yelled, and Rhona nodded vigorously.

Gideon raised his hands to settle the calls for brutal punishment. "I'm forming a counsel." His voice carried over everyone, and they hushed to hear. "Six peers, three men, and three women. They will hear the evidence against Alistair and discuss it to agree on a verdict of guilty or innocent, and they will advise me on a punishment. I'll take it all into consideration and decide according to their suggestions."

"Who will they be?" someone yelled.

"Those he wronged," another answered.

Gideon's voice overrode the budding questions, putting his plan out before his people. "The six will be chosen by me based upon their knowledge of the situation but not the victims themselves. And I'll continue this counsel of six, but those assigned to it will rotate through the people of Varrich so ye all will have a say in deciding the fate of your clan."

"Are my services needed today?" Bàs asked, his tone abrupt.

Everyone waited to hear Gideon's answer. "Nay, brother." He looked out at the crowd. "I've already chosen the first counsel and will alert them after we disperse. They'll convene at the castle tomorrow morn to discuss and deliver their suggestion to me. Alistair will be brought up from the dungeon to hear the decision and his fate. We may need the services of the Horseman of Death then but not today."

Bàs gave a nod and strode out toward the crowd, who opened for him, giving him a wide path so that they would touch no part of him. Children shied away, hiding their faces in their mothers' aprons. Men held their arms out wide, pushing the crowd behind them as if Bàs's very touch could bring disease. Gideon watched his brother walk solemnly out of the gate, shunned by everyone. Such a display used to fuel Gideon's convictions that he and his three brothers must be the brutal Horsemen heralding the end of days to keep the clan strong, but today it saddened him.

At the gate, Joshua dismounted his bay horse in the path that remained open. Arms out to his sides in question, he watched Bàs stride away. He dropped them and walked straight toward the platform. Keeping to the trees with his wife and bairn while the king visited, Gideon had sent Keenan to call Joshua back to the land of the living after the king had departed.

Joshua walked down the center toward the platform where two of Gideon's men were leading Alistair off. "What? No blood today?" Joshua asked, his grin annoying.

"Thank ye, everyone," Gideon called out, his gaze resting on Cait. "The initial six will be alerted this evening."

Slowly, the wide path narrowed and disappeared as the citizens of Varrich dispersed, a hum of voices rising. There'd certainly be much discussion today.

Cait remained where she stood, and Gideon watched her. Her face had been drawn and sad as she watched Alistair led out. Now there was a softness to her features, and her eyes met his. For a long moment their gazes connected, but then Viola tugged her arm. She gave a small bow of her head and let her and Rhona lead her back toward her home at the edge of the village.

"Seriously," Joshua said as he watched the people leave. "For three days, I've been closer to heaven." He chuckled at the double meaning, his brows rising to suggest his time with Kára in their house in the trees had been blissful. "And I return to earth and find the Horseman of Justice letting his executioner stride off with a clean ax? What the bloody hell has been going on?"

"Change," Cain said, and Gideon felt his brother's gaze on him. "And I anticipate there's more to come."

CHAPTER TWENTY-THREE

Court of Common Pleas, established by
Henry II of England, 1178 AD

A jury of twelve local knights has been created to
settle disputes over the ownership of land. To hear all
complaints of the realm and do right by the common
man, five members of the king's personal household,
made up of two clergy and three lay. They will be
supervised by the king and known as the wise men
of the realm.

"I heard Abigail and Richard were asked to be on the council," Rhona said as she ladled out some morning porridge.

"They'll be fair," Viola murmured from her seat on her bed feeding Henry.

"Fair?" Rhona scoffed. "He should be hanged."

"He very well might," Willa said as she finished tying Libby's apron. "But this way, 'tis not just Gideon deciding his fate."

Cait set the bowls of porridge around their table. After the gathering yesterday, everyone had hurried home to see if they would be chosen as the first council. The mood in the village was one of anticipation and lightness. To witness a conquering chief, the very Horseman of Justice, include them in judging a crime had lifted some of the anger the Mackays had harbored against the Sinclair. More so than any festival could ever do.

No visitor had come to the Orphans' Home. It wasn't that Cait expected one of them to be assigned to the council, not if Alistair were to get an impartial trial. But Gideon had stayed away, too. Was he busy? Had what they'd shared during the battle to save the king not mattered? Her heart squeezed.

Rap. Rap.

Athena, their now-named dog, barked, making Pickle flap her wings as she hopped out of her crate. Boo, the healing wren, leaped and fluttered upward to a basket hanging above her. Everyone inside the cottage stilled, faces turning toward the door as Athena continued to bark.

"The council has already been chosen," Rhona said as Willa hushed the dog.

Trix ran over to the window, peeking out through a crack in the shutter. "I see a big black horse," she said. "'Tis Gideon's, but there are two other horses." She turned back to the room, her face lit up. "I think one is Beauty."

"Beauty?" Libby whispered, running over to see if it was the horse that she and Trix had ridden into battle, the one they had named Beauty.

Rap. Rap.

Cait rose from her spot, her middle tight. Trix tried to run toward the door, but Viola caught her arm, keeping her back.

Cait walked over and opened it, Athena ran past her to inspect the three horses. Gideon stood just outside, the concern tightening his handsome features dissolving. "I've never heard the Orphans' Home so quiet," he said.

"Their mouths were full of porridge," she said, staring into Gideon's bright gray eyes. In the muted morning light, they seemed almost blue. He moved back when she stepped outside, closing the door behind her.

Even though he was alone, there were three horses, one of them being the older mare she had ridden. She walked over to rub her soft muzzle. "What are you doing here?"

"She told me that she missed your company," Gideon said, coming up behind her.

Cait looked over her shoulder. "She told you that, did she?"

He nodded. "And the other said she missed Trix and Libby."

She rubbed a hand along the mare's neck. She was much younger, quite tall, and strong. She'd also been gentle enough to keep Libby and Trix on her back when they'd hardly ever seated a horse before.

Gideon walked over to where Cait stood. "They are gifts for the Orphans' Home." Someone squealed inside the cottage, and Cait pulled Gideon farther away so that they stood behind the horses.

"There's no privacy here," she said with a smile. "And I thank you, but there's also no barn here or room for two horses. They aren't so easily housed as Pickle."

Gideon glanced away, his one boot shuffling the pebbles. "The horses can be housed up at the castle in the stables within the bailey. I was rather thinking…" His gaze found hers again. "I think Varrich Castle is too big for just one man to live in. Last night it was too quiet."

"I thought you liked quiet," she said, her eyes assessing. Her heart thumped hard as she hung on each word and the pinch of his brows. He looked nervous, which made her nervous. She'd said she loved him, was certain he felt the same after all he'd done, but he hadn't said as much.

Gideon rubbed the back of his neck. "I've found that I've gotten used to the sounds of children."

She frowned at the tremble running through her and rubbed her arms. "Whatever you're saying, say it quickly," she said, her words sounded breathless to her ears. "Or my heart might burst."

He inhaled fully, a small smile on his mouth. "I think the Orphans' Home should move to Varrich Castle. It can be your school, and it will house the children. There's room for all of them, Jack, Rhona, and even Viola, as well as others who come along. There are nineteen rooms above the keep."

Cait's breath completely halted as he gestured. He paused, watching her closely, and she inhaled. "We would…live in the castle?"

"The library is the perfect space for instruction. Others from the village can come. I'll move my ledgers up to my desk in our bedchamber. 'Tis certainly large enough."

Her mouth opened and closed. "*Our* bedchamber?" She shook her head slowly. "I cannot… I mean, thank you, Gideon. This is such a gracious offer, but if it's contingent on me being your mistress, the children would know and—"

"I don't want ye for a mistress, Cait," he said. His hand rose to gently set upon her shoulders. "I want ye for a wife."

She stared, blinking at his face where a pinch had developed between his brows. Giddiness spread through her chest, and her hand pressed there as if to keep her from bursting. "Wife?"

"Aye." The intensity in Gideon's face gave him the determined look of someone going to war. "I know your children come with ye to this union, as they should." He captured her hand in his large one, squeezing gently. "Ye have taught me so much, Cait; me, a man who has sought knowledge all his life and thought he knew everything." He shook his head. "But I was completely uneducated when it came to this feeling inside. I thought it was weakness at first, a softening, but I understand now that it is a strength."

He took a deep breath. "Ye said it on the field, and I knew then what it was, what it is." He touched the side of her cheek with his thumb, stroking along it. "I love ye, too, Cait Gunn Mackay. Will ye marry me?"

A squeal of happiness came from behind the horses, revealing the eavesdroppers had cracked open the door to hear better. A round of shushing followed, but it was clear that her family approved. Laughter bubbled up from Cait's chest, coming out sounding like pure joy. "Yes, Gideon Sinclair, I'll wed you, because I love you."

His tense features changed, lighting his face, and he pulled her into his arms. Behind the horses, cheers erupted as the children ran out of the cottage, the dog barking at the excitement. But Cait was wrapped up in Gideon, and his lips came down upon hers. The world became the two of them as the kiss stole her breath. She smiled against him when his deep chuckle broke the kiss.

"I will be a bridesmaid," Libby was saying.

"Me too," Trix said, jumping up and down so close that Cait felt her brushing against her.

"Willa will certainly be one," Rhona said.

"Willa, ye could marry Jack at the same time," Trix said.

"No, she can't," Libby scolded. "We've already discussed this."

The dog continued to bark, and it sounded like Pickle had escaped through the open door and was flapping around in the swirl of words, laughter, and bickering.

"Are you sure you want all of this under your roof?" Cait asked as she stared up into Gideon's face. "'Tis quite a messy, loud, spirited group."

He chuckled but did not break the gaze. "'Tis a big castle." He leaned in until she felt his warm breath on her ear. "And our bedchamber has a stout lock."

Cait laughed, pulling his mouth back to hers for an unhurried kiss. It filled her heart and body with warmth. No more the cold ice princess, Cait knew her future was full of passion, warmth, and love beside this amazing man.

"'Tis snowing," Willa called.

And Cait's eyes flickered open as she felt the cold flakes melt on her face. Breaking the kiss, she and Gideon looked up at the heavy sky where fluffy snowflakes fell. "'Tis snowing," Gideon said, his grin wide. "Ye know what that means."

She laughed. "No, actually."

He looked surprised. "'Tis time to twirl, of course." He took her hand, tugging her out before the cottage. He dropped her hands, spread his arms, and slowly began to turn. "Try it. I hear 'tis one of the best things in life."

The children, and even Rhona and Viola began to turn, everyone laughing at the spectacle of them all twirling in the falling snow.

Cait pressed against Gideon. "Twirl with me," she said, resting her back against his chest. Arms spread out together, she and Gideon twirled slowly. He leaned in to kiss the side of her neck, and she stopped, turning around to stare up into his handsome face. "I love you, Gideon Sinclair, with everything I am."

He smiled broadly. "Ye are everything, lass. I love ye, Cait."

The words coming from his lips coursed through her like warm honey. She cupped his head, guiding him back down to kiss her again while those she loved danced around, twirling and laughing in the softly falling snow.

EPILOGUE

30 April 1591 – Day before Beltane

Forest near the stream just beyond Varrich Village

Cait stared down through the newly unfurled leaves of the oak tree, her hand clutching her useless slippers and her toes curled around the branch on which she balanced. Her heart pounded, her breath coming quickly from her rapid climb.

"Nineteen… Twenty." Gideon's voice easily tore through the forest from his position at the edge. "Here I come," he yelled, his menacing voice making her smile. He hadn't wanted to play All Hid. They were hunting for trees that could be cut down to serve as cabers at the Beltane games tomorrow. But Cait had something to tell him and a promise to entice from him first.

Gideon broke through the bramble, not bothering with any type of stealth. "A rule was not to go into, across, or even near the stream," he yelled ahead of him. She knew better than to answer and give her position away.

Cait held herself completely still as he stopped below her perch. Good Lord, her husband never failed to make her insides flutter. He was brawny with well-hewn muscles making up every inch of him. Despite his cropped hair and short, precisely clipped beard, Gideon Sinclair always looked like the fierce warrior he'd been raised to be. He even walked like a predator on a hunt. And when he caught her… Cait's middle tightened with eagerness. His hands and mouth could do things to her that made her melt and then explode into a million shards of delicious pleasure.

Gideon turned in a tight circle, and Cait let her gaze slide along his broad shoulders that strained against his crisp linen tunic. He scanned the undergrowth. "She never follows the rules," he grumbled.

Cait's smile grew at his surly tone, and she lifted one of her slippers, throwing it. *Thump.* It hit him in the arse, and he spun around, tipping his head to frown up at her. "Ye don't follow any of the rules, do ye?"

"I don't remember a rule that says I can't hit you with a slipper," she teased.

"I said no climbing," he called, sounding like he was chastising Libby or Trix. They all lived up at the castle now, the three girls, Jack, and Rhona, along with Pickle the hen, Boo the wren, and Athena the rapidly growing dog. Viola and Henry had remained at their old cottage, which would become another place for abandoned mothers and children to live.

"I said the creek is running fast and dangerous so keep your feet on the ground," Gideon said. "And ye agreed."

She had to get him to play. "I was inspecting this birch as a caber," she said, smiling sweetly.

He snorted, but a smile grew across his mouth. Och, but that mouth could do wonderful things to her. As if her body remembered too well, it tightened in anticipation.

"Regardless, I've found ye," he said. "Come down and reward the victor."

The look on Gideon's face made the crux of her legs pulse as her body warmed. They'd been married four months already, but they still couldn't go long without hunting for a secluded corner or vacant room to indulge their insatiable appetite for each other.

He continued to stare up at her and shook the tree a bit. Cait laughed. "First, I have to tell you something."

"Come down and tell me."

She narrowed her eyes at him. "Whenever I come near you when you have that look on your face, we don't end up talking."

He laughed, throwing his arms wide as if claiming innocence. "I'll leave your lips free to talk." He dropped his arms. "Or groan or scream my name or praise God for sending ye such a talented husband."

"And one who is oh so humble," she said, laughing.

He waited below, and she bent over the limb holding her. "First," she said, "I want to hear you say something."

His brows narrowed. "Very well. What shall I say that will make ye come down?"

Cait took a deep breath. "Repeat after me."

He crossed his arms over his chest and waited.

"Cait is a strong, healthy, and capable woman," she said.

"I know that."

"Say it."

"Cait is a strong, healthy, and capable, and able to

render me hard and senseless merely by staring down at me from a tree." He adjusted the erection she could see pushing against his kilt.

"Gideon," she chastised.

"Very well," he said. "Ye are strong, healthy, and a capable woman."

"And even when she…" Cait paused to prompt him to talk.

"And even when she…" he said.

"Becomes round…with my child…"

Gideon's smile dropped away with his jaw. "With my child?"

"I will trust her to decide what is safe for her to do." Cait's words came faster with her sense that she was not going to be able to hold Gideon off much longer. "So, if she wants to ride or climb or swing from a length of fabric, I will let her."

"My child?" Gideon repeated as if numb. A huge smile slowly grew across his face that tilted up to her. "Ye are with child, Cait?"

She couldn't help but smile back, her eyes filling with happy tears. She nodded. "Yes."

"Molaibh Dia," he yelled, and Cait laughed as he lunged for the tree. His leap brought him halfway to her, and he easily pulled himself up the thick limbs until he reached her.

"You haven't said all the words," she said as he came level. She tried to maintain a stern face, but she couldn't keep her smile away as she looked at the joy in Gideon's expression.

"I will trust ye, Cait, to keep safe, but I am helping ye with it, every step of the way."

"That's the best I'm going to get, isn't it?"

"Aye." He leaned in over the branch separating them, his one free hand sliding along to cup her cheek. The caress held reverence. "I love ye, Cait, ye and our child, and all our children. Those of our bodies and those who come to us out of need. Ye've taught me love is not a weakness, even though it doesn't follow the rules, either."

Cait blinked back happy tears. "I love you with every bit of me, even the parts that break the rules."

"I wouldn't have it any other way, lass." Gideon leaned in, capturing her mouth in a kiss so full of love and acceptance that more tears swelled in Cait's eyes.

The snapping of limbs sounded in the distance along the creek, making them both look that way. Through the green of spring leaves, she caught the sight of someone running. Bàs leaped over the creek, traveling toward them and the edge of the forest. And he wasn't alone. Beside him ran a wolf. Silently, they watched Bàs and the wolf run past them and slow near the forest's edge.

"Falbh dhachaigh a-nis," Bàs said, and Cait's breath caught as the massive Sinclair patted the beast's large head. "Go home now," he repeated in English, and the wolf changed directions, running back toward the creek. It stopped to sniff Cait's slipper on the ground and raised its piercing eyes to the trees, making her shiver. It looked as lethal as Bàs. But then it ran on as Bàs continued toward Varrich.

"What was that about?" she whispered.

"I don't know," Gideon said. "My brother keeps his own counsel." His pinched expression relaxed, and he smiled. "And right now, I can think of nothing other than carrying ye and our bairn down to safety."

She rolled her eyes. "I knew this was going to be an issue. I should've waited until I was birthing to tell you." She looked pointedly at his fingers curled around her wrist as if to covertly anchor her so she couldn't fall.

He helped her lower to the ground and pulled her into his arms. They came together, their kiss full of promise, hope, and love. It was one of Cait's best things in life.

Make sure to continue the adventure with the fourth book in the Sons of Sinclair series. Bàs Sinclair has carried the guilt of his mother's death since the cradle. He keeps himself apart from his people, coming out of seclusion only when called upon to battle and play the executioner for his clan. He has never failed in his duty until now, when he discovers that the blue-eyed lass who he's helped in the forest is supposed to be his next victim.

A NOTE ABOUT GIDEON'S REFERENCES

The passages at the start of each chapter in HIGHLAND JUSTICE come from books, manuscripts, and rolls in Gideon Sinclair's extensive library. Gideon does not agree with or enact everything he has read, but he strives for understanding and wisdom by studying historical philosophy and law.

As his author, I too have learned a great deal about ancient, medieval, and renaissance law (and now have plenty of icebreakers with which to captivate people at cocktail parties). Digging through the various laws and codes sucked me right down into the research "rabbit hole" where I spent days checking references and taking notes, oftentimes with my eyes wide and mouth hanging open. Having consumed all this information, despite the fabulous gowns of the past, I can honestly say that I am exceedingly glad *not* to be an ancient, medieval, or renaissance woman or suspect!

ACKNOWLEDGMENTS

Thank you so much for reading Gideon and Cait's story in HIGHLAND JUSTICE! Every note or comment you send, or review you give, brings me such joy. You make all the hours of research and writing worthwhile! If I could, I would have you all over for tea.

Thank you to my mother, Irena, for being one of my biggest cheerleaders and for carting my kids around when I was in the middle of frantic writing and editing.

To Kyrra, my daughter, who is an amazing aerial silks artist—thank you for showing Cait and me the proper ways to "fly."

A huge thank you goes out to my fabulous agent, Kevan Lyon, for her constant support and guidance. Thank you also to my talented editor, Alethea Spiridon of Entangled Publishing for all you do to help me make my stories shine.

Also...

At the end of each of my books, I ask that you, my awesome readers, please remind yourselves of the whispered symptoms of ovarian cancer. I am now a nine-year survivor, one of the lucky ones. Please don't rely on luck. If you experience any of these symptoms consistently for three weeks or more, go see your GYN.

Bloating

Eating less and feeling full faster

Abdominal pain

Trouble with your bladder

Other symptoms may include: indigestion, back pain, pain with intercourse, constipation, fatigue, and menstrual irregularities.

Highland Justice is a sexy Highlander romance with a happy ending. However the story includes elements that might not be suitable for some readers. Mentions of kidnapping, sexual assault, and infertility are included in the novel. Additionally, there are scenes depicting beheading and sexual assault. Readers who may be sensitive to these, please take note.

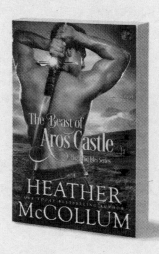

AMARA
An imprint of Entangled Publishing LLC